THE
HEART'S CHARGE

BOOKS BY KAREN WITEMEYER

HANGER'S HORSEMEN · 2

THE HEART'S CHARGE

KAREN WITEMEYER

BETHANYHOUSE
a division of Baker Publishing Group
Minneapolis, Minnesota

© 2021 by Karen Witemeyer

Published by Bethany House Publishers
11400 Hampshire Avenue South
Bloomington, Minnesota 55438
www.bethanyhouse.com

Bethany House Publishers is a division of
Baker Publishing Group, Grand Rapids, Michigan

Printed in the United States of America

Library of Congress Cataloging-in-Publication Data
Names: Witemeyer, Karen, author.
Title: The heart's charge / Karen Witemeyer.
Description: Minneapolis, Minnesota: Bethany House, a division of Baker
    Publishing Group, [2021] | Series: Hanger's horsemen; 2
Identifiers: LCCN 2020052792 | ISBN 9780764232084 (trade paper) | ISBN
    9780764239168 (casebound) | ISBN 9781493431588 (ebook)
Classification: LCC PS3623.I864 H434 2021 | DDC 813/.6—dc23
LC record available at https://lccn.loc.gov/2020052792

Scripture quotations are from the King James Version of the Bible.

Cover design by Dan Thornberg, Design Source Creative Services

Author is represented by the Books & Such Literary Agency.

21 22 23 24 25 26 27   7 6 5 4 3 2 1

Defend the poor and fatherless: do justice to the
    afflicted and needy.
Deliver the poor and needy: rid them out of the
    hand of the wicked.

—Psalm 82:3–4

To the four people I could not have
written this book without.

Toni and Jamie—Two incredibly talented
women. Your generous spirits proved so
wise and patient as you lent a perspective
to this project that I lacked. Your guidance
was insightful, personal, and such a
gift. Any lack in the finished version
of this manuscript is my fault alone.

John and Randy—Your knowledge of local
Llano County history and your willingness
to share your resources with me allowed
this setting to come alive. John—the
bridge scene never would have happened
without your historical research enticing
my imagination. Thank you both!

ONE

Llano County, Texas
Spring 1894

When Mark Wallace left Gringolet two days ago to deliver a prize gelding to a wealthy rancher west of Llano, he never dreamed he'd be called upon to deliver a baby too. Or that the mother of said baby would be waving a pistol back and forth between him and Jonah as if trying to decide which fellow to shoot first.

"Get outta here! I don't want your help." Her face contorted, and a muffled groan escaped as she wrapped her left arm around her swollen belly.

She might not want their help, but she sure as shootin' needed it. She looked as wrung out as yesterday's washrag.

Mark, palms out in front of him, took a step forward. "Easy, now, ma'am. I'm not going to hurt y—"

The pistol exploded. Mark flinched. He took note of the barrel pointing toward the sky but tossed a look over his shoulder anyway, to make sure his friend wasn't sporting any new holes. Jonah gave him a nod, his hand curling around the handle of his own revolver, ready to defend them if necessary.

Mark prayed it wouldn't be necessary. The lady in front of him might be a few cards short of a full deck at the moment, but she was still a woman. And a gentleman never abandoned a woman in need. Even if she shot at him.

The sound of the gunshot seemed to startle her as much as it had him. Her eyes widened, and her gun arm quivered. Seizing the opportunity, Mark rushed forward, grabbed her wrist, and knocked the pistol from her hand. She shouted, kicked, and pounded his chest and chin with her fists, but Mark ignored the pummeling. Well, until she nearly gouged his left eye from its socket. He couldn't ignore that. A man needed to be able to see, after all. Especially when dealing with a woman in a delicate condition who seemed to have taken leave of her senses.

Doing his best not to hurt her, he trapped her arms behind her back and gently but firmly pushed her inside the rickety cabin.

"No! I don't want you here. Only the angels are allowed." She struggled against him.

Angels? Mark believed such heavenly beings existed, but the way this woman referred to them sounded far from sane.

Then again, nothing about this woman had seemed sane since she emerged through the old cabin's doorway in her nightdress, hair falling down around her ears, gun in hand. They'd heard her pain-filled cries from the nearby creek where they'd stopped to water their horses and had approached the cabin to investigate, calling out to whomever might be inside.

Thankfully, the gelding they'd been tasked with delivering was no longer under their care. The buyer had taken possession of the horse an hour ago back in Llano, so they didn't have to worry about keeping track of an animal worth more than half a year's wages while wrestling a pregnant woman.

And wrestling was precisely what Mark was doing. The tiny, dark-haired woman was drenched in sweat and bent nearly in half, yet she continued to resist him.

"Sorry for the rough treatment, ma'am," Mark apologized as he inched her over the threshold. She nearly tripped trying to stomp his boot with her bare heel and would've fallen had Mark not supported her weight and kept her steady. "But you need to be in bed."

That was where a woman in labor ought to be, right? In bed? He remembered his mother closeting herself away in her room when his little sister was born. Not that he had an inkling of what actually occurred in the room besides a great deal of groaning, whimpering, and the occasional scream.

He heard Jonah scramble onto the porch behind him and secure the fallen weapon.

"I wish Dr. Jo was here," Mark murmured under his breath, thinking how much easier things would be if Matthew Hanger's wife, Josephine, were on hand. Not only was she a woman, but she was the best doctor in Texas, as far as he was concerned. She'd saved his life and most likely his arm after a rustler's bullet nearly took him out of commission.

The captain had married her last year, right after taking on a partnership with her father at Gringolet Farms, the US Cavalry's preferred horse breeder. Captain Hanger's new position gave the rest of the Horsemen a sense of permanence they'd lacked during the years following Wounded Knee, when they'd wandered from job to job, hiring themselves out to good people the law couldn't or wouldn't help. Mark didn't mind the ranch work—he loved horses, after all—but the permanence was a different story. He'd been itching for a while now. Itching to move on. To explore new territory.

Not that he didn't like the life he had at the moment. Good work. Good friends. The occasional job for Hanger's Horsemen to keep his thirst for adventure satiated. But the itch was growing harder to ignore. He had nothing against putting down roots. He just hadn't found the right soil yet. At twenty-eight, he wondered if he ever would.

"Maybe you should have taken stock of your lack of midwifery skills before you stuck your nose in this lady's business," Jonah groused as he sidled around Mark and the squirming woman trying to elbow him in the belly.

She castigated Mark with the name of every foul creature she could recall, from skunk to toad to snake. Some she even used twice. *Slimy slug sucker* seemed to be a favorite. That one came up at least three times. He had to give her credit— the lady knew how to throw a good insult. Not that her verbal bullets would slow him down any. His mission was to get her to the bed that stood ten feet away, and a cavalryman never allowed anything to stand between him and accomplishing his mission.

"Just because you ride a white horse," Jonah muttered as he straightened the crumpled bed covers, "it don't mean you always got to charge in like some kind of knight-errant. Not all women are innocent damsels, you know. Jezebel. Delilah. Belle Starr."

"Cooper's gray, not white," Mark corrected as he gave up trying to inch the struggling woman across the floor and just picked her up. His right shoulder protested the extra weight, the site of last year's injury making its presence known with agonizing clarity. He grimaced but managed to ignore the jabbing ache. That wasn't so hard to do when kicking heels and flailing elbows jabbed him in multiple other locations. "And I'm no knight in shining armor." Far from it. Not when he'd failed to rescue the one woman who mattered most. "I'm just a man who feels duty bound to help the weaker sex whenever the opportunity presents itself."

"I am *not* weak!" A small fist collided with the underside of Mark's jaw.

The unexpected impact caused him to bite his tongue. "That, ma'am, is abundantly evident," Mark said, his mouth throbbing. Thankfully, they'd reached the bed, and he was able to unload his ungrateful cargo.

Despite her claims of strength, the fight seeped out of her the moment she came into contact with the mattress. She curled up on herself and started rocking. "It hurts."

He imagined it did. *Ease her pain, Lord, and show me how to help.*

As her left hand splayed across her belly, sunlight from the open doorway glinted off something gold. A wedding band.

"Where's your husband, ma'am?" That fellow should be the one here, not him and Jonah. Maybe they could find him and drag his sorry, irresponsible hide back to take care of the wife who was laboring with his child.

"Wendell?" Her head came up, and something that almost looked like a smile passed across her lips. "Wendell's coming. He's meeting me here. We have it all arranged. I just have to get rid of the baby."

Get rid of the . . . ?

Mark jerked a sharp look toward Jonah. His stoic friend

usually hid his thoughts well, but not even the unflappable sergeant could hide the twinge of shock that knitted his brows together.

Surely she hadn't meant that like it sounded. She'd meant *deliver* the baby. Rid her body of the infant who was ready to enter the world. That had to be it. No mother in her right mind would—

"The angels will watch over our baby," she said even as her mouth turned down and her body stiffened. Another pain must be hitting her. Her breath came in ragged puffs, and her hands fisted in the sheets. "You hear me, God? Time to send them angels you promised." She threw her head back, the tendons in her neck standing out from her throat. "I did my part. Time for you to . . . uphold your end . . . of the bargain . . . 'cause this baby's . . . comin'!"

Jonah's footsteps pounded toward the door. "I'll go fetch a doctor."

And leave Mark alone with a deranged pregnant woman? Not a chance.

"I should go," Mark said, stepping away from the bed and following Jonah. "You grew up on a farm, right? You have at least a rudimentary understanding of what is happening here. I don't know the first thing—"

"You're white," Jonah said bluntly. He nodded toward the woman in the bed. "She's white. You can't leave a black man alone with a white woman. If word got out . . ."

He didn't need to finish that sentence.

"Either we both go, or I go," Jonah said, his voice like steel. "Ain't no third option."

Ashamed for letting fear of his own inadequacies temporarily overshadow his common sense, Mark nodded. "You're right. Sorry. I'll stay."

He glanced back at the woman muttering nonsense as her head tossed back and forth on the mattress.

"I'm coming, Wendell," she droned over and over. "I'm coming."

He had no idea how he was going to help her, but he couldn't leave her alone. Childbirth had been known to steal the lives of healthy, strong-minded women. There was no telling what it would do to this lost soul.

TWO

Jonah Brooks raced his chestnut gelding, Augustus, back toward Llano with a single purpose—retrieve a doctor and return before Mark ended up delivering the crazy lady's baby. Wallace was smart. Had good reflexes. He should be able to catch the kid, should it pop out on its own. But as much as he respected Mark as a fellow soldier, the younger man had grown up in privilege, protected from the rawer side of nature. He knew guns, horses, and music. Babies were way outside his areas of expertise. If anything went wrong . . . Well, they'd just have to pray that nothing did. At least not before Jonah could retrieve a doctor.

Coming upon several town buildings, Jonah slowed his pace to avoid endangering townsfolk but kept Augustus at a trot. He spied a pair of old-timers bent over a checkerboard set up on a barrel outside the livery.

"Which way to the doctor?" he called as he drew near.

One of the gray-bearded fellows pushed his hat back on his forehead before pointing down the street. "Last building on the left. Across from the Southern Hotel." He stroked his beard, then gave it a tug. "There some kind o' emergency?"

"Woman having a baby," Jonah answered as he passed them without slowing his pace. "Thanks." He waved to the helpful fellow and guided Augustus around the wagons and pedestrians on Main Street until he came abreast of the small office across from the hotel.

The shingle read *Michael Hampton, MD*.

Jonah dismounted, tossed his reins over the hitching post, and jogged up the boardwalk steps, leaping over the last one. He yanked open the door and hurried inside. Two faces turned toward him. One belonged to a woman in her mid-thirties with a reddened nose and a handkerchief at the ready. The other was attached to a rotund fellow wearing a dandi-fied gold brocade vest beneath his black suit coat. He didn't look particularly ill, though his disposition did lean toward the sour side, if his scowl was any indication.

"I need to see the doc," Jonah announced, hoping one of them would point the way.

Fancy Vest snorted. "You'll just have to wait. He's in with my wife."

"Can't wait." Jonah bypassed the snooty fellow and strode toward the hallway at the back of the waiting area. He wouldn't venture too far without permission, but he aimed to make sure the doctor heard him when he called.

"Cross that line, boy, and I'll have you brought up on charges."

There was no line. Just pine floorboards. But Jonah halted anyway, keeping his observation to himself despite the fact that being called *boy* when he was a year past thirty gouged his hide like a barbed wire blanket.

He didn't want trouble. Didn't have time for it.

The screech of chair legs against floorboards told Jonah the man had risen. He steeled himself for the confrontation, inhaling through his nostrils as he slowly turned to face his adversary. His father's words played through his mind, calming his soul.

You can't control what people say, what they do, or how they think. All you can control is what you say, do, and think. Control the mind first, son, and the rest will follow. Pain and anger narrow our vision. Take a higher perspective. Even the vilest man is made in the image of God and loved by him.

Jonah released his breath. Fancy Vest was trying to protect his wife's privacy. He was going about it in an unacceptably degrading manner, but that was on him. Jonah wouldn't rise to the bait. After all, he was here to protect a woman too. One who surely needed the doctor's attention more than whoever was down the hall behind closed doors.

Slanting a glance at the fellow who stood a good five inches shorter and at least ten inches rounder, Jonah said nothing—with his voice. His eyes, on the other hand, made it clear that he wouldn't be intimidated by insults and empty threats.

"Dr. Hampton?" Jonah called in a voice that boomed. "I've got an emergency. A baby coming."

Scuffling sounded on the other side of the door.

"Old Maisy is the midwife who delivers Negro babies in these parts," the woman with the red nose offered with a sniff that seemed to have more to do with disapproval than any ailment she was experiencing. "Ask for Tom Granger at the smithy. He'll give you directions. Maisy can assist your wife."

"Ain't my wife having the baby, ma'am," Jonah said, keeping his tone respectful despite the fact that the woman seemed determined to shoo him from the premises. "It's a white woman my partner and I ran across in an old line shack 'bout twelve miles southeast of here. But I thank you for the information. If Doc Hampton can't see his way to come, I'll fetch the midwife."

A door opened, and Jonah pivoted to see a man juggling a medical bag as he stuffed his arms into a black suit coat and made his way down the hall. As he crossed the threshold into the waiting area, he nodded to Fancy Vest. "Oscar, you can go in to your wife now."

Fancy Vest tossed a glare at Jonah, then hurried past them.

The doctor turned his attention to Jonah. "How long has she been laboring?"

"Don't know," Jonah said. "Just ran across her. But she looked like she'd been battling a good while. Sweaty, tired, and waving a pistol at anyone who tried to come close. I witnessed at least two pains come over her in the five minutes it took us to disarm her and get her into a bed."

The woman gasped behind him. "Disarm her? Who is this wild woman?"

Dr. Hampton picked up the black bag he'd set on the seat Oscar had vacated and stepped over to the red-nosed lady. "Jenny, why don't you head on home? I'll check on you later."

"But . . ."

He opened the door for her. "Try a steam treatment and some nice hot soup. That should get you feeling better."

She rose, her eyes darting between the two men, obviously more interested in the wild woman they were discussing than the recommended remedy for her cold. However, she seemed to sense the doctor's unwillingness to continue discussing a patient in front of someone not involved with the case and reluctantly gathered her belongings.

Once she had left, Dr. Hampton turned back to Jonah.

"Did you get a name?" he asked. "I know most of the expectant mothers in the area."

Jonah shook his head. "No, but she did say somethin' about her husband." He searched his mind for details and found precious few. "Can't recall the name. She was talkin' sorta crazy-like, though. Goin' on about angels and insisting her husband was gonna meet her at that old cabin. But there was no one there. No husband, no female relative to ease her time. Just her and that pistol. I didn't even see any baby things. It was as if she'd made no preparations at all."

An odd look came over the doctor's face. "Was the husband named Wendell?"

Jonah's memory cleared in an instant. "Yes! That's it."

"Dear Lord in heaven." The doctor's face paled. "Wendell Dawson died three months ago."

Jonah's gut knotted. Suddenly all the talk of angels made an eerie kind of sense. As did the pistol.

"Fern Dawson nearly took her own life after his death, so steeped was she in grief. She has no relatives here. Not many friends either. She and Wendell ran a small ranch southeast of town until his death. In her condition, she had no choice but to sell off the cattle. I thought she might keep the house, but she sold it off too, a couple of weeks ago. She's been staying in town since, waiting on the baby to come. I thought she was making progress, that she was shifting her focus from her loss to what she was about to gain—a child. Wendell's child. But now . . ."

His words drifted off, and Jonah's mind made short work of filling in the dark possibilities.

All at once, the doctor's expression firmed. "Oscar?" He yelled the name loudly enough to be heard in the next room.

Footfalls echoed in the hallway before Oscar appeared

with a petite woman hovering shyly behind him. "Yeah, Doc? This fellow giving you trouble?"

"It's Fern Dawson." The doctor cut straight to the point. "Her baby's coming, and she's cloistered herself away in one of Wendell's old line shacks. This gentleman is going to take me to her, but we're going to need a wagon and some female reinforcement. Tell Jake at the livery to hitch up a wagon and alert Mrs. Abernathy. If Fern will listen to anyone, it'll be the parson's wife. I'll tie a white handkerchief to a tree or bush at the place we turn off the road so he can find us."

Oscar remained wary as he jerked his head toward Jonah. "Are you sure we can trust this fella's—"

"Oh for pity's sake, man, we don't have time for this." Dr. Hampton grabbed Oscar by the shoulders and shoved him toward the door. "Fern is not well. Go fetch Jake before we end up having to deliver another Dawson to the undertaker."

Oscar's wife skittered after her husband, eyes wide, face pale. As she passed the doctor, however, she slowed and clasped his hand. "I'll find Mrs. Abernathy and let her know what has happened. If she's not available to attend Fern, I'll go myself."

Dr. Hampton smiled. "Thank you, Hannah. You've put my mind at ease."

She offered a small smile and released the doctor's hand, but instead of following her husband out the door, she hesitated in front of Jonah. She met his gaze, the pink spreading across her cheeks evidence of her embarrassment and unease. Yet there was an earnestness glowing in her eyes that could not be denied. "Thank you for going out of your way to help a stranger, Mister . . ."

Jonah tapped the brim of his hat. "Brooks, ma'am. Jonah Brooks."

"Mr. Brooks." She dipped her chin. "May God reward you for your kindness this day."

"A healthy mother and babe will be reward enough."

She nodded. "Amen to that." Her gaze darted to the doctor then back to Jonah. "Godspeed to you both. And may his grace abound."

As Jonah waited impatiently for the doctor to collect his horse from the livery so they could set out, he silently repeated Ms. Hannah's plea for grace. It was as good a prayer as any, he figured, and Jonah's gut told him that everyone involved was going to need a larger than average helping of the commodity before this day was through.

CHAPTER

THREE

Wendell! You should be here!"

Mark couldn't agree more. If he ever ran into good old Wendell, he was going to wring the fellow's neck. There were some things a man just wasn't meant to do, and bringing another man's baby into the world topped the list.

"It's all right, Fern." Mark had coaxed the name out of her about an hour ago, once the labor pains increased their frequency and she realized she was stuck with his company. "You can do this."

Whether or not *he* could was still in question. After years on the battlefield, he'd never considered himself squeamish, but injured soldiers typically didn't have live beings bursting from their bodies either.

He gripped her hand and ran a damp rag over her brow. She wagged her head back and forth, rejecting his offer of comfort. He tossed the rag back into the basin of lukewarm water he'd filled with the contents of his canteen. As midwives went, he had to be the worst in history. Why God had chosen him to aid this woman was a mystery he'd never comprehend. The Almighty must not have had anyone else in the area.

Fern grimaced, then gave in to the groan that tended to punctuate each push. Veins stood out at her temples. Strands of limp hair lay plastered against her face. Her dull eyes sought his. She squeezed his hand. "Sorry . . . I tried . . . to shoot you."

It was the first kind thing she'd said to him. First completely sane thing too. Mark grinned. "That's all right. I was a stranger to you then. You were afraid."

She wagged her head again. It seemed to be her favorite occupation. "'Be not forgetful to entertain strangers: for thereby some have entertained angels unawares.'"

She was quoting Scripture about hospitality? *Now?* Maybe he'd jumped the gun on the sane assessment.

He chuckled softly and gave a little head wag of his own. "I don't think God expects a woman in labor to play hostess."

She closed her eyes against another building contraction. "Not . . . that. Didn't recognize . . . you were . . . the angel." As if that statement were not shocking enough, she dug her nails into his hand and sat up away from the pillows he'd propped behind her. "Promise you'll take care of my baby." She gritted the words out through a clenched jaw.

"Of course." He'd agree to anything at this point.

I know I'm not an angel, Lord, but if you see fit to send divine reinforcements, I wouldn't argue.

"Good," she groaned, "because we need you . . . now!"

Now?

Mark chanced a peek at the place on the bed he'd been doing his best to avoid looking and spotted a dark, slimy dome emerging.

The baby was coming!

He jumped off the side of the bed and ran for the doorway, hoping he'd see the answer to his prayers riding down the

24

narrow path. He'd petitioned fervently on multiple occasions for the doctor to arrive before the baby, but apparently God had settled on a different plan.

He trusted that the cavalry was coming—Jonah would never leave him stranded—but in the meantime, he was the only officer on duty. Turning away from the doorway, Mark steeled himself, rolled up his sleeves, and marched back to the battleground.

For the next several minutes, Fern groaned and pushed, then pushed and groaned. A head emerged. Mark cupped his palm around the tiny face, spreading his fingers wide around the baby's mouth and nose as he did his best to support the child's neck.

"The head's out." A tiny person's head. Complete with a thin layer of dark hair, two ears, and all necessary facial features. Awe tightened his chest. He glanced up at the mother, whose face still contorted with excruciating effort. "Keep pushing, Fern. You're doing great."

She inhaled several panting breaths, then bore down again. As her groan coalesced into something closer to a scream, the baby's shoulders pushed through one at a time. After that, the rest of the kid slid out surprisingly quick.

It was a slippery little thing. Terrified he would drop the tyke, Mark turned the newborn over and seated the baby's bottom in his palm as he fumbled to support the head.

Her head.

"It's a girl!" Grinning like an idiot, he glanced up at Fern, but she wasn't looking at the baby. She stared straight up at the ceiling as she collapsed back on the pillows.

"I'm ready, Wendell," she murmured, her words eerily flat.

Mark grabbed a clean sheet edge and wiped the baby's face. The girl's forehead scrunched, and a tiny mewl of a cry escaped. Little arms flailed in jerky motions as the cry grew louder and more demanding.

"Don't worry, little beauty. Uncle Mark's here."

He cleaned her up as best he could, then wrapped her in the knitted blanket he'd found stuffed in a small bag under the bed. At least he thought it was a blanket. It hadn't been finished. Loops hung empty where a needle had been pulled free. He'd tied off the loose yarn end as best he could, but he knew as much about knitting as he did about delivering babies, so the blanket would probably unravel. But it was clean and warm, and that was all that mattered at the moment.

Once the little gal was presentable, Mark carried her around the edge of the bed to meet her mama.

"You have a daughter, Fern." The infant was red and wrinkly, hairy and noisy, and since he had no idea what to do with the umbilical cord, she had a tubular protrusion extending from her midsection. Nonetheless, the little charmer utterly captured Mark's heart as he cradled her close to his chest. "She's beautiful."

He bent low and extended the baby toward her mother.

Instead of reaching for her child, Fern recoiled. She turned her face away. "No."

No? What did she mean, no? Mark frowned. This was her child.

Trying to coax Fern into accepting her baby, Mark started to lay the little girl on Fern's chest, but the instant the baby's fist bumped against her breast, Fern winced and jerked forward.

Mark snatched the baby back to his chest.

The muscles in Fern's neck tightened again. "Something else is coming out," she moaned.

Something else? *Please don't let there be another baby. It's a miracle this one survived my ineptitude.*

Cradling the infant in his left arm, Mark maneuvered down the side of the bed, taking care not to tangle the cord even as he tried to hurry. He didn't see another head crowning, thank the Lord, but he did see blood.

"Help." The whispered plea was all he could squeeze out through the panic-strangled walls of his throat. Not that there was anyone around to hear it. Except the same God who thought it a brilliant idea to stick him with baby duty in the first place.

"Wallace?" A deep voice called from outside.

Jonah.

Relief hit Mark with such a keen edge, he had to blink away tears. Thank God. *I never should have doubted you.*

"In here!" he yelled back. "Hurry."

Footsteps pounded up the steps and into the cabin. Two sets. Thank God again.

"I brought the doctor." Jonah steered a shorter man in a black suit in front of him. "Name's Hampton."

Fern shook her head. "No. No doctor. Only Wendell. Wendell's supposed to come. I did my part." She moaned, her eyes sliding closed as tears slid from beneath her lashes. "I did my part."

Mark had given up trying to make sense of Fern, and frankly, he was a bit disgusted by her refusal to appreciate her daughter. So he ignored her ranting and turned his attention to Dr. Hampton. "The babe came about three or four minutes ago. I cleaned her up as best I could, but I didn't know what to do about the cord. And now Fern is bleeding, and I don't know why. Is there another baby?"

"Most likely it's just the placenta," Dr. Hampton said as he pulled off his coat and rolled up his sleeves.

Jonah took the doctor's coat, hung it on a nail protruding

from the wall behind him, then took up sentry duty in the most out-of-the-way corner available in the small room. Dr. Hampton shoved his hands into the water basin Mark had left by the edge of the bed, shook them dry, then placed one hand on Fern's abdomen and pressed down slightly.

"Fern?" He grasped her shoulder with his other hand and gave her a little shake so she would open her eyes. "You need to let your baby nurse. It will help your body purge the placenta."

"No." She started to sob. "Wendell's coming. I did my part."

Dr. Hampton sighed, then met Mark's gaze. "I'm going to cut the cord. Then I want you to wash the baby and place her against the skin of your chest. She needs to be warm, and that's the most efficient method. Plus, the human contact of skin against skin will calm her."

Mark gave a sharp nod, thankful to have someone with actual medical training giving the orders. As soon as the cord tethering mother to baby was cut, Mark moved to the corner where Jonah stood and set to work carrying out the doctor's instructions. Once the little lady was snuggled against his chest, her cries mellowed into sniffles, then quieted altogether.

"You know," Mark said as he leaned his back against the wall and secured his hold on the newborn, "I think I need to write my mother a letter of apology for all the pain I caused her during my arrival."

Jonah smirked. "That was only one day. What about all the rest of the trouble you caused her in the twenty-eight years since?"

Mark chuckled softly. "Valid point. Guess it'll be a long letter." His gaze returned to Fern as she feebly tried to fend off the doctor's ministrations, and he sobered. "At least our mothers accepted us."

Memories of his mother holding him in her lap, combing

his hair with her fingers, or singing a lullaby swamped him. So much love. He never once questioned his belonging in the family. Never doubted her affection.

He looked down at the babe snuggled securely against his chest. Felt the rise and fall of her breaths. "How can a mother turn her back on her own child?"

Jonah reached toward the windowsill where he'd stashed Fern's pistol before leaving to fetch the doctor. As Mark watched, he pushed open the cylinder and emptied the five unspent bullets into his palm, then tucked those into his trouser pocket.

Mark raised a brow. Fern wasn't exactly a threat, currently. Why empty the gun now?

Jonah set the empty gun back on the sill. "Her husband died three months ago. Doc said she's tried to join him at least once since the burial. Everyone hoped her grief would lift by the time the baby came, but I'm startin' to think she didn't bring this pistol with her to fend off interfering Good Samaritans. I'm thinkin' she planned to join her husband as soon as the babe was delivered."

"Lord have mercy."

The angels will take care of our baby. Fern's deluded words came back to him. *I've done my part.* She'd lived long enough to bring their child into the world and now wanted to reunite with her dearly departed Wendell.

Heart throbbing, Mark crooked a finger and caressed the baby's cheek. "Why can't she see that Wendell lives on in you?"

Dr. Hampton approached, drying his hands on a scrap of towel. "Fern is stable for the moment. At least physically." He shook his head. "I have reinforcements on the way who will hopefully be able to bolster her mental state. I've never seen such severe melancholia. She'll have to be kept under strict observation for quite some time."

"And the baby?" Mark tightened his hold on the tiny bundle. "Who's going to take care of her?"

"Kingsland is about as close to us as Llano, and there's a foundling home there. You'll have to ford the Llano River, but if you use Harvey's Crossing, you'll be fine. The ladies that run the home have contacts in the area and should be able to locate a wet nurse for the babe. Be sure to tell them the mother might want her child returned to her eventually. Some women experience a greater-than-normal sinking of the spirits during and following pregnancy. My prayer is that once the chemicals in Fern's body balance, her mood will improve and her mind will strengthen. I also plan to search out relatives who might be able to offer assistance. In the meantime, though, this little one has needs only another mother can meet."

"Just point me toward Kingsland, and I'll see she gets there," Mark vowed.

Dr. Hampton nodded.

After giving the infant a thorough exam and fashioning a diaper of sorts out of a square cut from the bed quilt, the doctor swaddled the babe in a flannel shirt Mark had in his saddlebag, then gave the men directions to Kingsland.

Mark had never been so nervous on horseback in his life. Then again, he'd never carried such precious and fragile cargo before. Thankfully, a large sandbar provided a smooth place to cross the Llano, so they made it to the outskirts of Kingsland with no incidents.

"There," Jonah said, pointing to a two-story farmhouse set back from the road. "White house, green trim, just like the doc said."

Mark turned Cooper onto the path and followed Jonah up the drive. The closer they got, the more run-down the place appeared. Chipped paint, loose railings, a dilapidated barn. Mark frowned. What kind of place were they taking his little lady to?

A wooden sign hung from the front porch eaves. A carefully carved sign that boasted a fresh coat of paint and read *Harmony House Foundling Home*. Beneath that, in hand-painted script, was a quote from Mark 10:14: *Suffer the little children to come unto me.*

Mark knew it was probably nothing but coincidence, but the fact that the establishment chose to quote from the gospel of Mark instead of Matthew or Luke resonated in his soul like a signal from heaven. He was meant to come here. Meant to trust these people with his little lady's care.

Jonah held Cooper steady while Mark dismounted. His lady fussed at the disturbance. Mark untucked her from inside his vest where he'd placed her for extra warmth as well as another layer of security as they rode. His left arm ached from being held in one position for so long, so he switched to holding her in his right, bouncing her slightly in an effort to mimic the horse's motion and hopefully lull her back to sleep.

He paid little attention to his surroundings as he climbed the steps and reached a hand up to knock on the door. All of his attention centered on soothing his little lady.

Until the door opened and a feminine voice inquired, "Yes?"

The intonation sounded vaguely familiar. Mark lifted his head and his stomach promptly lurched into his throat.

It couldn't be. She was supposed to be half a country away. Safe. Sheltered. In the bosom of her family. Yet here she stood, the same sky-blue eyes that had haunted his dreams for the past ten years widening in shocked recognition.

"Kate?"

FOUR

Katherine Palmer blinked three times, but the impossible vision before her failed to dematerialize. Mark Wallace was standing on her doorstep. *The* Mark Wallace. Favored son of Westfield, Massachusetts. Voted Whip City's best potential husband by the girls of the Prospect Street School three years in a row. Talented musician on track to earn a place in the Boston Symphony Orchestra. Until she'd accidentally destroyed his life.

Mark Wallace. The man she'd nearly married.

"Kate? What are you doing here?"

His voice was just as rich and smooth as she remembered. And his eyes . . . mercy, his eyes were like molten gold. She was melting into a puddle just looking at them.

"Miss Katherine?" a younger male voice piped up behind her. "Everything all right?"

Goodness. What was wrong with her? She was acting like the same besotted sixteen-year-old she'd been ten years ago. She gave herself a mental shake. She was an independent woman making her own way in the world. Responsible for others. One of said others being the nine-year-old boy trying to square off with an experienced cavalryman.

"Yes, Abner. I'm fine." Tearing her gaze away from Mark—who could have imagined that the handsome young man she remembered would look even better with a rugged beard hugging his jaw and a decade of living filling out his muscles?—she smiled at her self-assigned guard and touched his shoulder. "I was just surprised to find someone from my past on the other side of the door. This is Mr. Wallace. A friend from where I used to live in Massachusetts."

Abner's gaze shifted left, and he jerked his chin in that direction. "And the other fella?"

Other fellow? Katherine looked back through the doorway. Good heavens. There was another man standing on her stoop. She hadn't even noticed.

The black man pulled off his hat and dipped his chin. "Jonah Brooks, ma'am. We were told this was the best place to bring an infant in need of care."

A tiny fussing sound emanated from the region of Mark's chest. He bent his head and made soft shushing noises while gently bouncing his cradled arms. All thoughts of handsome swains and missed opportunities fled Katherine's mind the instant she caught a glimpse of the tiny babe's face peeking out from a mound of green plaid flannel.

"Yes. This is the right place. Come in." She opened the door and stepped aside to let the men enter. She positioned herself at Mark's elbow, however, and immediately began cataloguing pertinent information. "How old is the child?"

"A couple of hours," Mark answered, a dozen questions swirling in his gaze.

His questions could wait. Hers couldn't. Not if the baby was that new. Time was critical.

"Abner?" Katherine cast a glance over her shoulder at the boy who was closing the front door. "Fetch Miss Eliza. Quickly."

Abner dashed off, and Katherine steered the men into the front parlor that functioned as their office. They kept essentials on hand in here for any child brought to them. After Ruby arrived on their doorstep bloodied and broken last year, they'd started keeping this room ready for emergencies. Much more efficient than running upstairs to retrieve clothing or medical supplies.

Katherine led the way to an old sideboard that stood against the wall, snatching a quilt from the back of a nearby sofa as she passed. She folded the quilt into a pallet and laid it atop the sideboard, then pulled a clean diaper and baby gown from one of the drawers.

"Lay the child here."

Mark came alongside her. His large frame hovered so close, she might have been intimidated had he not been cooing to the baby in such sweet tones.

"Shh, little lady. It's all right," he said when she protested his pulling her from the warmth of his chest. "Miss Kate will get you all fixed up. Don't you worry."

The newborn's pink skin looked healthy, and her lungs appeared strong, as she worked up a full-blown wail when Katherine unwrapped her swaddling. "Sorry, sweetheart," she said. "But you'll feel better in clean clothes and underthings."

"Dr. Hampton checked her out," Mark said, pressing his belly against the sideboard as if worried the baby might roll off if he didn't create a barrier with his body. "Said I didn't mess anything up too badly."

She could hear the smile in his voice, even though she

didn't look up. She'd always found his tendency toward self-deprecation his most charming feature. Most handsome men had inflated egos from all the pandering they received, but Mark had always had a way about him that made others feel as though he considered *them* the special ones.

When she pulled herself away from memory lane, the impact of what he'd said finally sank in. *I didn't mess anything up too badly.*

Katherine halted, diaper in hand, and crooked a glance his way. "Did you deliver this baby?"

He shrugged. "Fern did all the work. I just caught the little one once she made her entrance."

Hearing another woman's name on his lips grated like scratchy wool against her skin, but she shoved the feeling aside. She hadn't seen him in ten years. He likely had a wife and a half dozen children by now. "Did the mother survive?"

Mark's smile dimmed, and Katherine turned her attention back to the child.

"Yes, despite her best efforts to the contrary." He sighed. "Dr. Hampton and some folks from town will be tending to her. Unfortunately, she refuses to have anything to do with her baby. Seems determined to join her dead husband in the great beyond."

A grieving widow. Katherine could only imagine the woman's emotional pain. She must have loved her husband a great deal if she was unable to imagine life without him. Yet a mother's life was not hers alone. She had a duty to her children. To love them and protect them and train them in the way they should go. Turning her back was not an option. Not to Katherine's way of thinking, anyway. She knew the sour taste of a mother's rejection. Oh, her mother hadn't kicked her out of the house or refused to feed and clothe her.

But she had withdrawn her support. Abandoned Katherine emotionally. No child deserved such treatment.

Katherine's heart ached for the babe as she fit the clean diaper to her tiny body and pinned it in place. Working at Harmony House these last few years had brought her more joy than she could have ever imagined, but her heart broke over the tragic stories behind each child's arrival. When she and Eliza had started Harmony House, they'd pledged that no child in their care would ever feel unloved or unwanted. They would accept all who came through their doors with open arms, no matter their background or situation. And that would be the case with this little one, as well.

Katherine fit the gown over the baby's head, then carefully slipped one arm at a time into the sleeves. "Does she have a name?"

Mark shook his head. "I've just been calling her Little Lady. It didn't seem right for a stranger to name her. Besides, the doc is hopeful that Fern will eventually emerge from her grief and want her daughter back."

Katherine lifted the baby, carefully supporting her head as she snuggled her close. "Well, if the mother decides to claim her, she can name her whatever she likes, but in the meantime, this baby needs a name. Every child that comes through our doors is special, created in our Lord's image, and deserving of a name." She met Mark's gaze. "You helped bring her into the world. You should name her."

His eyes widened. "Me?" He darted a nervous look toward his friend, the man standing so quietly in the corner behind them that she'd forgotten he was even in the room. Mr. Brooks offered no words of wisdom, however. Just a shrug.

Mark turned back to her, his usual confidence adorably absent. "I don't know. I . . ." He shook his head. "Something as important as a name shouldn't be doled out on the spur of the moment. She deserves something meaningful. Something . . ."

"Name or not," Eliza said as she swept into the room, instantly commanding both men's attention, "what the girl needs most right now is food." She strode up to Katherine and handed her a bit of moistened, tied-off cloth. "Here, I made her a sugar-tit. She can suck on this until we get her to a wet nurse. It should pacify her for a bit."

Katherine had never heard of a sugar-tit, but she trusted Eliza's judgment and offered the substitute nipple to the unhappy baby. Curling the babe near her own breast in order to mimic the instinctual position of mother and child, she rubbed the cloth bulb against the baby's lips until she latched on.

She smiled up at the woman who had become a big sister to her in the last five years. "It's working."

Eliza nodded. "Of course it is. There's not a babe been born that doesn't like sugar water."

Katherine longed for the self-assurance that came so naturally to Eliza. She was four years older than Katherine but seemed decades wiser. Katherine's sheltered upbringing hadn't prepared her for the challenges of raising outcast children in a world that would rather throw them away, but with Eliza's help, she'd come into her own. Taking care of *the least of these* was Katherine's God-given mission. In it, she'd found a sense of purpose. As a young girl who'd been raised to believe her value centered solely on being a godly wife and mother, she'd floundered after the fiasco with Mark left her reputation in tatters and her chances of securing a good match too low to bother calculating. But God had redeemed her future. Given her important work—work she never would have found if she'd accepted Mark Wallace's proposal all those years ago.

She stole a glance at the man she still thought about in her weaker moments. She told herself she was glad she'd rejected his offer of marriage. She never would have met Eliza otherwise. Never would have found the children. Found her purpose. It had been the right choice.

So why did her heart pound in her chest when she looked at him? And why couldn't she stop herself from hoping he *didn't* have a wife and a passel of kids tucked away somewhere?

Thankfully, Eliza cut into her thoughts with a healthy dose of pragmatism, just the medicine Katherine needed to get her mind back where it belonged.

"Abner will be down soon. I told him to dump out one of his dresser drawers and line it with a blanket. I'll hitch up the wagon and take the babe to Georgia. She'll know who can nurse the child."

Katherine caught Eliza's arm and dragged her a few steps away from the men. "We can't afford much compensation," she murmured softly. "Donations have dropped off this last year. We've run through nearly all our discretionary funds."

Eliza frowned. "We're not just asking for feeding. With the constant attention a newborn requires, we're asking someone to sacrifice sleep and time and energy. For four months. Once the baby can take solid food and tolerate goat's milk, we can take over her care, but until then . . ." Eliza didn't finish, but she didn't have to. Katherine understood the implication.

Georgia Harris and the women in her community had hearts as big as the Texas sky, and they'd never turn away a babe in need. But they had children of their own to provide for and woefully thin purses with which to do so. It wouldn't be fair to add to their burden without offering something in return.

"Take a few dollars from the kitchen crock. I'll figure something out."

Eliza smiled. "You always do."

Katherine wished it was as simple as Eliza made it sound. When they'd joined forces to establish Harmony House, Katherine had brought two things to the partnership—money and connections. Eliza supplied everything else: experience with children, practical competence, knowledge of the need and how to serve it. Katherine had possessed none of those necessary skills. All she'd been able to offer was an untapped dowry for purchasing property and connections with potential donors. That had been enough in the beginning. But the longer she stayed away from Westfield, the weaker her ties to those connections became. If she didn't find a new source of benefaction soon, Harmony House might take a decidedly discordant turn.

Without warning, a handful of banknotes appeared between the two women.

"Here."

Katherine followed the line of hand to arm to shoulder until her gaze reached the face of the man whose hearing had always been far too keen for her peace of mind. How had she forgotten that the very ability that made him such an excellent musician also made him an unbelievably gifted eavesdropper?

"If you need more, I can get it."

More? He had just shoved twenty dollars in her face.

"Sarah deserves the best care. Whatever she needs, I'll see she gets it." His jaw was set at a mulish angle, as if he expected her to argue.

The girl she used to be would have. She'd never been one to accept charity, after all, not even in the form of well-meant marriage proposals. But there was no room for personal pride when it came to providing for the children in her care.

"Thank you," she said. "That's very generous." She tipped her head and grinned at him. "Sarah, huh? After your mother?"

The defensiveness melted from his expression, and one corner of his mouth crooked up. "She's always hounding me in her letters about getting married and giving her grand-children." He shrugged. "This might be the closest I get to giving her what she wants. Figured I'd name the little lady in her honor."

Katherine barely made out the end of his explanation over the sudden roar of blood pumping furiously through her veins.

Mark Wallace *wasn't* married.

FIVE

If there was one thing Eliza Southerland could recognize on sight, it was trouble. And the man smiling at Katherine as if she were the sugar in his coffee had *Trouble* written all over him. Abner had mentioned their visitor was someone Katherine knew from back East, but this was more than knowin'. This was personal history. Romantic history, if she didn't miss her guess. Eliza's hackles rose. Katherine's tender soul had suffered enough damage over the last decade. She didn't need some sweet-talkin', woman-leavin' man adding new scars to her heart.

Katherine wasn't like Eliza. She hadn't built up callouses around her heart to keep the hurt out. She bled far too easily. Eliza had spotted tears in her friend's eyes yesterday when four-year-old Ted scraped his knee, for pity's sake. Katherine had too much backbone for this Wallace fellow to break her, but he could inflict serious bruising. A situation Eliza aimed to avoid. Loyal companions were a rare commodity on this earth, and she wasn't about to let some slick charmer hack away at the happiness of one of the truest friends Eliza had ever known.

It was time to get these fellows on their way.

"I'll hitch up the wagon," Eliza said, even though she could tell Katherine was only half listening. "Pack up a handful of extra diapers and a change of clothes for Miss Sarah, then meet me in the yard. The sooner she feeds on real milk, the better."

Katherine tore her gaze away from Mr. Wallace and put it back on the baby. "All right."

Satisfied, Eliza marched out of the room, her strides sharp.

The quiet fellow leaning against the wall inside the doorway fell into step behind her as she exited. "I'll join you."

"I can manage," she said in a tone designed to discourage without being rude.

"I'm sure you can," the irritating fellow responded, purposely ignoring her wishes by continuing to follow.

Once outside on the front porch, Eliza spun to face him. "Look, Mister . . ." Shoot. She didn't know his name. Abner had only informed her about Mr. Wallace.

His right eyebrow lifted slightly. He didn't smile. Nor did his eyes crinkle. But something about that twitching brow made her feel as if he found her lack of knowledge amusing. "Jonah Brooks."

"Eliza Southerland." The introduction slipped out automatically, her Southern manners apparently too ingrained to bypass. Even though her Western brain insisted that the less she and this stranger knew about each other, the easier things would be.

He dipped his chin. "Miss Southerland."

"As much as I appreciate you and Mr. Wallace bringing the babe to us, there is no need to linger." Unwilling to allow this conversation to slow down her progress, she continued her explanation by tossing words over her shoulder as she resumed her march down the steps. "Miss Palmer and I are well-versed in situations such as these, and I can assure you that young Sarah will receive the very best—ack!"

Eliza reared back and nearly fell on her rump. The largest horse she'd ever seen clipped the side of her head with its nose. Pulse racing, she stuttered backward a few steps and fought to rein in her fright.

Don't be a ninny. It's just a horse.

A decidedly large, muscular, could-trample-her-with-one-hoof-tied-behind-its-back horse, but still—just a horse.

"Are you all right?" All amusement had left Mr. Brooks's face.

He immediately moved between her and the oversized beast and placed a hand on her back. The warmth of his palm afforded a level of comfort she hadn't expected.

"Of course." Eliza moved away from his touch *and* his massive horse. She brushed at her skirt, embarrassed to show such weakness in front of a stranger.

She'd known there were horses in front of the house. She'd seen them when she exited. But they hadn't seemed so large while she'd been on the raised porch. And then she'd been distracted with putting this man in his place and had nearly collided with the big brown one. A shudder quivered over her spine as she added some extra distance between her and the equestrian giant.

Flashes from the past zipped through her mind. Chasing a kitten into the street. Twisting her ankle. Falling. A horse rearing. Sharp hooves hovering above her head. That horrible squealing sound the horse made. She could still hear it twenty years later.

"Miss Southerland?"

"I'm fine." Or she would be, as soon as she got away from that animal.

Making a wide circle around the visitors' horses, she headed for the barn, where Bessie and Tessie waited—two sweet-natured ponies who barely stood thirteen hands. She still preferred having someone else handle the chore of harnessing them to the wagon, but she could manage when necessary.

And today it was necessary.

Jonah gave Augustus a pat, then followed Miss Southerland at a distance. She possessed a powerful fear of horses, but then, everything about her was powerful. Back in the house, she'd taken charge of the room the moment she entered. Authority clung to her like a fine perfume. Intelligent, pragmatic, protective of those in her care—she was a natural leader. Reminded him a bit of Captain Hanger. Though she was far better to look at. His gaze traveled the length of her back, tucked in at the dip of her waist, smoothed over the curve of her hips, then danced along the swishing lines of her skirt.

Yep. Eliza Southerland was a fine-looking woman.

It had been a long time since a woman had drawn his notice. Jonah had made a point to avoid noticing them, for the most part. Too focused on his career. His father had taught him that the only way for a black man to find success in this world was to be the best at whatever he put his hand to. *Be skilled, and folks will notice. Be the best, and you'll earn their respect.*

So from the time he'd been a boy, he'd determined he'd be the best at something. As he grew, he came to recognize that God had blessed him with better-than-average eyesight and a steady hand. He'd turned that talent toward hunting, then shooting contests, then to becoming the best sniper in the US Cavalry. Not just the best among his fellow Buffalo Soldiers, but the best in the entire US Army. His skill was what led to him working with Captain Hanger and ultimately to joining the Horsemen, a brotherhood that had changed his life.

Maybe it was the respect of his brothers-in-arms that freed him now to notice the woman in front of him, or maybe it was the woman herself. Heaven knew the strength of her looks could arrest the attention of a blind man.

Her hair, a shade lighter than most black women's, lay coiled in a thick bun against the mulatto skin of her nape. And her face—high cheekbones, fierce eyes, proud chin. She possessed a warrior's beauty. A woman a man would fight beside, not in front of.

Jonah eyed the wagon standing outside the barn as he strode past, less than thrilled by its condition. *Weathered* and *rickety* were the two descriptors that came most readily to mind. *Reliable* and *sturdy* were not even in the running. He didn't care about fancy paint or padded benches, but a conveyance transporting women and children should at least promise not to disintegrate at the first hard jolt it received. The only promise this one seemed capable of making was that it would hold together in a still wind. Not exactly a ringing endorsement of dependability.

Turning his attention forward again, Jonah entered the barn and slid into the shadows out of habit, keeping his back to the wall. Not that he expected a threat more dangerous than a grumpy milk cow to emerge from behind one of the stall doors. Still, a man was better off keeping his back protected until he knew the lay of the land.

"Hello, girls," Miss Southerland was saying, her voice completely void of the command that had been so evident back

45

in the house. "It's me." She unlatched the first stall's half door. A piebald face nodded a friendly greeting. "Nothing to be afraid of."

Was she speaking to the horse or herself?

"We need to take a little drive, ladies. All right?" She reached for the first mare's halter, her body bending at an awkward angle as she tried to keep as much space as possible between her and the horse.

Horse might be too generous a term. The mares poking their heads over the stall door were ponies, at best. The tops of their heads would barely reach Augustus's withers. Jonah could understand Miss Southerland being uneasy around the large cavalry horses, but afraid of a pair of kid-sized animals? Something deeper than mere intimidation was at play here.

"Easy now," she urged, giving the halter a tug. "Come on, Bessie. Be a good girl."

Bessie tossed her head, obviously sensing her mistress's unease. She stomped her hoof and tugged her neck backward.

Miss Southerland gasped, released the halter, and lurched backward as if the pony had transformed into a two-headed dragon.

Jonah frowned. Interfering would curry him no favor with the lady, but not interfering would lead to unnecessary delays. He figured Miss Southerland cared more about meeting the baby's needs than coddling her pride.

Choice made, he crossed to the stall and took charge of Bessie's halter. He led her out to the tacking area without a single balk, his firm, authoritative hand calming the pony. He went back for the second horse, striding past a not-quite-pouting-but-definitely-disgruntled Miss Southerland.

"You don't have to—"

"I know." And he did. No doubt she had harnessed these animals dozens of times on her own. But why should she have to torture herself with the duty today when he was here and could accomplish the feat in half the time?

He led the second horse out to join the first and started tacking them up. Miss Southerland assisted, buckling harness straps, apparently more relaxed now that he had the ponies in hand.

"It doesn't seem right for them to respond so well to a complete stranger," she said with a sigh as she gave Bessie's neck a timid pat. "But then, I suppose you're much more accustomed to working with horses than I am. Horses have never particularly liked me, and I have to admit the feeling is mutual."

Jonah looked at her over the back of the second horse. "They sense your fear. It makes 'em nervous."

Her chin jutted upward as if to deny his charge, but no words followed.

"I'll finish hitching your team to the wagon," he offered, trying to salvage her pride by changing the subject. "Why don't you check on the others? Once you have everything ready, I'll drive you wherever you need to go."

"That won't be necessary." Head high, she moved away from the ponies. "While we appreciate you and Mr. Wallace bringing the babe to us, your duty is concluded. We'll take care of things from this point forward."

Harness in place, Jonah led the pair of ponies outside to the wagon. "With all due respect, ma'am, you won't be able to get where you're going and back before the sun sets, and it ain't safe for a woman to be out alone after dark."

Miss Southerland's skirt snapped as she hurried to follow him. "I'll have you know I've driven after dark on multiple occasions. I don't need an escort."

Jonah turned the horses and began backing them up to the wagon's tongue. Once they were in place, he craned his neck and gave the stubborn woman a look that brooked no argument. "Maybe not, but that babe is under the protection of the Horsemen. If you don't want me in your wagon, I'll accompany you on horseback. But I'm coming."

"The horsemen?" Miss Southerland's brows arched slightly. "What horsemen?"

"Hanger's Horsemen." Jonah watched as her brows arched even higher. Satisfaction puffed his chest. She'd heard of them. Good. She'd know he meant business. And maybe she'd be the tiniest bit impressed. Not that he threw around his association with the famed Horsemen as a way to impress women, but something about Miss Southerland made him itch to gain her good opinion. "Wallace and I are two-fourths of the team. The others, Matt Hanger and Luke Davenport, are currently in San Antonio."

The awe in her gaze didn't last long. In a blink, her eyes were narrowed and her hands had found their way to her hips. "I read that the Horsemen retired."

Jonah met her challenge and her glare head on. "Officially, yes. We are no longer actively seeking clients. However, we made a pact that if ever a situation arose where the Horsemen felt called to help someone in need, we would answer the call." He nodded toward the house. "Stumbling across that babe at just the right moment weren't no accident. The Almighty had his hands on this. He assigned the Horsemen this duty, and I ain't about to argue with him. Are you?"

SIX

The moment Jonah and Miss Southerland left the front room, Mark repeated the question his companion had yet to answer. "How did you come to be here, Kate?"

He still couldn't believe it. Kate Palmer. Here in Texas. It was either a miracle or some kind of cruel jest.

"I took a train, same as you, I suspect." There was the saucy smile he remembered from their school days, and the teasing sparkle in her blue eyes.

That sparkle used to tie his insides up in knots whenever she aimed it his way. Kind of like it was doing now. Apparently some things never changed.

But some things did. Instead of being in her family's home back in Westfield, Massachusetts, she was here co-running a foundling home. How had that happened?

Little Sarah's mouth slackened around the cloth Kate held to her lips, sleep overtaking her. Kate set the cloth aside, humming softly as she fiddled with Sarah's blanket. Did she still sing? He used to listen for her voice in church and harmonize his tenor with her alto, enjoying the way their voices blended.

The humming faded, and her gaze finally met his. "It's a

long story, Mark." The teasing light had been replaced with a spark of determined fire that almost hid the sadness behind it. "All that matters is that I'm right where I need to be. Where these children need me to be."

She gestured to someone behind him. Mark turned and encountered five faces taking his measure. Abner, he recognized. The sandy-haired kid looked to be about nine or ten. A reddish birthmark covered the top right quadrant of his face. His mouth was pulled tight in a belligerent scowl aimed at Mark, but uncertainty flashed in his eyes as his gaze darted between him and Kate.

"I got the drawer," Abner said, lifting the wooden rectangle for inspection as he moved toward the adults. "Ruby picked out the blanket."

A girl with jet-black hair framing a pale face and big gray eyes limped along beside him. "I gave her mine. It's the softest."

Kate smiled at the girl, who looked a couple of years younger than Abner. "Thank you, Ruby. That was very kind of you."

The girl stared up at Mark as if she'd never seen a full-grown man before. Not wanting her to get a crick in her neck, Mark dropped into a crouch and tipped his hat. "Hello, Ruby. I'm Mark Wallace." She inched closer to Kate, unsure of what to make of this stranger in her home. Mark smiled at her. "That's a real pretty pinafore you're wearing. And you've kept it clean all day? Wow! I never could keep my clothes clean when I was your age. Mud saw me coming and just jumped onto my trousers without me so much as offering an invitation."

A small giggle escaped before Ruby clamped her lips shut. Those lips curled into a shy smile, though, one followed by a proud little swirl of her dress to flare out the pristine pinafore.

"Mud jumps on me too," a third child declared. Then, as if to demonstrate, the little black boy leapfrogged, hop after hop, until he landed in front of Mark, nearly colliding with Ruby in the process.

"Careful, Ted," Kate warned.

The boy didn't seem to hear, however. He was too busy pointing out all the dirt smudges on his pant legs and even one impressively large jam-colored smear on his shirt. Mark steadied Ruby with a hand to her shoulder even as he *oohed* and *aahed* over Ted's badges of honor. It was all Mark could do not to chuckle. This one must be a handful.

The last two children lingered in the doorway. A girl and a boy with nearly identical facial features. Definitely related. Same height, so possibly twins or cousins. They had the olive complexion of those with Mexican or Spanish heritage.

"Ubee?" the little girl said.

Ruby waved the young ones forward. "It's all right, Pris. You and Quill can come see the baby."

"Twins," Kate murmured, confirming his theory. "Priscilla and Aquila."

Priscilla took her brother's hand and led him into the room, though she gave Mark a wide berth and planted herself squarely behind Kate.

"The baby's sleeping," Kate said as she turned to face the twins, who couldn't be more than three years old. She bent down to let the little ones see the baby, and the sunlight from the window transformed her honey-blond hair to a vibrant reddish-gold. He'd forgotten that bit of magic. The way her ordinary veneer slipped every now and then to reveal a glimpse of the truly extraordinary treasure within. How had no other man noticed and snatched her up?

Or maybe his proposal wasn't the only one she had turned down. Somehow that idea didn't offer the comfort it should have. He didn't like the idea of another man courting her, even if his suit proved unsuccessful. Which made him a rather self-ish blackguard, not wanting her to find happiness with someone else just because she'd been unwilling to find it with him.

Quill made a grab for little Sarah's nose, and Kate straightened, pulling the baby out of the toddler's reach.

Not wanting to be left out, Ted tugged on Kate's skirt. "We gonna keep her?"

Kate smiled. "She'll live here at Harmony House when she gets bigger, but she's too little right now. Miss Eliza is going to take her to a home where there are other babies so she can eat and grow. After a few months, we'll fetch her back, and she can stay with us."

Mark pushed to his feet, in awe of the way Kate interacted with the children. So patient. So nurturing. A natural mother.

These could have been *their* children, had she accepted his proposal all those years ago. Although they'd both barely been more than children themselves at the time. He'd been eighteen. Kate sixteen. How green he'd been. How cocky yet utterly ignorant. He'd thought himself a grown man, believed he could support a wife and family. Maybe he could have, to some extent, either with his music or by working in his father's buggy whip factory. But he'd known so little of the world back then. He'd known so little of himself. The military exposed a fellow's weaknesses. Made him face them and either grow stronger or run home a failure. He'd become a better man, a stronger man for the path he'd taken. Yet seeing Kate again stirred old feelings that opened doors to questions about the life he could have had if her answer had been different.

Best to keep those doors closed, though. One busted heart was plenty. Mark tore his gaze away from Kate and focused on the kids. As nostalgic as it was to see her again, he'd be wise to learn from the past instead of dooming himself to repeat it.

"Did her mommy and daddy die like mine did?" Ted asked the heart-wrenching question with such matter-of-fact bluntness, it took Mark aback. The boy lifted up on tiptoes and reached for the baby, his fingers making it as far as Kate's elbow.

Kate rubbed the boy's head. "Her daddy died, but her mama is still alive. She's just not able to take care of Sarah right now."

"Or doesn't want to," Ruby said in a quiet voice that resonated with personal pain.

Before one of the adults could respond, Abner set the drawer-turned-baby-bed on the sofa and planted fists on hips. "It don't matter if our folks didn't want us, Ruby. Miss Katherine wants us. Miss Eliza too. So no poutin'." Having said his piece, he dropped his hands from his hips and picked up the drawer. "Now, let's get our new little sister taken care of before she wakes up and starts cryin' again."

Abner eyed each of his siblings, then turned and marched out of the room. Like troopers following their commanding officer, all four of the remaining kids fell into step behind him. Ruby with her lopsided gait and slightly abashed countenance, Ted with his jumping enthusiasm, and the twins with their waddling toddle and determination not to be left behind.

Kate met Mark's gaze, a smile quirking the corners of her mouth. "And now you know who's really in charge of Harmony House."

She tacked herself onto the end of the train and followed the children out the door, but Mark wasn't fooled. Abner's confidence stemmed from his faith in Kate. She and Miss Southerland had created a place where discarded children felt not only safe, but wanted and loved.

Perhaps she really *was* where she needed to be. A humbling thought, seeing as how she hadn't required his assistance in the slightest to get here. He'd fancied himself her rescuer all those years ago, but she hadn't needed his rescue. She'd managed that maneuver all on her own.

Katherine bit the inside of her cheek as she exited the house, leaving Mark behind. Again. Oh, she knew he was still there. She could feel him following her, but her heart already ached at the thought of sending him away a second time. How would she manage it? Sending him away the first time had shattered her heart. It had taken years to fit the pieces back together and get the mechanism working again. She'd thought herself healed, but Mark waltzing back into her life unannounced had magnified the cracks and fissures, making them impossible to ignore.

Why, Lord? Must I really do this again? Send him away when my heart yearns for him to stay?

Maybe God was testing her faith—testing her dedication to her calling. The children had to come first. Her desires came second. Mark was simply her Isaac. The human love she must sacrifice upon the altar in order to stay true to divine love.

Katherine lifted her chin. She'd done it before. She could do it again. It wasn't as if they'd truly gotten reacquainted or anything. They'd spent less than an hour in each other's company. They were still strangers. Strangers with a common past, perhaps, but strangers nonetheless. People changed a lot in ten years. Heaven knew she had changed. There was no telling what a decade of waging war had done to Mark. His gentle musician's soul had probably been hardened into something unrecognizable.

Then again, he'd seemed plenty gentle cradling baby Sarah in his big warrior arms.

Doing her best to banish that heart-softening picture, Katherine focused her attention instead on Eliza and Mr. Brooks. They seemed to be arguing about something. Not that their voices were raised, but Eliza had that annoyed expression on her face that only appeared when someone attempted to derail her plans. The fact that the quiet Mr. Brooks had elicited such a response from the strong-willed Eliza was unexpected. And exceedingly interesting.

"Here's your baby bed," Abner announced as they came alongside the wagon.

Eliza, still exuding an aura of miffed-ness, turned to face the approaching children. "Thank you, Abner. This looks splendid. However, I might not need it after all." Her gaze found Katherine. "Mr. Brooks has taken it upon himself to play escort and drive me to Georgia's home."

And she was going to *let* him? Katherine bit back a smile. She couldn't wait to hear the story of how Mr. Brooks convinced Eliza to capitulate. For there had to be a story. Eliza Southerland wasn't one to surrender easily.

"Well, Sarah just drifted off to sleep, so she might be content to ride in the bed." Katherine looked down at the peaceful babe in her arms. "Though she is awfully sweet to hold."

"Yes, well, I better take her." Eliza came around to stand in front of Katherine and held out her arms, her militant bearing softening as her gaze fell upon Sarah. Her voice lowered to a murmur. "The child needs to nurse, the sooner the better."

Katherine nodded. "Of course." She started to hand off the baby, but a shadow fell over them.

"Wait," Mark said softly. "I'd like to say good-bye." He held out his arms, his gaze imploring. "May I?"

Katherine shifted directions and lay the babe in his arms.

"Thank you." Holding Sarah in his left arm, he tugged his hat off with his right and set it on the wagon seat. Then he bent down and placed a kiss on her tiny forehead. "You had a rough start, little one, but you're strong. Never forget that God wants you to be on this earth. He sees you and loves you and has a special plan for your life. Miss Katherine and Miss Eliza will take good care of you, and Uncle Mark is only a telegram away if you ever need me."

As he spoke, Katherine's gaze fell on Abner, then Ruby, then the little ones. They all stared up at Mark as if the words of blessing he spoke over Sarah were meant for them too. Perhaps they were. Katherine's heart swelled. These children were so thirsty for affirmation, for acceptance. She resolved to speak such blessings over them until they all believed they were loved, wanted, and created with a purpose.

Her attention returned to the man who seemed to have deepened over time, not hardened.

Mark's gaze bored into her. "I mean it, Kate. If she ever needs anything, send word. I'll take care of it."

Unable to speak from the emotion welling in her throat, Katherine offered a nod instead.

Mark handed the baby over to Eliza and reclaimed his hat, his eyes suspiciously bright as they followed the baby's progress. "Take care of them, Jonah." He tipped his chin toward his friend as Mr. Brooks moved to help Eliza climb into the wagon.

Mr. Brooks met his gaze. "I will." His tone carried the weight of a sacred vow.

Katherine gathered the children around her, making sure they were well out of the wagon's path. She picked up Quill and propped him on her hip and placed a staying hand on Ted's shoulder while Ruby clasped Priscilla's hand. Abner stood stoically at her side as the wagon rolled away.

Only as the conveyance disappeared down the road did it occur to Katherine that Mr. Brooks had left his horse behind. Meaning he'd be coming back for it. Meaning his friend would probably wait on him before making his own departure. Meaning she would no longer be able to avoid his questions.

And the more they talked and shared with each other, the harder it would be to send him away again. The more it would hurt to lay him on the altar.

Quill bounced in her arms, then patted her cheek with a cry of "Bunny!" He pointed at the tall grass along the side of the road, then squirmed to get down.

Struck by the sight of an animal emerging from a thicket, Katherine lowered Quill to the ground with only half her mind, paying little heed to the children bounding off to give chase to the unsuspecting rabbit.

When Abraham offered Isaac on the altar, the Lord stopped him at the last moment, giving him a ram, instead, to offer in Isaac's place.

Her focus shifted to the man who had gathered the reins of his mount and the mount of his friend. As he led them past her, their gazes caught and held.

"What?" he asked, his pace slowing.

She shook her head. "Nothing." Then, to keep from sounding like a complete idiot, she added, "There's a water trough at the east end of the barn. Fresh hay inside."

He tugged on the brim of his hat in a motion of thanks and continued past.

Katherine bit her lip, much more than *nothing* going through her mind. Complicated thoughts. Worrisome thoughts. Hopeful thoughts that could easily lead to devastating disappointment. Yet all of them centered on a single dangerous question.

Might God restore Mark to her as he did Isaac to Abraham?

And if so, what would that mean for the children?

—CHAPTER—
SEVEN

I t took thirty minutes to reach the turnoff to Georgia Harris's home, plenty of time for Eliza to take the measure of the man at her side. Or it would have been, had Jonah Brooks possessed the decency to fit into any of the tidy pigeonholes she'd constructed in her mind for the categorization of men. Unfortunately, he had barely uttered a dozen words to her since they'd left Harmony House, making classification difficult. A fact that left her quite uneasy. Until she understood his temperament, she wouldn't be able to manage him properly.

After growing up in the South, being educated in the North, and making a life for herself in the West, Eliza had fine-tuned her male-identification system, with the majority falling into one of three major categories.

Master types needed to believe they were fully in power. Blatant disagreement only brought out the bully in them. One had to employ subtlety, hinting at suggestions while wearing a veil of subservience, so as to make them believe a planted idea was actually their own.

Intellectual types were impervious to emotional pleas and must therefore be approached with logical arguments. Even better if a woman supported her logical argument with documentation provided by men—quotes from male philosophers, scientists, and historians proved most effective.

Savior types wanted to feel strong and necessary to the women around them. Independent women constituted a threat to their masculinity. Managing this type required one to mask her strength and defer to the gentleman's capabilities and protective instincts. This type was susceptible to emotional displays—tears, in particular—though Eliza had never had the stomach, nor the acting ability, to manipulate to that extent.

"That the turnoff?" Mr. Brooks asked, raising his left hand to gesture to the overgrown path twenty yards ahead.

How had he spotted it so early? She only knew its location because of the frequency of her visits to Georgia's home, not because the grass-covered ruts were actually visible. Most people missed the turn altogether the first handful of times they searched it out. And even once a person knew what she was looking for, she had to be right up on it to see where to go, especially this time of year, when the vegetation was at its peak.

Eliza eyed him more closely as she adjusted her hold on the baby. "Yes. That's it."

He nodded and resumed his silence.

She'd initially placed Mr. Brooks in the savior category, with his insistence on playing escort combined with the way he'd stepped in and taken charge of hitching the team for her. Yet he'd been slow to interfere with the ponies, allowing her to struggle on her own before taking them in hand, and he'd made it clear that his escort was prompted more by a sense of duty toward the child than the belief that a woman couldn't handle driving a wagon on her own.

His reserved demeanor gave one the impression that he preferred thinking a matter through before speaking, which could indicate an intellectual typology. On the other hand, his bearing radiated the authority of a natural leader, more in keeping with the master type. When he'd made the proclamation about escorting her, she'd recognized instantly that there would be no dissuading him. Yet he hadn't bullied or insulted her in any way.

Not to mention that he was a *Horseman*, for goodness' sake. A warrior confident in his skills and experience. For good reason. Yet he was not the *leader* of the Horsemen. Which meant he was content to let others take charge. At least other men. Whether or not he'd bend to the wisdom of a woman was yet to be seen.

She utilized other, more minor, categories as well: scoundrels, cowards, charmers. Mr. Brooks definitely did not fit any of those descriptions. Then there was the decent type. Kind fellows, unfailingly polite, and always ready to lend a hand. One need not manage the decent type at all, which made them comfortable to be around, yet exceedingly bland. Jonah Brooks was anything but bland. There was a roughness around his edges and secrets behind his eyes. Secrets that intrigued and invited investigation as much as they cautioned her to keep her distance.

Mr. Brooks clicked to the ponies and effortlessly steered them onto the rutted path that led to the Harris homestead. Bessie and Tessie responded to him like a pair of lovestruck schoolgirls eager to please the new boy in town. Not a hint of stubbornness emerged when the wagon made the corner, unlike when Eliza drove. It usually took her two or three attempts to get the pair to turn off the road and into the high grass, but apparently Bessie and Tessie would traipse right off a cliff with Mr. Brooks at the reins.

He turned to look at her at that exact moment, precisely when her pique was at its, well, peak. He said nothing. Neither in words nor expression. No smirk to indicate a feeling of superiority. No brow raised in challenge. Not even a polite smile to put her at ease. Just a brief, nondescript glance that heightened her curiosity to disturbing levels.

Why did she care so much about discerning the inner workings of this man? He was a stranger who would be on his way in a few hours, never to darken her doorstep again. She should simply ignore him and focus on the baby who'd inspired this little drive in the first place.

Eliza straightened her spine, faced forward, and ordered her mind back to the task at hand. Only the task at hand was currently sleeping and had no need of immediate attention. Which left her mind free to travel elsewhere. And, of course, the elsewhere it chose sat three inches away from her on the driver's bench.

Stoic. Inscrutable. Frustratingly capable. And far too handsome for her peace of mind. Not that a man's looks were worth anything. Character was the true measure of a man's worth, though she'd yet to meet one who didn't come up short in that department. Her father included. Nevertheless, a well-put-together face with a strong jawline, a pair of broad shoulders covered in lean muscle, and an impenetrable gaze that dared her to probe deeper could all be extremely distracting. Even for someone who knew better than to be taken in by such meaningless superficiality.

Girl, get your head on right.

"What was that?"

Good grief. Had she actually muttered that bit of self-instruction aloud?

Mr. Brooks turned those far-too-keen eyes her direction. Eliza stiffened, refusing to give him the upper hand. She wouldn't be intimidated. Not by him. Not by anyone.

Pasting a smile on her face that had nothing in common with the flash of embarrassed panic thumping in her chest, she pointed to the homestead that had just come into view. "The house is ahead, on the right."

He held her gaze for a heartbeat, just long enough for her to be certain he hadn't been fooled by her word switch. But he didn't call her on it. Nor did he exhibit any hint of smugness, suspicion, or even amusement. He simply nodded his acceptance of what she'd said and steered the wagon toward Georgia's yard.

Why couldn't he just fall into one of her tidy categories and cease being so intriguing?

As he drew the wagon to a halt and came around to assist her, however, the confidence of his stride, the sureness of his arms, and the penetration of his dark brown eyes boded ill. She very much feared that Jonah Brooks was not a man to be pigeonholed. Which meant he was a man who needed to fly her coop as soon as possible.

Jonah intended to lift Miss Southerland to the ground, babe and all, but apparently the contrary woman had different ideas. She handed the infant to him, then turned to clamber down from the wagon under her own power. Which would have been fine had he possessed any clue how to hold a baby. Hands that had been prepared to circle a woman's waist nearly clapped together as the space shrank to engulf a newborn's torso. Twisting his grip at the last moment, he planted one palm on the little one's stomach and the other against her back like bread on a sandwich.

Sarah's eyes popped open. Taking one look at him, she scrunched her face and howled. Jonah winced.

Don't drop her. Don't drop her. Don't drop her.

Afraid to move, he held Sarah at arm's length and prayed for Miss Southerland to hurry up. It seemed an eternity passed before she reached the ground. When she turned, he swore he heard amusement in her voice, though he didn't dare take his eyes off the baby to confirm his suspicion.

"Held a lot of babies in your day, Mr. Brooks?"

"First one," he muttered.

He hated looking incompetent in front of a woman as dynamic and efficient as Eliza Southerland, but if looking the fool knocked a crack in that veneer she'd hidden behind for the last half hour, maybe it was worth the dent in his pride.

"I would have never guessed."

Why was she teasing him instead of rescuing the kid from his ineptitude? Wasn't that her job? Rescuing children?

Jonah swiveled until his outstretched arms nearly bumped Miss Southerland's shoulder. "Here."

He chanced a quick glance away from the baby and caught a diabolical twinkle in her eyes.

"Oh no. I held her the entire ride out here." She brushed past him, pausing just long enough to give his back a patronizing pat as she went. "It's definitely your turn."

He looked at the baby. Then at Miss Southerland's retreating back. Then back to the baby, her cries boosting his panic and galvanizing his feet.

"Hold up."

She spun to face him but continued backing away. "What was it you told me? Something about this baby being an assignment from the Almighty?" Her lips twitched at one end. "I certainly wouldn't want to interfere with your sacred duty." Her gaze dropped from his face to the wailing babe, blanket unswaddled and dangling, feet kicking. "I'm sure you have everything"—her eyes met his again—"well in hand."

Her skirt billowed as she executed a perfect about-face and strode away.

Jonah eyed the baby. "She don't think I can handle you," he murmured as determination fired in his blood. "Time to prove her wrong."

As if the babe understood him, she ceased her wailing and blinked at him.

A team player. Good.

Cupping his right hand more firmly around the back of Sarah's skull, Jonah positioned her along the length of his forearm, then tucked her close to his body like a sack of potatoes, and marched after Miss Southerland, his longer strides allowing him to catch—and pass—her before they reached the front porch. As if not to be outdone, her strides lengthened to keep pace with his so that they reached the house at the same time. The urge to win pulsed strongly through his veins, but good manners took precedence. Halting at the base of the porch steps, Jonah pivoted sideways and gestured for Miss Southerland to precede him.

She glared at him instead.

Then, all at once, her face was directly in front of his as she moved not to the steps but to his position. Close enough for him to smell roses. From her soap, maybe? Whatever it was from, it was mighty distracting. Made him notice other things. Like the fact that her waist was only four inches away from his left hand, a hand that suddenly itched to fit itself to that particular curve. And her mouth. Just two inches below his. Her lips weren't smiling, but they weren't exactly frowning neither. More like suspended halfway between, still deciding on a direction. Which result would a kiss achieve?

Get your mind back on business, Brooks.

At the same moment the silent scold pierced his mind, Miss Southerland reached for the baby and reclaimed Sarah from his potato hold, her mind obviously on nothing *but* business. Yet when a loud creak announced the opening of the front door, a touch of color darkened her cheeks as she lurched away from him.

Maybe her mind hadn't been *completely* on business after all.

"Eliza Southerland." A thickset black woman, hair streaked with silver, walked out onto the porch, her eyes shining nearly as brightly as the yellow apron she wore over a drab gray gown. "Did you go and catch yourself a man without tellin' me a thing about it? Shame on you for keepin' secrets, girl. 'Specially when they's as handsome as this'un."

Miss Southerland's cheeks darkened further. Jonah bit back a grin.

"I did *not* catch myself a man, Miss Georgia," she insisted in a voice haughty enough to belong to Queen Victoria herself. Jonah half expected to see the back of her skirt lengthen into a fancy train covered in beads and lace as she made the short climb up the porch steps. "I caught myself a newborn foundling in need of a wet nurse. You know full well that children are my only concern."

"And you know my thoughts on a woman closin' herself off to opportunities the Good Lord drops in her lap because she's too blinded by her own notions."

Miss Southerland's head dipped slightly. "Yes, well, just because you were right about Katherine doesn't mean you're right about everything."

Georgia Harris placed a hand on Miss Southerland's shoulder, her face softening. "'Course it don't, sugar. I make as many mistakes as the next woman." She gave a small chuckle.

"Prob'ly more, since I got a weakness for meddlin'." Her gaze fell to baby Sarah. She pushed down the fabric that had bunched up around the infant's neck to get a better look. "Let's get you and this sweet child in the house. I got just the nurse in mind. Tildy James is fixin' to wean her youngest. I'm sure she'd be willin' to feed this young'un for a spell. Might even help keep her womb empty a little longer. Heaven knows that gal has a talent for gettin' herself with child."

"A hazard of catching oneself a man," Miss Southerland muttered.

Miss Georgia cackled as she steered her charge toward the front door, shaking her head as she went. "You got yourself a point, there, 'Liza. Though there's nothing sweeter than holding a babe created from the love shared between a wife and her husband." She paused on the threshold, her voice growing nostalgic. "I thank God ever' day for the three children he done gave Abe and me. Havin' them's the only thing that made losin' Abe bearable." Her work-worn hand circled Miss Southerland's arm. "Takin' care of children like you do is a holy callin', 'Liza girl, but so is bein' a wife and mother. And in all my Bible readin', I ain't never come across a passage that says you can't do both. Keep your eyes and your heart open, child. That's all I'm sayin'."

Pretty sure the womenfolk had forgotten his existence, and *certain* he didn't want to be roped into any conversation centered around marriage and procreating, Jonah eased his steps back the way he'd come. Tending horses might not be as holy a calling as tending children, but about now he was definitely feeling the urge to get as far away from Miss Georgia and her meddling as possible.

Before he could make a clean escape, however, Miss Georgia turned and speared him with a gaze as targeted as any sharpshooter's. "Come on into the house, mister," she said.

"I've got coffee on the back burner and fresh bread in the pie safe."

Jonah tugged his hat from his head in a show of manners he hoped would cover his retreat. "Maybe in a bit, ma'am." After the conversation had shifted to something safer. Like Comanches. "I need to see to the horses."

"Uh-huh." Skepticism dripped from her tone, but she didn't press him. "I'll send Samuel out to help ya."

"Much obliged." More for her allowing his escape than for the help, but she probably knew that too.

Samuel turned out to be a boy of around ten, one of Miss Georgia's eight grandchildren who apparently took weeklong shifts living with her throughout the year. To keep the *lonelies* away, according to Samuel, who had inherited his grandmother's chatty nature.

Since there was no point in unhitching the wagon when they'd be headed off to another homestead soon to deliver the baby, Samuel fetched a bucket of water for the ponies to share while Jonah double-checked rigging he knew to be secure. He did take a closer look at the rear axle, though, not liking the cracks in the wood. A broken axle could strand one of the Harmony House ladies out in the middle of nowhere the next time they went out. The thought of Eliza alone on the road with nothing but her pride to protect her soured his stomach. The wagon needed serious repairs.

"Which are you, Mr. Brooks?"

Jonah straightened from his crouch, realizing too late he'd not kept up with Samuel's prattling. "What?"

"A gunslinger or a lawman?" The kid pointed to the pistol strapped to his thigh. "Mama says only two types of men wear guns like that, and I'm supposed to steer clear of both."

"Sounds like your mama's a smart woman." Steering clear

of trouble of all sorts, no matter which side it came from, was a good idea. "I'm actually neither. I'm a Horseman. Rode with the 10th Cavalry until a few years ago. Then with Captain Hanger. Now, I suppose, I'm retired. Still carry the gun, though." He shrugged. "Habit, I guess."

"You're a Buffalo Soldier?" The awe in the kid's voice made Jonah uncomfortable.

He'd felt much the same as a youngster, idolizing men who served their country with courage and distinction. Men who looked like him. Shared his heritage.

But being on the other side, having experienced the ugliness of war, the brutality and injustice, Jonah didn't feel comfortable being cast as a hero. Not after Wounded Knee.

"Not anymore, kid." Jonah thumped Samuel's back and strode forward to check on Bessie and Tessie, two old girls who wouldn't have the energy to tangle their traces even if they discovered the inclination.

"But you used to be, right?" The boy was persistent, trailing after him like an eager puppy. "Maybe you can stop the kiddy-snatchers."

Jonah spun around. "The what?"

"The kiddy-snatchers." Samuel's wide eyes blinked up at him, nothing but sincerity shining in their depths. "Rawley told me about 'em. They come out of the woods when no one's around and snatch up boys old enough to be out on their own but too young to put up a fight. Once a boy is snatched, he's never seen again. Ever."

"Samuel Crawford Harris! What have I told you about tellin' tales?" Georgia Harris stood with hands planted firmly on hips, a glower darkening her previously pleasant countenance.

"But Gramma Georgia, it's the truth!"

His adamancy didn't leave a dent. She raised a brow. "Have you seen a child be snatched?"

"No, but Rawley said—"

"Rawley is a boxcar boy who rides the rails with a gang of troublemakers who steal from honest folk and stir up mischief. He probably made up the story just to frighten you."

Samuel's expression turned mulish. "He wouldn't! He's my friend."

"Even though your mama told you not to see him again?" She wagged a finger in the boy's direction. "Do I need to have a conversation with your daddy when he comes to pick you up tomorrow?"

All defiance leaked out of Samuel with the speed of water passing through a sieve. "No, ma'am."

Miss Georgia nodded in satisfaction, and a smile returned to soften her face. "That's my good boy. Now, run up to the house and help yourself to a slice of Gramma's bread for helping Mr. Brooks. There's jam on the counter too."

Samuel headed for the house, defeat drooping his shoulders. He passed Miss Southerland along the way. Her brow crinkled, and she twisted her head to watch him go but made no move to interfere.

"Let me give you the directions to Tildy's house," Miss Georgia was saying, but Jonah only listened with half an ear, his focus on the boy.

When Samuel reached the porch, he grabbed the railing, then stopped and glanced over his shoulder. Directly at Jonah.

A small shiver vibrated against Jonah's nape. Tall tale or not, he couldn't leave the kid hanging.

He dipped his chin. Samuel dipped his in return.

The Horsemen had just been hired.

—CHAPTER—
EIGHT

Mark leaned against the side of the house and watched the kids play in the yard. Kate was avoiding him. Had been for the last hour. After he'd seen to the horses, he searched her out in the kitchen and found her peeling potatoes. He'd offered to help, hoping to spend some time with her and maybe wheedle past whatever reluctance was keeping her from answering his questions. He'd start with some innocuous questions about her family. Share a few tidbits about his own from his mother's last letter. Do a little reminiscing over old times. Then gently move into the unknown territory of what had transpired between the past and present.

He'd barely managed the opening smile of his campaign before the little minx retreated. She'd thrust the bowl of peelings at him, thanked him for his help, then left. Left! With no explanation beyond a muttered excuse about needing to restock the baby supplies in the downstairs cabinet. As if that were a matter of great urgency. Supper seemed a more imminent need, in his estimation, but he had let her go, staying behind to peel potatoes.

He conquered the tower of tubers heroically, determined

to impress the fair maiden with his knightly knife skills. He even went so far as to chop the spuds into chunks and dump them in the pot of water waiting on the worktable. All for naught. Kate had not returned. And unless *restocking supplies* included knitting new blankets by hand, her excuse had run out of viable duration.

The Kate Palmer he'd known wouldn't abandon a guest, especially not an old friend she hadn't seen in a decade. She was kind and hospitable, always cognizant of the feelings of others. Sometimes *too* cognizant, he thought, frowning at the memory of the way she'd rejected his proposal all those years ago, insisting that she wouldn't allow him to sacrifice his future to salvage her reputation. As if a future with her would have been some kind of punishment.

Therefore the fact that she'd abandoned him to finish potato duty alone meant he had spooked her. The trouble was, he couldn't decide if that was a good thing or a bad thing. Had dormant feelings awoken in her the way they had in him, or had his feelings always been one-sided? Maybe her rejection of his proposal had not been as noble as he'd thought. Maybe she'd just been sparing his feelings, covering the fact that she had no actual desire to tie her life to his, preferring to live with a tattered reputation rather than as his wife.

Thankfully a squabble breaking out amid the younger ranks saved him from pondering that particularly depressing thought any further.

"That's mine!" Ted yelled, stomping his foot for good measure. "Give it back, Ruby!"

The girl shook her head and handed the wooden horse on wheels to the smaller boy behind her. "You've had it long enough. It's Quill's turn. Miss Katherine told us we have to share. Remember?"

Mark pushed away from the side of the house and eased his way toward the confrontation in the middle of the yard.

"I'm not done with it yet!" Ted grabbed the toy and yanked it away from Quill, who immediately commenced crying.

Ruby made a grab for the toy herself, but Ted ran off, knowing she'd never catch him with the limp that slowed her down. "I'm gonna tell Miss Katherine!" She shouted the threat after him, but Ted just turned and stuck his tongue out.

"Hold up there, partner." Mark scooped Ted up from behind in a one-armed hold. "A gentleman never sticks his tongue out at a lady." He gently but firmly removed the toy horse from Ted's grip. "Neither does he refuse to share with those around him."

Ted's legs kicked Mark's knees as he squirmed in protest. "Not fair! It's my turn."

"Tell you what. Why don't we play a different game altogether?" Mark strolled over to a small elm a few feet away that tethered the end of the empty clothesline stretching across the yard from the back porch. Raising the wooden horse above his head, he secured it in a *V* formed by two branches.

Ted's squirming slowed, and his head tipped back as he frowned up at his captor. "What kind o' game?"

"It's called Cavalry."

"How do you play?" The quiet question came from Ruby, who approached slowly with one twin on either side, their hands clasped in hers. Quill sniffed and rubbed his teary eyes with the heel of one hand.

"Well," Mark said, "when I was in the Army, I was a trumpeter. It was my job to sound the bugle."

Abner, who had been building some kind of structure out of sticks and rocks at the edge of the barn, abandoned his project and jogged over to join the discussion. "You mean like the battle charge?"

"Yep. But there were a bunch of other calls too. Mostly used in camp to tell the soldiers what to do and where to be. One tune told the men it was time to wake up; one called them to the stable to take care of their horses; one told them it was time to eat; one told them it was time to practice their drills; one told them it was time to get ready for bed; and the final tune—"Taps"—signaled that all lamps were to be extinguished and all talking was to cease. How about I teach you a few of the calls, and we see if you can remember what to do for each one?"

Ted's face scrunched as he craned his neck to meet Mark's eye. "But you ain't got no bugle."

Mark grinned. "Actually, I do. In my saddlebag. Shall we fetch it?"

A chorus of excited *yeses* had them setting off for the barn.

Mark had removed the saddles and gear from Cooper and Augustus earlier, so the bag he sought sat near the barn entrance on a low shelf. It took only a moment to throw open the flap and pull out what he sought.

"That's jus' a bunch o' old clothes," Ted said, disgust lacing his tone.

Mark chuckled and hunkered down so the boy could better see the odd lumps inside the bundle. He unwrapped a trouser leg to expose the top of the bugle's bell. "When I was in the Army, I would wear it strapped around my chest so the bugle was always close at hand in case my captain needed me to signal the men. But now that I'm retired from the cavalry, the horn stays in my bag. I cover it with spare clothes to protect it."

He finished unwrapping it, taking a moment to shine a fingerprint off the bell before shoving the clothes back in the pouch. It wasn't the concert trumpet he'd once hoped to play in the Boston Symphony, but this one carried memories as well as music. So many that he'd purchased the instrument from the

Army when he'd mustered out, not wanting to hand it over to another trumpeter who might think it merely a piece of brass.

"Now," he said, straightening, "let's start the game!"

Mark set his lips to the mouthpiece and sounded the most recognizable call in his repertoire. At the same time, he pointed dramatically with his left arm, straight as a cavalry saber.

Abner was the first to yell. "Charge!"

The rest joined in as they ran out of the barn and charged into the yard.

What kind of a coward hid behind baby clothes? Katherine blew out a sigh, shook her head, and clicked the cabinet door closed. One could only count a pile of diapers so many times, and she'd exceeded that number by about fifteen.

Setting her shoulders, she slowly unfolded from her kneeling position and gained her feet. He was just a man, for heaven's sake. A friend, even. One didn't desert one's friends. At least not without an extremely good reason. And while preserving her sanity had seemed a viable justification when Mark appeared in her doorway oozing charm and chivalry, now that her more mature self had retaken command of a mind temporarily infected by a sixteen-year-old girl's panic, she could admit that she'd taken the wrong path.

Time to correct her course.

She glanced at the clock on the parlor mantel and gasped when she spied the hour hand nearly atop the five. Good heavens! An hour? Her mother would be horrified by the extent of her rudeness. She'd left the parlor a handful of times to check on the children, but she'd made a point to use the front door in order to avoid the kitchen. Of course, by now the kitchen was probably empty. Mark had no doubt abandoned the potatoes minutes after she'd abandoned him. But where had he gone? She would have heard him had he moved about in the house. Yet she hadn't spotted him in the yard either. He must have retired to the barn and the company of his horse. A friend who wouldn't bolt the moment they were alone together.

Another sigh escaped her before she stiffened. Fisting her hands, Katherine lifted her chin and threw back her shoulders. No more sighing. If she could face down closed-minded charity matrons and bigoted bankers without cowering, she could converse with Mark Wallace.

Barely two steps into her march of redemption, the piercing call of a horn echoed through the house. Short staccato notes. Immediately recognizable. A set of low notes followed by a set of higher notes before returning to the lower. Katherine ran to the kitchen and peered out the side window just in time to see the children charging out of the barn. Mark brought up the rear, a bugle in his hand.

He still played. Her heart leapt. When he joined the Army, she thought she'd driven him away from music altogether. God had gifted Mark with an incredible facility for music. Believing she had inadvertently stolen that gift from him had left her morose and depressed for months after he'd left. Lingering guilt was probably what sent her into hiding today too. But she should have known better. A gift bestowed by God couldn't be stolen by man. Or woman. It might be neglected or stifled, but never stolen. The Lord had simply provided a new way for Mark to put it to use.

As he was doing with her children. They sat around his feet, attention rapt as he spoke, excitement building as he raised the bugle to his mouth and played a different tune. One that ran up and down the scale so quickly she felt like she should jump into some sort of action.

He stopped playing, then gave some instruction she couldn't hear but could easily guess when all of the children lay down. He played the tune again, and the children jumped up from the ground and started pantomiming something that resembled the making of a bed before standing up stiff and straight and giving a salute.

A delighted laugh bubbled out of her.

"'Reveille.'"

Katherine bit her lip and turned away from the window. He was so good at creating fun and putting people at ease. Even children, apparently. He would make a wonderful father someday. A pang low in her belly brought an unexpected tear to her eye, but she blinked it away. She had potatoes to peel.

Except she didn't. The worktable was clean. No potatoes, peelings, or even a knife in evidence. Only the pot. She stepped close and peeked inside. That man. Going above and beyond the call of duty. Not only had he prepped the potatoes, he'd cleaned up after himself. He deserved so much more than a woman too afraid to dredge up the past that she neglected him in the present. At the very least, he deserved a proper thank-you.

Resolved, Katherine marched out the back door and into the yard, where Mark was retrieving a toy horse from the elm tree. How it came to be there in the first place, she couldn't imagine.

"The next bugle call is the stable call." He walked halfway to the barn, used the heel of his boot to draw a rectangle in the dirt, then placed the wooden horse inside. "After a trooper wakes up, his next duty is to see to his horse."

He lifted the bugle, pursed his lips, and blew. She hadn't heard this call before. It moved up the scale in stairstep fashion, but on each platform note, he tongued a complex, exceedingly fast rhythm that exhibited impressive technical skill. He might actually be better now than when he'd been training for the symphony.

She hung back, not wanting to interrupt or distract from the game. Plus, she enjoyed watching him. Listening to him play. Remembering the happy times they'd shared. The laughter. The music.

"When a soldier hears this call, he hurries to the picket line to muck out the area and feed, hay, and groom his mount. So when you hear this call, I want you to hurry to our picket area here and pretend you're wielding a pitchfork. Yes! Just like Abner's doing."

Soon all the kids were mimicking Abner's shoveling charade.

Mark sounded the stable call. A herd of children descended upon the toy horse and mucked for all they were worth.

"Excellent! You all would make perfect troopers. The next call was always my favorite because it meant it was time to eat." Mark pooched out his flat belly and thumped it like a drum. "Mmm."

The kids giggled. Katherine grinned.

"Where do you normally eat dinner?" Mark quizzed the assembly.

"Kitchen!" Quill called out as he pointed a chubby finger at the precise location where Katherine was standing.

"The kitchen. Right!" Mark pivoted toward the house, and his gaze stumbled onto Katherine. He fell silent for a moment, his eyes locked on hers, before he recalled the game and turned his attention back to the children. "When you hear this next call, run to Miss Katherine and pretend to eat a bowl full of"—he glanced over his shoulder at her and winked—"potatoes."

Katherine's face warmed, but she held her ground and gave him a nod of concession. She deserved that gentle jab.

The game continued for a good thirty minutes. Mark played different calls—"Reveille," "Stable Call," "Mess Call," and "Taps"—while the kids tried to keep them straight and act out the appropriate charade. At first there was much confusion. Most of the kids just waited for Abner to act and followed him. But by the end their confidence had grown, and they were soon racing each other to see who could get to the correct station first.

Mark drew the game to a close with a final call for "Taps." The mournful sound echoed through the evening air as the children dropped to the ground and pretended to sleep.

Ruby was the first to sit up. "Can you play any other songs? Like 'Here We Go Round the Mulberry Bush'?"

Mark sat on the ground and crossed his legs in front of him. "I could if I had my valve trumpet." He wiggled his fingers above the midsection of the bugle. "It has . . . buttons, I guess you could call them. When you push the buttons in different combinations, you can play any note a song could have. Bugles like this one, though, can only play five notes." He laid the bugle in his lap and grinned at Ruby. "But we can *sing* your song!" He inhaled an exaggerated, and impressively loud, breath and launched into a rousing rendition of "Here We Go Round the Mulberry Bush."

After that, every child clamored to pick a song. Mary's little lamb made an appearance, followed by London's bridge. But when Ted picked "Home on the Range," hilarity ensued. Mark gave the most melodramatic performance she'd ever seen, his mournful cowboy so comically wretched, the children laughed more than sang along.

She hummed and swayed, the music drawing her closer without conscious thought. Before she knew it, she stood directly behind Mark's back.

Once Abner caught his breath from laughing so hard, he smiled up at her. "What song do *you* want to sing, Miss Katherine?"

"Oh, I don't need to—"

"I know!" Without giving her the chance to demur, Mark handed his bugle to Abner and leapt to his feet. "There's a park . . . and a fountain . . ."

She shook her head. He wouldn't.

His eyes danced with equal parts mischief and pleading as he held out his hand to her. "Sing it with me, Kate. The kids will love it."

The song they'd performed ten years ago in the Westfield Follies, their annual school production. That number had led to her own Westfield folly a few months later by making her believe she and Mark had a special connection. Making her far too bold for her own good. But oh, how she'd loved singing with him.

Singing. Holding hands. Playacting a couple in love. She'd adored every minute of it. Being in his home so his mother could accompany them on the piano. Mark's handsome smile, his teasing flirtation whenever his mother left the room. The way he could harmonize with her using notes that weren't even written on the sheet music. As if his voice just instinctively fit with hers.

It had been the most perfect two weeks of her life.

"Sing, Miss Katherine," the children demanded. "Sing!"

She stared at Mark's outstretched hand, then met his eyes.

"Come on, Kate. For old times' sake."

Oh, what was the harm? It was just a song.

"All right."

The children cheered, but it was the excitement sparking in Mark's amber eyes that set her stomach to somersaulting.

Ten years, and she still hadn't built up an immunity to those eyes. Best not tempt fate by actually touching him.

"If we're going to do this," she said, spinning away from him and his outstretched hand with a swirl of her skirt, "we might as well give them the full performance."

Mark tipped his hat. "Yes, ma'am." He strode in the opposite direction before pivoting to face her. He straightened his clothing, put on a dandified persona, and took a step in her direction.

"'While strolling in the park one day,'" he sang, his pitch impeccable despite the lack of accompaniment.

She took a step in his direction, looking anywhere but at him, and sang, "'All in the merry month of May . . .'" She placed a hand to her chest and leaned backward as her eyes flew wide. "'A roguish pair of eyes . . .'"

Mark waggled his brows. Their audience giggled on cue.

"'They took me by surprise,'" she lilted. "'In a moment my poor heart they stole away.'"

Mark strutted forward and offered her his arm as he took over the song. "'Oh, a sunny smile was all she gave to me.'"

She tipped her head and beamed a smile at him while batting her lashes. He hummed the instrumental interlude, and then, as if ten years hadn't passed, they came in together in perfect harmony. "'And of course we were as happy as could be.'"

He spun her around, then led her in a prance around the children for the refrain. "'So neatly I raised my hat.'" He lifted his hat from his head. "'And made a polite remark.'"

She gazed at him with theatrical adoration. "'I never shall forget that lovely afternoon . . .'"

"'. . . When I met her at the fountain in the park.'"

They did a little vaudeville-style dance as Mark whistled the interlude, then took up their parts again for the second verse, alternating lines.

"'We lingered there beneath the trees.'"

"'Her voice was like the fragrant breeze.'"

"'We talked of happy love until the stars above.'"

"'When her loving "yes" she gave my heart to please.'"

Katherine stumbled a bit at that line. Mark caught her arm smoothly and carried on as if no great irony lived in the lyric.

They continued through the rest of the song, singing of happiness and tipped hats and shared memories. But when Mark twirled her around for the big finish, dropping to one knee so she could perch on his upraised thigh and strike the final pose, memories of another time he went down on one knee flew through her mind in a distracting wave, causing her to overshoot her seat. As Mark's gorgeous tenor voice belted out the last note, she slid off the back of his leg. Her feet flew up as she toppled. She squealed, he tried to catch her, and they both ended up in a heap on the ground.

"Kate? Are you all right?" Mark lifted up on one arm to take his weight off her. He searched her face, concern etched into his features.

Laughter burst from her. A snuffle at first, but it soon broke into a glorious guffaw that brought tears to her eyes. He matched her with a chuckle of his own, and the children joined in. Rolls after rolls of mirth convulsed through her, stealing her breath and leaving her weak. But she didn't care. The laughter felt so good. It cleansed away all the unnecessary worry tied to the past and allowed her to revel in the simple joy of the present.

A present that included both Mark *and* her children. It might only last for this single, precious moment, but she would absorb the elation of it and store it away for those days to come when loneliness tried to weigh her down.

⟶ CHAPTER ⟵
NINE

Jonah sat atop Augustus, swaying in rhythm with the horse's walking gait. Years of military training had him scanning the road and surrounding area for signs of trouble as he and Mark meandered toward Kingsland, but his mind paid scant attention to what he saw. His internal cogitations took precedence.

Miss Southerland's stubborn silence after they'd dropped baby Sarah off at the James home should have given him plenty of time to strategize the best way to investigate the mysterious kiddy-snatchers. However, Eliza Southerland, even when silent, proved to be a powerful distraction. And not just because of her looks, though they certainly contributed to the problem. It was the curiosity she whetted in him.

The touch of Southern drawl in her voice made him wonder at her upbringing. Had she been born on a plantation? Illegitimate daughter to some entitled white man who thought he could take whatever he wanted from his female slaves? What had it been like for her growing up? She'd obviously been educated. Likely at her father's expense. So what kind of relationship did that imply? Did she treat all men as if they carried some kind of contagion, or just him?

That last question had shaken him and caused him to urge Miss Southerland's team to greater speed as they made for home. He'd hoped that putting some distance between himself and Harmony House would settle his mind back on matters of actual importance—like missing children. Unfortunately, leaving the foundling home brought trouble of its own.

"We should've stayed for supper," Mark grumbled as he rode at Jonah's side. "I spent a good thirty minutes prepping those potatoes."

Jonah raised a challenging brow. "It ain't taters you're missin'. It's the lovely Miss Palmer." At least he wasn't the only one with a woman glued to his brain.

"Yeah, well, you would be too, if you suddenly found yourself face-to-face with the girl you nearly married ten years ago."

Jonah's face jerked sideways. He reined Augustus to a halt. "Married?"

Mark shrugged. "Nearly."

Jonah let out a low whistle. Mark "the Lady's Man" Wallace, a husband? Hard to believe. Sure, Wallace had a soft spot for the ladies, but Jonah had never pictured him settling down with any particular one. He seemed the type to enjoy a variety of women without the tangles of commitment. But maybe that had less to do with enjoying his freedom and more to do with pining for the one who got away.

"Close call, eh?" Jonah smirked, but Wallace failed to rise to the bait.

Instead he just stared off into the air, his expression pensive. "Sometimes I wonder if it wasn't close enough."

Jonah wanted to ask more but held his tongue. A man's past was his own to share or not as he chose. If he started peppering Wallace with questions, his friend might expect Jonah to answer in kind. And he'd just as soon keep his thoughts—at least about women—to himself.

"If you want to head back to Gringolet in the morning," Wallace said, nudging his gray back into motion, "I'll give you the papers and payment from the sale to give to the captain. I'm going to stay around here a few more days."

"Oh?"

"You saw the place." A touch of defensiveness slid into Wallace's tone. "Harmony House is in desperate need of repairs, and from what I can tell, they don't have the funds to pay anyone to do the work. I thought I'd volunteer some manpower. Put a few things to rights. Wouldn't want one of those kids to fall through a rotted floorboard, you know."

Or a horse-phobic woman to be stranded with a broken axle.

"I think I'll join you."

Wallace turned in his saddle, the intensity of his gaze warming the back of Jonah's neck. "Why?" The simple word packed a wallop of suspicion.

Jonah rolled his shoulders, trying to rid himself of the uncomfortable weight of eyes that probably saw too much. "I got my reasons. Most of which are tied to a job I just signed us on for."

"What kind of job?"

Jonah looked straight at his partner. "A Horseman kind of job."

Wallace, to his credit, didn't immediately pester him for details. "Do we need to bring in Matt and Preach?"

Jonah shook his head. "Not yet. I ain't even sure we have

a real case. There's some question about the reliability of the witness."

"But you think it's worth digging into?"

"Yep."

Wallace nodded acceptance, confirming that Jonah's opinion was reason enough on its own. No justifications required.

Jonah sat a shade taller in the saddle. He never took trust and respect for granted. Captain Hanger and the rest of the Horsemen had never been stingy with extending those commodities to him, but a lifetime of dealing with others who viewed his opinions as inferior simply because his skin color differed from theirs made him appreciate the gift each time it was given.

"Any pay?" Wallace asked.

Jonah grinned. "Nope."

"Guess we better not break the bank on accommodations, then." Mark winked at him as they reined in at the livery on King Street.

A young boy ran out to meet them. "Can I help you, sirs?"

The redheaded kid's trousers exposed an inch of ankle, his shirt was missing a button, and he kept jerking his head to keep his overlong, curly hair out of his face, but he wore a friendly, welcoming grin. 'Course, the grin seemed more for the horses than for either him or Wallace. The kid barely looked at them before lowering his gaze to Augustus and Cooper. Jonah couldn't blame him. They were fine horses.

He and Wallace dismounted and led their mounts to the stable door. "We need to board them for the next couple of nights. Feed, water, and a nickel for you per animal if you give them a thorough brushing."

The kid bounced in his shoes. "Yes, sir!"

Jonah pulled two nickels from his vest pocket and flipped

them to the boy, who snatched them out of the air with the skill of a circus juggler.

"I'll take real good care of 'em." He stuffed the coins into his trouser pocket, then reached for the reins of both mounts. "We don't get too many horses from outside Kingsland. Most folks ride the train in. Usually I'm rentin' horses out, not takin' 'em in. Especially not ones as nice as these."

Augustus snuffed at the boy's hair, earning a laugh from the kid.

Jonah collected his saddlebags and rifle from his gear, then patted the gelding on the rump to signal him to follow the stable boy. Wallace did the same, except he patted his gray's neck and whispered something in the animal's ear before stepping aside.

"His name's Cooper," Wallace said as he moved away from his horse. "And he likes his belly rubbed once the saddle comes off."

The boy nodded. "I'll rub him good."

Wallace held his hand out to the boy. "Name's Mark Wallace." He tipped his head Jonah's way. "That there's Jonah Brooks."

The boy shifted both sets of reins to his left hand, wiped his right on his trousers, then fit his palm to Mark's. "Name's Edgar, but you can call me Wart."

"Nice to meet you, Wart." Somehow, Mark managed to pronounce the name as if it were a royal title and not an unsightly skin growth. But then, he'd always had a knack for makin' folks feel special.

Instead of extending his hand, Jonah opted for a silent nod and a tip of his hat. He didn't want to put the kid in an awkward spot.

"Will you be working here in the morning?" Wallace asked as he released the kid's hand.

"Yes, sir. Mr. Donaldson lets me sleep in the loft."

Mark swung his saddlebags over his shoulder. "Great. If you have our horses saddled and ready by seven, there'll be another pair of nickels in it for you."

Wart straightened his thin shoulders. "They'll be ready."

"Thanks."

Wallace paid the boarding fee, then turned to leave. Jonah started to follow but caught sight of another kid hiding behind the livery wall. Wart made a shooing motion with his hand, and the second kid's face disappeared. Wart glanced over his shoulder, probably checking to see if either of his customers had noticed. Jonah kept his face blank and continued his departure.

"If you need a place to stay for the night," Wart blurted, his voice shakier than it had been a moment ago, "the saloon might have rooms. People been talkin' 'bout how the railroad's gonna build a big hotel here one o' these days, but they ain't done it yet."

Jonah faced him. Met his gaze. The kid's eyes pleaded, as if he knew Jonah had seen the other boy. He probably wasn't supposed to have friends around while he was working. Jonah saw no reason to tattle.

"That's all right," he said. "I don't cotton much to fancy hotels anyhow. Prefer mindin' my own business and lettin' other folks mind theirs."

Wart's posture sagged in relief. "I know whatcha mean." A smile stretched across his freckled face. "See ya tomorrow."

Jonah tapped his hat brim, then lengthened his stride to catch up to Wallace. The railroad depot was placed prominently in the center of town, surrounded by pens for livestock. Cattle and hogs, mostly. A two-story school building stood proudly nearby, an impressive building for such a small town. But with darkness setting in, a fellow need only follow the noise to find the saloons.

Wallace led them to the larger of the two and strode up to the bar while Jonah took his customary place in the shadows near the door. Some places tolerated *his kind*, but few offered genuine welcome. More than one establishment had encouraged his departure with a loaded shotgun or the belligerent escort of a group of locals eager to work out their frustration over a poor hand of cards on a black man who dared breathe the same stale air as them.

So far, the folks here seemed more interested in the entertainment down front than the stranger keeping his own company at the back of the room. A fella banged out a peppy tune on a piano and sang while a group of three females in bright dresses that dipped low in the front and high at the ankle danced to the beat. They swirled their skirts and stamped their feet, showing off a thick froth of petticoats as the patrons clapped along.

Jonah didn't waste time watching the show. He examined the room instead, keeping an eye out for trouble. A few hostile looks came his way, but no one cared enough to leave their drinks, cards, or companions to follow up on them.

"They're full up." The sour look on Wallace's face told the true tale. The lack of vacancy was tied directly to the company Wallace chose to keep. "Bartender said there's a couple who sometimes take in boarders on the other side of the tracks. He recommended we check there."

A Negro couple, no doubt.

"Truth be told," Wallace ground out as he strode for the door, "I was glad to learn about the Jacksons' place. I'd much rather give decent folks money than contribute to a place whose business is liquor and cards. Probably has better food too."

Jonah knew better than to offer to go to the Jacksons' alone. The Horsemen always stood together. It was one of the things he appreciated the most about Hanger's group. They all had equal standing, not only within their foursome, but in presenting a united front to outsiders as well.

'Course, things might get dicey if the Jacksons didn't feel comfortable having a white man under their roof. "Better let me do the talkin' this time."

"Glad to." Mark winked. "My tongue's plumb tuckered out."

Jonah scoffed. The day Wallace grew tired of talkin' was the day Jonah would grow tired of sittin' a horse.

Thankfully the Jacksons proved more hospitable than the saloonkeeper once Jonah vouched for his partner. The boarding space they offered was part of an old carriage house out back. Half the place was being used for storage, but Mr. Jackson had laid brick to corner off a section to accommodate guests. It had a bed, a chair, a washstand, and a small bureau that would suit their needs fine. A room away from the main house meant more quiet. More privacy. Two things that would come in handy if a pair of Horsemen needed to discuss how best to investigate a case that may or may not be legitimate.

Once inside, Wallace tossed his saddlebags onto the bed. Jonah dropped his into the corner and stood his rifle against the wall. Wallace propped his rifle next to the head of the bed, then sat on the edge and started pulling his boots off. Jonah claimed the chair but left his boots on. He never put himself at a disadvantage when staying in a strange place. He'd learned long ago that it was best to be ready to run or fight when surrounded by strangers. No matter their skin color. So, boots on, valuables stored on his person, and guns within reach. Hence the lack of debate over who got the bed. Whichever Horseman bunked with him knew not to ask. He always opted for the floor.

"So, what case did we pick up?" Wallace asked, his patience holding out an entire thirty seconds longer than Jonah had expected.

"Might be nothin'," Jonah warned.

Wallace didn't blink. "But it might be something."

"Yeah." Jonah frowned. His gut hardened as disturbing possibilities darkened his mind. "Someone in these parts might be snatching children."

"W here's Wart this morning?" Mark slid the dime in his palm back into his trouser pocket as he grinned up at the bowlegged fellow traipsing out of the livery.

Donaldson scratched at a scraggly beard more gray than brown, his bushy brows angling down in a V of frustration. "Scamp ran off in the middle of the night. No warning or nuthin'. Just left me high and dry. If you gave instructions, I'm afraid I wasn't aware of 'em. I'm guessin' the gray and the chestnut belong to the two of you. I can have 'em saddled in fifteen, if ya don't mind waitin'."

Mark's nape tingled as it did when he was out on patrol and something didn't seem right about the landscape. He glanced at Jonah. His partner's face confirmed his own unease.

"I'm sorry to hear that," Mark said, keeping his tone light and sympathetic despite his concern for Wart. Folks tended to talk more freely when they believed their audience possessed an understanding ear. "The boy seemed eager to make a few coins last night. I'm surprised he didn't stick around to earn them. Maybe an emergency came up at home?"

"Wart ain't got no family in these parts. No home neither, unless you count the loft I been lettin' him sleep in." The livery owner stretched his suspenders out and ran his thumbs up and down beneath the elastic bands. "He's one of them boxcar boys. I knew I shouldn't o' trusted him. Bunch of thievin' scalawags. He swore he gave up riding the rails, and he had a good way with the horses, so I took him on. 'Sides, I ain't gettin' any younger. Need help watchin' the place at night. Worked out good for a while. Then this." His arms gestured wide, and the suspenders popped off his thumbs to snap against his chest. "Guess I learnt my lesson."

Mark and Jonah shared a look.

Jonah stepped forward, touching his hat brim in deference. "You can hold off on the chestnut for now. I got a few errands to run around town. I'll be back in about an hour."

The liveryman jerked his chin toward Mark. "You still want the gray?"

"If you don't mind."

Donaldson waved a hand as he pivoted back toward the livery. "I'll have him ready in a jiffy."

Jiffy was a bit optimistic, Mark thought, watching the man's slow, lopsided gait. But he wasn't in a hurry. Kate wasn't even expecting him.

He leaned close to Jonah, careful to keep his voice low. "Let me know what the deputy has to say. And if you get the sense he's not being forthcoming with you, I can take a run at him this afternoon when I come back to question the teacher."

During their plotting last night, they'd decided Jonah would question the local law to see if anyone had reported missing children. Mark would take charge of the schoolmarm, see if she'd noticed anything unusual lately or heard any chatter about *kiddy-snatchers* during recess patrol. If anyone had heard about children disappearing, surely it would be one of those two community members.

"I think I'll pick up a train schedule while I'm at it," Jonah said. "If we come up dry with the adults, we might get some answers by running these boxcar kids to ground."

Mark nodded. "Good idea. I'll ask Kate about it as well." Hopefully in a subtle enough manner to avoid causing alarm. He didn't want to scare her. Just see what she might know.

"Hey, Donaldson," Jonah called to the livery owner, who'd just led Cooper into the tacking area. "You handle wagon repair? I got an axle that needs replacin'."

Donaldson shook his head as he retrieved a bridle from a numbered hook on the livery wall. "I can do minor stuff, but any axle work will need to go to the wheelwright in Llano."

"Got it. Thanks."

Mark shot his partner a questioning look.

"Noticed a significant crack in the wagon's rear axle yesterday." Jonah fit his hat lower over his eyes as if worried his gaze might give away more than he wanted to reveal.

Like an attraction to a certain Harmony House headmistress.

Mark pushed his hat higher on his forehead, letting all the smirkiness in his eyes dance around in full view.

Jonah grunted and turned away.

Mark chuckled. Nice to know he wasn't the only one with an ulterior motive for hanging around a foundling home.

Five minutes later, Donaldson had Cooper saddled and ready to go. Mark slung his saddlebags behind the cantle, then slid his rifle into the scabbard. In a well-practiced motion, he fit his left foot to the stirrup and mounted. "I'll be back this afternoon," he said.

But not before he and Kate finally got around to those explanations that had never quite materialized yesterday.

"So. Are you going to tell me about Mr. Wallace voluntarily, or am I going to have to order the twins to tickle it out of you?"

Katherine lifted her gaze from where she'd been hiding it in her teacup and looked across the table at Eliza. Her best friend had sacrificed her normally perfect posture in favor of a more intimidating stance that included crossed arms, a single raised brow, and the Southerland death stare. The one that brought misbehaving children to their knees in the classroom and spurred bureaucratic feet-draggers into action when a child's welfare was at stake. Unfortunately, it had a similar effect on Katherine, crumbling her resistance as if it were no sturdier than the day-old biscuit she'd used to break her fast.

"It's not a story I'm particularly proud of," she confessed. Yet ever since Mark had appeared at the door yesterday, she'd been able to think of little else. Their history had even invaded her dreams, twisting into a convoluted mess of emotions and obscured facts that had left her more tired than rested when she awoke.

Eliza's intimidating expression melted away in an instant. She leaned forward in her chair, scooted her empty breakfast plate out of the way, then reached for Katherine's hand. "If you don't want to tell me, you don't have to. Just know that nothing you say will diminish my respect for you. I know your heart. Your passion for those discarded by others. None of us is perfect." A smile broke across her face. "Especially when we're sixteen. That's how old you would have been a decade ago, right?"

Katherine nodded. Her pride insisted she sprint down the escape path Eliza had kindly ungated, but her conscience wouldn't allow such cowardly behavior. Perhaps if she got those memories out of her head and into the real world, she could finally put them to rest.

"We were so young," Katherine said, thankful the children were out of earshot, occupied in the schoolroom upstairs. Eliza always let them play for thirty minutes before she started lessons. It helped them expend some energy and allowed the adults a quiet breakfast before the day began in earnest.

Nostalgia relaxed her tense muscles and tugged her lips into a small smile. "All the girls were infatuated with him. Handsome. Tall. Athletic. But that's not what drew their attention. Not really. Mark had this way about him that was just so genuine. He got a little cocky at times, yet never in a cruel way. He cared about people. Listened to what they had to say. It didn't matter if they were cranky old men with a laundry list of complaints or children barely old enough to have a full set of teeth. He charmed them all."

A small *harrumph* emanated from Eliza's side of the table.

Katherine shook her head. "I know you think charm is a weapon wielded by manipulators and the insincere, but that wasn't the case with Mark. His sincerity *was* his charm."

Eliza looked less than convinced. "So how did this Prince Charming break your heart?"

"He didn't. I managed that feat for both of us." Katherine sighed. "Mark was two years older than me in school, but our families were close. We both shared an interest in music as well, so we were often paired together for school and church functions that involved singing or performing. I had a terrible crush on him, although Mark never let on that he knew. He didn't show favoritism to any of the girls. My mother explained his need to be careful in that regard. Handsome young men from fine families were considered a great coup, and some girls—and their mothers—would not be above trapping such a young man into marriage. The Wallace family honor would never allow a lady's reputation to be marred, so even if Mark was the victim of a self-serving girl's scheme, he wouldn't cry off."

Katherine swallowed the last bit of her tea, her face scrunching at the lukewarm temperature. Strange how something so perfect when hot left a bad taste in her mouth after the passage of time. Much like her own folly with Mark. In the heat of the moment, she'd been so sure she was doing the right thing, but time proved her choice not only foolish, but distasteful.

"There was another girl my age, Paulina Higgins, who was determined to catch Mark's eye. She flirted with him outrageously and went out of her way to thrust herself into his path whenever possible. I was terribly jealous of her. Even at seventeen, she possessed one of those figures that turned men's heads. Including Mark's. She acted as sweet as pie when young men or their mothers were around, but she turned viper-mean with the girls she considered competition."

Katherine forced her fingers to unclench from around the teacup. Taking a breath, she moved her hands to her lap so she could wring her napkin into a wrinkled mess without fear of her old resentments breaking the china.

"Paulina bragged about how she and Mark were destined to be together. How they were perfectly suited, although I couldn't find anything they had in common beyond youth and good looks. She didn't care about Mark's musical talent or his dreams to join the Boston Symphony. But then, Paulina sang like a drowning cat, so music wasn't exactly on her list of interests. She couldn't even play a phonograph in tune."

Eliza made a choking noise that sounded a great deal like a stifled guffaw. "I don't think I've ever heard you say an unkind word about anyone, Kat. This girl must have really gotten under your skin."

Shame welled in Katherine's breast, and she bit her lip. God called his people to grace and mercy, not bitterness and gall. She knew better. She'd thought she *was* better. That she had matured over the last decade. Apparently, the road to bitterness was paved with castor oil. Lose focus for a moment, and one's spiritual feet could shoot right out from under her.

Forgive me, Lord.

"Sorry. That was not well done of me." Katherine straightened in her chair and lifted her chin. "As much as I want to blame Paulina for what happened, I can't. She might have faked an injured ankle in order to finagle her way into Mark's arms and have him carry her halfway down Elm Street, but my jealousy brought us to disaster. Not Paulina's shenanigans."

"What happened?" Eliza was not a woman given to excessive gentleness, so to hear her soft tone and glimpse the sympathetic gleam in her eyes nearly undid Katherine.

Blinking away the unwanted moisture, she stiffened her spine. Best just to spit out the rest all at once.

"Mark and I had grown close during the months leading up to the Paulina-ankle incident, close enough that I believed he might actually feel something beyond friendship for me. But after Paulina's conniving, he avoided me. Or so I thought. In hindsight, I think Paulina scared him with her forwardness, and he reacted by backing away from all girls. At the time, though, I was sure his affections had shifted to Paulina. In desperation, I did the very thing I condemned Paulina for—I threw myself at him."

Katherine swallowed hard, but the unpalatable truth stuck in her throat.

"He'd taken a job as a piano player at one of the dance halls in town and walked home every Friday at midnight after his shift. Going out alone that late at night was terribly improper, but I'd been unsuccessful at cornering him in private in any of the usual social venues. Desperation drove me to be bold. And foolish. I snuck out of the house one Friday night and hid myself in the bushes at the edge of a vacant lot along the route he took home. When he passed by, I intended to step out of the bushes with ethereal grace and confess my feelings. Instead, my hair caught in the branches, and when I moved, the tangle nearly snatched my scalp bald. I yelped in pain, and Mark startled so badly, he tripped over the edge of the walkway and tumbled forward. By the time he saw me, it was too late. His momentum carried him down, straight on top of me.

"I cried out again as he fell onto me, my hair ripping free of its mooring. Things would have been fine had Mr. Owen not been out walking his pregnant dog. He heard my cry and discovered us before Mark had time to rise. Mr. Owen started whacking Mark over the head with his cane, accusing him of molesting an innocent. I did my best to correct him, vowing that Mark hadn't even known I was there. That it was all a big misunderstanding. I had only screamed because my hair had gotten snagged. Which led Mr. Owen to turn his accusations on me, questioning what a young girl was doing out alone after curfew. And why she would hide in the bushes. Proper young ladies were abed at that hour, not lying in wait for young men to ensnare in their seductive webs."

She could still hear his voice grate on her conscience, his words falling like acid on her soul.

"Mark defended me, of course, but to no avail. Mr. Owen woke both our parents and told them what he'd witnessed. He painted it as an assignation, giving us both equal blame." Katherine would never forget the look of horror on her mother's face or the deep disappointment on her father's. "I confessed everything, not wanting Mr. and Mrs. Wallace to think their son had done anything wrong, but it didn't matter. My reputation had been ruined. Mark proposed to me that very night. I turned him down.

"My scandalized mother insisted I accept, fearing that shame would fall on the entire family if I refused, but I would not be swayed. Even when Mark took me aside and tried to convince me that he wasn't angry. He urged me to reconsider, told me he cared for me, and swore we would have a good life together.

"But I couldn't do that to him. Couldn't trap him in a marriage he didn't really want. Couldn't steal his freedom, his dreams. What about his music? If he had a wife to support, he wouldn't be able to chase his symphonic dreams. He'd be stuck in his father's buggy whip shop, toiling at a job he hated. So I held firm.

"He left the next day. Joined the US Cavalry and never returned." Katherine hung her head. "Not only did I drive Westfield's favored son away from the people who loved him, I drove him to the most dangerous occupation on the planet. His life could have ended on any of a hundred battlefields, and it would have been my fault."

Eliza pushed out of her chair, came around to where Katherine sat, and yanked her to her feet. "Katherine Palmer, his choices were not your fault." Eliza gripped her shoulders.

"He could have stayed. He chose not to. He could have pursued a career with the symphony. He chose not to. You are responsible for your choices, but you're not responsible for his. Got it?"

Katherine sniffed. What would she do without Eliza? She was a treasure. A grin stretched Katherine's cheeks. "You really are bossy, you know that?"

Eliza pulled her into a rough hug, then stepped away. "Yes, well, women have enough obstacles to overcome without weighing themselves down with blame that's not theirs to carry."

"I suppose that's true." Though guilt was rather sticky stuff. Hard to shake off even when one's mind understood it didn't belong.

All of a sudden, a herd of children stampeded down the staircase. "Miss Eliza! Miss Katherine! The bugle man's back!"

Katherine and Eliza shared a look, then rushed to the front room and pulled back the curtains. Sure enough, a man on a white horse was riding into the yard.

Eliza dropped the curtain back into place and grumbled, "Looks like he's going to be harder to get rid of this time around."

Katherine mirrored her friend's frown, but inside, her heart leapt with something that felt suspiciously like hope.

— CHAPTER —
ELEVEN

"What are you doing here?"

Mark grinned at the puckered look on Kate's face as he reined Cooper in and dismounted. She'd come out onto the front porch a moment ago and closed the door behind her. Now she stood with arms firmly crossed over her chest and legs braced apart, barring the path to Harmony House as if he were a desperado set on pillaging. He'd received warmer welcomes from Lakota warriors on the battlefield. Good thing he didn't chill easily.

After patting Cooper's neck and murmuring a few words of praise to his faithful steed, Mark unhooked the sack of supplies he'd picked up from the hardware shop that morning. He held the sack aloft as he strode toward the house. He placed one boot on the lowest stair but didn't ascend. Not yet. Best to be invited.

"I noticed a healthy dose of wobble in your railing," he said, tipping his head toward the wraparound porch balusters. Some leaned inward, some outward. Some were missing entirely. "Thought I could fix those up for you. I brought nails, sandpaper, and paint. Wasn't sure what you'd have on hand."

The pucker around her lips softened just a hair, and her shoulders relaxed a smidgen. "That's kind of you, but we're managing. I wouldn't want to delay you from whatever business brought you this way in the first place."

"My business is complete. And before you ask," he said, holding up his hand as if he could hear her next argument, "my boss agreed to let Jonah and me take a few days off before heading back to San Antonio. I wired him this morning."

Kate's arms uncrossed completely, and a hint of a smile curled her mouth. "Mr. Brooks is coming too?" She glanced behind her toward the house, as if thinking about how that news might affect someone inside. Like the sassy headmistress who'd opted to let Kate handle guard duty on her own.

"Yep." It was going to be interesting to see how things played out between those two later today. "He'll be here in a bit. He mentioned something about repairing a wagon axle."

Kate's smile faded. "I know it needs work, but we don't have the funds to cover that expense right now. It'll have to wait."

Mark grew serious. He climbed two of the four porch steps. "I'm not sure it can, Kate. Not if you want to ensure the children's safety. I'll cover the cost. Think of it as an investment in Sarah's future."

"I can't take your money, Mark. It feels too much like taking advantage of our past friendship."

Was that what she called it? Friendship? In his mind it had been a lot more.

"This is a charitable organization, isn't it?" he pressed. "One funded by donations?"

"Yessss," she hedged, obviously not wanting to go down the road he was steering her toward but unable to refute his logic.

He took the third step then the last. Watched her blue eyes lift to follow him. His heart kicked in his chest as he drew nearer. When he finally stood with her on equal footing, her head tipped back in order to hold his gaze. A gaze currently absorbing the beauty of her face. Sky-blue eyes framed by long auburn lashes. Slender nose that turned up just enough to be adorable. A delicate jawline that invited a man's hand to cup her cheek, and a chin that attested to her determined nature. Until yesterday, he'd never thought to see this face again. What a tragedy that would have been.

Mark grabbed hold of the banister to keep from reaching for the woman in front of him. "Consider any work and expenses incurred by either Jonah or myself over the next few days a donation."

"But . . ."

"If it makes you feel better," he said with a waggle of his brows and a mischievous grin, "I'll let you reimburse us with two home-cooked meals a day."

She shook her head. "I swear, Mark Wallace, you could convince a tree stump to uproot and move to a different yard with that smile of yours."

His grin widened. "Is that a yes?"

"I suppose, but I won't have you traipsing around the house uninvited and disrupting the children's lessons. Eliza's liable to take a rolling pin to your skull if you interfere with her teaching." Her arms crossed again, as if she'd decided to retrieve her armor. "Besides, we are two single women responsible for the raising of children and reliant on the good opinion of potential donors. I know the cost of a damaged reputation, and while I was happy to pay the price when I was the only one to suffer the consequences, I won't put Eliza or the children at risk. They have to come first, Mark."

The weight of those words slid over him like a leaden blanket, but he accepted it willingly. She hadn't let him rescue her from scandal a decade ago, but he could take steps to ensure he didn't endanger her reputation in the present.

Placing his hand on his chest, he said, "You have my word, Kate. Jonah and I will remain outside at all times unless invited in for a specific repair. We can eat on the porch steps like any other hired hands, and if we need to speak with one of you, we'll knock and await your pleasure." He pulled his hand down and extended it to her. "Deal?"

She eyed his hand for a long moment, then slowly untangled her arms and slid her palm into his. "Deal."

The moment their skin touched, something jerked in his gut. Rather like a loose peg driven back into its proper place by the firm swing of a carpenter's hammer. Shock waves rippled out from his core to shiver along his extremities as his attention riveted on her eyes. They widened ever so slightly when his fingers closed around hers, as if she too had felt the tremor.

He'd thought he'd made his peace with leaving Kate behind all those years ago. Thought the hole inside him had been filled with the purpose he'd found in military service and in the brotherhood forged with the Horsemen. He'd never felt like anything was missing.

Until now.

Kate drew out his protective instincts like no other, but he wasn't the naïve kid he'd been the last time he'd seen her. He remembered the sting of her rejection far too well to get carried away by the excitement of seeing her again. He'd test the waters, see where this reconnection led, but he wouldn't make the mistake of handing his heart to her on a silver platter again, not unless she offered hers first.

An hour later, Mark had dismantled much of the railing on the east side of the wraparound porch. He'd extracted the weakest spindles, leaving more than a dozen gaps in the railing. He needed to inspect each one for rot. See how many could be salvaged and how many would require replacements.

As he examined one spindle missing a hefty chunk of wood from around the nail hole, the sound of a door opening brought his head up. Running a sleeve over his forehead to wipe away the sweat that had accumulated from laboring in the morning sun, Mark straightened in anticipation of seeing Kate. Who else could it be? The children wouldn't be released from their lessons until noon when they took a break for lunch.

Yet it seemed a pupil had escaped, for instead of the lovely Kate rounding the corner, Abner strode down the porch, a glass of water sloshing slightly in his hand.

"I finished my reading early, so Miss Katherine asked me to bring you a drink."

Mark set his hammer aside and accepted the glass. "That was kind of her." Although he would have appreciated the gesture more had the lady seen to the task herself. But that wasn't Abner's fault. Mark nodded to the boy. "Thank you for the delivery."

Abner shrugged.

Mark lifted the glass to his lips and took a good, long swallow, expecting the kid to scamper away and return to the house now that his job had been completed.

But he didn't. Instead, Abner strolled over to the dismantled railing and hunkered down to examine one of the spindles. "You fixin' it?"

"Yep. Trying to, anyhow." Mark set his half-full glass on a floorboard near the house, then joined Abner in a crouch. "I'm a mediocre carpenter at best, but I figure I can repair some of the spindles, replace others. Make it safer for the little ones. It might not be the prettiest job ever, but when it's finished, it should be sturdy enough to hold up to Ted's romping."

Abner craned his neck around to look at Mark. "How'd you know he used to climb on the railings?"

Mark chuckled as he tipped his head toward the place where the railing had started to buckle. "See how the paint's practically worn off that section? And how it bows out away from the house?"

"Yeah."

"Well, having once been a rather adventuresome tyke myself, I know all about the temptations of railings. Hanging. Swinging. Turning flips over them." Mark rose to his feet and peered over the railing to the ground beneath. "Especially when there's a soft patch of grass on the other side to break my fall."

Abner stood as well, walked to the railing, and peered over the edge to see for himself. He had to lift up on his tiptoes, but when he settled back down on his heels, he measured Mark with a look.

"Why'd ya assume it were Ted and not me?"

Mark winked. "Easy. You're the oldest. You have to oversee the others. Frolics aren't exactly your thing. Ted, on the other hand, is a Texas tornado trapped in a four-year-old's body. He's constantly in motion. Running, jumping, spinning. To be honest, I'm amazed your teacher manages to keep him contained in the classroom in the mornings."

"She doesn't." A touch of a smile quirked Abner's mouth

for the first time. "She lets him and the twins play with the alphabet blocks and dominoes while she gives Ruby and me our morning assignments. Then, while we work in our readers, Miss Eliza sits on the floor with the little ones and goes over the different letters on the blocks. She counts the dots on the dominoes with them too. Quill and Prissy can already count to twelve and say their letters, but Ted's more interested in building houses with the blocks and knocking them down than learnin' anything."

"You might be surprised," Mark said as he leaned against one of the supporting pillars near the railing. "Just because he doesn't learn the same way you do doesn't mean he's not learning."

"Maybe. Seems like he's just makin' things harder on Miss Eliza, though. She has to trick him into learnin'. Tellin' him things like he can't knock his wall down until it's five rows tall or only lettin' him play with dominoes that have six dots on 'em."

"Sounds to me like Miss Eliza is a smart lady."

"Yeah."

"What about Miss Katherine?" Mark probed gently, hungry to learn more about the woman Kate had become. He knew the girl she'd been ten years ago, but who was she *now*? "Does she help with the schooling?"

Abner shrugged again. "Not really. She mostly tends the little ones after Miss Eliza shoos them outta the schoolroom."

"Is that why you're so protective of her? Because she cared for you when you were little?" Mark forced casualness into his tone, trying to disguise how interested he was in the answer. "I remember how you guarded her at the door yesterday when I showed up unannounced."

"Miss Katherine didn't care for me when I was little." Abner's voice grew quiet. Small. "No one did."

Guilt stabbed Mark square in the chest. He hadn't intended to dredge up painful memories for the kid. He floundered for a moment, debating whether it would be better to apologize or pretend there was nothing shocking in Abner's revelation.

Before he could choose, though, the boy filled the silence. "The other kids were brought here," Abner explained, "by family that didn't want 'em or do-gooders tryin' to help. Not me." He kicked at one of the loose spindles, his attention fixed on the ground.

Mark matched his soft tone. "How'd you get here, Abner?"

He lifted his face, and his eyes took on a fierce glow. "She *chose* me." His jaw tightened before his gaze dropped again to the porch floor. "My ma worked in a saloon in Llano. Took men to her room every night, spent whatever she made on drink the next day. Blamed me for stealin' her looks and knocked me around whenever she got frustrated. I learned to stay outta her way. Earned my keep by cleanin' spittoons and runnin' errands for the owner, until my ma bashed him over the head with a whiskey bottle during one of her spells. Trammel didn't even wait for the doctor to stitch up his head before he kicked us out.

"Ma was cussin' and hollerin'. Makin' a scene. Slapped me across the face when I tried to calm her down. She woulda hit me again, but Miss Katherine scooped me up and pulled me outta Ma's reach. Ma lit into her good, but Miss Katherine didn't balk. She held me tight and told my ma that she would have her arrested for saltin' a child. She took up for me. No one had ever taken up for me before. Made me feel safe. I didn't wanna get down for nuthin'."

Mark struggled to keep his emotions masked, not wanting the kid to see the pity welling inside him.

"They argued for a while," Abner continued. "I don't know 'bout what. All I remember is my ma shouting about how she never wanted the brat anyway and if Miss High-and-Mighty thought she could do better, she could keep him. I raised my head and called out to my ma, but she kept walking and never looked back.

"I was so scared, sure the nice lady would put me down and leave me too. But she didn't." Abner lifted his chin and stared into the yard. "She held me tighter. Promised that everything would be all right. Told me she and her friend were starting a home for children just like me. That I could come and live with her." A half smile tugged at his mouth. "I didn't believe her, of course. But I wanted to. So bad that I wrapped my legs around her waist and my arms around her neck so she couldn't put me down.

"That's when the church lady stepped out of the crowd. Miss Eliza was with her. I think they'd been meeting with the lady before Miss Katherine left to get me. I knew who the church lady was. Trammel used to talk about her. Said she was a meddlin' do-gooder who wanted to close down his den of inkwitty. She didn't like drinkin' or gamblin' or what the girls did upstairs. Said we were all of the devil. That church lady took one look at me, at the mark on my face, and told Miss Katherine that if she and Miss Eliza wanted her charity money, they couldn't take me to Harmony House. She said a child born in sin and bearing its stain had no place in a Christian foundling home. I knew then that Miss Katherine would let me go. Money and power always won. With my ma, with Trammel, with everyone. The church lady had both.

"I unwrapped my legs and starting sliding to the ground, but Miss Katherine wouldn't let me. She grabbed me around the middle and held on tight. She looked right at the church lady and said she was sorry they wouldn't be working together. Then she carried me to her wagon and held me on her lap all the way here."

Abner finally looked at Mark. "She chose me, Mr. Wallace. Even though she got nothing in return. She chose me."

"She's a remarkable woman," Mark said, his voice thickened by the emotion he couldn't quite contain. Pride in a woman who would trust God to provide for her calling instead of bending to the demands of prejudiced wealth. Triumph for a hurting kid who'd found a love that would change his life. And just the smallest twinge of jealousy that he couldn't yet make the same claim Abner had.

She chose me.

TWELVE

Jonah held the railing steady while Mark nailed in the last makeshift spindle. Jonah had arrived at the foundling home about an hour ago and joined Mark in his work. Not wanting to bring up their investigation so close to the house, where an open window or ill-timed visit around the corner could lead to one of the kids overhearing, he'd held his tongue and focused on helping Wallace with the repair work instead.

They'd found a handful of dowel rods in the barn to serve as substitute spindles. Jonah had cut them down, whittled the ends, and sanded them smooth while Mark straightened and refastened the spindles he'd deemed salvageable. The new rods might not match the rest of the balustrade, but they'd hold the railing secure.

After Mark hammered the final rod in place, Jonah signaled with a tip of his head for them to take a walk across the yard. Once at the barn, Jonah moved inside and braced his back against the nearest stall, choosing a position that allowed him to keep an eye on the door.

Mark dropped his hammer onto the workbench, then

massaged his right shoulder, rotating his arm in a wide circle to loosen the tightness in the joint. Wallace had regained full mobility in his arm after taking a bullet last year, but the old wound still pained him from time to time. Especially after heavy use. Jonah didn't insult him by asking about it, though.

"What'd you learn from the deputy this morning?" Mark winced slightly as he made one final rotation with the shoulder.

"I learned he's young." Jonah had been less than impressed with Deputy Bronson. He seemed like one of those kids who got the job because he knew the right people, not because he had any particular aptitude for the post. "He answered my questions, but I got the impression he wouldn't make a move on anything without the sheriff's say-so."

Mark raised a brow. "The sheriff in Llano?"

"Yep. Name's Porter. If I take that axle in for repair tomorrow, I'll stop by his office and have a word. I doubt he'll have any more to offer than Bronson, though." Which had been precious little.

Jonah reached into his trouser pocket and closed his fingers around his father's pocket compass. The feel of the smooth brass casing never failed to focus and orient him when he lacked direction. This compass had led his father north to freedom when all he'd known was slavery. With it, his father had taught him how to gain one's bearing in unfamiliar territory and how to find his way home in the dark after long days of hunting. With it, his father had taught him about the unchanging nature of God. How his presence was always ready to guide those who sought him.

This one's murky, Lord. If you could see your way to pointin' the needle in the right direction, I sure would appreciate it.

"So what did Deputy Bronson offer?" Mark asked.

Jonah released his hold on the compass and brought his hand up to rub at an itchy spot at the back of his neck. "Said no one had reported any missing children."

Mark frowned. "So either no children are truly missing . . ."

"Or children *are* missing, but no one has reported it," Jonah finished.

Mark scowled and pushed away from the workbench, agitation sending him pacing across the barn floor. "Who wouldn't report a missing child?"

"Not all kids have family, Wallace. And of those who do, not all would trust a lawman."

Mark ceased his pacing. "You're right." He blew out a breath. "Just this morning Abner told me the story of how he came to be here. His mother worked in a saloon. Abner was an . . . unintended consequence of her profession. She never wanted him. Treated him abominably. Drank so much she probably wouldn't have noticed for days if he went missing. I'm thinking it's a blessing she abandoned him so he could find a home here. Something tells me Kate and Eliza would tear the town apart if one of their flock went missing."

A flash of lavender skirt at the edge of Jonah's vision had him straightening away from the wall and standing at attention in a heartbeat. But it wasn't soon enough.

"Who's missing?" Eliza Southerland swept into the barn, her eyes piercing his with all the ferocity of a tigress preparing to fight for her cubs.

Mark spun to face the headmistress of Harmony House, but for once his smooth tongue failed him. Of course, it wasn't Mark she was looking to for answers. No, her gaze had locked on Jonah, pinning him to the stall wall as effectively as a javelin.

Eliza marched into the barn on a mission. Katherine might have sent her to call their uninvited handymen to lunch, but the moment Eliza heard Mr. Wallace mention Abner's name, her objective changed. Halting just outside the door, she'd shamelessly eavesdropped, determined to learn as much as she could about why these men were truly here. Wallace might have courting on his mind, but Mr. Brooks?

A little tickle stirred in her belly, but she eradicated it with ruthless force. She was far too headstrong to attract a man. Friends and family had been expressing that opinion for years, hoping she'd take a softer stance, she supposed. Not that it had the desired effect. She didn't have time to worry about attracting a man. Not when there were needy children to care for. And if there were children in danger here in Kingsland, no *man* was going to keep her in the dark.

Without slowing, she bypassed Mr. Wallace with his half-open mouth and strode straight to Mr. Brooks. "Explain."

The irritating man just stood there, his stoic face giving nothing away, his uncooperative tongue frustratingly still.

Well, two could play the stubborn game. Widening her stance, she crossed her arms over her chest and jutted her chin. She'd stand here as long as it took. Stare him down. *He* was the interloper here, not her. This was *her* barn, *her* property. And the children of Kingsland were *her* responsibility. She wouldn't let him go until he told her everything he knew.

The silence grew heavy. Tense. One minute passed. Then another. The urge to repeat her demand for an explanation became harder to ignore. She shifted her weight. The man in front of her shifted his mouth. Into an incredibly annoying half-smile. As if he knew her struggle and found it amusing.

Which only made holding her tongue more difficult, as the desire to flay him with it nearly overwhelmed her.

"Hey, Wallace," the obnoxious man finally said, breaking the silence as well as their eye contact as he glanced at his companion. "Why don't you fetch Miss Palmer? Might as well fill them both in at the same time."

"The children—" Eliza began to protest.

"Will be just fine," Mr. Brooks finished for her. "Abner can be in charge while they finish their lunch. He seems more than capable."

She couldn't argue with that. Abner was a born leader, one the other children idolized. She and Katherine had depended on him more than once to tend the younger ones when their attention was required elsewhere.

The scuff of shoe leather on hard-packed dirt echoed behind her. She didn't turn to look, preferring to continue glaring at the man in front of her.

"Be right back," Mr. Wallace said as his footsteps retreated.

Once his partner was gone, Mr. Brooks straightened away from the wall, making him taller and . . . closer. Eliza swallowed.

"It's not polite to listen at doorways, you know." His voice was low, almost intimate. Her pulse fluttered in response.

Eliza frowned. Her pulse never *fluttered*. She didn't have time for fluttering.

"Yes, well, it might not be polite, but it is certainly informative." Her gaze darted away from his, but she ordered it back to the front line. Embarrassment had no place here. She lifted her chin. "When one has neither the privilege of being white nor the privilege of being male, she must find other ways to balance the playing field."

"Did your mother teach you that? Or your father?"

"What difference does it make? The lesson was learned." And she'd really rather not share personal details of her up-bringing with a man she'd just met. One just passing through.

"It makes a difference." The statement was so simple, yet the depth ringing inside it rocked her back on her heels. "Lessons taught from love bring wisdom. Lessons spawned from fear and pain often come with cynicism and bitterness attached, which can cloud the truth."

"And you're the all-wise seer of truth, are you?" she snapped, not liking the way his words made her skin itch.

Something changed in his deep brown eyes as he gave a small wag of his head. "Nope. Just someone who's spent a lot of years expecting the worst instead of looking for the best. It's kept me alive, but sometimes I wonder if it's also kept me alone."

Eliza rubbed her arms, a stone or two shaking loose from her defensive wall. "What about your fellow Horsemen? Aren't you close with them?"

From what she'd heard, only one Buffalo Soldier rode among the four. Mr. Brooks didn't seem the type to ride with a group who didn't respect him, but respect of a man's skill and respect of the man himself were two different things. She'd been fighting for both types her entire life.

"They're my brothers," he said, his tone adamant. "But a man don't live with his brothers forever." Something in his gaze shifted. Warmed. Made her belly tighten. "Captain Hanger married Dr. Jo a few months back. Hung up the Horsemen's spurs and took on a partnership with Miss Josephine's daddy. Matt gave us all jobs at Gringolet, puttin' our horse know-how to work. But seein' him settle down, realizin' there'll be little Hangers running around afore long, the rest of us read the writing on the wall. The time's comin' for us to set up lives of our own. We'll always be brothers, but we gotta be our own men too."

"I can't imagine anyone who is more his own man than you."

It wasn't until his lips tipped up at one end that Eliza realized she'd spoken the thought aloud. Heat rose to her cheeks, but she refused to look away like some foolish schoolgirl caught in a flirtation. She would not pretend to be anything other than who she was. Not for the father who had treated her like a daughter in private and a servant in public. Not for professors who warned she'd be too white to teach in black schools and too black to teach in white. Not for the wealthy donors who disliked the lack of segregation in her foundling home. She owned her thoughts, her beliefs, her principles, and she would not hide.

The longer she held his gaze, the more his smile widened. Yet the light in his eyes was not amusement. It almost looked like . . . admiration. Unsure what to do with that, Eliza fidgeted with the fabric covering her elbows until approaching footsteps signaled the blessed end of her torture.

"Eliza?"

She turned at Katherine's voice and moved to clasp her friend's hand even as she noted Mr. Wallace's palm at the small of her back. Unbidden, thoughts of sisterhood and Jonah's comment about how one didn't live with siblings forever flooded her mind. Ever since she and Katherine made a pact to run Harmony House together, she'd envisioned this being their life's work. The two of them ministering to children until their hair turned gray. But what if Katherine's old flame rekindled their romance? What would happen to Harmony House? Katherine wasn't the type to back out of her commitments, yet Eliza couldn't expect her to continue serving at the same level if she started having children of her own.

A squeeze of her hand brought Eliza out of her thoughts. "Is it that bad?" Katherine whispered, her brows raised and her face growing pale. "Mark wouldn't tell me anything beyond the fact that they needed to talk to us about some children who might be in trouble."

Eliza patted Katherine's hand and forced a smile onto her face. "Mr. Brooks told me nothing either. I just got caught up in my imagination for a minute. Sorry. I didn't mean to alarm you."

Some of the color returned to Katherine's cheeks. "I am well acquainted with the dangers of an unhindered imagination." She slanted an accusing look over her shoulder at Mr. Wallace and raised her voice. "So let's end this subterfuge and get down to the facts. Who is in trouble, and how can we help?"

Mr. Wallace stepped deeper into the barn, but instead of starting the explanations, he gestured to his friend to take the lead.

Mr. Brooks glanced at Katherine momentarily, but his attention fixed on Eliza. "Yesterday when we stopped at Miss Georgia's home, Sam and I had a chat."

Eliza frowned. "Samuel Harris? Georgia's grandson?"

"Yep. Seems he's heard tales about kids going missing in the area. Miss Georgia is of the opinion that the source of the tales can't be trusted, since the stories come from a gang of rail-riding boys, but I promised Sam I'd look into it."

Rare for a grown man to take a child's concerns seriously, especially when adults more acquainted with the child discounted those concerns. Eliza peered more closely at the man in front of her, a man who just might be worth heeding.

"I talked to Deputy Bronson in Kingsland this mornin'," he continued. "No missing kids have been reported, but he did mention that cattle thieves and outlaws have been known to hide out in the hills by Honey Creek. He said if anyone was up to mischief, it probably came from that quarter."

Eliza nodded. "I've heard the same rumors, but what would rustlers or outlaws want with children?"

"Dunno. Sam told me only young boys have been taken. Boys around his age." Jonah shrugged. "Miss Georgia could be right. It could be nothin' but a tall tale made up by a group of troublemakers to scare young boys."

"Or it could be true."

He nodded.

Katherine leaned forward. "If it *is* true, that would mean whoever is taking children is targeting those who wouldn't be missed."

"Like the boxcar boys," Mr. Wallace added.

Eliza's mind spun. "The villain would have to be familiar with the families in Kingsland to know who belonged to who." A rather unsettling prospect to think that someone she passed in the mercantile could secretly be kidnapping children.

"Mark is going to chat up the local teacher this afternoon," Jonah said. "See if she's heard any rumors among her students."

Eliza turned to Mr. Wallace. "Peggy Williams has been teaching here for years. She and her husband are good people. They live out by Honey Creek too, so she might have some insight into any unsavory element inhabiting that area. But if you want to know what the *children* are saying, you'll probably want to talk to Miss Gordon. After Peggy had her second baby last year, they decided to bring in another teacher to help manage the workload. Althea Gordon works with the younger children. She'll be the one on duty at the school-house this afternoon."

Mr. Wallace nodded, a thoughtful look transforming his usually carefree countenance into one befitting a scholar. Perhaps there were greater depths to him than she'd originally postulated. "What can you tell me about her?" he asked.

"Not much, unfortunately. Her specialty is local history. I heard she took the children out to Packsaddle Mountain a few weeks ago to teach them about the last major battle between the settlers and the Apache back in '73, when the three Moss brothers and five other local men defeated a band of twenty-one Indians who had stolen their horses and cattle. The kids in town were talking about it for days afterward."

"I see her at church sometimes," Katherine added. "She travels to Llano a couple weekends a month, I think. Something about a sick father? She made a point to visit Harmony House after she started teaching. Introduced herself to the children and asked Eliza about her schoolroom. Even donated a set of old history books to our limited collection. It'll be a few years before Abner and Ruby are old enough to read them, but it was a thoughtful gesture."

"That's helpful," Mr. Wallace said. "Thank you."

Eliza looked at Katherine. "I can speak to Mrs. Fieldman at church on Sunday. See if she's heard anything." She shifted her gaze to Jonah. "Mrs. Fieldman teaches the Negro school out by Miss Georgia's homestead. If Samuel has heard tales, there's a good chance other children from that community have as well." Feeling a sudden sense of urgency rise in her spirit, Eliza amended her offer. "On second thought, I think I'll drive out this afternoon. Meet her when school lets out."

Mr. Brooks shook his head. "Not in that hunk of rotted boards you call a wagon, you won't."

Eliza bristled at his audacity. "It's not your place to dictate to me, sir. I'll go where I choose, when I choose, and in whatever conveyance I choose."

He moved only one thing, his eyebrow, yet he might as well have been lowering the barrel of a pistol at her for the level of challenge the gesture delivered. "I ain't stoppin' you from going anywhere, Miss Southerland. Shoot, I'll even give you a ride there myself. You just ain't takin' the wagon. It's not safe."

And to think she'd almost thought him pleasant a few minutes ago.

Eliza planted her hands on her hips and glared at the overbearing soldier who thought he could order her about. "She's tougher than she looks."

Mr. Brooks advanced a single step. "Stubborn ain't the same as durable."

Why did she get the feeling he was talking about her more than the wagon?

The two eyed each other, neither giving an inch.

Until Katherine's conciliatory voice interrupted the strained silence. "They've offered to have the wagon repaired for us, Eliza." Her hand came to rest lightly on Eliza's arm. "You know how much we need that. I fret every Sunday when you take Ted and the twins to church that something will happen. I know you don't like to ride, but if Mr. Brooks is willing to take you up on his horse, you can still visit Mrs. Fieldman today without worry of being stranded or injured."

Without worry? Had Katherine *seen* the size of his horse? Eliza would be nothing *but* worried. No. She'd be terrified.

"Good. It's settled," Mr. Brooks said, as if having one woman on his side meant the other would timidly fall in line. "I'll meet you out here at two. Will that give you time enough to finish up your lessons?"

Eliza bit back the retort perched on the tip of her tongue.

This battle might be better fought from behind enemy lines than in face-to-face combat. She'd let him think he'd negotiated her surrender. For now. It would make her victory all the sweeter when she thwarted him.

Eliza lifted her chin. "I'll be ready."

At one-thirty. And she'd take that wagon whether he liked it or not.

The only problem was, when she made her way to the barn to hitch the team after an abbreviated geography lesson, she found her wagon propped up on a pair of wooden stilts, back wheels removed and rear axle missing. No, not missing. The axle stood upright, leaning against the side of the barn, right next to the arrogant cavalryman who'd outmaneuvered her.

THIRTEEN

"Do you think she'll be all right?" Kate shot a worried glance at Mark as Jonah and Miss Southerland finally set off down the road, Eliza clinging to Jonah's back like a barnacle to a ship.

She clearly feared horses, yet her drive to assist in their investigation had proven stronger. Jaw clenched, face pale, she'd barely breathed as Mark assisted her onto the back of Jonah's horse, where she'd taken one look at the ground and immediately squeezed her eyes shut. After a single step by Augustus, she forfeited all pretension and hugged Jonah's waist with both arms, hiding her face in his back.

"She'll be fine." Mark grinned at the departing couple, thinking how fine *Jonah* must be feeling with the lovely Eliza pressed so close against him. "Jonah will keep them to a walk. And you don't have to worry about Augustus spooking." He turned his attention to Kate and moved a step closer. "He's a cavalry mount, trained to hold his position even amid cannon fire. She'll be safer with him than one of those cart ponies."

Mark cupped Kate's elbow and steered her back toward the house. Pleasure warmed his chest at the simple touch.

Did the contact affect her as well? She made no protest at his taking the liberty, yet her face dipped away from him as they walked, making her reaction hard to decipher.

Touching her was far too pleasant. His hand at her back earlier. Now this. Each touch made him want another. He'd assumed his packed-away feelings for her had been atrophying from disuse over the last decade, but apparently they'd been fermenting and intensifying during their dormancy. And now that they'd awoken, he worried they might outgrow his sense of caution.

"Would you sit with me for a minute?" he asked, not wanting her to disappear inside the house again when he finally had her to himself.

She slowed but didn't meet his eyes. "I have bread dough rising."

He tugged her to a halt at the base of the back stairs. He debated trying to tease or challenge her into changing her mind, but playing the rogue felt wrong. So when she finally raised her face, he opted for straightforward sincerity.

"Please, Kate."

She hesitated, her eyes peering into his. Gauging his motives. Mark held his breath and opened himself to her scrutiny.

Please.

After an eternally long moment, she nodded.

Air rushed from his lungs in a relieved sigh as he grinned and gestured for her to take her pick of stairs. She settled on the third step, scooting over to ensure he had plenty of room. He joined her on the same step, angling his body so that he could lean his back against the railing and see her face. Not that she looked at him. Her attention seemed glued to the children playing in a pile of sand a few yards from the barn.

"I'm proud of what you've accomplished here, Kate. It's good work. Meaningful work."

She shook her head. "It's not my accomplishment. Harmony House was all Eliza's idea. Her vision. Her expertise. Her training." A rueful smile quirked her lips. "She's the teacher. I'm just the silent partner."

"That's not the way I hear it."

Her head snapped around, her brows arching high in question.

Mark nudged her knee with his. "Abner told me about your valiant rescue. How you argued with his mother until she capitulated into giving him into your keeping. How you refused to be intimidated by a wealthy donor's threats. That's heroism in my book, not silent partnering."

Pink tinged her cheeks. "I'm surprised Abner told you about that day. He doesn't like talking about his mother."

"But he does like talking about *you*." Mark winked at her, even as he infused his voice with absolute sincerity. "You're his hero, Kate."

She ducked her head and nibbled on her lower lip.

Not wanting her to hide from him, he reached between them, covered her hand, and gave her fingers a gentle squeeze. "You're quickly becoming my hero too."

Her head popped up, and her eyes widened.

"It's true," he insisted, reading the doubt in her expression. "It takes a lot of courage to leave the only home you've ever known and take on a job you feel unqualified to practice. I know. I was terrified out of my mind when I joined the Army."

"Then why did you leave?" She shifted to face him more completely, all trace of shyness disappearing. "I thought you'd pursue the symphony in Boston. You weren't supposed to join the military and put yourself in constant danger. You could have *died* because of me!"

He rubbed his thumb over the back of her hand. "No, Kate. I could have died because of *me*. Joining the Army was my decision. Heaven knows my parents tried their best to talk me out of it, but I wouldn't be dissuaded. My pride was hurt, and my heart was hurt, and music no longer held the same appeal. It was something *we* had shared." He swallowed, wanting to turn his head but forcing himself to hold her gaze. "I was a foolish kid, Kate. Too young to realize how much I actually cared about the girl whose music harmonized so perfectly with mine. Until I lost her."

Her head wagged slightly back and forth. "I thought I was saving you from a forced marriage. The last thing I wanted to do was trap you into something you didn't want. I cared about you too much to force such an injustice upon you." Her lashes lowered slightly. "I couldn't have borne it if you came to resent me, and I couldn't imagine that not happening. Not when I was the one responsible for compromising us."

Mark's pulse throbbed at the revelation that she cared for him. Or at least had, once upon a time.

"You know," he said with a playful shrug, trying to lighten the mood so he wouldn't feel quite so vulnerable as he bared his heart, "there was a part of me that was glad Mr. Owen found us."

Her dubious look made him grin.

"Sure, I was embarrassed and frustrated the old fellow had jumped to such improper conclusions, but his outrage created an opportunity. An excuse to propose. I'd already been picturing the two of us together. I might not have expected the timetable to be so short, but when I considered the future, you were the one I envisioned by my side. So when you turned me down, it didn't feel like you were freeing me from an unfair trap. It felt like you were rejecting me."

Mark pulled his hat from his head and tapped the brim against his knee. "That's why I joined the Army. I sought a distraction. A way of life that would demand all of my attention so I could forget about the young woman who'd chosen to live with a damaged reputation instead of living with me."

"Oh, Mark." She leaned close, her face mere inches from his. "It wasn't like that at all. I swear."

He believed her. How could he not, with those earnest blue eyes imploring him? And that mouth. So close. So ripe for the kiss he'd been waiting a decade to taste. He leaned in. Took aim. Approached the target.

"Miss Kafrin! Look!"

Mark jerked backward as Ted thrust a dirt-colored creature at Kate's face. The ugly critter resembled a squashed lizard covered in spiky armor.

"I caught a horny toad!" the boy crowed as if he'd just captured a fire-breathing dragon.

Kate chuckled. "I see that." Her gaze darted to Mark's, a remnant of warmth still visible beneath the humor.

"Wanna pet him?" Ted shoved the horned lizard closer.

Her answer was clear when she lurched backward and pulled her hands behind her. But Mark knew her tender heart would not be able to bear Ted's disappointment. Time for a diversion tactic.

He waved his hat toward Ted to grab his attention, then set it back on his head, out of the way. "Let me see him, partner."

Ted swiveled, his shrinking smile quickly gaining new life and returning to its full width. "Abner said he's a big 'un."

"He sure is." Matt held out his palm and mentally braced himself for the scaliness about to descend. He'd never been particularly fond of reptilian creatures, but if he could play Kate's hero and spare a kid's feelings in the process, it'd be worth it.

Ted placed the horned lizard in Mark's palm. "Careful. He's fast."

Debatable. It didn't move a muscle when Ted released his hold. Just sat there blinking. Mark cupped his fingers around its body anyway, not wanting to be responsible for losing Ted's prize. The lizard's belly contracted as it breathed, the motion growing rapid and shallow.

"Hey there, little fella." Mark brought his other hand around and patted the critter's head.

The lizard's body puffed. Then, without warning, blood shot out of the creature's eye.

Kate squealed. Mark blocked the stream with his left hand and jerked the lizard away from her. Thankfully, he kept the presence of mind not to fling the thing through the air.

"Whoa!" The wonder in Ted's voice almost made the mess worth it. "I gotta show Abner!" He snatched the bloody lizard from Mark's hand and ran off for the sandpile.

Mark grimaced at the red staining his hand and the handful of drops marring his sleeve cuff. "Might want to release him after you show him off," he called after the boy. "The poor critter's probably scared to death."

Most animals had defense mechanisms, but this was the first time he'd ever fallen victim to squirting blood. He supposed it was better than a skunk. At least this he could wipe off without smelling like old garbage for the rest of the week.

Kate touched his shoulder as he shifted to retrieve his handkerchief from his trouser pocket. "Are you all right?"

He quirked a grin. "Sure. Just a little mess. No harm done."

Though he might need to change his shirt before he interviewed the teacher this afternoon.

"I'm so sorry."

"Don't be. It'll make a great story." He shook his handkerchief open and wiped the streak of blood off his hand and wrist. "And there's the proof." He nodded toward the sandpile, where all the kids huddled around Ted while he gave an animated retelling. "They're captivated."

"Ruby looks more disgusted than captivated," Kate said, a smile in her voice.

"I don't know. Seems to me like she's both."

Mark turned to study the woman at his side. Love for the children in her care emanated from her like rays from the sun. It warmed him. Drew him in. Brightened his outlook on life. Even as it made him realize that if they had married all those years ago, neither of them would be the people they were today. He wouldn't have met Captain Hanger, the man who turned him from a wild kid with a thirst for reckless adventure into a hardened cavalryman with a purpose beyond himself. And Kate—well, he couldn't imagine her being anything less than extraordinary, but he had to concede that her joining Miss Southerland in this ministry had lent a depth to her spirit, a maturity that he found even more attractive than the vivacious girl he remembered.

"You seem happy here," he observed.

She grinned, her gaze hovering over the children. "I am." Her face softened into a more introspective mien. "After you left, I think I lost myself a bit. Friends distanced themselves from me to guard their reputations. My relationship with my mother deteriorated. She was so angry at me for turning down your offer, convinced I'd thrown away my life for no good reason. Your parents never blamed me for your leaving, but everyone else in town seemed to. Westfield no longer felt like home. It was just . . . a place."

A lonely place, by the sound of it. A heaviness settled over Mark as he listened to her tale. He'd been so consumed with his own hurt, his own need to escape and forget, that he'd never allowed himself to imagine what things had been like for her, living in the aftermath of scandal.

"I shouldn't have left," he ground out between clenched teeth, disgust at the selfish youth he'd been tingeing his tone with bitterness.

"No." Kate turned to him and clasped his arm. "You did nothing wrong, Mark. I knew what I was doing when I made my choice, and even now I wouldn't unmake it. Not when I can see how God used those years of loneliness for good."

How could loneliness be good?

She must have read the question on his face, for a small smile curved her lips. "A strange thing happens when you find yourself on the outside of society. You start to see the world from a different perspective. Satan uses loneliness to isolate and depress. But God uses it to build compassion."

She sat back, her gaze drifting to the sky. "It took me a few years to get over my self-pity, I'm ashamed to say. I focused so much on what I had lost that I failed to appreciate what I still had. Good health. More wealth than most of the inhabitants of Westfield. And a heart that God was actively reshaping at his potter's wheel." She shook her head a little, her eyes lighting with a happy memory. "Do you know there are people who don't care a fig about a woman's reputation? Hunger, sickness, ostracism—people afflicted with such things care only about a warm meal, healing medicine, and a compassionate touch. Once I pulled my head out of the sand, I realized I was not the only lonely person in Westfield. I was one of many. Most of whom were far worse off than myself.

"Mother refused to allow me to tend the sick, fearful I'd catch some contagion and spread it to the rest of the family, but she couldn't stop me from befriending the hurting. Instead of sitting in my parlor alone with my needlework in the afternoons, I started visiting various widows in the area and plied my needle in their company. Some would chatter; others would work their own embroidery in silence. One elderly lady whose eyesight was failing had me read aloud to her, usually from the Bible. Many times she would quote passages as I read them, her knowledge of the Word inspiring me to spend more time in the Scriptures myself. And as I did, I felt a stirring within my soul calling me to something bigger. To a ministry that focused on *the least of these*.

"A few months later, I attended a revival meeting that emphasized mission work. The preacher delivered a rousing sermon, urging members to lend their financial support to one of the organizations whose representatives were in the missions tent. The sermon highlighted the Great Commission and our call to spread the gospel to every nation. People flocked to the missionaries raising funds to carry the good news to foreign lands. Others proved eager to support medical outreaches and charities geared toward helping the poor. But as I wandered through the tent, I steered clear of the crowds, seeking the fringe instead. That's when God led me to Eliza. She was so passionate about discarded children and the foundling home she believed would serve them. Her ministry was small compared to the others. And she was a single black woman. Easy for many to discount and ignore. Most visitors that day passed by without even pausing to listen."

"But not you." Mark's heart swelled as he pictured Kate

slowing her step, smiling in encouragement, and asking pertinent questions.

"No," she said softly, her face radiating with something beyond physical beauty. "I made an outright pest of myself, I'm sure. It's a miracle she agreed to let me visit her in Texas. But I knew I had to come. God had opened a door for me, and nothing was going to stop me from walking through it."

CHAPTER
FOURTEEN

Augustus tossed his head for the second time in as many minutes. He was antsy. Not surprising when the woman behind Jonah radiated enough tension to rival fencing wire. He needed to find a way to help her relax before Augustus started sidestepping. The jerky gait wouldn't bother Jonah, but any unexpected movement was bound to send Miss Eliza into a panic.

Maybe if he got her talking . . .

"So how'd you and Miss Palmer meet up?"

No response.

All right. Maybe a little prod to her pride would get her going. "Seems like an odd partnership."

Her arm twitched at his waist, and the sudden circulation of cool air against his shoulder blades testified to the removal of her cheek. "Why is my partnership with Katherine any odder than your partnership with the Horsemen? We work together, using the different skills and talents we possess, to accomplish shared goals. Isn't that how the Horsemen operate? Or do you think us incapable of working well in tandem because we're female?"

Jonah bit back a triumphant grin.

"The Horsemen bonded during wartime," he said, ruthlessly keeping all amusement from his voice. "I know kids can be a handful, but it's not exactly the same as dodging bullets while trusting the man beside you to keep you alive."

"You think not?" Air flow traveled a little farther down his back as her indignation separated them a hairsbreadth more. "Try facing down condescending donors who are certain their ideas are better than yours or navigating the political tightrope when black churches want to provide funds only for needy black children and white churches want to provide only for white. If I didn't trust Katherine to watch my back while I watched hers, Harmony House would have closed its doors years ago."

Eliza's hold on him loosened just a little, and her body relaxed enough to begin finding the rhythm of the horse. Augustus seemed to sigh in relief.

"So did she start out as one of them do-gooders who thought she knew better than you? I bet she came out here from back East with a passel of naïve ideas and wrongheaded notions."

"I thought so when I first met her," Eliza admitted, "but she quickly proved me wrong." Her torso became more pliant behind him, and he couldn't help wondering if she were smiling. "The summer of 1889, I traveled from gospel meeting to gospel meeting all over the East Coast, trying to drum up financial support for Harmony House. I had given up teaching in order to start a foundling home in this area, determined to create a place where no child would be turned away. Black, white, Mexican, Indian—none of that mattered. Healthy, sick, abandoned, orphaned—Harmony House would be open to all."

Admirable goal. Yet one fraught with political dynamite. For if all children were treated as equals, what did that say about the adults they represented? Yet who better to champion the cause of children from multiple walks of life than a woman whose own childhood straddled two worlds?

"By the time I made it to Westfield, Massachusetts," Eliza continued, "I had nearly given up hope of finding the financial support I needed. My project was too small to attract large congregations and too controversial to attract personal donors protective of their reputations.

"Then Katherine showed up. She was so young, barely twenty-one at the time. I doubted she could be of any real help, but I gave her my pitch anyway, hoping she had a rich daddy who might be influenced by her recommendation. We talked that afternoon, then met again the following day. I appreciated her compassionate nature, yet I needed money, not sympathy. So I decided my time would be better spent courting the favor of others." Eliza made a scoffing sound. "Here I was, a single woman determined to run a foundling home on my own, and I was discounting a possible donor because of her gender, youth, and inexperience. How the Lord must have laughed at the irony."

"What made you change your mind?"

"She did." A tiny chuckle escaped, and Jonah silently cheered. She had all but forgotten she was on a horse. "Katherine might seem soft and dainty on the outside, but she's got a backbone of steel. She showed up at my boardinghouse the morning I planned to depart, traveling bag in hand. Said she was prepared to donate a sum large enough to purchase the property I had told her about, while leaving enough funds in reserve to supply basic furnishings and teaching materials. She offered to use her connections to drum up monthly support for the continued sustainability of Harmony House as well. But she had one condition—partnership in the ministry.

"It's not unusual for donors to want to see how their money is being spent. I told her I would be glad to send her monthly accounting reports and host her any time she wished to travel to Texas for a visit. She turned that offer down flat. Said the Lord was calling her to give not just her money, but herself to this mission."

Eliza huffed out a self-deprecating breath. "That wasn't what I wanted to hear. Harmony House was *my* mission. *My* dream. The Lord hadn't laid the need for a partner on *my* heart. I made it abundantly clear to her that purchasing property did not constitute ownership of this mission. I would run Harmony House as I saw fit with no interference, and if she couldn't agree to those conditions, she could keep her money."

It was a good thing Eliza couldn't see his grin. She'd probably find it insulting. In truth, he rather liked her straight-shooting mentality. "Not exactly the diplomatic type, are you?"

"Not when it comes to issues of freedom."

That statement sobered him in a flash.

Her arm shifted at his waist, her fingers stretching out of their fisted state to flatten against his ribs. Suddenly *he* was the one with the racing heart and shallow breaths. Symptoms that had nothing to do with being on a horse's back and everything to do with having a compelling woman's arms around him in a way that felt less like a death grip and more like companionship.

"I needed her money," she continued as Jonah struggled to pay more attention to her words than to the feel of her fingertips splaying across his midsection, "but I wasn't about to compromise my vision in the process. I also wanted to set the ground rules up front. Both for her sake and for mine. The rules didn't matter to Katherine, though. She agreed on the spot. So fast that I became suspicious. But I agreed to take her to Texas with me and show her the property.

"She purchased the place after being in Texas for two days. With money I later learned had been set aside as her dowry. She insisted both our names be recorded on the deed, and when she signed the document, she told me she considered the agreement as sacred and binding as any marriage. She committed herself to Harmony House, to me, and to whatever children God brought through our doors.

"I still expected her to lose interest in a month or two, grow homesick, and run back to Massachusetts. Then I saw her fight for Abner, take him under her wing, and love the fear right out of him. That's when it became clear that I had misjudged her. This wasn't a silly, impetuous girl who would quickly grow bored. This was a woman with a deep spiritual calling. The partner God knew I needed even when I stubbornly insisted on carrying the burden alone.

"By the time we officially opened the doors of Harmony House in the spring of 1890, I had a dear friend and partner whose opinions I respected. I might have thought I wanted unilateral control, but what Harmony House needed was the strength of two differing perspectives working in balance. *Harmony* was in the name the Lord had supplied, after all." Eliza fell silent for a moment, then spoke again in a soft tone he barely recognized. "To this day, Katherine insists that Harmony House is my brainchild and gives me full credit for its work, since I am the one with the teaching degree. However, while it might be true that I am the head and hands of the foundling home, Katherine is most definitely its heart."

"Sounds like a healthy partnership." Though he'd argue her last point. Miss Palmer might possess the more affectionate nature of the two, but he didn't doubt for a second that Miss

Eliza loved those kids. Fiercely. Her love simply manifested through meeting practical needs instead of through hugs and games. After all, that love was what got her on this horse. And for a child who might or might not actually be in peril.

Jonah spotted the turnoff that led to Miss Georgia's homestead and lifted an arm to point. "Do we turn there?"

The question startled her out of her reverie. The reality of where she was and what she was doing crashed over them both. Her arms tightened about his middle, and her posture resumed the pliability of a brick.

"No. Stay on the road another half mile. The school will be on the left."

A few minutes later, they came upon a group of five Negro children of varying ages on the road, books and lunch buckets in hand. Jonah scanned their faces, looking for Sam, but didn't see him. No doubt there was a more direct path to his grandmother's house than the road.

Jonah nodded and tugged the brim of his hat as he drew near the kids. Conversations quieted, and their eyes widened. He wasn't sure if their reaction was due to timidity at having a stranger in their midst, awe at the fine specimen of horseflesh Augustus presented, or disbelief at seeing Miss Southerland in the company of both a strange man and an overlarge horse. The group came to a halt in the middle of the road and craned their necks as Jonah passed.

"Does Miss Eliza have a beau?" The not-quite-whispered question and the groan it elicited from the woman behind him brought a smile to Jonah's lips.

Not yet. But she definitely had a fella intrigued, and intrigue could lead to all sorts of interesting possibilities.

Possibilities that would have to wait, because they'd reached the schoolhouse.

Jonah reined Augustus to a halt in front of the small one-room building, then carefully assisted Eliza to the ground.

"Fit your foot in the stirrup," he instructed quietly, not wanting to cause her any further embarrassment. "Then hold my arm. I'll lower you slowly to the ground."

He expected her to need a moment to gather her gumption, but she surprised him. She followed his instructions without hesitation or reservation. Her grip on his arm was tight enough to cut off circulation, but that only proved her courage. Eliza Southerland's fear of horses might be massive, but she had grit to match.

She hastened away from the horse, cleverly disguising her desperation to separate herself from Augustus with a cheery greeting for the young black woman standing by the school-house door, her arms filled with books.

"Candace! So good to see you. How's the teaching going?"

Jonah hid a grin and started to dismount. As he shifted his weight into the left stirrup, however, a movement behind the schoolhouse caught his eye. He froze. Swept the area with his gaze, then zeroed in on the kid running head-down toward the school.

Wrong way. School was over. Kids were headed home. Not back.

Jonah's right hand moved to his gun. He glanced over the kid's head, looking for someone or something giving chase, but nothing else moved. The kid finally glanced up. Recognition stabbed Jonah in the gut.

"Sam."

In a flash, Jonah was urging Augustus into action. The horse responded instantly, and the two raced to intercept the boy.

He heard Eliza's concerned call behind him, but Jonah

didn't stop to explain. Only one thing drove a kid to run that hard for the nearest adult—danger.

Sam must have heard the approaching hoofbeats, for he stumbled to a halt, his eyes widening in his face. He backed up a step or two, obviously thinking he'd run across a new threat.

"Sam!" Jonah called, hoping to reassure him.

The boy's face cleared. All backpedaling ceased, and he took off toward Jonah.

The distance shrank between them. Jonah reined Augustus in and leapt from the saddle before they'd fully halted. He ran to Sam and dropped to one knee. "What is it, son? What happened?"

The boy struggled to catch his breath, his exhaustion doubling him over. "Kiddy . . . snatchers. I saw 'em . . . by the . . . old oak." He pointed to an ambiguous spot behind him. "They got Rawley."

— CHAPTER —
FIFTEEN

Jonah's insides stilled, then hardened as if he were sighting down his rifle for a long-range shot. No room for unnecessary data. Only his purpose. His target.

He squeezed Sam's shoulder. "Can you show me?"

Sam's nostrils flared, but he nodded.

Jonah stood, swinging the boy up into his arms as he went. In two strides, he was beside Augustus. Gripping Sam beneath his arms, he set him in the saddle, then mounted behind him, scooting the boy into the small space between himself and the saddle horn. Sam was still panting from his run, but he immediately directed Jonah with a jutting arm and pointed finger.

"That way."

Jonah nudged Augustus into a slow canter—fast enough to give chase, but not so fast they would miss evidence.

Like the scuff marks in the dirt around the old oak and the hoofprints leading west. Jonah pulled Augustus to a halt and ordered him to stand while he examined the area.

"This is where me and Rawley meet when he's in town,"

Sam explained as Jonah picked out details about the horse he'd be following.

Average size. Heavy rider. No, not heavy. He had the boy with him, weighing down the horse. Jonah zeroed in on one of the rear hoofprints. It had a small nick at the front of the arc. Likely from a chipped hoof overdue for trimming.

"I was late gettin' away from school," Sam said, self-blame coloring his voice. "Miz Fieldman asked me to clean the blackboard. I tried to hurry, but she wouldn't let me go 'til it was perfect. If I'da been faster . . ."

Jonah had seen enough of the ground. He remounted Augustus. "If you'd been faster, you would've been taken too, and there would've been no one to go for help. You should thank God for dirty blackboards. Now, let's find your friend."

Jonah nudged Augustus into a lope, keeping his gaze locked on the hoofprints glaring up from ground more accustomed to the feet of schoolchildren.

Rawley had put up quite a fight, by the look of the disturbed dirt and leaves by the tree. The kid was a scrapper. One didn't ride the rails without learning how to fend for himself. Even against someone twice his size.

Come on, kid. Make some trouble.

The kidnapper had too much of a lead for Jonah to catch him unless he was forced to slow down or stop.

Give me an opening, Lord. Anything.

A horse's scream shot through the air. Jonah pinpointed the direction, tightened his hold on Sam, then urged Augustus into a full gallop. No need to watch for tracks if he knew the location of his target.

When they crested a small hill, the target came into view. A bucking horse. Something protruding from its flank. A man picking himself up from the ground and retrieving his hat.

Steadying the horse. Removing the foreign object. A knife, by the look of it, its blade red with blood.

Where was the kid?

Jonah reined Augustus in and reached for his rifle. There. Rolling toward the brush. The kid was smart. Staying small, making himself less noticeable.

The man shouted a curse and pivoted. His eyes searched for the boy. Found him. Lunging forward, he gave chase.

"Put your head down, Sam," Jonah murmured. "And don't move."

The boy obeyed, bending over the saddle horn.

Jonah levered a cartridge into the chamber of his repeater. Calculated the distance—only a hundred yards. The wind—southwest, maybe ten miles an hour. Adjusted his aim. Fired high. The Horsemen didn't shoot to kill if they could help it, and while anyone who would abduct a child deserved a bullet in his backside, Jonah's first priority was protecting the child. Which meant shooting high, so that even if the kid jumped up unexpectedly, the bullet wouldn't be anywhere near him.

At the sound of the shot, the snatcher jerked toward Jonah's position. The kerchief tied around the lower half of his face made him impossible to identify. All Jonah could tell from this distance was that he was white with brown hair and a medium build. A description that probably fit two-thirds of the men in Llano County.

"Leave him!" Jonah yelled the command, then took a second shot, this one close enough to whiz by the fellow's ear, since he'd done him the courtesy of standing still.

The man ducked. Cursed again. Then ran for his horse.

Jonah took a third shot. Kicked up dirt by the horse's front hooves. The horse reared and bolted. His rider sprinted after him.

Jonah took up the reins and made for the boy who was busy scrambling into the brush.

"Rawley!" Sam cried. "It's me. Hold tight. We're comin'."

Augustus covered the ground in a pair of heartbeats. Jonah reined him in long enough to let Sam down.

Rawley rolled over to face the newcomers, his gaze leery as he continued scooting backward.

Jonah pinned him with a glance. "You injured?"

"Not bad," the kid ground out.

Jonah wasn't sure he believed him, but his only chance to catch the kidnapper hinged on pursuing now. "I'll be back." He reined Augustus around and gave him his head. "Yah!"

"Mr. Brooks! Wait! Rawley's bleedin'!"

Sam's call was barely audible above the combination of Augustus's pounding hooves and Jonah's pounding pulse, but it reached its target at the same time the kidnapper reached his mount. Jonah slowed. Debated. Sam might be overreacting. The injury might not be too bad. He still had time to catch the snatcher.

"Please, Mr. Brooks!"

The fear in Sam's voice brought him to a full halt.

Jonah grimaced as the masked bandit pulled away. The man would have his reckoning one day soon. The Horsemen would see to it. In the meantime, more important matters demanded his attention.

It only took a moment to return to the boys, but by the time he got there, he could tell Sam had been right to call him back. Rawley had a nasty gash in his side, one his arm had been covering earlier.

"I'm fine." Rawley pushed Sam's hands away. "Leave me be."

The kid was tough as weathered boot leather despite the

fact that he was probably no older than twelve. Experience had turned him cynical. Guarded. Traits necessary for surviving alone in the world. He had the heart of a lion and the grit of a warrior. He wouldn't take well to coddling.

Steeling himself to ignore Rawley's youth, Jonah strode forward and hunkered down beside the scrawny black boy with hard eyes.

"You shouldn't've stopped." Rawley glared an accusation at Jonah as he curled his arm over his side and tried to sit up taller. Facing him man to man. "He'll jus' find some other kid to snatch. One that won't have a knife in his pocket to fight back with."

Jonah made no move to touch him, just met his defiant stare with stoicism. "That the same knife that ended up in the horse's flank?"

A glint of pride flashed in the boy's dark eyes, quickly followed by a touch of regret he tried to hide behind a callous shrug. "Couldn't stop the man, so I had to stop the horse."

"Bold move. You break anything in the fall?" Jonah eyed him more closely, examining his limbs for any subtle deformities.

Rawley shook his head with a vigor that spoke more of impatience than denial. "You kiddin'? I jump from moving trains all the time. I know how to tuck and roll."

Maybe. The maneuver would be much more complicated when tangled with a grown man who didn't want to lose his prize.

Jonah tipped his head toward the boy's midsection. "Hard to control a knife while bein' jostled by a horse."

"Weren't the horse." Rawley turned sideways and spat at the ground. "Once I got it out of my pocket, the snatcher spotted it. Tried to knock it out of my hand. I didn't feel like letting go."

Even when the blade sliced into his own side.

"Danglin' over his lap, I didn't have much choice. I could stab the snatcher's calf or the horse's flank. One gave me a better chance of escapin', so I took that 'un." The toughness faded from Rawley's eyes for a brief moment, and a tinge of uncertainty slipped through. "You don't think I hurt him too much, do ya? The horse?"

"I doubt you caused him any permanent damage." Pain, yes. But the kid already knew that. No need to pour salt in the wound. As much as Jonah hated the idea of anyone doing intentional harm to a horse, if it meant saving human life—a *child's* life—it was justified.

Jonah turned his attention to Sam. "Why don't you see if you can find Rawley's knife? The snatcher prob'ly dropped it when I took that first shot."

The younger boy pressed his lips together and met Jonah's gaze. Reading the question in his eyes, Jonah nodded. Yes, he'd take care of Rawley.

Once the assurance had been given, Sam scurried away to search the path and surrounding brush for the missing pocketknife.

"Thanks," Rawley murmured. "I didn't want him to see." He slowly lifted his arm away from his side and hissed in a breath. "Sam reminds me of my kid brother. Jack never did have a stomach for blood."

Taking care to keep his movements methodical and deliberate, Jonah raised the boy's shirt and got his first look at the wound. Not too deep, thankfully. Might need a few stitches, though. For the second time in as many days, he wished Dr. Jo had come on this trip. Captain Hanger's wife would have the boy fixed up in a heartbeat. 'Course, she probably woulda fussed all over him too. Rawley would hate that. Or

146

at least he would pretend to. Deep down, Jonah was pretty sure this tough guy hungered for kindness, love, family. What man didn't?

"I'm gonna fetch my canteen and pour some water over that wound," Jonah said as he pushed to his feet. "Then we'll wrap it."

Rawley gave a tight nod, already bracing himself for the discomfort to come.

After fetching the water, Jonah hunkered back down into position. "What happened to your brother?" he asked as he unscrewed the canteen lid. "Jack."

"Rosemary took him back to Houston with her after Pops died. She weren't my real ma. Just took up with Pops after my ma passed. Jack was her boy, so he went with her."

And left Rawley to fend for himself. Jonah's jaw ticked.

"Lean to the side," Jonah said, hardening his heart against the ache throbbing for this boy who'd been so callously abandoned. Rawley wouldn't want his sympathy. Not that Jonah was the sympathetic type, anyway. Emotions clouded a man's judgment, hampered rationality. Better to lock them away and focus on the problem in front of him. He tipped the canteen. "This might hurt." Not as much as whiskey would have, but it still wasn't gonna be comfortable.

Rawley braced one arm against the ground and used the other to hold his dusty shirt out of the way. "I'm ready."

Jonah poured.

Rawley flinched but didn't cry out. A muffled groan was all the sound he made. Had he been a few years older, Jonah would've recommended him to the Army. The kid would make a great soldier.

Once he'd flushed the wound, Jonah pressed a clean handkerchief to the site of the injury. It was only about an inch long and maybe a half-inch deep. It looked to be more of a glancing slice than a stabbing penetration.

"Hold this," Jonah ordered, waiting for Rawley to comply before he released his hold on the dressing. "Push tight. It'll help stop the bleeding."

Now he just needed something to use as a bandage. All his spare clothes were back at the roomin' house. That left him with what he was wearing. He glanced at his coat and trousers. Not exactly the cleanest duds to work with. Although . . .

Jonah stripped out of his coat, then unsheathed the hunting knife at his waist. Holding his left arm out like a chicken wing, he slid the tip of the knife into the shoulder seam of his shirt, then yanked it through. Holding the knife blade with his teeth, he grabbed his left sleeve and jerked downward until the sleeve tore free of the shirt's torso. He repeated the action on the other sleeve, then pulled his coat back on.

The kid was skinny enough that one sleeve ought to do the trick, but Jonah wanted to double up the protection. Hopefully it would cut the chance of infection in half.

He'd just finished tying off the second bandage when Sam ran up to them, a triumphant grin on his face. "I found it!"

"Good work, Sam." Jonah squeezed his shoulder and took the small knife from his hand. "Let me clean it off."

He took the canteen and stepped a few feet away before pouring water over the small blade encrusted with blood and dirt. He rubbed it clean with his fingers, rinsed it with another splash of water, then wiped it dry on his trouser leg.

"You gotta tell 'im." The boys' whispers became distinguishable words as Sam's volume rose. "He was a Buffalo Soldier. He can help."

Jonah closed the pocketknife blade and walked back to

where the boys sat huddled together. Rawley was shooting daggers at Sam.

Jonah handed the knife to Rawley. "Help with what?"

Rawley said nothing as he snagged his knife and jabbed it into his pocket. He glared at Sam in a manner that made it clear he expected the younger boy to keep his trap shut. Sam, however, wasn't feeling particularly obliging. After firing off a mutinous glare of his own, he jumped to his feet and faced Jonah.

"Another boxcar boy went missing last night."

"*Former* boxcar boy," Rawley growled. "And it ain't none of this fella's concern. We take care of our own."

Sam, angry tears shining in his eyes, fisted his hands and spun to face Rawley. "Yeah, well, you can't take care of your own if you get snatched too, can you? We need help, Rawley. Mr. Brooks saved you. Maybe he can save the others."

"I saved myself," Rawley grumbled, but his gaze dodged away from both Sam and Jonah as he said it.

"I respect a man who takes care of his own," Jonah said as he crouched between the boys.

Sam imitated his posture, squatting down and balancing an arm on one knee. Rawley frowned, no doubt displeased that his protégé had found a new role model.

"If you don't want to work with me, that's your choice," Jonah said, offering the boy some semblance of power over a situation that had no doubt shaken his confidence. "But I've been hired to do a job, and I aim to see it through."

Belligerence hardened Rawley's face. "Who hired you?"

Jonah tipped his head toward Sam. "He did. Yesterday. Asked me to look into the kiddy-snatchers. I ain't gonna walk away from that commitment. Now, we can either both do our own digging and possibly get in each other's way, or we can work together. Coordinate our efforts. Share information. Work as allies to defeat a common enemy."

Rawley raised a skeptical brow. He wouldn't trust an adult easily. Yet he was smart. He'd recognize the advantage. The question was, did he care enough about his comrades to sacrifice his pride and let someone else lead?

"Allies means equals." Rawley jutted his chin. "You gotta share as much with me as I do with you. This ain't no one-way street."

"You have my word." Jonah extended his hand.

Rawley made no effort to take it. "Prove it," he demanded.

Jonah nodded. It was a risk to tell the kid anything without an agreement in place—shoot, it was a risk to tell him even if they *did* have an agreement in place—but he and Mark needed the intelligence Rawley and his gang could provide. Trust had to start somewhere. Might as well be on his end.

"I've spoken to the local law. No one has reported missing kids. We've shared our concerns with Miss Southerland and Miss Palmer at Harmony House, and my partner is going to speak with the Kingsland teacher this afternoon. We need eyes on kids, and these ladies have the best view."

"Not of the boxcar boys." Rawley turned and spat again. "There's a reason no one's reportin' the snatchin'. It's 'cause the only kids being snatched are those with no family. No one to know or care that they're missin'."

"We figured the same. Which means that whoever is taking the kids knows which ones have families or caregivers in the area and which don't. Only way for them to figure that out is to study the local kids. Watch them. At school. At church."

Some of the belligerence fell away from Rawley's face. "So you ain't just askin' about missin' kids, but about who might be hangin' around those places. Watchin'."

Jonah dipped his head. "Yep."

A light that looked suspiciously like approval lit Rawley's eyes. "You might be worth more than firepower after all."

"What can you tell me about the man who took you?"

Rawley blew out a breath. "Not much. His face was covered." His brows lifted. "He smelled like peppermint, though. Like those sticks you can buy in the mercantile." His brows sagged back down. "Probably don't mean nuthin'."

"I wouldn't be so sure." Jonah offered the boy a hand and carefully pulled him to his feet. "Could help us identify him. Can't be too many outlaws packin' peppermint sticks in these parts."

Sam chuckled. Rawley almost smiled. Progress.

"So, about this kid that was taken last night," Jonah pressed as he lifted first Sam, then Rawley, up into the saddle. "What does he look like?"

"Little taller than Sam," Rawley said. "Curly red hair. Freckles."

A sick feeling churned Jonah's stomach.

Rawley circled his hand around the saddle horn and gripped it. Hard. "Worked in town at Donaldson's livery."

Jonah's hand faltered as he lifted Augustus's reins over his head to use as a lead.

The snatchers had taken Wart.

⟞CHAPTER⟝
SIXTEEN

Eliza tried to concentrate on what Candace Fieldman was telling her about the rumors she'd overheard from her pupils, whispers about the latest bogeymen they were calling *kiddy-snatchers*. Unfortunately, Candace's recitation couldn't compete with the arresting image lingering in her mind of Jonah racing to meet Sam. He could have been a centaur, as one with the horse as he'd been. The sight had stolen the breath from her lungs, and not for the usual reason. She hadn't feared for his safety. No, she'd been in awe of his mastery. Though as magnificent as the sight had been, her belly knotted for the unknown cause behind it.

Then there'd been the gunshots. They'd been faint. Distant. But unmistakable. She would have taken off running if Candace hadn't grabbed her arm and held her back.

"It's just hunters," she'd said, but Eliza hadn't believed it. She was fairly certain Candace hadn't believed it either. Nevertheless, she'd stayed behind. Talking. Distracting herself from the hundred questions rattling around in her brain.

Jonah would protect Sam. She was sure of it.

Unless one of those bullets had taken him down.

Her gaze darted to the trees again. Where were they? What had happened? Was someone hurt?

A hand touched her arm. "Eliza?"

She blinked and focused once again on Candace. "Sorry." She offered a weak smile to apologize for her inattention. "You were saying . . . ?"

The teacher speared her with a concerned look. "Just that I've had no unusual absences lately. All of our children are accounted for." She turned to peer in the same direction that had captured Eliza's attention. "If they don't return in ten minutes, we'll search them out, all right? But we have no weapons to lend to whatever fight is going on, and showing up unannounced will only make things more complicated. Unless you doubt that man of yours can handle whatever trouble he stumbled upon?"

"Jonah's *not* my man." The sharpness of her denial might have been a tad excessive, but it seemed essential to clarify the point. "However, he is more than capable of handling whatever trouble he comes across. He's one of Hanger's Horsemen and a former Buffalo Soldier."

A whistle of admiration leaked through Candace's pursed lips. "One of the Horsemen? I say we give them fifteen minutes, then." Her eyes crinkled at the corners. "I always knew it would take someone special to turn your head. Guess a Horseman qualifies."

"He hasn't turned my head," Eliza protested.

"No?" Candace looked at her sideways. "You called him *Jonah*."

Had she? Eliza bit back a groan.

"Not that I blame you," Candace continued, enjoying her friend's discomfiture far too much. "If I wasn't such a happily married woman, I'd be scheming to get close to that handsome hunk of man too. The slow ride from Harmony House—with your arms around his waist and your body pressed close to his—must have been quite pleasant."

Heat suffused Eliza's cheeks. "It was terrifying, I assure you. You know how I feel about horses."

"Which makes your appearance on one that much more remarkable."

Was it poor manners to stuff a handkerchief into the overactive mouth of one's friend?

Candace grinned as if she'd read Eliza's mind. She probably had. Or her face, anyway. Eliza never had been one to hide her thoughts.

"I'm sure having such a capable man to hold must've eased your fears considerably."

"Not really." Though his talking to her had. There'd been a few minutes when she'd actually managed to forget she was perched upon a mammoth beast who could abandon its training at any moment, throw them off, and trample them into the earth. "I'm not at all looking forward to getting back on that animal for the ride home."

Candace smirked. "Liar."

"Candace Fieldman! I ought to—"

Her diatribe evaporated the moment she caught a glimpse of Jonah cresting the hill behind the schoolhouse, leading Augustus. She couldn't make out faces from this distance, but she could count heads. There were *two* boys in the saddle. Not one.

"It's a child." Eliza's feet immediately started moving toward the horse. "He might be hurt."

Candace's demeanor shifted in a heartbeat. "Bring him into the classroom. I'll fetch the medical box."

154

The two diverged, the teacher disappearing into the schoolhouse while Eliza grabbed a handful of skirt and ran to meet Jonah to assess what damage had occurred. However, the closer she drew, the more puzzled she became. She didn't recognize the taller boy behind Samuel. Who was he, and where had he come from?

Slowing to a walk to ensure she didn't spook the horse, she finally looked to Jonah—*Mr. Brooks*—for a hint of what had happened. The frustrating man's face was as stoic as ever, giving nothing away. Nothing except an invigorating intensity she found oddly comforting. Almost like a reassurance that everything was under control. Then he lifted his right brow, and all that lovely reassurance disappeared beneath a not-very-subtle warning for her to maintain her composure. As if she were the type of woman to fall apart in a crisis. Exasperating man!

Lifting her chin, Eliza stepped around Mr. Brooks and came alongside the boys, keeping a good three feet between her and Augustus as she walked. She trusted Jonah to control his horse under normal circumstances, but she didn't trust herself not to do something accidentally that would spook the animal. Heaven knew she tended to bring out the worst in the creatures.

"Who's your friend, Samuel?" She tried to imitate the cheerful tone Katherine used when meeting a child for the first time instead of her authoritative teacher voice, but she must not have done it correctly. After tossing a questioning look over his shoulder and receiving a glare in response, Samuel faced forward and ignored her.

Fine. Teacher voice it would be.

"Don't pretend you didn't hear me, Samuel Harris."

His chin jerked sideways, and his gaze flew to hers. "Sorry,

Miz Southerland. I heard ya just fine. But Rawley doesn't want me sayin' nuthin'."

Rawley? The leader of that ragamuffin gang of boxcar boys the men had been talking about earlier? The one Miss Georgia had warned Samuel to stay away from?

Eliza shifted her gaze to the taller boy with the pugnacious expression. And the dirt-encrusted clothing. And the posture of one who seemed to be cradling a wounded side. The child had obviously suffered some kind of injury. How, she didn't know, but the cause wasn't nearly as important as the remedy at the moment. His health and well-being took precedence.

"Mr. Rawley?" She banished all sympathy from her voice. Eliza had dealt with independent types before. Emotion wouldn't soften them. The only way to bend them to her will was to gain their respect. "I see you've run into some difficulty."

"Nuthin' I couldn't handle."

A soft cough from the man in front of the horse confirmed her suspicion that the boy had bent the truth to some degree.

"And those injuries?" she inquired with a raising of her brows. "Are you handling those as well?"

He sniffed. "That's right."

Jonah glanced over his shoulder, stoicism giving way to sternness. "Not alone, you're not. We're gonna get you stitched up and bandaged proper. Even then, it'd be best for you to lay low for a while. Heal up before you go traipsing around the rail yard. You got people dependin' on you. Won't do them any good if you take a fever 'cause that gash got infected."

Rawley sat forward, his eyes glittering like shards of black obsidian. "Won't do them any good if I'm holed up someplace where they can't find me neither."

156

"Well then," Eliza said, a touch of cheerfulness creeping back into her tone, "I guess it's a good thing I have a place where *all* of you can stay." She turned her attention back to Samuel. "Sam, do you know how to find Rawley's people?"

"Yes'm."

"Perfect. Then get a message to them that Rawley will be staying at Harmony House, and they are all welcome to join him."

Rawley sputtered. "I ain't goin' to no orphanage!"

"Of course you're not. You're coming to a place where children go when they have no other safe place to stay." He started to argue, but she glared him into silence. "From what I understand, you and the boys who run with you are the main targets of whoever is snatching children. How better to keep your comrades safe than by hiding them away in a home with protective walls, three free meals a day, and two of Hanger's Horsemen guarding the fort?"

Rawley's gaze flashed up to where Jonah walked. "You're a *Horseman?*" For the first time, no trace of belligerence marred the young man's face.

Jonah didn't bother turning around. "Yep."

"Then that settles it," Eliza said, willing it to be the truth and not giving Rawley a chance to argue. "How many new boys should I expect for supper?"

CHAPTER

SEVENTEEN

Six?" Katherine was certain she'd heard incorrectly. But then Eliza nodded in confirmation of the number, and Kate's stomach knotted.

Six new boys? Tonight? That would more than double their occupancy.

Lord, I know I've been praying for Harmony House to reach more hurting children, but so many all at once? I don't know if I—

"It'll be fine," Eliza said, her no-nonsense tone batting away Katherine's rising anxiety as if it were no more significant than a gnat buzzing by her ear. She crossed the kitchen, grabbed a mixing bowl, and started dumping cups of flour inside. "These boys are used to sleeping in railcars. We don't need beds. Pallets will do."

Katherine forced a calming breath into her lungs. "For now, yes, but if they decide to stay with us permanently, we'll need to have beds made." And how she would pay for that, she had no idea. But that was a problem for tomorrow, not today.

She gave herself a mental shake and bent to open the door

on the icebox. "'My God shall supply all your need according to his riches in glory by Christ Jesus.'" She murmured the beloved promise beneath her breath as she fetched the half-filled milk bottle and butter crock and set them on the worktable beside Eliza to aid in her biscuit-making.

If it was God's will for these poor motherless boys to find a home at Harmony House, the Lord would provide the beds. *Trust and obey, Katherine. There's no other way.*

Reaching back into the pie safe, she pulled out the ham she'd been saving for tomorrow's breakfast and joined Eliza at the worktable, slicing it into thin strips. The leftover beef and potatoes they'd planned to eat wouldn't stretch far enough. Ham, biscuits, and Eliza's red-eye gravy might be rudimentary, but it was filling. And on hand. The most important factor at the moment.

Eliza had returned barely twenty minutes ago and had left Mr. Brooks and a boy named Rawley in the barn with a washtub, a kettle of hot water, a cake of soap, and an order to clean up. Since then, she'd shared the few details she knew about Rawley's near kidnapping and warned Katherine of the impending arrival of an army of boxcar boys. Dozens of additional questions begged to be answered, but they'd have to wait. A meal needed to be served in less than an hour to twice as many mouths as they'd originally anticipated.

Katherine did a bit of mental calculation. Not all mouths were created equal. Since Mark and Mr. Brooks were staying, it would probably be wise to triple, not double, the amount of food. Eliza had invited the Horsemen to take up residence in the barn until they caught whoever was abducting children. A security measure Katherine fully supported. The children must be kept safe.

Not to mention that housing the Horsemen offered the

additional benefit of increased opportunities for her to see Mark and explore what was resurrecting between them. After spending several hours in his company today, her urge to explore had expanded to Lewis and Clark proportions.

Once she finished slicing the ham, Katherine scraped it from the cutting board into a skillet and covered it. They'd fry it up later when their company arrived. Wiping her hands on her apron, she looked over at Eliza, who was flouring the worktable surface for biscuit kneading.

"I'm going to collect blankets and pillows for our guests."

Eliza nodded, her attention focused on the sticky dough coating her fingers. "I'll set extra water on to boil. Those boys will need a thorough scrubbing before laying their heads on our linens. Can't allow lice or other vermin into the house."

Katherine hesitated in the kitchen doorway. "Will forcing a bath on them scare them away?" As much as she appreciated cleanliness, she also realized that feral boys were about as fond of bathing as feral cats.

Eliza dropped the biscuit dough onto the floured surface and jabbed the heel of her hand into the middle of the lump. "They'll follow where Rawley leads." She glanced up and grinned. "I made Jonah promise to see the boy clean before coming up to the house. If Rawley is forced to bathe, he'll make sure the others suffer the same indignity."

"You don't think Mr. Brooks will sympathize with the boy and let him off the hook?"

Eliza ducked her head and refocused on her kneading. "He's not exactly the soft, sympathetic type. If he says he'll see a job done, he'll see it done."

The words painted a rather harsh picture, but the way Eliza spoke them made a smile tug at the corner of Katherine's mouth. Eliza admired him. She might not admit it in so many words, but something had definitely shifted between her and Mr. Brooks during their excursion. Respect had blossomed, and Eliza didn't give respect easily. One had to earn it.

The tension in her friend's shoulders revealed her wish for a change of subject, however, so Katherine obliged. "Would you prefer I set out the pallets in the front parlor or upstairs in the classroom?"

"The classroom, I think." Eliza pressed the dough into a uniform height with her fingertips. "Better to keep some distance between them and the front door. Just in case."

Katherine frowned, concerned for the new boys' safety. She was tempted to arrange a seventh pallet so she could keep an eye on them, but stealing their privacy might goad them into an escape attempt, and she didn't want that. Children needed a home. Love. Protection. But until she and Eliza could gain their trust, these boys would be more likely to value their independence over anything Harmony House offered. Life had taught them that freedom equaled survival. It would take time to show them that life had more to offer than mere survival. For tonight, she'd have to be satisfied with leaving her bedroom door ajar and trusting the Lord to wake her should a need arise.

Perhaps Mark would have a recommendation. He'd been a boy once. She'd speak to him as soon as he returned from his interview with Althea Gordon. Katherine headed to the stairs, a swirl of anticipation eddying through her midsection at the thought of sharing her concerns with Mark. Seeking his perspective. Inviting him more deeply into her world. It was enough to make her a touch light-headed as she climbed the stairs. Gripping the railing, she pretended it was his arm and grinned all the way to the top.

Mark fiddled with his hat as he stood in the hall outside Miss Gordon's classroom. He'd been cooling his heels for about twenty minutes, waiting for her to finish a tutoring session with one of her students.

The other teacher, Mrs. Williams, had been on her way out when he arrived and had graciously escorted him upstairs. He'd asked if she'd heard any rumors about missing children, and she'd seemed genuinely shocked by the idea. Kingsland was a close-knit community. If a child were to go missing, everyone would be called to action. Searches would be made until the child was found.

The rising panic in her eyes reminded him that she had two young babes at home. Mark quickly reassured her that the local law had confirmed that no children had been reported missing in Kingsland. He also abandoned his original plan to ask her about unsavory characters lurking around Honey Creek. She didn't need any more reason to fret. She made her excuses and left, no doubt hurrying home to check on the safety of her children. Mark made no effort to detain her. He simply leaned against the wall, hat in hand, and waited for Miss Gordon to conclude her lesson.

Finally, the door clicked open, and a young girl emerged. "Thanks again, Miss Gordon." The girl looked to be about ten. When she caught sight of Mark, she blushed and ducked her head.

Mark smiled and nodded as she skittered by, and then he pushed away from the wall and stepped through the doorway. "Excuse me, Miss Gordon?"

The woman standing at the blackboard paused her erasing to glance his way. Green eyes widened at the sight of him, though more in curiosity than startlement. "Yes. Can I help you?"

"I hope so." Mark grinned and crossed the threshold. "My name's Mark Wallace. I need to ask you a few questions."

She smiled, set down her erasing rag, and moved to the edge of the teacher's desk. "Of course. Do you have a child to enroll in school?"

"No, ma'am." He chuckled lightly and shook his head. "'Fraid I've not been blessed with a wife and children." Yet. Crossing paths with Kate again had put ideas in his head, though. Ideas regarding roots and proper soil. He needed to till things up a bit more, ensure the ground would prove fertile before he risked another planting, but early signs indicated promising possibilities.

Mark didn't miss the flare of interest that sparked in the teacher's eyes at the mention of his bachelor status. Miss Gordon leaned a hip on the corner of the desk and twisted slightly to show off her figure to full advantage. Usually he welcomed such a response. It made his work easier, after all. Charming information out of ladies required the ladies to actually be *charmed*. But something about this situation felt different. Flirtation no longer seemed like a harmless means to an end. It felt . . . disloyal. To Kate. Not that they had an understanding between them, but a man considering a commitment to one woman should not behave in a way that could lead her to believe him fickle in his affections. Nor should he give another woman reason to believe his interest lay anywhere other than where it did.

So even though past experience urged him to move closer, to capitalize on the flash of attraction he'd seen in the teacher's eyes, Mark retained his position near the door. He retained his smile as well. Friendly was different than flirty.

"I was told you were the one to talk to about rumors that might be circulating among the grade school crowd."

Althea Gordon's brows lifted. "Oh? And what interest could a man with no family and no ties to the Kingsland community possibly have in childish gossip?"

She was smart. Protective too. Excellent qualities in a teacher. Unfortunately, such qualities made extracting information a little more complicated.

Mark pointed his hat at her and kept his voice light. "Fair question." Using his most disarming grin, he took one step deeper into the room. "My partner and I have been hired to look into some rumors about area children who have gone missing."

His statement knocked Miss Gordon backward. She gripped the desk for support. "M-missing children?" Her posture started to crumple, but she restored her composure in quick order. Straightening her spine, she met his gaze. "I've not heard a word about such things. Neither in the classroom nor among any of my acquaintances in town." She leaned away from the desk and stood to her full height, which was tall for a woman. Her head nearly stood level with his. "I don't know who hired you, sir, but I can't help wondering if it might have been under false pretenses."

Mark shrugged, hoping to put her at ease. "It's possible. We're still in the very early stages of our investigation. But I'm sure you'll agree that if there is even a sliver of a chance that these rumors are based in truth, we need to pursue any leads we uncover."

"Of course." Miss Gordon paced away from him, her fingers tracing the edge of her desk until she reached the far corner. When her fingertips ran out of real estate, she pivoted sharply to face him. "What can I do to help?"

"Just listen for any talk among the children about kiddy-snatchers. That's the terminology used in the rumors we've heard. Also, if you see any strange men hanging around the school or watching the kids, jot down a description and bring it to me over at Harmony House. I'm doing some repair work at the foundling home, so that will be the best place to find me. If I'm not there when you visit, you can leave a note with either Miss Palmer or Miss Southerland. They'll see that I get it."

"I'll be sure to keep an eye out," Miss Gordon said, a thoughtful look coming over her face. "Harmony House. Is that where these rumors first surfaced?" She hesitated, but not long enough for him to insert an answer. "The children there come from rough, sometimes tragic circumstances. From my experience, children lacking a stable home environment are prone to seek adult attention in whatever way they can. Some strive for perfection in order to please their guardians, others act out, and some invent wild stories to elicit sympathy or reassurance."

Mark couldn't argue with her observation, yet it riled him a bit to have her assume that the children of Harmony House would be the only ones to fall into such behavior patterns. He'd known plenty of rowdy boys back in Westfield who had acted out or made up wild stories despite being raised in traditional homes.

"The one who brought this matter to our attention has no ties to Harmony House, ma'am, but we have spoken to the two proprietresses there about the matter, just as we've spoken to you and Mrs. Williams."

"Of course." Althea Gordon's tight smile showed her to be less than pleased.

Did she resent not being the first teacher approached on

the matter? Or had she picked up on the fact that he didn't fully buy into her theory?

"Who else do you plan to share your concerns with?" she asked, a touch of stridency tightening her voice. "I would hate to see the town thrown into a panic."

Mark lifted a conciliatory hand. "We are being very discreet, I assure you. My partner spoke to the deputy this morning, and by now, he and Miss Southerland have spoken with Mrs. Fieldman at the Negro school. We agree that it's best to keep things as quiet as possible. If the rumors prove unfounded, we avoid unnecessary panic. And if there *is* something afoot, the fewer people who know, the slimmer the chance that someone will inadvertently tip off the guilty parties. So while we would appreciate your vigilance, Miss Gordon, we would also appreciate your silence."

She gave a stiff nod. "You have both, sir. Thank you for taking me into your confidence." Her tone made it clear their conversation had come to an end.

Mark dipped his chin and fit his hat onto his head. "Thank you for your time, ma'am. I'll let you get back to your duties."

"Good day, Mr. Wallace."

"Good day, Miss Gordon."

Mark left the school and collected his horse, preparing to return to Harmony House for supper and an update on what Jonah and Eliza had learned from their meeting with Mrs. Fieldman. He'd just mounted and turned Cooper to the west when he caught sight of Jonah and Augustus approaching at a fast clip.

Instincts on alert, Mark nudged his gray into a canter. As he and Jonah met, they each reined in their mounts.

"Wart's been taken," Jonah said with no preamble.

Mark's stomach clenched as the unspoken fear he'd been

carrying in the back of his mind ever since the boy failed to show at the livery that morning turned into harsh reality.

"Sam's friend Rawley was nearly snatched too. Managed to escape on his wits, but he's injured. Eliza convinced him and the rest of his boys to hole up at the foundling home for a few days." Jonah eyed him meaningfully. "We're standin' guard."

A hundred questions bubbled through Mark's mind, but he stuffed them down. There'd be time later for explanations. Right now, they had a duty to perform.

He turned Cooper in the direction that would take them to the Jackson place. "Let's grab our gear and get back to Harmony House."

—CHAPTER—
EIGHTEEN

A n hour later, Jonah had scouted out a spot in the barn loft and measured out the best lines of sight from the open hay door. He knew exactly where to position himself to have a clear shot to the foundling home's back stoop. The path to the privy. The tree line to the east. Any position from which an enemy might advance from the rear. Wallace would guard Harmony House from the front, passing the night in a rocking chair on the porch, where he could monitor the road and the country lying southwest. Being on the ground would give Wallace the defensive advantage of speed in getting to the women and children should the need arise. But the higher ground of the barn loft provided Jonah the offensive advantage. The gable end sat sixteen feet above the ground. A protected position. Not to save his own hide, but because a sniper was only as effective as his vantage point allowed.

Jonah shouldered his rifle and sighted down the barrel, taking aim at the two windows that faced his direction. One from the kitchen. The other from the upstairs classroom where Rawley and his gang would be sleeping. Shooting into either room was out of the equation. Not with the women and children inside. Even with better-than-average night vision, he wouldn't risk hitting a friendly target. So if the enemy made it into the house, he'd need a fast way inside. Wallace would be there, of course, but if more than one combatant breeched the house, or if one managed to take a hostage, things could turn ugly fast. Jonah would need to even the odds.

Sticking his head out of the hay door, he eyed the hook used for loading hay into the loft. Lassoing a rope to the hook should work. He'd keep the rope coiled inside the loft. If the need arose for a quick exit, he could toss the coil out the opening, climb down, cross the yard, and be in the house in thirty seconds. Maybe less. Jonah frowned. It might be a good idea to do a few practice runs just to ensure there'd be no surprises.

He stashed his rifle in the rafters, out of the reach of any curious young'uns. Boys were attracted to guns like mosquitoes to a swamp. Even with the loft declared off-limits, Jonah knew better than to assume those limits would be accepted without challenge. Rawley and his bunch were masters at skirting the law and doing as they pleased. Jonah wouldn't underestimate their cageyness.

After descending the loft ladder, Jonah crossed to the tack room and sorted through the lengths of rope available. The ladies didn't keep much on hand, and what they did have was old and frayed. He tossed aside a length that failed to hold together when he wrapped it around his hand and shook his head in disgust. This stuff probably came with the house. Who knew how many years it had been sitting out here deteriorating? He didn't trust any of it to hold his weight. Better to use his own. He strode over to where he and Mark had stowed their gear and unbuckled the rope strap on his saddle.

He had just slid the coil free of its mooring when Augustus nickered in his stall.

Jonah stepped into the barn's aisle and watched his horse's ears prick and his head turn toward the north.

Someone approached.

Hanging the rope on a protruding nail with one hand, Jonah reached for his pistol with his other and eased the weapon from its holster. Moving silently down the aisle, Jonah positioned himself behind the partially open rear barn door. Back pressed to the wall, he inched toward the opening and peered into the twilight of early evening. The rapidly dimming light made it hard to distinguish shadow from reality, but he caught movement to the east.

Movement too low to the ground for a man. About right for a kid, though.

Jonah holstered his gun and stepped through the cracked doorway, keeping his right hand hovering near his hip. After a moment or two, the blob of shadow moving toward Harmony House separated into six distinguishable shapes. A few minutes later, he could make out general features. Sam led, while the others traipsed along in his wake. One fellow lagged behind. Smaller than the rest. Head darting side to side as if nervous, feet tripping over themselves.

Jonah strained to make out more of the smaller kid's features. There was something familiar about him. It nagged at his brain.

Stepping out of the shadow of the barn, Jonah lifted a hand in greeting. "Howdy, Sam."

The little fellow at the end of the group jumped at the unexpected sound, and wide, startled eyes flashed Jonah's way. Recognition hit him. The kid from the livery. The one Wart had been trying to hide. If anyone knew what had happened to the missing stable boy, it would be this kid.

Too bad he looked as skittish as a cockroach in a lamp factory. He'd run if too much attention was shone on him too quickly.

"Mr. Brooks!" Sam waved a greeting and jogged over. "I found 'em."

Jonah pushed his hat back on his forehead. "You sure did. Why don't you run inside and tell Rawley his crew is here? Then I'll see you home."

"On Augustus?" The boy's eyes lit with excitement.

Jonah chuckled. "Yep."

"Yes, sir!"

Sam sprinted to the back porch, leaving Jonah with a handful of wary-eyed strangers. The wariest being the tyke at the back.

Jonah met each gaze but said nothing. Not because he didn't want to, but because he had no idea what to say.

Where was Wallace? He needed his friend's glib tongue.

The boys said nothing either. Their attention darted from him to the house to the road as if weighing all options. Some challenged him with defiant glares and jutting chins. Others avoided eye contact altogether, choosing to stare at the ground and kick at the dirt. But when the kid at the back with the freckles finally found the courage to look Jonah in the face, the pleading in his blue eyes kicked Jonah in the gut.

Doggone it. He couldn't just ignore him.

Moving slowly down the line, Jonah came to the end and crouched down in front of the sandy-haired kid with the big eyes. "I heard about Wart. He a friend o' yours?"

The boy gave a tiny shake of his head. "Brother."

Ouch. Hard enough to lose a buddy, but a brother? The tighter the connection, the more it hurt when severed.

Jonah held the lad's gaze. "Me and my partner are going

to do everything we can to find him and get him back." He leaned back on his heels and tipped his hat a little farther back on his forehead. "Ever heard of Hanger's Horsemen?"

The young'un nodded, and the rest of the crew started crowding around, suddenly very interested in the conversation.

"Well, me and my partner ride with Matthew Hanger. We're Horsemen, and we ain't about to let a kid go missing without hunting down the one who did it."

Quiet murmuring broke out among the older boys. Elbows nudged neighbors, and heads bobbed in some kind of coded communication.

Until a whistle pierced the air.

As one, all the boys turned at the sound.

"Rawley!" One of the boys called out their leader's name, and then the herd ran off to meet him where he stood on the back porch with Sam.

Only one little dogie lingered behind. "You really gonna find Wart?"

Jonah nodded. "A Horseman don't quit until the job's done." He just prayed that when they found Wart, the boy would still be alive.

His gut told him that someone was taking these boys for a purpose. The fact that no bodies had been found lent credence to his assumption, but that knowledge didn't comfort him as much as it should have. Death wasn't always the worst option in cases like these. He prayed the boys who'd been taken were still in the area. Hidden somewhere. Waiting to be found. If they'd been sold, or shipped off to places unknown, they'd be much harder to track down.

"It's my fault the snatchers got 'im."

The small voice sharpened Jonah's focus back on the child

in front of him. "Why d'ya say that?" He tried to keep his voice patient, sympathetic, but his hunger for details that could provide a solid lead made restraint difficult.

"I didn't want to stay at the livery with him last night." The kid stared at the ground, his hands balling into fists at his sides. "I knew you'd seen me." Blue eyes tinged with accusation rose to glare at Jonah. "If you squealed, told Mr. Donaldson what you'd seen, Wart could lose his job. He weren't supposed to let any of his riffraff friends into the livery after dark."

The kid tossed a glance over at the boys by the porch, then turned back to Jonah. "Rawley has a place outside of town where we stay sometimes, a lean-to with a stash of food and blankets hidden in an old trunk. I was gonna meet up with some of the others there. But with the snatchers on the loose, Wart wouldn't let me go alone. We had to wait 'til after dark so Wart could sneak away without anyone noticing, but we'd barely made it to the edge of town before he started looking over his shoulder. He told me it was nuthin', but I knew he was lyin'. He started walkin' faster. Grabbed my hand. I looked behind us but didn't see anyone.

"After we left the road, Wart calmed down some. I thought whatever had spooked him was gone. Then I heard the footsteps. Running. Getting closer. Wart shoved me away from him, grabbed a tree branch off the ground, and yelled for me to run. But I couldn't. I couldn't leave him there. I looked for a branch I could use, but all I found was a bunch of useless twigs. Too small to help. Just like me. That's when he yelled at me again. Told me to fetch Rawley."

The boy swallowed. Glanced away. Almost fast enough to hide the moisture shimmering in his eyes, but not quite. "I ran as fast as I could." His voice clogged. He shut his mouth and kicked at the dirt.

Jonah pushed to his feet and clasped the kid's shoulder, surprised at how thin the bones felt beneath the baggy coat he wore. He must be wearing three or four layers. Probably every stitch of clothing he owned.

"You did the right thing," Jonah said, his voice gruff. There was nothing worse than feeling helpless in battle. Unable to help a brother under attack.

"I let my brother be taken!"

Jonah narrowed his gaze. "No. You accomplished his mission."

"What . . . mission?" The kid's face scrunched as he sniffed and rubbed his nose with his coat sleeve.

"Any good soldier puts his mission first. Wart's mission was to ensure you arrived at your destination unharmed. His own safety was irrelevant. All that mattered was protecting you. If you had stayed behind and tried to help him, both of you would have been taken, and no one would know anything about what had happened. Wart's mission would have failed. But when you obeyed his order to retreat, you accomplished his mission. Not only did you escape harm, but you collected valuable information that we can use to track down Wart. In war, information is as vital to mission success as guns and bullets. Sometimes more. You're a witness, young man. A witness who can help us track down the snatchers and rescue their captives."

"Me?" Disbelief clouded the kid's eyes, but hope edged those clouds with a golden glow. "I didn't hardly see nuthin'."

Rawley strutted toward the barn, his gang dogging his every step. Wallace and Miss Katherine followed, Mark toting a second washtub and Miss Katherine a kettle. Jonah thumped Wart's brother gently on the back. "Don't worry, kid. You know more than you think you do. Trust me."

"Hey, Al," Rawley called as he approached. "I know ya don't like baths, but we're all takin' one. The ladies here are strict about dirt. They got hot food ready to set on the table but won't let us in unless we're clean."

Al adamantly shook his head.

The older boy came alongside and draped his arm over Al's shoulders. "It ain't so bad. See?" He held out his other arm for inspection. "They even gave me clean clothes to wear. There's enough new duds for everyone."

"I ain't doin' it, Rawley." Al pushed away from his mentor, eyeing Wallace as if he were the devil incarnate carrying a tub full of brimstone instead of hand-me-down clothes. He backed away. "I'll just stay in the barn. I don't need no dinner."

Rawley's face hardened. "All the boys is doing it, Al. You included. Now get goin'." He jerked his chin toward the open barn door. "I ain't gonna miss that food I been smellin' 'cause you're too baby to get in a tub of water."

The other boys snickered.

Wallace came up to Rawley and handed the tub to him. "Get some of your boys to fill this at the pump and drag it inside. Al and I will be inside in a minute."

Al was gonna bolt. Jonah could feel panicked energy coiling up in the kid. Miss Katherine's sweet smile and calm manner didn't even help. She described warm bathwater first, then went on to list all the mouth-watering details of what dinner would entail.

It didn't matter a bit. Al bolted between the fresh buttered biscuits and fried ham. Kid was fast too. If Jonah hadn't been anticipating the move, Al probably would have gotten away. Instead, Jonah scooped the kid off the ground with an arm around his midsection and did his best to dodge the flailing arms and kicking legs. But when a high-pitched, blood-curdling scream nearly busted his eardrum, it was all Jonah could do not to drop the little beggar on his hind end.

The shriek brought Rawley running out of the barn, knife out, ready to defend one of his own. Wallace winced and plugged his ears with his fingers. But it was Miss Katherine who surprised Jonah the most. She set down her kettle and walked up to the wild child as if her ears were completely unaffected. Jonah did his best to hold the kid still so he couldn't head-butt the teacher or ram his heels into her ribs, but she proved intelligent. She circled around behind Jonah, then tapped his shoulder.

"Could you bend down, please, Mr. Brooks?"

The kid squealed and squirmed, but Jonah squatted down as best he could, leaning his head as far away from the little banshee's mouth as possible.

Miss Katherine reached over his shoulder and grabbed hold of Al's head. Then she leaned close and spoke into the child's ear. Her words so shocked Jonah, he nearly dropped the kid then and there.

Al stilled instantly. Jonah's arms loosened. Al slipped free and took Miss Katherine's hand.

"Al has consented to a private bath in the washroom," the teacher announced as the boys all looked on, gaping. Jonah was pretty sure he was gaping too, though hopefully not quite as loose-jawed as the others. "Dinner will be served in thirty minutes. I suggest you have yourselves presentable before then."

No one moved as she turned and strolled away, Al walking meekly at her side.

"C'mon, boys," Rawley finally said, breaking the spell. "There's biscuits waitin'."

As the boys disappeared into the barn, Wallace came over to Jonah. "What did Kate say to him?"

Jonah shook his head, still a bit rattled. "She promised to keep the kid's secret."

Wallace frowned. "What secret?"

Jonah met his partner's gaze, hating to admit that the Horseman with the keenest eyesight had failed to see what had been right in front of his face. "Al's a girl."

— CHAPTER —
NINETEEN

Katherine leaned over the washtub and scrubbed her fingernails against the young girl's scalp. The poor child had enough dirt caked on her head to start a garden.

"What's your real name, sweetie?" Katherine asked as she worked the soap through the girl's shorn locks, trying to engage the too-solemn child.

Al hadn't fought her as Katherine helped her out of her boy's clothes and into the warm hip bath, but she hadn't welcomed the chance to wash either. Even with the privacy of a closed washroom door. She huddled unresponsive in the tub, shoulders slumped, eyes downcast, as if every speck of dirt that left her body took a piece of hope with it.

When Al made no effort to respond, Katherine tried a different tactic.

"Hmm. Maybe I can guess. Alexandra?"

A tiny shake of the girl's head signaled participation. Katherine seized on that victory and continued, racking her mind for all the names she could think of that started with those two letters. She let her arms lie slack against the edge of the tub, giving both herself and Al a break as they played their name game.

"Alberta?"

Another shake. Though her posture was perking up a bit.

"Allison? Alfreda? Alleluia?"

Two shakes and a small burst of air through the nostrils that Katherine chose to interpret as a giggle.

"How about Alabama?" Might as well throw a little geography into the mix. Especially since she'd drawn a blank on other traditional names. "Alaska? Maybe Albany?"

An actual smile emerged. A small one, but it was terribly encouraging.

The shake this time was vigorous enough to splatter tiny specks of suds on Katherine's bodice.

"Then what is it, pray tell?"

The girl's lips curved wide enough to show a hint of teeth. "Alice."

"Alice. Of course." Katherine made a theatrical face complete with rolled eyes and wagging jaw. "I should have known. Were you named for the girl who visited Wonderland?"

Another head shake. "No. It was my granny's name."

"Ah. A family name. Those are extra special." Katherine gently resumed the washing.

Alice sat up straighter in the tub and leaned her head back to keep the soap out of her eyes. "My brother doesn't think so."

Katherine reached for the small ewer of rinse water waiting at the side of the tub. "No?"

"He was named for our great-grandpappy Edgar."

"That's not so terrible." She placed her hand at Alice's nape. "Lean your head back a little farther, honey. I'm going to rinse you."

Alice obeyed with the habitual ease of one who'd been

bathed countless times in the past. By a loving mother? How long had she and Wart been on their own?

"I don't 'member Grandpappy, but Wart said he was grouchy and smelled like old turnips. He didn't want to end up like that."

"So he chose to be called Wart instead?" It seemed an odd choice. Didn't exactly draw the finer things to mind.

Alice closed her eyes and let Katherine pour the water over her head. "He didn't choose it. I did."

"You did?" Katherine helped her sit up. "Why would you choose such an odd name?"

Alice shrugged as she clasped the sides of the hip bath and stood. "I was just a kid at the time. About four or five."

And she was so *old* now. Maybe as ancient as seven.

"When Mama got sick, Wart had to take care of me. One day I heard Mama praise him for being such a good big brother. She called him a knight. A stall-wart knight. I thought it was 'cause he liked workin' with horses, but our teacher said it meant strong and brave. I liked it."

Alice eased one leg over the side of the tub.

"He was the best big brother in the world, so I started calling him Stall Wart. It made Mama laugh. And Mama hardly ever laughed after she took sick. I wanted to make her happy, so I kept sayin' it, but I got tired of wrapping my mouth around the whole thing, so I trimmed it down to just Wart." Alice shrugged as she finished climbing out of the tub and stood on the towel Katherine had laid out on the floor. "After Mama passed last year, calling him Edgar didn't feel right no more. Edgar was just a kid. Wart was a knight. Strong and brave."

And now he was missing. Katherine's lashes fluttered as she batted away the tears pooling in her eyes. She wrapped a second towel around Alice's slim shoulders, wishing she could wrap the girl in a warm hug as well. What this poor child had been through. Losing her mother and now her brother as well.

Please, Lord, let Wart still be alive. Alice needed a home. A sanctuary. She needed Harmony House.

Alice pulled on the secondhand clothes Katherine had provided, stepping into the trousers and extending her arms over her head so Katherine could help her into the masculine shirt.

"You think they'll know I'm a girl?" Alice caught a glimpse of herself in the rectangular mirror hanging over the washstand. She finger-combed her short hair onto her forehead in an unbecoming manner. "Wart rubbed dirt on my face every mornin'. Said it would help with the disguise."

No wonder the bathwater looked like mud.

Unable to help herself, Katherine gently pushed Alice's hands away and combed her hair in a more natural style, parted on the side with her bangs pulled across her forehead in a fetching swoop. With her delicate features, clean freckled skin, hair that now gleamed more red than brown, and the flip of a damp curl at her nape, Alice could pass for a pixie from a fairy story. There was no way the boys wouldn't notice.

"Would it be so bad if the others learned the truth?"

Before Katherine could stop her, Alice snatched her filthy wool cap from atop her discarded clothes and slapped it on, pulling the brim down low over her forehead. "Rawley's crew is boys only. If they find out I'm a girl . . ." She hugged her arms around her middle as if trying to stave off the threat of further abandonment.

Katherine knelt in front of her and placed her hands on her shoulders. "If they find out you're a girl, you'll just come stay at Harmony House," she said fiercely. Softening her voice, she tried to paint an inviting picture. "We have a girl staying here named Ruby who is about your age. And another named Priscilla who's three and lives here with her twin brother. They would love to have a new friend. You'll meet them at dinner."

Alice shook her head. "I can't stay here. Rawley told us all about orphanages. They feed kids gruel, make 'em work all day, and take a strap to their backsides whenever they so much as sneeze wrong."

"Well, as smart as Rawley is, he doesn't know everything." Katherine bundled up Alice's dirty clothes before the child decided to reclaim something else from the pile. "Harmony House is not an orphanage. It's a foundling home. Emphasis on *home*. Miss Southerland and I established this home for children in need. Not only do we provide meals and a place to sleep, but Miss Southerland is a teacher, so anyone staying with us will also receive a first-rate education. We do ask our wards to help with chores around the house, but straps are never utilized. Ever."

Alice looked skeptical but slightly less mutinous.

"Why don't you ask Abner and Ruby about it after dinner?" Katherine suggested as she wrapped the dirty clothes in a sheet and set them aside to launder later. "They can tell you everything you need to know about what life is like at Harmony House."

"You gonna give those back?" Alice jerked her chin toward the laundry bundle, her voice cracking with challenge.

Katherine smiled. "Of course. They belong to you. I'm just going to wash them first. They will be returned to you tomorrow evening, cleaned and pressed."

Alice said nothing aloud, but her expression clearly said, *We'll see.*

Yes, you will. Katherine opened the washroom door and placed a hand behind Alice's shoulders to guide her through. *You'll see that we follow through on our promises. Give us a chance, and we'll shower you with all the love and kindness you can stand.*

She'd be surprised if Rawley and the others could be convinced to stay once the snatchers were caught. That crew was too free-spirited to willingly tie themselves down to a permanent dwelling. But Alice and Wart? Katherine's heart throbbed with the need to shelter them. It was the same way she'd felt when she'd first encountered Abner all those years ago. Alice and Wart belonged at Harmony House.

Watch over her brother, Father. I haven't even met him, but I feel your calling to bring him into our home. Maybe this is the true reason you brought Mark here. To rescue Wart. I stand ready to assist, however I can. Bring him home unharmed, Lord. Home to Alice. She needs him so.

Alice halted suddenly, causing Katherine's prayerful thoughts to scatter as she bumped into the girl's back. Abner stood before them, his arms filled with plates intended for the dining room.

He met the newcomer's stare head on without his usual defiance. Katherine's heart soared. It was so difficult for Abner to meet new people. They never failed to stare at the red birthmark on his face, leaving him angry and embarrassed. This time, however, he ignored Alice's shock and offered a friendly grin.

"Welcome to Harmony House. My name's Abner."

Acting the perfect host. Katherine bit back a grin. She hadn't had much time to prepare the children for their influx of visitors, so she'd simply explained that these were children who had no home and needed a safe place to stay. She'd asked

Abner and the others to be kind and hospitable, and here he was doing exactly that. Putting his own discomfort aside to ease the discomfort of another. No mother could be prouder.

"I'm . . . Al."

"Al, huh?" Abner didn't look too sure about the boyish name, but he shrugged it off as unimportant. "Ruby and me are settin' the table in the other room. Wanna help?"

A tight, bristling voice cut into the conversation. "Al's not goin' anywhere until I find out exactly why *she's* been lyin' to me for the last six months." Rawley scowled at Alice, his eyes dark with betrayal.

Abner turned and glowered at the older boy, moving to place himself in front of Alice. "Back off."

Rawley did no such thing. He advanced, his narrowed gaze switching from Alice to Abner. "I don't back away from nuthin', tomato face."

Abner's cheeks reddened to match his birthmark, and the plates rattled ominously in his hands.

Before the boys could come to blows and break half the plates in her pantry, Katherine jumped between them. "That's enough." She looked first at Abner. "Please see to your duties in the dining room."

He peered up at her, a question in his eyes. She nodded, assuring him she'd look after Alice. He tossed one final glare at Rawley before making a silent departure.

Katherine turned to Rawley next, doing her best to keep her own hackles from showing. Reminded herself that this boy had been surviving on his own, possibly for years. Striking first before someone could strike him. Living by his own code, one that obviously valued honesty and trust. Perhaps she could build on that.

"While you are staying with us, Rawley, I must ask you to

abide by our rules. We do not allow name-calling or other disrespectful behavior. Is that understood?"

The boy's face closed down, his jaw clamping tight as he visibly struggled with his response. He glanced at the door and the other boys standing just inside, staring at him, waiting for him to decide their fate. Temptation to leave warred with his need to protect those in his charge.

"You and the others are welcome to stay here as long as you like," Katherine said, saving him from having to verbalize a response to her edict. For now, it was enough to communicate her expectations. Collecting his agreement could wait. "Perhaps some of you will even choose to make Harmony House your permanent home."

She placed a hand on Alice's shoulder, and understanding flashed in his eyes. Understanding and . . . relief? Something clicked in Katherine's mind. It wasn't the dishonesty that bothered this leader of young men so much. As a survivor, he would know precisely what had motivated Alice's disguise. However, to be in charge of a young girl, especially if her brother was no longer around, was a layer of responsibility he hadn't anticipated or been prepared to accept. And what would happen as she grew older? Would she continue to be treated like one of the crew, or would she be a source of distraction and strife among them?

"However long you stay," Katherine continued, meeting Rawley's gaze, "you will treat the others as you would wish to be treated yourself. With kindness and respect. Can you agree to those terms?"

He sniffed and raised his chin. "I s'pose."

"Excellent!" Katherine beamed a smile at him. "Then why don't you ask Miss Southerland what you can carry to the table for supper? I'm sure you're all starved."

Her prediction proved true, as the giant batch of biscuits Eliza had made disappeared with staggering speed. Every drop of gravy and scrap of ham was consumed in record time. A bit of tension lingered in the air between Abner and Rawley, but Ted's constant questions about railcar living and Rawley's yarn-spinning skills kept a lively conversation going throughout the meal. Katherine had been happy to see Ruby and Alice engaging in a quiet side conversation of their own, both undoubtedly hungry for connection with another girl their own age.

Despite all the activity at the table, Katherine's mind kept turning to Mark. He and Jonah had opted to eat outside, taking their plates of food onto the back porch. Whether in an effort to protect the ladies' reputations or to discuss their investigation in private, she didn't know. Both, most likely. Mark had hinted that they'd want to speak with Alice after the meal, and when the knock she'd been straining to hear finally rapped against the back door, she practically flew from her chair to answer.

She pulled the door open. Mark's eyes lit with pleasure upon seeing her, and her insides hummed in response. She dipped her gaze and noticed the plates he held, one stacked upon the other.

"Here, let me take those." She reached for the dirty dishes, and her fingers accidentally overlapped his.

His roguish smile made an appearance, as if he thought she'd touched him on purpose. She hadn't. Not really. Had she? In truth, she'd been so enamored by the delight in his eyes upon seeing her that she hadn't paid much heed to where her hands were going.

"Sorry," she mumbled, quickly adjusting her hold so as not to trap his fingers against the plates.

"Don't be." Mark slipped his hand free of the dishes, then lifted it to caress the edge of her cheek with the back of one knuckle. "I like it when you touch me."

She liked it too. Enormously. But she couldn't bring herself to admit as much aloud. He didn't seem to mind, though. Just smiled at her, his roguish grin softening into something infinitely sweeter as the teasing melted away to reveal a warmth that revived every dream she'd ever had of spending her life with this man. And there'd been many, *many* of those dreams over the years.

But the children must come first.

Dipping her chin away from his touch, she retreated a step into the kitchen. "Would you like to conduct your interview in the front parlor?"

Mark cleared his throat and nodded. "That would be fine. Would you join us? I'm sure Alice would be more comfortable with you there. Jonah and I will do our best to keep things friendly and nonthreatening, but two grown men facing down a little girl is going to be intimidating no matter how gentle we are."

"Of course." With romance safely set aside for the moment, the friendly camaraderie Katherine had always felt with Mark returned. "I was planning to horn in on your conversation anyway, but it's much nicer to be invited." She winked.

He chuckled, the sound seeping into all the cracks and crevices of her battered heart, soothing them like a healing balm.

"I thought you might." Their eyes met and held, so many comfortable, happy memories zinging between them like messages on a telegraph wire. Yet it wasn't only memories they shared. It was this moment. The miracle of finding each other after years apart and the hope of a second chance.

"We ready?" Jonah Brooks stood at the bottom of the porch steps, his voice cutting through the gathering dusk.

How long had he been there? She didn't recall seeing him when she'd first opened the door, but then, Mark had so filled her vision that a coyote could have been padding around the yard and she wouldn't have noticed.

"Absolutely." She forced a smile as she withdrew from the open doorway. "Come through to the parlor. I'll fetch Alice as soon as I put these dishes up."

Katherine made a point not to look back as she set the plates by the sink and hurried into the dining room. Eliza was instructing the boys on how to clear the table while Ruby corralled the little ones. Alice stood behind her chair, glancing between Rawley and Ruby, not sure which group to join.

Katherine took a step in her direction. "Al, would you come with me, please?" Not sure which name the girl would prefer now that the truth was out, Katherine thought it best to stick with the old one. Things were changing fast enough as it was. "Mr. Wallace and Mr. Brooks would like to talk to you. About Wart."

Alice complied, taking Katherine's hand when she offered it. Squeezing her fingers warmly, Katherine led her to the parlor. They sat together on the settee, leaving the men the armchairs across from them.

Surprisingly, Mr. Brooks did most of the questioning. Apparently Alice had opened up to him earlier. Mark added a question here or there, but he let Jonah guide the conversation. One that centered around pinpointing the exact location where the attack occurred and a physical description of the man Alice had caught a glimpse of before she ran to get help.

"I really didn't see him," she insisted when Jonah asked a third question about what the man had been wearing.

All she'd given them so far was that he wore a hat, dark clothes, and a bandana over his face. She mentioned that he was tall, but didn't every man look tall to a child? Hearing Alice's rising frustration and the sound of tears nearing the surface, Katherine decided to call a halt to the interview. But before she could, Jonah snuck in one more question.

"Did he have dark skin like me or white skin like Wallace over there?"

"Dark," Alice said without hesitation, "but not like you. More like Mr. Lopez from the train yard. Everything about him was dark. His clothes. His hat. His skin. It's why we never saw him coming."

Jonah snapped a look at Mark, who sat up straighter in his chair.

"What?" Katherine asked, her gaze flitting between the two men. "Does that mean something to you?"

Jonah nodded. "The fellow who snatched Rawley was white. Means there's at least two of 'em. Workin' together. Probably hired by someone."

Hired? For what purpose? Who would hire thugs to steal children? Were they being sold? Used as unpaid labor in some horrible factory or textile mill? She wanted to demand answers, but she feared frightening Alice. The girl was already burrowing into Katherine's side like a rabbit into its den. Besides, the men had no answers. Only God knew the truth.

You see them. Wart and the others. You know exactly where they are and who the perpetrators are. Lead us to them, Lord. Please. Show us the way.

"One more question, Al, then we'll be done, all right?"

Katherine felt the little girl's chin rub against her arm in a nod.

"Before you ran away, while you were looking for a way to help your brother fight, did you hear the man say anything?"

"Maybe? I don't . . ." The tears were too close to the surface.

Katherine lifted Alice into her lap and wrapped her arms around the trembling child. She wanted to put an end to the questioning that very moment, but she knew the answers were too important. "Close your eyes, sweetheart," she said instead. She cupped the girl's face in her hand and gently urged her to lay her head against her chest. "Sometimes when you close your eyes, it helps you remember."

Alice lay against Katherine and squeezed her eyes closed.

"I know it's scary, but you're safe here. I've got you. Feel my arms around you?" Katherine tightened her hold, and Alice nodded. "Now, go there in your mind. To that tree where you were looking for fallen branches. Listen to what's happening around you. What do you hear?"

"Footsteps. Heavy, fast footsteps."

"Good. What else? What is Wart doing?"

"Telling me to run."

"Before that." She stroked Alice's hair. "Did Wart say anything to the man?"

Alice stiffened. "Yes. He said, 'Get out of here!' Then yelled and ran at the man, swinging his branch."

"Did the man say anything back?"

Alice said nothing for a long minute, then jerked away from Katherine so fast, the top of her head slammed into Katherine's chin.

"He called Wart a little thief. Said he had it comin' to him." She leaned toward Jonah. "Does that help?"

Katherine didn't see how it could, but Jonah nodded.

"It just might. Where does Rawley's gang do most of their

swiping? I'm not talking about snitching food here or there. I'm talking about coins or other valuables."

Alice shook her head. "I-I can't tell you. It's a secret."

"Across the river, on the Burnet side of the bridge." Rawley strode into the room. He must have been eavesdropping from the hall. "When there's no train, the only way into Kingsland is over the bridge. Folks'll leave their wagons or horses on the Burnet side and walk across the bridge. They don't usually leave much of value behind, but if a fellow knows to search deep and look for holes in linings and secret pockets under stirrup straps, well, the pickin's can be pretty good." He crossed his arms over his chest. "You gonna turn me in to the law?"

"Nope." Jonah pushed to his feet and took a few steps in Rawley's direction. "But I just might kiss you for givin' us the first real lead in this case."

Rawley pulled a face and backed up a step, earning a soft chuckle from Jonah. "Me and the boys'll be movin' on after we help you get Wart back. We won't be workin' that spot no more."

Mark stood and joined Jonah. "That's probably a good thing. Thieving ain't that great for long-term security anyhow. You should consider heading out toward San Antone. I know a ranch where the group of you could earn an honest wage. If you're interested."

Rawley shrugged. "Don't know where we'll be headin' just yet." His gaze shifted past the men and settled on Alice. "But I do know you won't be coming with us."

Alice's breath caught on a tiny sob.

"Now, don't start bawlin' like a stuck calf. It ain't 'cause I'm mad at ya for lyin' to me about bein' a girl. I got over that halfway through dinner. You're one of us, Al, and you always will be. But Wart would want you to stay here. At Harmony House. That's why he took that job at the livery, ya know. To find a way to provide for you away from the rest of us. Railcar ridin' ain't no life for a girl. Now that I know the truth about ya, I ain't so mad at him for leavin' us behind. A man's gotta take care of his womenfolk or he ain't much of a man. When we get him back—and we *will* get him back— the two of you should stay here. Together. It don't seem so bad. Food's good. And I checked all the closets. No straps." He pointed a finger at her. "But I do think you need to start wearin' dresses." Rawley looked at Katherine. "Ya got any girl's duds she can use?"

Confused by the strange turn of the conversation, Katherine crinkled her forehead. "Yes. But if she prefers trousers, I don't see why—"

"Disguise," Rawley interrupted. "If the fella who took Wart saw Al, he saw a boy. If he decides to look for her, he'll be lookin' for a boy."

Not to mention that the snatchers, in general, were looking for boys. Not girls. The best way to keep Alice safe was to hide her in plain sight as the girl she was.

Katherine grinned approvingly at Rawley. "You are one clever young man."

He grinned back. "I know."

Early the following morning, Jonah led Tessie and Bessie from the barn and hitched them to the poor excuse for a wagon he and Mark had pieced back together last night after shoring up the cracked axle with some sturdy leather straps. They'd plotted while they worked and decided it best to divide and conquer today. Jonah would drive the dilapidated wagon to the wheelwright in Llano and inform the county sheriff of both Wart's abduction and the attempt on Rawley. Wallace would remain at the foundling home to guard the place and keep the boys busy assisting with property repairs. Tomorrow they'd switch roles. Jonah would guard the house while Mark crossed the bridge into Burnet County and visited nearby Hoover's Valley in search of information about a man who liked to dress all in black.

Questioning locals and getting them to open up was Wallace's talent. Not Jonah's. So even though a black man was less likely than a white one to gain a Texas sheriff's full cooperation, it was still the best division of labor. Jonah could wield his connection to Hanger's Horsemen to buy a decent measure of respect. It had worked in the past. With their reputation for bringing in wanted criminals and collecting bounties, most lawmen in the state were sufficiently amiable. And really, all he needed to do was report the crime. The sheriff could decide whether or not to investigate. With as shorthanded as the man seemed to be, he'd probably jump at the chance to have the Horsemen do his work for him. Especially when the only kids missing were vagrants whom the voting members of the county cared little about.

The trip would take a full day. Four hours there. Four hours back. He could have cut the return time in half by taking Augustus, but the ladies had insisted on renting a replacement wagon so they could drive the children to church on Sunday, two days from now.

At the sound of the back door clicking shut, Jonah glanced up and caught an eyeful of Eliza sauntering down the porch steps with a basket of vittles hanging over her arm. Nice of her to pack him a lunch. Nice of her to deliver it too, Jonah thought as he tipped his hat brim downward to watch the sway of her approach without her noticing.

She looked good first thing in the morning. 'Course, she looked good night and noon too, but there was something about morning that suited her. She was just a little bit softer now than after the responsibilities of the day caught up to her. A tad more vulnerable. He'd already studied her in the kitchen that morning while shoveling down eggs, bacon, and grits as the rest of the house slept. Shoot, he'd probably stolen enough glances at her to earn his own wanted poster, but he didn't regret a one. Not even when she'd caught him in the act. It just allowed him to target those expressive eyes of hers. Watching them shift from surprised to embarrassed to flustered had been pure pleasure. But it had been the hint of interest that flashed right before she'd turned away that had really gotten his blood pumping. No doubt he'd be reliving that flash a few hundred times during the twenty-mile drive to Llano.

Recalling her lack of love for horses, Jonah stepped away from the team in order to intercept her in neutral territory. Quirking a grin, he reached for the basket she'd so kindly packed for him, then frowned as she swung it over his outstretched palm and sidestepped him to place it in the wagon bed herself. Tracking her as she sailed past, it occurred to him that she looked different than she had at breakfast. No apron. And she'd donned a bonnet. Something flipped in his gut.

"I'm going with you." She released the basket handle, then spun to face him, hands finding their way to her hips.

Schooling his features, he raised a brow. "Oh?"

His pulse kicked up a notch at the thought of her company. 'Course, she probably had a practical reason for wantin' to make the trip. It wasn't as if she suddenly couldn't bear the thought of being parted from him. Though *he* had experienced a few twinges at the thought of not seeing her for a full day. Which was crazy. Women didn't get under his skin. At least they hadn't before now. What was it about *this* one that was so different?

He looked her up and down. The gentle curves softening her statuesque figure. The warm glow of her tawny skin. The fire of challenge sparking in her large dark eyes. The sass in her posture. The determination in her raised chin.

Everything. *Everything* about her was different.

A slow smile stretched across his face.

One of Eliza's hands slid off her hip. She jerked it back into place. "I canceled school for the day. Rawley and his crew need time to settle in before lessons are enforced, and

195

Friday is a terrible day to start a new routine. We'll start fresh on Monday. Besides, we need supplies. We have twice as many mouths to feed now."

Her rambling boosted Jonah's confidence. Maybe *he'd* gotten under *her* skin as well. Only fair.

He stalked forward, his gaze locked on hers. "They got stores in Kingsland," he said. "No need to travel all the way to Llano for supplies."

"My *wagon* is going to Llano," she volleyed, "so if I wish to have a conveyance to cart my supplies, it appears I'll need to go to Llano with it."

While she spoke, he closed in on her. She reached out to halt his advance. Four fingertips pressed against his chest, and lightning charged through him from each contact point. His pulse jumped. As if she felt it, she snatched her hand back and curled her fingers into a fist.

Spend the day with Eliza Southerland? Yeah, he could suffer through that torture.

Jonah gestured to the wagon seat. "Hop in, Teach. Daylight's a wastin'."

She nodded with a regal dip of her head, as if his compliance had never been in question. Let her believe herself the victor, he thought as he handed her up onto the seat. He didn't mind a strategic surrender every now and again. Especially when the reward gained outranked the forfeiture. And seeing as how all he was forfeiting was eight hours of boring, solitary drive time with nothing to entertain him but God's scenery, he figured he'd come out on top of this deal. The rolling hills, rivers, and trees of Llano County were fine, indeed, but they couldn't compare to the handiwork evident in Eliza. The Lord had outdone himself there.

Too bad the Almighty hadn't seen fit to give Jonah a bit

more fine-tuning in the verbal exchange department. It was hard to impress a woman when a fella ran out of conversational ammunition within the first five minutes. His pride suffered a serious blow when, not thirty minutes into their drive, she fetched a book out of the basket she'd packed and started reading. So much for his theory that she'd used Harmony House's dearth of supplies as an excuse to spend time with him. She'd probably been trying to escape the clamor of a dozen rambunctious children. Who wouldn't want some peace and quiet after the day they'd had yesterday?

Oddly enough . . . he wouldn't. Usually he preferred solitude. A man alone with his thoughts and his God. It kept him grounded. However, a man alone with a beautiful woman who was ignoring him . . . well, that just kept him frustrated. And lonely. And silently berating himself for not having anything of consequence to say.

Paper crinkled slightly as she turned a page. Her gaze shifted closer to him as she searched out words printed on the left side of the binding.

And if he was noticing that, he was in a sorrier state than he'd thought. Enough with the reconnaissance. Time to take action.

Jonah cleared his throat. "Whatcha readin'?"

She fit her finger between the pages to mark her place, then folded the cover over to show him the title. "*Illustrated School History of the United States* by G. P. Quackenbos."

"Quackenbos?" Jonah choked on a partially stifled laugh.

Enough amusement escaped, however, to elicit one of those warning looks womenfolk were famous for. The raised brows, the tilted head, the slanted eyes designed to let a man know his behavior was edging toward unsuitable. Were they at a fancy dinner where using the wrong fork might shame him, he probably would have heeded that warning. But out in the middle of nowhere? Not a chance.

Jonah released a full-on chuckle. "I would've thought a teacher would know better than to read a book written by a quack."

Eliza pulled her finger free from the book and jabbed it into his shoulder. "I'll have you know that George Payn Quackenbos is a well-respected educator and the author of numerous texts not only in history, but in arithmetic, grammar, composition, and phil—why are you laughing?"

The affront in her tone only made Jonah laugh harder. "His middle name is *Pain*?" His eyes started to water. "Oh, that's rich. I bet the kids *love* his lessons."

He expected her hackles to bristle into weaponized porcupine quills, so the smile that blossomed across her face as she shook her head caught him off guard.

"I had never actually thought about it, but you're right." Her eyes sparkled. "There's a lot of"—she interrupted herself with a giggle—"irony in that name."

Laughter changed her face completely. Before his eyes, this strong, independent woman relaxed into a woman so approachable, he had to struggle to keep his hands on the reins. His fingers itched to cup her cheek, to caress the skin along her jaw, to tilt her lips up to his.

Easy, partner. Eyes on the road.

Jonah forced his head around, dragging his gaze back where it belonged. "So, ah . . . where'd you get your training? To be a teacher?"

"Howard University."

Jonah's head swiveled sideways. He'd known she was smart, but Howard? She put his education to shame. "Impressive."

198

"Thank you." Pride rang in her voice and straightened her shoulders, but it wasn't the kind of pride that looked down on others from a lofty perch. It was the type that remembered the arduous climb it took to reach the pinnacle and felt a sense of responsibility to help others make their own ascents.

"With your accent, I supposed you had grown up in the South somewhere."

"I did. In Georgia."

"Then how did you—" He cut himself off, afraid he might offend her.

She raised her brows, but her expression didn't frost over. "I was blessed with a mother who understood the value of education. Mama might have started off an illiterate slave, but she craved knowledge like a starving man craves bread. Her good looks earned her a place serving in the house of a respected apothecary, but it was her intelligence that seized upon the opportunity to learn. When the mistress gave her a shopping list to take to market, she'd ask for items one at a time so she could learn to recognize which words matched which item. Flour. Sugar. Eggs. Carrots. Peaches. She picked apart the letters to learn their sounds, then started trying to guess items she didn't recognize by sounding out their similar letters."

Jonah suddenly felt guilty for complaining as a boy about being stuck in the schoolroom reading when he'd rather have been fishing or shooting targets. Hearing how Eliza's mother had taught herself to read through painstaking determination, effort, and creativity made him realize just how precious was the gift of literacy.

"It took months, but she started recognizing simple words in newspapers and shop signs. But she hungered for more. Not just words, but the knowledge they unlocked. Knowledge that didn't care about her age, her gender, or the color of her skin." Passion rang in Eliza's voice. Passion and pride in what her mother had accomplished. "She'd sneak books out of the master's library one at a time, careful to fill the shelf space so no one would realize a volume was missing. She dared not let anyone discover her secret. Slaves who could read were considered threats to the household. Instigators of unrest."

Jonah's jaw tightened. He knew it was true, but hearing her admit it aloud brought a righteous anger to the surface inside him. Just one more way his people were leashed by their oppressors.

"Although she kept her growing literacy a secret," Eliza continued, "the master noticed her intelligence and capability. He started trusting her with more and more responsibility. Even trained her to assist him in the preparation of his medicinal powders and elixirs to cut down on his workload when his wife grew ill, allowing him to spend more time nursing her at home."

Was this *master* Eliza's father? Jonah longed to hear more but didn't want to pry. He glanced her way to show his interest, then held his tongue, letting her dictate the conversation's direction.

"Papa used to brag that she could work a mortar and pestle with more skill than half the men in his profession."

Papa. Something boiled inside Jonah at the sound of that name on her tongue. A name associated with the man who'd *owned* her mother. A name she'd spoken with a hint of affection. How could she call him Papa when he'd abused his position so thoroughly? He'd taken advantage of a woman in his household. Fathered a child on a woman not his wife.

Clenching his jaw, Jonah turned back to the road. Eliza couldn't change who her father was. How she came to be. He should be glad that she *could* speak of her father with affection. Hopefully that meant he had treated her with some level of kindness. Better than a cruel man who inspired hatred.

Yet Jonah couldn't let it go. His mother had been a slave too. A laundress. Her work would have brought her to the big house on a regular basis. What if her master had taken a liking to her and decided he wanted more than just her work? What choice would she have had? Disobedience earned the lash. Even if she'd had the courage to refuse his advances, the master could've taken her by force. No one would've stopped him from doing what he wanted to his property.

Jonah's thoughts churned as Eliza continued narrating the story of a young woman's love of books, science, and education. He listened with only half an ear until that name jumped out of her mouth again and grabbed him around the throat.

"After the mistress died, Papa relied on my mama more and more."

His grip tightened reflexively on the reins. "Why do you call him that?"

Eliza's sweetly reminiscent smile flattened into a frown of confusion. "What?"

"Your father. How can you call him . . ." His throat constricted.

"Papa?" Eliza's eyebrows arched, silently questioning his right to make such an inquiry.

He had no right, and they both knew it. But that didn't stop him from wanting to know the answer.

"Your mother was his *property*. Like a horse in his stable or a painting on his wall. No rights. No freedom. She had to hide her ability to read, for pity's sake, as if she were a criminal. How can you condone that?"

Her eyes flashed fire. "You think I *condone* his owning slaves?"

Offense radiated through her with such ferocity that he worried for a moment she might jump off the moving wagon to escape him.

"I grew up in the deep South," she said, her words sharp, angry. "I heard the tales of field hands whipped to death for even speaking about a freedom run before the war. I saw the scars, the broken spirits, the . . . lynchings." Her voice cracked and she turned her face away for a moment. "Slavery is a vile, dehumanizing practice," she said once she had her emotions under control. "A practice my father once participated in. That knowledge shreds my heart with shame." She looked at him, and Jonah felt the dissonance of her position tugging on his soul, cooling his temper. "But if each man and woman were defined solely by their greatest sin, what hope would there be for any of us?"

Dousing the last flames of his indignation, Jonah considered her words. Thought of Wounded Knee. The acidic shame that ate at him whenever he recalled the horrors of that massacre. What if no one ever saw him as anything more than a soldier who'd participated in that slaughter? Equating him with those who killed women and children even though he did everything he could to preserve innocent lives?

He needed grace as much as the next man, even if the next man was a slave owner with a mixed-race daughter.

Jonah met Eliza's gaze and softened his heart. "Tell me about him."

---CHAPTER---
TWENTY-ONE

Eliza bit her lip. Her family situation was . . . complicated. Uncomfortable. Both to talk about and to accept. Even for her. How could she expect Jonah to understand?

Slowly, she lifted her chin and claimed her identity. Illegitimate. Mulatto. Female. All classifications the world looked down upon. Yet she was the person God created her to be. His fingers had formed her in her mother's womb. With purpose. She was fearfully and wonderfully made, and she would not hide.

"My father was far from perfect, but he wasn't evil." Eliza held Jonah's gaze until he looked away to check their position on the road. "His wife passed away in the winter of 1861. She'd always been frail and spent more time abed than in company, but he mourned her loss. Mama hated seeing the man of science she respected retreat into a hollow shell. He started making mistakes at the shop, mixing up orders and forgetting ingredients. Mama worried his patients would suffer and couldn't in good conscience sit idly by and let things deteriorate without doing something to intervene."

Jonah craned his neck and raised a brow, a light of teasing

in his eyes. "Hard to imagine an interfering female in your family tree."

Eliza's lips twitched. "Yes, well, we Southerlands aren't afraid to have opinions."

"So I've noticed." His tone offered no censure, only admiration. A fact that sent warmth through her midsection and up into her cheeks.

Good heavens. Was she actually blushing?

Clearing her throat, Eliza returned to her story. "Mama refused to let him languish away. She became downright impertinent. Throwing open draperies when he said he preferred them closed. Taking food to his study when he neglected to come to the table and not leaving until he ate to her satisfaction. She watched every move he made in the workshop and challenged him when she spotted an error.

"Respect blossomed in that workshop. A respect that grew into something . . . more."

Eliza repositioned herself on the wagon bench, uncomfortable speaking of her parents' immorality. No matter how many times her mother tried to justify their relationship with talk of love and how it was only because of society's intolerance that they'd never wed, the truth was still the truth. Her mother had given herself to a man without the benefit of marriage vows, and her father had not had the courage to defy convention and marry her mother, even in secret. He could have taken her to New York or Vermont, states with no anti-miscegenation laws. He'd had sufficient wealth to pay someone off and ensure secrecy. Even if he never acknowledged the marriage publicly, she and Mama would have had the comfort of the truth. The blessing of legitimacy in the eyes of God, if not in the eyes of society. But her parents had chosen to walk a different path.

"When he was a young man, Papa fell ill with the mumps,

and the physicians told him he was sterile. After having no children with his first wife, the last thing he expected was to beget a child on my mother." Eliza tried to pretend she hadn't noticed the tightening of Jonah's mouth or the clenching of his jaw. "But Mama discovered the truth mere weeks before Lincoln issued the Emancipation Proclamation in January 1863. Papa was so obsessed with the idea of having fathered a child, *any* child, that when my mother demanded he draw up freedom papers on the day I was born, just in case the South found a way to win the war, he didn't argue. When the Union prevailed and the Thirteenth Amendment was ratified, she informed him that the two of us would stay with him only if he agreed to her terms."

The muscles in Jonah's face relaxed a bit. The corner of his mouth even twitched. "Somehow I don't find that hard to imagine."

Eliza smiled. Her mother's fearlessness in standing up for herself and for her child was the trait Eliza most strove to emulate. Reckless when necessary, but always intelligent. Never haphazard. Risks were always assessed but seldom allowed to stand in the way of progress.

"She had three conditions for staying. First, he could never marry or have relations with another woman. Second, he had to settle the equivalent of a dowry upon me, placing the funds in an account that only she and I could access, to ensure that should something happen to one or both of my parents, I would not be left destitute. And third—and to my mother, the most important—he had to commit, in writing, that he would educate me at the same level he would a legitimate son and heir. My mother believed education to be the true road to equality. Not only between races, but between genders as well.

"My father proved true to his word on all three counts. He allowed me to attend the local freedmen school and even tutored me himself some evenings once I was old enough to study the sciences. He took such pride in my scholastic accomplishments, sure it was his bloodline that enabled my success, never realizing that it was Mama who taught me my letters well before I started school. Mama who snuck books to me and encouraged me to read at every opportunity. Mama who helped me with my sums and quizzed me in history.

"He never took another wife. And when he and I were together, he treated me as his daughter. Playing with me. Reading with me." One memory in particular rose to settle softly on her heart. "I learned to dance by standing on his shoes." She sought out Jonah's gaze. "It was only natural for me to call him Papa."

The fond memory faded, replaced by others wrapped not in velvet but in stinging nettles. Her gaze fell to her lap, where her fingers gripped her book far too tightly. "However, whenever we were out in public or when visitors came to the house, Mama and I addressed him as *sir* or *Mr. Farmington*. I remember Mama coaching me over and over when I was a girl about what to call him, depending on where we were or who was around. I was always so careful. Until the day Mrs. Bellows called at the house with her daughter. Widow Bellows hoped to make a match with my father. He'd done his best to avoid her company, but when she showed up at his door, hospitality had to be offered. Mama ordered me to stay in the kitchen, away from the guests, but my curiosity got the better of me.

"Remembering I had left my doll in the parlor, I decided to fetch it. I wouldn't say a word. Just creep in, retrieve my doll, and leave. I yearned to see the woman and little girl who wanted to steal my papa away."

How foolish she'd been. How impetuous. She'd never blindly followed a whim since that day.

Jonah turned at her silence, his voice gentle as he prodded, "What happened?"

Moisture pooled in Eliza's eyes at the tenderness in his voice. She ruthlessly blinked it away. "The doll wasn't where I'd left it. Nelda Bellows, the widow's daughter, had found it and was playing with it on the rug next to the hearth. She had it cradled in her arms and was murmuring a quiet lullaby.

"Seeing that doll in her arms, I realized for the first time how wrong everything was. That doll, *my* doll, looked nothing like me and everything like Nelda. I used to think the doll's brown hair and eyes were like mine, but they weren't. Not really. My frizzy spiral curls were nothing like the silky tresses of the doll, curling only at the ends. My brown eyes were two shades too dark. And my skin, while a good deal lighter than Mama's, looked more like dead leaves than the snowy perfection of the doll's white porcelain face. Nelda's face was white. Her hair long and silky. Even her blue dress matched the doll. All I could think in that moment was that *she* was the daughter my father must have wanted. Why else would he buy a doll with white skin and silky hair?" Eliza shook her head. "It never occurred to me that china dolls only came in one color."

"What'd you do?"

Not one to let maudlin emotions control her, Eliza straightened her shoulders and raised her brows in mock haughtiness. "I marched directly over to Nelda, held out my hand, and demanded she give me my doll. At once."

"At once, huh?" His tone lightened, as she'd intended, but the sympathy in his gaze lingered, as if he could guess how the story would end.

"Indeed. And when she refused to do so, I stomped over to where my father was taking tea with Mrs. Bellows and said, 'Make her give me my doll, Papa.' Mrs. Bellows gasped. Papa's face reddened. Then his hand shot out and cuffed me across the mouth. It was the first time he'd ever struck me. I ran from the room, devastated. Not because he had hit me, but because I'd realized he was ashamed of me. Ashamed of my very existence. I never forgot myself in company again."

Jonah said nothing, but his hand covered hers. Its warmth soothed and strengthened, helping her pack away the painful memory.

"He apologized later, of course, but our relationship was never the same after that."

Jonah traced the line of her thumb with his. "I'm sorry, Eliza."

She nodded, those simple words having a profound effect. They freed something inside her, some small piece that still believed that shame was hers to carry. It wasn't. She knew that in her head. But in the dark of night, as she lay alone, there were times when her heart still doubted. Perhaps that was why she'd never told Katherine this story. Despite her being the most compassionate person Eliza had ever met, she didn't know what it was like to live in brown skin. To wear the stain of illegitimacy. To pretend to be a servant around the man who was supposed to be her protector and defender.

Jonah might not relate to the details, but he understood the core conflict. The fight to believe oneself worthy in a world that communicated the opposite.

"All that to say, my father has made his share of mistakes, but he's also done much to provide for me. Especially in my education. He financed my college tuition—anonymously, of course. Couldn't risk his customers and neighbors learning he'd paid to educate a servant." His hypocrisy still left a bitter taste in her mouth.

He'd commended himself for being so progressive, so kind to her and Mama. But time after time, when push came to shove, he succumbed to society's dictates. Refusing to take a stand anywhere other than in his mind. Yet, he was still her father, and even with the growing rift between them, she had to acknowledge the truth. "Without him, I never would have attended Howard and earned my teaching degree. My *doorway to freedom*, as Mama likes to call it."

"I've got one of those too," Jonah said, releasing her hand to dig in his trouser pocket.

"A teaching degree?" Eliza asked with a raised brow.

"Nope." He finally pulled whatever he'd been searching for out of his pocket. "A doorway to freedom." He opened his hand and revealed the worn brass casing of a small compass. "Only my daddy called it the *key* to freedom. He and my ma used this very compass to find their way north on the Underground Railroad before I was born."

He gestured for her to take it. She held it reverently, recognizing at once the treasure it represented. She opened the lid and watched as the needle wobbled with the movement of the wagon yet held true to its course.

"Daddy passed it on to me when I left to join the Army. Said it would guide me to freedom just as it had guided him."

Eliza's brow scrunched. "But weren't you already free?"

"Free from slavery, sure, but there's a lot more out there that will enslave a man if he surrenders to it. Hatred. Bitterness. Greed. Drink." Jonah snorted softly and shook his head. "Daddy feared war would steal my soul. That the wandering lifestyle of a cavalry unit would leave me untethered, and I'd forget who I was." He caught her gaze. "Your mama believed education brought freedom. My daddy believed freedom lay in the land. Owning it. Working it. Building a homestead and raising a family on it. He's been after me for years to buy a piece of property somewhere and settle down. Says a man don't really know who he is until he's got his own land under his feet and a family at his side."

Eliza peered closer, her heart thumping a touch faster as she studied his face. "And what do *you* say?"

Dark eyes melded with hers, eyes that had experienced their own pain and disillusionment. "I say nothing teaches a man who he is more than war."

He turned back to the road, making it clear he'd welcome no probing on that particular topic. At least not today. But what about the other topic? The one his daddy had found such value in?

She carefully closed the lid to the compass, the quiet *click* barely audible above the rattle of the wagon wheels and harness. "What about the land? Do you plan to settle down and buy a piece someday?"

He shrugged. "Maybe. Never really had a thing for farming, but running cattle has possibilities."

And family? Eliza longed to ask, but such a question would be far too presumptuous. Besides, it would make her sound like she was applying for the position. Which she wasn't, no matter what her wildly thumping heartbeat said to the contrary. She'd known him less than a week.

Yet she felt as if she'd known him half her life.

Maybe it was the danger heightening things. Or maybe it was just the man himself. Stoic. Contrary. Stubborn as new shoe leather. Yet there was a solidity to him that invited leaning. Like a Greek column that still stood straight and tall after thousands of years. He could be relied upon. Perhaps that was why she'd shared more of herself with this man in the last few days than she had with any other person of her acquaintance.

Eliza turned Jonah's compass over in her hand and found an inscription etched on the back. The writing was shaky, as if etched into the brass by an amateur hand, but she made out a pair of letters and four numbers. "PS 3278. What does that stand for?"

Jonah lifted his chin and smiled, his eyes lighting. "Psalm 32:7–8. My daddy scratched that into the back before I left home." His gaze moved toward the sky as he spoke the scripture from memory. "'Thou art my hiding place; thou shalt preserve me from trouble; thou shalt compass me about with songs of deliverance. I will instruct thee and teach thee in the way which thou shalt go: I will guide thee with mine eye.'" When he finished the recitation, his attention came back to her. "Daddy said the first verse was a prayer for my safety, and the second was to remind me not to get too big for my britches." His grin widened. "I've always been a crack shot. Eyes like an eagle, folks like to say." He shrugged away the praise. "Daddy liked to say that no matter how keen a man's eyesight, he still couldn't see everything. He needed the Lord's eye to guide him and instruct him on the way that he should go."

Eliza traced the crude lettering with her fingertip. "Your daddy sounds like a wise man."

Jonah nodded, his gaze traveling to a distant spot in front of the wagon. "That he is."

She handed the compass back to him. He shoved it into his pocket, and silence resumed. It was a different type of silence than before, however. There was no awkwardness. Just quiet—as if both passengers had weighty notions to contemplate and neither wanted to interrupt the other. Eventually, the mood lightened and chatter resumed. He pointed out rabbits and prairie dogs when they scampered near the road. She asked about his life as a Horseman. He told her stories of criminals brandishing guns and branding irons. She regaled him with tales of troublemaking boys brandishing snakes and spiders. By the time they rolled into Llano, they were completely at ease in each other's company. The history book had been neglected for the majority of the trip, and Eliza hadn't missed Mr. Quackenbos's scholarly exhortations one iota.

After dropping the wagon off at the wheelwright for repairs, Jonah rented a replacement wagon and drove Eliza to the general store so she could stock up on supplies while he ran the other errands that had brought them to town.

As he saw to the horses, slipping a feed bag over each of their heads so they could replenish their energy before making the long journey home, he searched Eliza out on the boardwalk in front of the general store. He couldn't recall the last time he'd spent four uninterrupted hours with a woman, let alone enjoying it. It almost made him want to tag along at the store instead of seeing to his own business. But then, the faster he took care of his business, the faster he could have her to himself again. Maybe he'd see if she wanted to stop by the river to eat their lunch on the way back to Kingsland. He'd noticed a pretty spot on the way into town. Far enough from the road to afford them some privacy, but close enough to maintain propriety.

The thought gave his stride extra length and pace as he cut the corner of Main and Ford and headed along the courthouse square to the county jail at the end of the block. Sheriff Porter proved a fair-minded fellow when he learned of Jonah's connection to the Horsemen. He took down Jonah's information and filled out a report on Wart's disappearance as well as Rawley's attempted abduction. The lawman also offered to wire his deputy in Kingsland and encourage him to poke around Honey Creek a bit, see if any of the locals had noticed a change in outlaw activity in the area.

"Most folks out there stay to themselves," the sheriff said, "but it's possible someone might have seen something. I'll tell Bronson to expect a visit from you middle of next week for a report."

It was more cooperation than Jonah had expected, so he tipped his hat and thanked Porter for his assistance. "I'll wire you if we turn up a lead," he promised, even as he realized that wasn't the only wire he needed to send.

Leaving the jailhouse, he headed for the telegraph office, only to pull up short when he heard his name being called. He turned to the east, his right hand inching closer to his weapon, but he relaxed when he recognized Dr. Hampton hailing him from the boardwalk in front of a barbershop.

"Mr. Brooks!" The doctor hurried down to the street and wove between two ladies out for a stroll and a farmer toting a bag of chicken feed on his shoulder as he crossed to meet Jonah on the other side. "Oh, I can't tell you how glad I am to see you."

"What can I do for ya, Doc?"

Hampton took a handkerchief from his pocket and dabbed at his face where perspiration had gathered after his short jaunt. "Did you and Mr. Wallace make it to Harmony House with the baby? How is she doing? Have you heard?"

Jonah nodded, impressed that the doctor took such a personal interest in a child who had never really been under his care. "Little one's doin' well, as far as I know. Miss Southerland found a wet nurse in the area, and we delivered the babe to her that very day. The ladies at Harmony House have pledged to give the child a home with them once she's weaned."

Had it only been a couple of days since baby Sarah brought him and Wallace to Harmony House? It seemed like ages ago. So much had happened since.

"Thank the Lord, she's all right." Dr. Hampton shoved his folded handkerchief back into his suit coat pocket. "I've been praying for her. Poor little thing, thrust into the world under such harsh circumstances. I should have known the ladies of Harmony House would set things to rights for her. They are a godsend to this community, I tell you. A godsend."

"Yes, sir." Jonah couldn't agree more.

"I'm hopeful their services will not be needed permanently in this case, however."

Jonah frowned. "What do you mean?"

Excitement lit the doctor's face. "I've written to the Dawsons. Wendell's folks. I'm hoping they'll take Fern and her baby under their wing. I've been checking on Fern every day. She's not the first expectant mother I've tended who has struggled with depressed mood, though her grief certainly compounded things. My prayer is that, in time, her mind will heal and she will want to be a mother to her child. If not, perhaps the baby's grandparents will want to raise her."

"It'd be good for the girl to have family."

Though Harmony House could be that for her too. In fact, he'd kinda suspected that Wallace might want to adopt Sarah himself if he and Miss Katherine got around to tying the knot. Most kids were stuck with whatever parents biology dictated, but little Sarah had options. He prayed the Lord placed her with the best one.

"Will you be staying in the area long?" Dr. Hampton asked. "Last time we met, I got the impression you and your partner were passing through."

"Something came up in Kingsland that requires our attention. We'll be sticking around a while. If you hear from the Dawsons, you can send word to Harmony House. Wallace and I are helping the ladies there with some repairs."

"Excellent! I'll send word as soon as I hear anything. Thank you again for all you did for Fern and her baby."

Jonah waved off the gratitude. Wallace had done all the work. All he'd done was fetch the doctor. But still, he was glad he'd made a contribution, no matter how small. Kids had a hard enough row to hoe in this world without adults making things worse. If he could help one of them get a fair shake, he was glad to do it.

Too bad helping the other kids God had placed in his path wasn't quite so clear-cut.

Excusing himself from the doctor, Jonah hiked the rest of the way to the telegraph office, composing his missive in his head as he went. He had it slimmed down to close to a dozen words by the time he walked through the door.

Dropping sixty-five cents on the counter, he grabbed a telegram blank and filled out his message.

To: Matthew Hanger, Gringolet Farms, San Antonio, TX
   KIDS MISSING IN KINGSLAND
   STAYING TO INVESTIGATE
   WILL SEND FOR HORSEMEN IF NEEDED

Matt would put Preach on alert. They'd be ready to come at a moment's notice. Jonah hated pulling the captain away from his work and his new wife, but there was no one he trusted more to have his back.

Once he and Wallace figured out where Wart and the others had been taken, he'd call in the cavalry.

TWENTY-TWO

Y ou are *not* going to use yourself as bait!" Katherine dropped the wooden clothespin from her hand as if it had suddenly combusted into flames.

Leaving a sheet half secured on the clothesline, she ducked around the flapping fabric that had hidden her from view and marched over to the cluster of boys who'd been too busy plotting their own demise to pay attention to who might be listening. And thank God for that!

The five boys jerked their faces toward her, their expressions varying from guilty to embarrassed to mutinous. The mutinous one concerned her most. Focusing her full attention on Rawley, she wagged her finger as she approached.

"You are children, not worms, and you will *not* purposely put yourself in danger. Is that clear?"

Rawley's chin lifted and his eyes narrowed as he stepped away from his compatriots to meet her on the field of battle. "It's been over a week, and we still ain't got a clue as to where Wart and the others are." His gaze darted over to Alice and Ruby sitting beneath a tree near the house, a picture book stretched over their two laps. "It's takin' a toll on Al." He looked at his gang. "It's takin' a toll on all of us."

Heads nodded in agreement.

Katherine's heart ached for the boy. She fretted over Wart and the others too. Mark and Jonah didn't even know how many boys in total were missing. Stolen children forced into an unsavory situation—the horrible possibilities didn't bear thinking about. She had to focus on hope. Not only for herself, but for those around her. She wasn't a warrior like the Horsemen. She couldn't fend off evil with her fists or a gun. All she could contribute was prayer and a steady diet of optimism.

"I know waiting is hard," Katherine soothed, "but Mr. Wallace and Mr. Brooks will find them. We just have to be patient."

Rawley huffed and crossed his wiry arms over his chest. "Look, Miz Katherine, you and Miz Eliza are nice and all, and I gotta admit that the eatin's been real good around here, but me and the boys are gettin' itchy. We don't belong in a place like this. All the rules and schoolin' and stuff. I only agreed to stay until I was healed up, and I am now. Good enough not to slow the boys down, at least," he qualified when she raised a brow in challenge. "Truth is, we can go places Brooks and Wallace can't. We can do more to help Wart and the others out there than we can hidin' out here."

"And who will take care of your boys if you get taken?" she asked, making a desperate appeal to his protective nature. It had worked in the past. But this time he just smirked.

"*You* will."

Katherine's mouth hung open, her protest evaporating on the breeze.

"He's got you there."

Mark! Katherine turned, thankful to see him. Rawley would listen to him, surely.

"Of course I would take care of you boys," she said, pivoting back to Rawley and his cohorts, taking the time to smile at each one. "Every one of you is welcome here anytime. For as long as you wish. No strings attached." Her gaze zeroed back in on their leader. "But that doesn't give you permission to recklessly endanger yourself." She glanced over her shoulder at Mark. "I overheard him plotting to use himself as bait to try to lure the kidnappers out. Tell him that's a horrible idea."

"I can't."

Katherine's stomach clenched. "What?"

Mark shrugged, his gaze as apologetic as his jaw was firm. "It's a good idea. One we would have tried days ago if Jonah or I could pass for a ten- or eleven-year-old boy. But since neither of us is *that* clever with disguises, we took the option off the table."

"Well, put it back on. I'm volunteerin'." Rawley jutted out his chin, daring Mark to naysay him.

Mark took the dare. "Nope. Even with both Jonah and I watching, there are too many factors outside our control. If the snatcher spots one of us, he could decide you aren't worth the trouble, put a bullet in you, and dump you on the trail to halt our pursuit."

Katherine shivered, her imagination painting the scene in vivid detail. *He won't let him do it,* she told herself. Mark was not the type of man to endanger a child, not even to save others.

Rawley, on the other hand, was just wild enough not to care. The rebellious gleam in his eyes made it clear he wasn't one to abide by an adult's ruling if he didn't agree with it. And he obviously didn't agree with this one.

Mark acted as if he didn't notice the rising insubordination. "Besides," he said offhandedly, "neither of the snatchers would consider you an easy mark. Not after the way you stabbed that horse and fought your way free. These types of criminals go for the easy pickin's. Safer that way."

A bit of the fight faded from Rawley's gaze, but he wasn't fully convinced yet. "It don't hurt to try. If nuthin' else, bein' back on the street will let me keep an ear to the ground. There's other fellas that ride the rails. They mighta heard somethin'. Seen somethin'. Can't learn nuthin' hiding out here."

You can't get hurt hiding out here either. Katherine had to bite her tongue to keep the words from escaping.

Things had been quiet over the last ten days. Mark's and Jonah's presence proved a comfort to the children and a deterrent to anyone bent on mischief, yet she couldn't deny the truth of Rawley's words. They'd made little progress in their search for the missing boys. And while she insisted on guarding the children in her care, she couldn't neglect the ones who'd been taken. They needed to be found. Soon.

Mark had grown unusually quiet. Katherine glanced his way. His face looked far too thoughtful, as if he were actually considering Rawley's plan.

She touched his arm. "Mark, you can't. . . ."

He didn't look at her. He addressed Rawley instead. "Jonah just returned from town. He's in the barn seeing to Augustus. Go fetch him, and we'll talk."

Rawley nodded and strode off to the barn, his gang flanking him.

Katherine yanked her hand away with enough vigor to jostle Mark's arm. "You can't seriously be considering putting those boys in danger. They're children!"

Mark's jaw ticked. "They're boys on the cusp of manhood, Kate. Far too eager to prove themselves. You saw that look in his eyes. If we don't find a way to involve him, he's going to leave and do it on his own."

She pressed her lips together and shook her head, wanting so badly to deny the truth staring her in the face.

Mark curled his hands around her upper arms and tugged her close. "I don't like it either, sweetheart, but in all honesty, we might actually need them out there if we're going to make any progress with this investigation."

Katherine peered at his face and noted the haggardness of his features, the dark smudges beneath his eyes, the flat line of his mouth. The late nights standing guard and the frustration of a less-than-fruitful investigation had taken their toll. He was worn out. Fighting discouragement. She didn't want to add to his burden. She wanted to lighten it. But how? She couldn't just agree that they throw Rawley and the others to the wolves.

Reaching for him, she bent her arms upward and clasped his elbows. She'd listen. Stand with him. Love him. Even if she didn't agree.

Mark stared at the blond topknot belonging to the only woman he'd ever loved. He hated that he had to disappoint her, sure her protective instincts toward the children would put them on opposites sides of this argument. Yet as he rubbed her arms and sought the right words to assuage her concerns while not shying away from doing what had to do be done, she surprised him.

Instead of pulling away, she leaned closer. Her palms curled around his elbows. And when her face tipped upward, it wasn't anger or disillusionment he read in her eyes. Nor was it surrender. It was commitment. A decision to stand by him no matter where the upcoming discussion led.

A weight he hadn't realized he'd been carrying shifted and fell off his shoulders. She wasn't holding their burgeoning relationship hostage. If he displeased her with his decision, she wasn't going to send him away. Her affection wasn't shallow.

His hold on her arms tightened, and if there hadn't been half a dozen sets of footsteps tromping across the yard behind him, he would've bent his head to hers and kissed her. Ah, horsefeathers. He *had* to kiss her. There were too many fireworks shooting off inside of him to ignore. Releasing her as if nothing earth-shattering had just occurred would be a crime. She'd offered him freedom, love, and trust. He had to respond in kind.

So he tugged her close, leaned down, and pressed his lips to the top of her forehead. His eyes slid closed for a precious heartbeat as he savored the feel of her skin on his lips. Inhaled the fragrance of her hair. Heard the tiny sigh that escaped her lips. Felt the slight softening of her posture and the caress of her thumb against the crook of his elbow.

It was the best moment of his life. But that was all he could allow it to be. A single, glorious moment.

He lifted his head and set her away from him, trailing his fingers along the length of her arms as they separated.

By the time Jonah and the boys reached them, Mark had his mind back on the question at hand and preempted the conversation before anyone could comment on what they'd just witnessed.

"Learn anything at the livery?"

Jonah shook his head. "Still no word about a knife-injured horse. I hoped Rawley's snatcher would have sought out a healing salve at one of the liveries in the area or called someone out to treat the animal, but no one's heard anything. Not here or in Llano or in Hoover's Valley. The farrier's done a handful of trimmings in the last week, but only for local customers, and none had a nick on the right rear hoof. Our two strongest leads have gone cold. We got no choice but to mix things up. Try something new."

Mark nodded. He'd come to the same conclusion when his two forays into Burnet County had turned up nothing substantial on the dark-skinned man clad all in black. The fellow probably only dressed that way when hunting kids at night, using the camouflage to conceal himself in the darkness.

Mark had been widening his search, trying to learn about any *vaqueros* in the area who might match the description and checking on their whereabouts on the night Wart had been taken. But of the half-dozen men he'd tracked down, none raised any suspicions.

Not even the Mr. Lopez Alice had mentioned. Mark had checked on him first, seeing as how his job as porter at the train station gave him access to the boys who had been targeted. But Lopez was pushing sixty and far from spry. With his bum knee, Wart and Alice could have easily outrun him. The old fellow seemed harmless. He was the friendly sort who could talk a man's ear off. Told Mark all about the boys who rode his train. Rawley confirmed Mr. Lopez was an ally. The porter had never turned them in and even gave them a few coins when they carried the heavier luggage for him. He wouldn't hurt the kids.

However, his garrulous nature could have endangered them unintentionally. He'd shared all kinds of stories with Mark despite the fact that Mark was a newcomer to town. What if he'd told another stranger the same stories? He could have unwittingly painted a target on the boys' backs. Yet when Mark had asked if any other men had questioned him about the boys in recent weeks, Mr. Lopez had shaken his head. Said most people just wanted their luggage, not conversation.

"What do you think about letting Rawley and the boys sniff things out around the train station during the day?" Mark kept his gaze locked on Jonah, knowing he'd be tempted to waver if he looked at Kate.

Jonah rubbed his chin. "I think Miss Eliza won't want them missin' their lessons."

Rawley scowled. "Addin' numbers on a slate ain't gonna get Wart added back to his sister. Schoolin' can wait. Wart can't."

Something moved to Mark's right. Alice and Ruby must have overheard the commotion and come to investigate. They eased close, eyes wide, ears probably open even wider. Abner neared too, though he hung back, not mixing with the other boys. It was a good thing Miss Eliza had the youngest ones upstairs in the schoolroom, or they'd have a three-ring circus on their hands.

Scraping the bottom of his diplomacy barrel, Mark quickly hatched a plan he hoped would grant Rawley enough freedom to satisfy while still keeping some protective measures in place. "How about this?" he said. "You and the boys conduct your investigation, but keep in groups of two or three at all times. And report back to Harmony House once a day to let us know what you've learned and help us plot our next moves."

"There'll be food waiting for you," Kate inserted. "Whenever you come. And cookies."

Mark couldn't hide his grin. Bribery wouldn't keep Rawley at Harmony House permanently, but the kid had enjoyed more than a week of regular meals and probably wasn't all that eager to scrounge for scraps and leavings again.

Jonah tucked his thumb into his gun belt and nodded

toward Rawley. "If you get a lead on someone you suspect as a snatcher, send a runner for us right away. I got the wagon back yesterday, so I won't be making any more trips to Llano. But if we ain't here when you come, Miss Eliza or Miss Katherine will get word to us."

"If you don't report in," Mark warned, "we'll round you up and lock you in the classroom with Ted, Quill, and Prissy for an entire afternoon."

The inane threat elicited a round of groans, but it also elicited unanimous avowals of agreement.

"We still got a good five or six hours of daylight left," Rawley said, squinting up the sky. "Let's get a move on, boys. Leave your gear here for now. We'll fetch it tonight when we come back to make our report."

Mark chanced a glance at Kate. She looked a tad ill, but she made no protest.

"I'll be in town later today, chewing the fat at the saloon to see if I can learn anything new," Mark said, for Kate's benefit as well as Rawley's. "If you run up against any trouble, you can find me there."

However, it wasn't Rawley or one of the boys who came to fetch Mark from the card table later that afternoon. It was Kate. Flushed. Out of breath. And far too beautiful for a room smelling of stale beer, sweat, and tobacco spit.

Mark dropped the full house he'd been holding as if it were no more valuable than a pair of twos and pushed to his feet. "Kate?"

Every head in the room turned to stare, but she ignored them all and ran straight to him, not stopping until her hands pressed against his chest.

"It's Alice. She's gone."

—CHAPTER—

TWENTY-THREE

Katherine grabbed the lapels of Mark's coat, ready to drag him out of the saloon if need be, but he required no urging. Without a backward glance, he abandoned his cards and his winnings, clasped her hand, and headed for the door. She trotted to keep pace with his long quick strides, the strength of his hand calming her panic.

Mark would find Alice. He was a Horseman, after all. The fact that he hadn't yet found Wart nipped at her confidence, but she shook off her doubts. Mark would find her. He *would*.

He ushered her around the corner of the building and halted, giving her a chance to catch her breath before asking the inevitable question. "What happened?"

"After Rawley and the others left, I asked Alice and Ruby to help me finish hanging the laundry on the line. I worried how she might react to the boys leaving and wanted to keep her close. She was so quiet and withdrawn. Her gaze constantly drifted to the road. I tried to reassure her that they would be safe, thinking she must be afraid for them. I never guessed she wanted to join them."

Foolish error, assuming Alice's thoughts would mirror Katherine's own. The girl had grown accustomed to traipsing around like a boy, making her own decisions, forging her own destiny. Her brother had been gone for over a week. She'd want to be part of the hunt.

"How long has she been gone?" Mark cut through her rambling, disordered thoughts, searching for the pertinent facts.

Katherine straightened as if she were a trooper under his command. "I don't know," she admitted. "The last time I saw her was around four this afternoon. She told me she wasn't feeling well and wanted to lie down. I went to fetch her for dinner around six and found the room empty. Her dress was on the bed, and her trousers were missing. I questioned Ruby, but she didn't know anything. Somehow Alice snuck out of the house without anyone noticing."

"She probably went looking for Rawley." Mark grabbed her hand and took off for the street. "Come on. Let's check at the depot."

Katherine took nearly two steps for every one of his, but she didn't mind. Every moment that ticked past was another moment Alice was in danger. If she had rejoined Rawley's gang, things might not be so dire, but Katherine remembered how firm Rawley had been about Al staying at Harmony House. He'd probably send her back. And if she was too stubborn to obey, she'd be off searching for her brother on her own. Vulnerable. The *easy pickin's* the snatchers were looking for. Katherine started jogging, moving ahead of Mark and dragging *him* along.

Once they reached the train station, she slowed her pace, happy to let Mark take the lead. He was the one who knew how to siphon information out of people. All she knew right now was how to fret over the child she'd lost.

226

They circled around to the rear of the depot, both of their gazes scouring every shadowy nook they passed for any sign of the boys. Suddenly, Mark jerked to a halt.

"Look." He pointed to a uniformed man setting out a pair of luggage carts on the platform near the tracks.

Her heart thudded. Mr. Lopez. God could not have sent them a better source of information.

Katherine nodded agreement to Mark's unspoken suggestion and hurried with him to the platform steps. Mark released her hand so she could precede him up the stairs. Without a speck of hesitation, she dashed onto the platform and made a beeline for the porter.

"Mr. Lopez!" Katherine waved her arm in the air to draw his attention as she hustled to intercept him before he could duck back inside the baggage room. "Might we speak with you a moment?"

The porter grinned at her and lifted his own hand in greeting. "*Señorita* Palmer. How nice to see you. And *Señor* Wallace." His smile brightened as he saw Mark come alongside her. "*Mi amigo.* Did you bring me another batch of those oatmeal cookies I like so much?" His eyes twinkled as he turned to Katherine and confessed, "I have a terrible sweet tooth."

She smiled. She couldn't help it. "Well, at least I know my missing cookies went to someone who would appreciate them."

Mr. Lopez thumped a hand over his heart. "Ah, *mi ángel.* No one could love your cookies more than Fernando Lopez."

"Well, I'll be sure to bring you some the next time I bake."

If cookies encouraged him to talk, she'd promise him a baker's dozen.

"Fernando," Mark began, "we need your help. Do you remember the youngest of Rawley's boys?"

"You mean little Al? *Sí*."

"We're trying to find him. He was staying with Miss Palmer at Harmony House, but he ran away. We think he may be in trouble."

The porter wagged his head, a quiet chuckle on his lips. "Ah, those boys are slippery. They're good kids. Not too fond of boundaries, though." He patted Katherine's arm. "Don't worry, mi ángel. He'll turn up when he's ready."

That wasn't good enough. "You don't understand," she said, but the stationmaster's call cut her off.

"Lopez! Stop lollygagging and finish prepping the carts. The 6:50 will be here in fifteen minutes."

"Yes, sir. I'll have them ready." Mr. Lopez shot her an apologetic glance, then started shuffling back to the depot building. "Sorry, mi ángel. I have to go. Al's a good boy. He'll show up."

Sensing they were about to lose their only lead, Katherine leapt forward, took hold of the older man's arm, and played the only card she could think to play. "Al's not a boy. She's a girl. Alice. Rawley kicked her out of his gang when he learned the truth, so she's out there all alone. *Please*. If we don't find her before dark, there's no telling what might happen to her."

Mr. Lopez looked stricken by her pronouncement. "Little Al *es una niña*? I . . . I never would have let her go had I known."

"Let her go where?" Mark asked, his voice sharpening.

Mr. Lopez twisted to face the Horseman, his face etched with remorse. "She came by about an hour ago. Asked if I had seen Rawley and the others. I told her they'd hopped the spur into Burnet County. They said something about looking for the man in black."

Katherine darted a glance at Mark.

228

"Al said she'd take the bridge. Mumbled something about how Rawley didn't know what to look for, but she did."

Katherine's stomach clenched. Alice was going after the snatcher alone? She'd barely seen the man. She'd said so herself. How did she think she would recognize him? Especially if he wasn't wearing his black camouflage? Katherine clutched Mark's arm. It didn't matter if Alice could recognize the snatcher or not. She was putting herself in his path, and if he spotted her, she could be taken, just like the others.

"We've got to get to her. Now!"

Mark nodded but took the time to shake the porter's hand in thanks. Katherine didn't. Leaving the men behind, she hoisted her skirt above her ankles and sprinted across the platform and down into the street. People turned to stare as she raced past, but she paid them no mind. Her only thought was to follow the railroad tracks and get to the bridge.

Mark called out to her, but she didn't look back. He'd catch up soon enough. Nor did she hesitate to mount the tracks and start across the bridge. People crossed this bridge on foot every day. Heavens, children from Hoover's Valley walked across it every morning to come to school in Kingsland.

Once on the bridge, she hiked her skirt up a bit more and watched the placement of each hurried step. There were no railings and no trestles to protect her from falling into the Colorado River below should she lose her balance.

"Kate!" Mark called, much nearer now. "Stop!"

She lifted her head to judge how far she'd come. Almost halfway. And there, across the river, she spied a pair of horses at the end of the bridge. A small child in boy's clothing moved between them. *Alice!* Katherine's heart soared.

"I see her!" She halted momentarily and glanced over her shoulder, her excitement building.

Mark stood on the tracks at the edge of the bridge, waving her toward him. "Come back!" he yelled.

Go back? No. They had to go forward. Get to Alice before she was lost to them again. She shook her head and resumed picking her way across the bridge. Faster now. Nearly at a run. Alice was on the other side. In danger. Nothing else mattered.

But two-thirds of the way across, she realized she was wrong. Something else *did* matter. Something barreling toward her with such speed that the tracks convulsed beneath her feet. The deep, haunting moan of a train whistle pierced her ears and her heart.

The 6:50 from Burnet. Heading straight for her.

TWENTY-FOUR

The instant Kate turned away from him, Mark sprinted forward, his heart pounding faster than his feet.

God, help her!

She might make it. Might clear the bridge before the train arrived. He calculated and recalculated distances as he ran. The distance to the shore. The distance between each stone pier. The distance between him and the water. Fifteen feet. Maybe twenty. He could survive the plunge if necessary. But Kate? Between the currents of the Colorado and her layers of petticoats dragging her down, she'd never make it. For the first time, he prayed for her to run faster.

Then the train appeared. Its whistle blew. And Kate stopped in her tracks.

No! Run, darlin'. Run!

The toe of Mark's shoe jabbed an uneven railroad tie and nearly sent him sprawling. He caught his balance at the last moment and righted himself, but it cost him precious seconds. By the time he looked up, Kate had already started running toward him, away from the train. The train traveling at least twenty-five miles per hour. Impossible to outrun.

Mark stopped. Assessed. Decided.

A stone pier stood between him and Kate. Narrow at the top, widening gradually into a slender pyramid as it stretched toward the water. Not ideal, but it presented a better option than drowning or butting heads with a locomotive. He reached it first. Dropped to one knee. Peered over the side. A ledge of stone blocks about eight inches wide jutted out roughly two feet from the edge of the tracks. Too precarious to stand on. The force of the train would blow them into the river. They needed a more secure position, and he could think of only one that might work.

"Mark!"

He stood at Kate's cry.

She slowed as she neared him, but her eyes were wild with fright. "We have to run!"

He shook his head. "No time," he yelled. The thunder of the train was rolling closer, making it hard to hear. "Get on my back."

Her brows lifted. She glanced over her shoulder. The train was nearly to the bridge. Her head whipped back around. Tears glistened in her eyes.

Mark took hold of her arms. "Trust me. It's the only way."

She nodded and hiked her skirts up past her knees. He turned his back to her and bent down, arms reaching behind him. As soon as he felt her legs against his hips, he grabbed hold and bounced her up to his waist. She wrapped her arms around his neck, not tight enough to choke him, just enough to secure her hold.

Her unquestioning faith in him boosted his determination as he stepped onto the ledge. Her face pressed against his nape. Her legs squeezed his midsection.

Lord, strengthen me.

The bridge shook as the train left the shore.

Releasing his hold on Kate's legs, Mark carefully turned his back to the water.

The train blasted another warning whistle. The stone pier trembled beneath his feet.

No time.

Thighs burning, he squatted and fit his hands to either side of the pillar, then dropped over the edge.

Kate squealed in his ear. Her knees knocked against the stone and slid off his waist. Her arms strangled his neck. The wind from the locomotive tugged at his hat. His fingers dug into the stone ledge while his knees gripped the pillar as if he were on a rearing horse. Only this horse stayed upright for minutes, not seconds. He clung to the pier, locking his face against the cold stone, praying Kate would hold on.

Train car after train car sped by. The pillar shuddered like a bronc trying to buck him off. Kate whimpered softly but thankfully held still against him.

The extra weight of her on his back drained his endurance at an alarming rate. How much longer could he hold on? The angle of his arms, initially ninety degrees from wrist to shoulder, grew more obtuse as his strength waned. His knees slipped an inch. Then another.

Like the blind Samson in the Philistine temple, Mark squeezed his eyes shut and prayed for strength. For Kate. *Just until she's safe, Lord. Please.*

He slipped another inch. And another. His arms were fully extended now, his knees weakening.

Hurry up, he begged, the train's length seemingly eternal.

His grip faltered. He fought against his muscles' rebellion. Concentrated on his fingers, ordering them to hold their position, no matter the pain. Push through the tremors. Overcome the weakness. A Horseman never quit. Not when an innocent depended on him. Not when the life of the woman he loved hung in the balance.

A swirling *whoosh* of air finally declared the passing of the last railcar. The vibrations of the pier lessened, and Mark's spirit cried out in thanks.

But the ordeal wasn't over. He still had to get Kate safely onto the bridge, and with his arms shaking like fall leaves during a blue norther, hoisting her up himself wasn't an option.

"Kate," he groaned, hoping she could hear him now that the train's thunder was in decrescendo. "You gotta climb up. Use me . . . as a ladder."

She gave no indication that she'd heard. Her arms remained locked at his throat, her legs limp behind his hips.

"You can do it." He moved his head slightly, so his lips were closer to her ear. "I need you to, Kate. I can't hold on much longer."

"But I don't want to make you fall." Tears filled her voice, cracking his heart.

"You won't." Any falling would be his fault, not hers. "Now, go."

As she shifted, he tightened his hold, giving everything he had to keep his grip a few moments longer. Her foot found his gun belt and used it as a toehold. He clenched his teeth as she pushed herself up. His knees gave out and slid down the stone. Kate gasped.

"It's all right," he ground out. "Keep going."

Her arms released his neck, and she reached for the ledge. Her second foot braced against his hip, then a knee pressed down on his shoulder. He felt her hands brush against his on the ledge before they reached higher.

"I've got the rail!"

"Good girl! Now stand on my shoulders and pull yourself up."

With her holding the rail, the weight on him lessened, providing a tiny surge of energy.

Her feet found their way to his shoulders, then the ledge. She accidentally trod on the fingers of his left hand, and his grip failed.

"Mark!"

He hung by one hand, too exhausted to pull himself up. Then, all at once, she was there. Her belly flat against the ledge, her hips tucked against the rail. She grabbed his flailing arm and pulled his hand back to the ledge.

He tipped his head back, his gaze melding with hers.

"Don't you even think about leaving me again, Mark Wallace," she ordered. "I won't have it."

He smiled. "No, ma'am."

"Good." She fisted her hands in the fold of his coat collar behind his neck and pulled. "Now . . . get . . . up . . . here."

Her grunts mixed with his growls as they poured all they had into getting him off that pier. His feet scratched at the pillar until the edge of one boot sole finally caught on a minuscule lip between stone blocks. It wasn't much, but it was enough to propel him upward since his arms were too depleted to do the job. He got an elbow on the ledge, then his chest. Finally, he secured a knee and allowed Kate to drag him the rest of the way onto the bridge.

Mark lay on his belly for a moment, too thankful to do anything more than breathe. Then reality bombarded him with hailstones of panic.

He could have lost her! If he'd been a few seconds slower or the train a few seconds faster . . . He rolled over onto his side and reached for her. Needing to reassure himself that she was safe. But touching her hand wasn't enough.

Tucking his knees beneath him, he took hold of her arms and helped her rise to a sitting position. "Kate. Tell me you're all right." He scanned her face. Rubbed her arms. Then slid his hands up to cradle her cheeks.

Her deep blue eyes met his, misty but brimming with emotion. "I'm all right. We're *both* all right. Thank God."

Yes. Thank you, God.

He couldn't lose her. Ever. The clarity of that single thought obscured everything else and drove him to action. He pulled her face up to meet his and kissed her with the desperation of a man who'd nearly lost everything he valued. His fingers tangled in the hair at her nape as he drew her closer, needing to feel her pressed against him, to prove she was alive and still within his grasp.

Her hands clutched at his shoulders, and she rose up to meet his kiss. To return it. Mark's pulse throbbed, her passionate reaction lighting a fire inside him. They belonged together. Always.

She tasted so sweet, so . . . right. He tore his lips from hers, his breath ragged and loud in his ears. But he couldn't stop from dropping tiny kisses on her cheeks, her closed eyes, her forehead.

"Marry me, Kate." The proposal slipped out before he'd even fully formed the thought, but he didn't regret the impulse. In fact, as soon as the words left his tongue, they solidified in his brain. She was what he wanted. More than anything. More than *everything*. "Marry me."

He pulled away just enough to see her face clearly. Her lashes fluttered open to reveal dazed blue eyes.

"I love you, Kate. I always have."

Her face softened, her beautiful eyes misted. "I love you too. With all my heart. But . . ." She bit her lip.

But? The euphoria that erupted in his chest like a geyser gushing toward the sky at her declaration of love froze mid-surge.

"Miss Katherine?" A tiny voice, wobbly and timid, brought Mark's head up.

Kate swiveled. "Alice! Oh, thank goodness." She opened her arms to the little girl standing so despondently on the bridge six feet away.

Alice hesitated. Guilt clouded her gaze as she darted a glance at him before focusing again on Kate. "Are you and Mr. Wallace all right? I saw you . . . and the train . . . I thought . . ."

A sudden sob burst from her throat, and the child ran into Kate's waiting arms.

"Shh, sweetheart. It's all right. We're both safe. Everything's fine." She rocked Alice back and forth, stroking her hair.

"It's my fault," Alice wailed. "If I hadn't run off—"

"It's not your fault, sweetheart. I was the one who should have listened to Mr. Wallace when he called to me to get off the bridge, but I didn't." She glanced his way, an apology in her eyes.

But an apology for what? Rushing across the bridge or refusing his proposal? Again.

Don't get ahead of yourself. She hadn't actually refused. That *but* could have led to a hundred different statements. Many of them innocuous. Besides, he wasn't the wet-behind-the-ears kid he'd been a decade ago. He'd battled raiding Indians, survived being shot by rustlers, and outsmarted deadly outlaws as part of an elite military squad. He could lay siege to a woman's heart and wear down her resistance. After all, there was already a significant weakness in her fortifications.

She loved him. With all her heart, she'd said. That was the important bit. Not some dangling conjunction that could lead a hundred directions.

Besides, there was only one direction they needed to focus on right now. Home.

Mark pushed to his feet with an exaggerated moan, sure to draw attention. Although, in truth, the moan wasn't all that feigned. He ached everywhere.

"Let's get you two ladies back to Harmony House, shall we?"

Alice scrubbed at her eyes with the heel of her hand, then scowled up at him. "I gotta keep lookin' for the man in black." She twisted and pointed back toward the mounts on the other side of the bridge. "One of them horses could be his. I was looking through the saddlebags for papers with names on 'em."

Mark hunkered down, shocked at how sore his legs felt while carrying out the simple task of folding. "Those look like farm horses, built for pulling plows and wagons, not for speed," he said gently. "I doubt the man in black rides a plow horse."

Al crossed her arms. "He might. You don't know."

"No, I don't. Not for sure. But it's more likely those horses belong to someone else."

Al shrugged. "It wouldn't hurt to hide out and wait for the owners to come back. I was gonna lie down in the grass and keep watch. One of 'em might be the fella that snatched Wart."

Mark gave her a steady look. "What if he's not wearing black today? Will you still recognize him?"

She jutted out a quivering chin. "Maybe. If he said something. I'd remember his voice."

Huh. Mark hadn't thought about her being able to identify the man's voice.

"What if I promise to take you out with me tomorrow? To places where men congregate. Places where you can listen to their voices without anyone suspecting what you're about."

Kate laid a hand on his arm. Her concern weighted the air like impending rain, but she didn't give it voice. She gave him trust instead.

Man, but he loved this woman.

As much as he wanted to look at Kate and reassure her with silent promises, Mark kept his gaze locked on Alice. "What do you say?" he challenged. "Do we have a deal?"

She peered at him long and hard, then thrust out her hand. After he took it and gave it a firm shake, she declared her answer. "Deal."

TWENTY-FIVE

Eliza cast a final glance over her shoulder as she drove the wagon out of the yard and onto the road. Was she making the right choice? Leaving the children alone with Jonah?

The man in question lifted his hat from his head and waved it at her as if he could see her furrowed brow. With his sharp eyes, he probably could.

Eliza returned her attention to the road in front of her. Jonah was one of Hanger's Horsemen, for heaven's sake. He could corral a half-dozen kids for an hour or two. Besides, he wasn't truly on his own. Abner and Ruby would help him. They knew all the routines.

"I'm sorry for putting you out like this."

Eliza smiled at the thin, wan woman on the wagon seat beside her. "It's no trouble."

When Fern Dawson had shown up on Harmony House's doorstep a mere quarter hour after Katherine left in a panic to fetch Mr. Wallace, Eliza had known this wouldn't be a short visit. Mrs. Dawson could only have one reason to travel all the way to Kingsland. Her baby.

"I know you must think me a terrible person," Fern said, her head bowed, her fingers tangled in a white handkerchief that stood out in stark contrast to the black widow's weeds that covered her from chin to bootheel.

Eliza bit back her agreement, reminding herself that God called his people to mercy, not judgment. Even toward those who abandoned their children. "I think you . . . a woman beset by grief."

Fern's unnaturally stiff posture buckled at the kind interpretation of events. "I *was*. God help me, I still am." Tears clogged her voice as she turned pleading eyes on Eliza. "Wendell was my whole world. When he passed, I begged God to take me too. I couldn't imagine living without my husband. I had no one else. No family. No friends. No desire to walk this earth alone."

She wouldn't have been alone. She *had* family. A child.

The words perched at the top of Eliza's throat, ready to jump forth in admonishment. But the Spirit bridled her tongue. Fern was here now, taking steps to fix what she'd broken. Which meant the Lord had been working on her heart since the birthing. Eliza wouldn't undo that work by handing out recriminations and lectures.

Fern hung her head. "I was out of my head when the baby was born."

The baby. Not *my* baby.

"I didn't even look at her." Fern glanced up again. "Did he tell you that? The man who brought her to you."

"Mr. Wallace." Eliza neatly sidestepped the question.

"Wallace." Recognition rang in Fern's voice. "That's right. I remember the doctor mentioning him. I'm afraid I didn't pay much heed to his name at the time. All I remember is being angry that he wouldn't take the baby and leave so I could . . ."

241

Join her husband.

Fern shifted on the bench and turned her gaze to the horizon. "That same anger clawed my insides for three days. But with Mr. Wallace gone, I directed it at the church ladies who forced themselves into my home. Fussing over me night and day. Not giving me a single moment to myself." She fiddled with a pleat in her skirt. "They took shifts. All Mrs. Abernathy's doing. She organized my guards better than her husband organizes his sermons. They cleaned my house. Made sure I ate. Prayed over me." Her voice hitched.

"No matter how much I yelled at them and demanded they leave, they stayed. Mrs. Peabody bathed me and combed my hair. Mrs. Green brought me quilt squares to appliqué and praised my stitches even though they were a shambles. And when my breasts became so swollen it hurt to move, Mrs. Hawthorne made cool compresses and offered a distraction by reading a novel to me.

"They were all so patient and kind. To someone they barely knew." Fern spoke softly, a touch of disbelief coloring her voice. "Living miles from town, Wendell and I didn't make it to Sunday services very often. Yet the women came anyway. Cared for me despite my ingratitude."

Eliza's heart warmed at the testimony. "'Pure religion . . . is this,'" she said. "'To visit the fatherless and widows in their affliction.' They were living out their faith. Loving you as Jesus does."

"But how can Jesus love me after I turned my back on my own child?" Fern wailed.

Eliza tugged Tessie and Bessie to a halt, then turned to her companion and gently touched the distraught woman's arm. "How can Jesus love any of us? We've all broken his heart with the poor choices we've made. Yet the Good Book teaches that God delights in showing mercy. He has compassion on us, treads our sins underfoot, and hurls all our iniquities into the depths of the sea." She squeezed Fern's forearm. "*All* our iniquities. Pebbles, boulders, even mountains. Nothing is too heavy for him."

Fern shook her head. "That's a nice thought, Miss Southerland, but mountains? Really? Such a thing's not possible, and you know it."

Eliza smiled. "Nothing's impossible with God. Jesus himself said as much." She stared into the distance, concentrating on the verse she'd memorized as a child. "'For verily I say unto you, That whosoever shall say unto this mountain, Be thou removed, and be thou cast into the sea; and shall not doubt in his heart, but shall believe that those things which he saith shall come to pass; he shall have whatsoever he saith.' Mark 11:23." Eliza returned her focus to Fern's face. A spark of hope flared in the younger woman's eyes. "He can forgive anything, Mrs. Dawson. Move any mountain. No matter how large. All you have to do is believe in him and ask."

Fern's gaze remained locked on Eliza's for a long moment before she ducked her head to stare at her lap. Eliza snapped the reins and clicked her tongue to set Bessie and Tessie in motion once again, but the clop of their hooves on the road rang louder and louder in Eliza's ears the longer her companion remained mute.

"What brought you to Harmony House today, Fern?" she prodded gently. "Why now? You could have waited until tomorrow." She'd arrived so late in the day that the trip couldn't have been planned. It had to have been an impulse.

"Laura Thomas came to see me this morning." Fern twisted her handkerchief in her lap. "The ladies aren't staying with me around the clock anymore. They only come by for an hour in the morning or afternoon to check on me. Laura came today. With her baby."

Fern spoke the words with a reverence that caused Eliza's heart to thump painfully against her breastbone.

"I couldn't take my eyes off of him. She must have noticed, because she asked if I wanted to hold him. I shook my head, but she brought him over to me anyway. Sat beside me on the sofa. Handed him into my arms. He seemed impossibly small, but he already had two teeth cutting through his bottom gum. He smiled at me and grabbed the buttons on my blouse." Fern paused and raised her handkerchief to wipe her eyes. "For the first time since Wendell died, a pinprick of light penetrated the black dungeon of my grief. But it hurt my eyes. I'd gone too long without it. I thrust the baby away from me, and as soon as his mother took him back, I ran from the house. I didn't know where I was going, only that I needed to get away from the hope that light had stirred. From the truth I couldn't bear to admit. I had abandoned my baby. *Wendell's* baby."

"And so you came," Eliza concluded, but Fern shook her head.

"No. The shame was too stark. I told myself I didn't deserve to be her mother. That I had lost my chance and there was no going back."

Eliza frowned. She'd hoped Fern's mental state had lost its fragility over the last week and a half, but listening to her confess events from mere hours ago tempted Eliza to turn the wagon around.

"Even so, I couldn't escape the urge to learn what had become of my daughter. I needed to confirm she was safe. So I visited the only person in town who could give me the answers I sought."

Eliza adjusted her grip on the reins. "Dr. Hampton."

Fern nodded. "He'd called on me a couple of times after the birthing to check on my healing and give instructions to the ladies overseeing my care. So I went to his office and asked him to tell me everything he could about my baby. He assured me my daughter was well. That she'd been taken to Harmony House, and that a wet nurse had been found. But his answers didn't satisfy. He urged me to come see for myself, but I couldn't. I just . . . couldn't." She shook her head as if she still didn't believe it a good idea, even though she was on a wagon barely a mile from where her daughter was being fostered.

Then she grasped her purse, which sat on the bench between them, and pulled it onto her lap. She unfastened the clasp and pulled out a folded sheet of paper. "That's when the doctor gave me this letter." She unfolded the page, smoothed it against her legs, and inhaled a long, shaky breath. "From Wendell's mother. The doctor had written to her about the baby. About me."

Jonah had told Eliza as much. Said the doctor hoped the Dawsons might provide a home for Fern and the child. Or at least the child. But how would they react to a daughter-in-law they barely knew? To a child they might be too old to care for themselves? What if they had health problems? Or were harsh taskmasters? Or were lazy and overindulgent in nature?

"I was afraid to read the letter at first," Fern said, "sure it would be full of blame and anger. How could it not? I'd only met them twice. At the wedding and then three months ago at the funeral. They'd offered to stay a few days and help around the house, but I sent them away. I couldn't bear hearing Yancy's voice when it sounded so much like my Wendell's. And his face—he had the same eyes, the same cleft in his chin. It hurt too much to look at him.

"But when I read Myrna's letter, there was no hate in evidence. No anger. No blame. Only the most amazing grace." She ran her fingers along the words inked onto the page. "I've read this a dozen times and still find it hard to believe."

She met Eliza's gaze. "They've made up a room for me in their home. Invited me to live with them. Said I was family and that I could stay as long as I liked. Even permanently, if I wished." Fern swallowed. "Myrna said that Dr. Hampton had explained about my . . . complications following the birth. About how the baby was with a wet nurse while I . . . recovered. She's already talked to one of the young mothers at her church, and that woman has agreed to nurse my daughter along with her own should I decide to move to Houston."

A chance to rebuild her family. Not many were given such an opportunity.

"They are coming next week."

"So soon?" Eliza asked as she steered Bessie and Tessie onto the side road that led to Tildy James's house.

Fern shrugged. "They're probably anxious to meet their granddaughter." She ran her hand over the letter a final time, then carefully folded the page and slipped it back into her purse. "I decided I better meet her first. See if what they proposed was even possible."

"Remember what I said earlier, Fern. With God—"

"—all things are possible. I know. I'm just not sure I believe it yet."

"Well, I guess today's as good a day as any to start." Eliza grinned.

A tiny smile curled the edges of Fern's mouth, proving she *wanted* to believe, she just needed some practice.

"Now," Eliza said, turning the conversation to more practical matters, "don't take it personally if little Sarah cries when you hold her. Crying is what babies do. She'll get used to you quick enough. She was part of you for nine months. She'll remember."

"You call her Sarah?" Fern's nose wrinkled slightly.

Either she didn't care for the name or it bothered her that someone besides her had selected it. Well, Eliza's sympathy only stretched so far, and here was where it stopped. "Every child deserves a name," Eliza said, perhaps a little more force-fully than gentleness dictated. "When your daughter came to us, she didn't have one, so Mr. Wallace named her after his mother."

Bessie tossed her head and snorted at the front of the wagon, bringing Eliza's awareness to her too-tight grip on the reins. She relaxed her hold, offering a silent apology to her ponies and her Lord. Passion for the children in her care served her well most of the time, but perhaps this particular instance called more for compassion than conviction.

"Of course," she said, taking pains to soften her voice, "if you take the babe back into your keeping, you may name her whatever you like. Did you and Wendell have a name picked out?"

Fern shook her head. "No. And after he passed, I stopped caring."

"But you don't like the name Sarah."

Fern's nose wrinkled again. "No. I had an Aunt Sarah who took me in after my parents died. She was a miserable old hag who was impossible to please. When I met Wendell, I couldn't escape fast enough."

Eliza spotted the James homestead and turned the team down the short drive.

Fern sat up straight, smoothed her bodice, and lifted a hand to her hair. "I do like the idea of honoring the man who brought my daughter into the world and kept her safe for me, though. Just not with the name Sarah. What is his first name?"

"Mark." Eliza chuckled. "Doesn't really lend itself to a little girl, does it? I guess you could call her Marcia."

Another wrinkled nose. Apparently Marcia didn't sit well either.

"You've got time to decide," Eliza assured her as she halted the wagon and set the brake. "Why don't you wait until you see her? Maybe the perfect name will come to you."

Fern tucked her handkerchief inside her sleeve and ran her palms over her skirt. "I . . . I don't know if I'm ready."

Eliza patted her hand. "No first-time mother is ever ready."

Fern still made no move to disembark.

"Come on," Eliza said as she climbed down from the driver's seat. "I didn't drive you all this way so you could sit in the wagon. Let's go."

Eliza made a wide circle around the ponies and reached the front stoop about the same time Tildy opened the door. "Eliza? What brings you out here so close to sundown?"

"Tildy James, this is Fern Dawson. Sarah's mother." Eliza gestured for Fern to come closer when she hesitated at the base of the porch. "Fern, this is Tildy, your daughter's nurse."

Fern blinked back tears as she stared at the other woman, but Tildy wasn't one to stand on formality.

"Well, come on in, Miz Dawson." Tildy threw the door wide and waved them into her tiny cottage. "I'll fetch baby Sarah for ya. She's a sweet little thing. Don't hardly cry unless she needs somethin'. I wish all my young'uns were so well-behaved. This 'un here," she said as she rubbed the head of a boy around five years old, "used to keep me up all hours of the night, hollerin' like the Lord Jesus was comin' back and he'd been assigned trumpet duty." She chuckled and shooed him toward the back portion of the room that served as their kitchen. "Go help your sister with the dishes, Zeke."

The boy trod off without a word as Tildy led them deeper into the room. A three-year-old girl ran up and grabbed her mama about the leg, her thumb planted firmly in her mouth as she stared, wide-eyed, at the white woman entering her domain.

A toddler, barely over one year, waddled over and lifted his arms to his mother. "Uh. Uh!" he demanded, not shy in the least around the strangers in his home.

Tildy complied, plopping him onto her hip. "This one wasn't too happy about sharing his mama when Sarah first came to stay with us," she said as she pulled a piece of lint out of his hair and straightened his shirt to cover his brown belly, "but he's gotten used to her now. Even comes to get me if I'm not fast enough in respondin' to her fussin'. He'll be sorry to see her go."

Fern's eyes widened, and her hands waved in front of her. "I'm not taking her. Not yet, at least. I just . . . wanted to meet her."

"Of course you did," Tildy said as if she'd never considered any other possibility. "And here she is."

On the far side of a small sofa was a cradle, one that had been invisible until they came deeper into the room. Tildy set down her son, then reached into the hand-hewn baby bed. "Wake up, little Sarah," she cooed as she pulled the babe, blanket and all, from the cradle. "Your mama's come to call."

Tildy straightened, a wide smile on her face as she held the child out for inspection. Fern didn't reach for her child, however. Just stared in wonder at the tiny babe.

"Here," Tildy said, "why don't we sit on the sofa? I'll show you how to hold her."

It took only a minute to execute the transfer, and once Fern had her babe in hand, it became clear that to her, nothing else existed. As she unwrapped the blanket to take inventory of every finger and toe, Tildy left her to her exploration and joined Eliza a few steps away near the hearth.

"Miss Georgia told me you been lookin' into those kiddy-snatchers the young'uns been talkin' about," Tildy said in a low voice. "Those men staying with you find anything yet?"

Eliza grimaced. "Not enough. We know one's a white man who rides a horse sporting a shallow cut on its haunches and a nicked rear hoof, and the other's likely a Mexican who tends to dress all in black when he goes out at night."

"Sounds like Miguel Ortega," Fern said.

Eliza's attention jerked to the sofa, shocked that Fern had heard a word they'd said. "Miguel Ortega?" She didn't recognize the name.

"Mm-hmm." A flick of a glance was all the attention Fern spared them as she continued studying her dozing daughter. "He worked a couple summers for Wendell at the farm, though I can't say I cared for him much. He had a coldness about him that made me uncomfortable. He sure did like black, though. Wore it nearly every day."

Eliza's breath caught. Their first real lead, and from the most unexpected of sources. She approached Fern and lowered herself onto the sofa beside her. "Do you know where we might be able to find Mr. Ortega?"

Fern shook her head. "No, he seemed the roving type. Moving from job to job." She ran a finger over the dark hair at Sarah's forehead, then suddenly looked up. "Wait. I think I remember Wendell saying something about Honey Creek." She nodded to herself. "Yes. I was upset when he told me about it, because I worried we'd welcomed an outlaw into our barn. Wendell scolded me for jumping to conclusions. Said the man sought honest work and should be judged on his performance alone and not on the shady reputation of the place where he spent his winters. Does that help?"

"Very much." Eliza's pulse vibrated through her veins with a humming energy that demanded they return to Harmony House as soon as possible. She needed to tell Jonah. Fern might have just handed them the clue that could break the snatcher case wide open.

TWENTY-SIX

M ark delivered Alice and Kate back to Harmony House before returning to Kingsland for his horse. Crazy how hard it was to walk away, even knowing he was coming right back. He didn't want to let Kate out of his sight. The Army had trained him to shake off death's close calls for himself, but not for those he cared about. He wasn't sure he'd ever recover from that trauma. His hands still shook from the shock of seeing that train barreling down on her.

Thankfully, he maintained enough dexterity to untangle Cooper's lead from the saloon's hitching post without much trouble. Mounting felt good. Almost like he was back in control. With a click of his tongue, he turned Coop and rode straight for home.

The thought jarred him. When had he started thinking of Harmony House as home?

Mark wagged his head in self-deprecation as he nudged Cooper into a canter. Probably the moment he discovered Kate inside. *She* was his home. He just needed to convince her that he was her home too.

Once back at the foundling home, Mark unsaddled his

horse, rubbed him down, then saw to Coop's food and water. His own belly rumbled with hunger, but no cavalryman worth his salt would feed himself before tending his mount.

He'd just exited the barn when movement near the road caught his eye. In a flash, he had his revolver out of its holster and ready to fire, but he lowered it when he recognized Bessie and Tessie at the head of the approaching wagon.

Jonah had mentioned that Eliza had run an errand. What he hadn't mentioned was with whom. Spying Fern on the wagon seat made Mark's chest tighten in concern. He'd been praying for her, but he hadn't actually expected to see her again. At least she wasn't raving like a lunatic and threatening to shoot him this time.

Once his weapon was safely holstered, Mark lifted a hand in greeting.

"Whoa, girls," Eliza called to the team. "Whoa."

The ponies didn't seem to pay her much mind. Just kept plodding forward. Mark moved in front of Bessie and held up a hand. The old girl stopped and bobbed her head against his palm as if to say howdy. It made him grin.

And it made Eliza sigh. Loudly, and with great exasperation. But only for a moment.

"Did you find Alice?" Eliza asked.

Mark ran his hand along Bessie's neck, then patted her side as he made his way back to the wagon. "Yes. She's safe. We had a bit of a scare"—*that* was the understatement of the decade—"but all's well now. Kate's seeing to her in the house."

"Thank the Lord." Eliza's gaze briefly tipped toward heaven before settling back on him. "I wanted to check in here before taking Mrs. Dawson home."

"Would it be possible," Fern murmured, "for me to have a word with Mr. Wallace before we go?" She clasped the wagon seat with both hands before turning to face him. "If you don't mind, that is."

Mark nodded. "Of course. In fact, why don't I see you home, and we can talk on the way?"

Eliza wasted no time relinquishing the reins. In less than a minute, she had disembarked and he had climbed aboard. Taking the lines in hand, he clicked to the ponies and offered them a few warm words of apology for taking them back out when they'd thought themselves finished for the night.

"There's a good girl, Tessie," he praised as he looped them around and aimed them toward the road. "That's right, Bessie, steady on."

"Do you talk to everyone like that, or just horses and women in the throes of labor?" A tiny smile played at the corner of Fern's mouth.

Mark chuckled, the tightness in his chest easing. If she could tease, she must be doing better. "Mostly just horses."

Her smile flattened into a serious line. "I wanted to thank you."

"Ah, you don't have to—"

"Yes, I do." Her adamancy took him aback. "If you hadn't happened by . . ." Emotion clogged her voice. She steadied herself by grabbing the edge of the wagon bench and inhaling a long, slow breath. "My daughter would not be alive today if it weren't for you. She wouldn't be healthy and beautiful and absolutely perfect."

Mark braced his boot against the footboard. "So you've seen her."

She nodded as she raised a hand to wipe at her eyes. "Wendell's parents have offered the two of us a home with them."

"That's good." He smiled despite the misgivings running through his head. She was the babe's mother. And it sounded like she'd have help. Just because he'd entertained a few fuzzy notions about him and Kate adopting little Sarah didn't mean he had any right to stand between a mother and her child. Besides, his future with Kate was fuzzy enough on its own.

"I think it will be. Yancy and Myrna are good people. Wendell would want them to be involved in their granddaughter's life."

Mark tried to read her face, but there was so much uncertainty etched in her features that he had trouble seeing anything else. "What about you? Do *you* plan to be involved in your daughter's life?"

She timidly met his gaze before dropping her chin to stare at her lap. "I don't deserve to be." Slowly her posture straightened and her head lifted. When she looked his way, he spotted a hint of hope shining through the guilt. "But when I held her today, something shifted inside me. I swore I could feel Wendell looking over my shoulder, whispering in my ear. Telling me how proud he was to see his girls together. How much he loved us. How much he believed in us."

A tear slipped down her cheek. "God sent you at just the right time, Mr. Wallace. You saved my daughter. Saved *me*. I didn't think I could live without Wendell. I thought he was the only person in the world who loved me. But I was wrong."

Thank you for opening her eyes, Father. No one loves better than you do.

Fern wiped the tear from her face and lifted her chin. "I'm ready to build a new family," she said. "To tell my daughter about her amazing daddy and be the mother Wendell always believed I could be."

"I'm glad, Fern." And he was. Life shone in her eyes, something that had been missing the last time he'd been with her.

Talk of babies and families drifted away as the buildings of Kingsland cropped up. Fern directed him to a ladies' boardinghouse, and Mark steered the wagon to the side of the road and set the brake. As he turned to climb down, however, Fern stopped him with a hand to his arm. He resumed his seat and waited for her to speak.

"I want to name her after you," she blurted. "I know you named her Sarah after your mother, but I had a horrible aunt named Sarah, so that name just won't do, even though I'm sure your mother is a lovely woman—"

"Whoa, now." Mark grinned and held up a hand to stop the runaway rambling. "She's your daughter. She should have a name that means something special to *you*. My preferences are inconsequential."

A relieved smile touched her lips. "Thank you. I was worried you'd be offended."

"Not in the slightest." Though it was probably a good thing he hadn't had time to write to his mother about her namesake. As much as she fussed about him settling down and giving her grandchildren, she would be distraught to learn she'd lost her connection to a pseudo-grandchild. Then again, if the news came sandwiched between his rediscovery of Kate and a wedding invitation, all would likely be forgiven.

"I do still want to name her after you, though," Fern said, drawing his mind away from Kate.

"As much of an honor as that would be, ma'am, no pretty little girl deserves to be saddled with a name like Wallace. Sounds too . . . sturdy. Like something that holds up a roof on a house."

Fern smiled. "Only the first part. The last half of the name is rather feminine."

He frowned. "Ace? Like the playing card? Makes me think of saloons and gambling. What's feminine about that?"

Her smile broadened. "Take off the first three letters and leave the rest."

Wal-lace. *Lace.* Of course.

His face must have cleared, for she nodded and said, "I want to name her Lacy. If that's all right with you."

Warmth spread through his chest, and he had to clear his throat before he could answer. "That sounds mighty fine, ma'am. Mighty fine."

Fern smiled in return, a touch of pink coloring her cheeks.

She was going to be all right, Mark thought, as he climbed down and moved around to assist her. He offered his arm and escorted her to the door of the boardinghouse.

Once there, she turned to face him a final time. "Thank you, again. For everything."

Mark relinquished her arm and tipped his hat to her as he stepped back. "God bless you, Mrs. Dawson. And Lacy too."

"He already has, Mr. Wallace," she said as she twisted the door buzzer. "He already has."

❧

By the time Mark made it back to the foundling home, unhitched the wagon, and took care of the team, his stomach was growling something fierce. Yet supper wasn't the only thing stirring his hunger. He needed to get Kate alone to talk things out. Between taking care of Alice and tending to Fern, there hadn't been time for him to follow up on his marriage proposal. To discover what had caused her to hesitate. Whatever it was, he'd find a way to fix it. God had brought them back together for a reason, and Mark wasn't about to squander this second chance.

He stomped the dirt off his boots before entering the kitchen through the back door. Kate walked into the kitchen from the dining room at the same time. Had she been listening for his return? The thought made his chest expand. He tugged his hat from his head and hung it on a hook by the back door.

"I kept a plate warm for you," she said as she moved to the stove and pulled a plate from the warming oven above the range.

"Thanks." He rounded the table to meet her by the drawer where she was extracting flatware with her free hand. "Kate, I want you to know—"

Her blue eyes crashed into his. "Not now," she murmured in a low tone. "Jonah and the others are waiting for you. He seems a little . . . perturbed."

Jonah, perturbed? That didn't bode well. And why did Kate look guilty? Only one way to find out.

Taking the plate from her, he tilted his head toward the dining room. "Lead the way."

A spot at the foot of the table sat open. Kate placed his utensils down, then moved to the sideboard to pour him a glass of water. Mark slid into the vacant chair and met Jonah's eyes across the length of table. Alice sat to Mark's left with Abner a couple places up. Dirty plates on both sides evidenced where the other children had eaten before heading upstairs to play. Eliza sat next to Jonah near the head of the table, leaving Kate to slip into the chair at Mark's right.

"So, what's up?" Mark asked as he stabbed a piece of roast with his fork and lifted it to his mouth.

"Besides you and Miss Palmer hanging off the side of a railroad bridge?" Jonah raised an accusing brow at him. As if Mark were still some wet-behind-the-ears recruit prone to unnecessarily reckless stunts.

So, she'd told him. Either that or Alice had. He couldn't blame them. It was too good a story not to tell. Still, Jonah didn't have to get all bent out of shape simply because Mark had gotten within spitting distance of the pearly gates.

Mark chewed his mouthful of beef and prepped a bite of mashed potato. "Yeah," he said after a quick swallow. "Besides that."

Being the youngest Horseman, Mark was used to the others acting like overprotective big brothers. Shoot, the captain had hovered over him like a mother hen for weeks when he'd taken that bullet in the shoulder back in Purgatory Springs. Jonah had always treated him like an equal, though. Which meant the train story must've really rattled him to have him shooting Mark chiding looks across the table.

"Alice just told me you promised to take her out tomorrow to listen for one of the snatcher's voices. You really think it a good idea to take a child into the kind of places where a man of that caliber is likely to be found?"

All right. So maybe the chiding look had nothing to do with the bridge.

"Better with me than on her own, don't you think?" Mark kept his voice affable, but that didn't fool Jonah. His eyes glared his displeasure as hotly as before.

Apparently his tone didn't fool Kate either, for she placed a warning hand on his forearm. "Perhaps we can discuss this later?" She glanced meaningfully at the two youngsters still sitting at the table.

Unfortunately, the kids caught the look and understood exactly what it meant. Alice jumped from her seat and jabbed a finger in Mark's direction. "You promised! Wart's been gone for *days*. We gotta find him. *I* gotta find him, and if you won't help me, I'll do it myself."

Mark was sorely tempted to toss Jonah an I-told-you-so look, but Alice needed his attention more than he needed satisfaction. So he set his fork down and leveled a stare at the girl. "I gave you my word, Alice, and I won't go back on it."

"You won't have to." This came from Eliza, the last person Mark expected to enter the fray. "And you won't have to take Alice out searching either."

Mark swiveled to give the teacher his full attention. She knew something. Something so big, she looked ready to burst from it.

"I know who took Wart."

Jonah's head snapped toward her. "And you're just telling us this *now?*"

She glared at him with such vexation that Mark would have chuckled had he not been so keen to hear what she had to say.

"Because I just found out."

"When? During your trip to Tildy's house?" Jonah tried the raised brow on Eliza, but she was having none of it.

"It was *at* Tildy's house, if you must know."

"Oh, for pity's sake, Eliza," Kate exclaimed. "Who is it?"

Eliza turned away from Jonah to face the table at large. "Miguel Ortega. Fern recognized his description. She said he'd worked a couple of summers for her husband, and he wore black nearly every day."

Miguel Ortega. The name clicked in Mark's mind. "I heard that name at the saloon too. Along with a handful of others. Men willing to set scruples aside to take on a job if the money was good enough."

"Fern wasn't too fond of him. Said he made her uncomfortable." Eliza twisted back to face Jonah. "She also said he hailed from Honey Creek."

Jonah met Mark's gaze, his face as soft as a rock. "Looks like we're goin' huntin' tomorrow."

Mark nodded. "Indeed."

TWENTY-SEVEN

K atherine took her time with the dishes, extending the chore to its maximum duration. Mark and Jonah remained in the dining room talking strategy, and Eliza had all the children except Abner upstairs. Abner had gone out to the front porch to keep watch while the men plotted and schemed. Things had been quiet, so no one actually expected him to spot any trouble, but he'd been uneasy after dinner and had volunteered for the duty.

Katherine didn't blame him for wanting some time alone to think. The dishwater had turned her hands to prunes with the tortoise-like pace she'd set, but it offered an excuse to ponder things without the distraction of the children. Her excuse held as much water as a big-eye colander, but it sufficed. Or it would for a few more minutes. She was down to drying her last two pots.

The men's murmuring was too low for proper eavesdropping, but that was probably for the best. Hearing their plan would likely increase her anxiety, not relieve it. Still, she'd wanted to stay close. To Mark.

He'd asked her to marry him. *Again.* Oh, how she wanted to say yes. Her heart ached with the desire. But she'd made a vow to God and the children of Harmony House. She couldn't just run away with the man she loved and leave those commitments behind.

What do I do, Lord? You brought him back to me, but for what purpose? To test my resolve or to restore our lost love?

How did one decipher God's will when multiple paths seemed viable?

They had time to figure things out, she reminded herself as she placed the thrice-dried baking dish on the shelf and reached for the upended saucepan—the last item waiting for a swipe of the dish towel. Mark had only proposed a few hours ago. And kissed her with enough passion to leave her heart sizzling long after his lips departed. Her eyes slid closed as she hugged the pan to her chest. She pressed her lips together. Remembering. Reliving.

I love him, Lord. So much. But I want to love you more. Show me how.

A burning bush or wet fleece would certainly come in handy. She glanced down at the damp spots on her bodice where she'd clung to the pan. Too bad her dress was made of cotton instead of wool. Katherine shook her head, blowing air from her nose in a silent snort. She was such a ninny.

No longer dragging her feet, she shoved her towel inside the pan and wiped every droplet dry. God would make things clear when he was good and ready. She just needed to wait and prepare her heart to accept whatever answer he provided.

"Need any help?"

Mark's voice startled her. Katherine spun to face the man who refused to leave her thoughts. "Are you and Mr. Brooks finished talking?"

Mark nodded and crossed the kitchen to stand directly in front of her. "He left out the front. Going to walk the perimeter before heading to the barn for the night." He took the pan from her hands and set it on the table behind him, the soft *thud* ringing with the volume of a fallen tree in her ears.

Heavens, but he was handsome. Odd to have such an observation jump into her head now, though. He'd *always* been handsome. Mark's chiseled features and lean, muscular frame had been making young ladies swoon since their school days. And while she appreciated the way the Good Lord had put him together as much as the next woman, his looks were no different today than they'd been yesterday. So what had suddenly magnified her attraction to him?

His eyes, Katherine decided as Mark stepped even closer, causing her to tilt her head back to meet his gaze. She peered into those golden depths, and her pulse fluttered. They seemed . . . darker. More intense. More . . . focused. On her.

Mercy. How had she never noticed the way his eyes glowed? Like amber lit by the sun.

Mark reached for her. His hands cupped around her arms and slowly slid down until he captured her fingers within his own. "I love you, Kate." His thumbs rubbed back and forth across the backs of her hands, sending delightful tingles dancing over her skin. "I want you to hear me say those words in an ordinary kitchen surrounded by ordinary items, not just in the middle of a railroad bridge while the tracks are still shaking from the train that nearly ran us down. Those words weren't born from the momentary exhilaration of having cheated death. They were born from deep admiration. I don't want you to doubt them, not even for a minute."

"I don't." She gazed into his face, her heart swelling by

the second as love for this man flooded her. "I love you too. Wherever you might be standing."

He smiled, his eyes softening with a tenderness that weakened her knees. "I'm not leaving you this time," he vowed. "Whatever hesitancy you have about accepting my proposal, we'll work it out. Together." He squeezed her hands, his voice tightening with fervency. "God reunited us, Kate. How else can you explain the two of us finding each other almost a decade after we parted, in a place half a continent away from where we started?"

"I can't," she said. "He *did* bring us together. Of that I am certain." She swallowed, then looked away. "I'm just not sure why."

His hold on her tightened. "I am. He's giving us a second chance for a life together."

"I'm not so sure." Katherine tugged her hands free. This was too hard to talk about while he was so close. Touching her. All she could think about was their kiss and how badly she wanted to repeat it.

Retreating until her hips bumped against the dry sink, Katherine crossed her arms over her midsection and bit her lip. Mark didn't follow. He just sat on the corner of the table and waited, his eyes a little duller than they'd been a moment ago. Her heart ached at the sight.

Give me strength, Lord. And wisdom.

"I made a promise. To Eliza. To God. That the children would come first." She uncrossed her arms and clutched the edge of the counter, needing to feel something solid. "As much as I love you, Mark, I can't abandon the work God has called me to. Even if Eliza were to find another partner willing to step into my shoes, leaving would haunt me. I made a commitment, and I don't take it lightly. A vow made to the Lord is sacred, and only he can release me from it."

"All right. So we stay here."

Katherine blinked. Men didn't follow their wives. Wives followed husbands. It was how marriage worked. Every marriage she'd ever seen, at least. Husbands provided for their families through the sweat of their brow. They made the decisions. Wives made the home, bore the babies, and served as helpmeets. They followed where their husbands led. Single women—widows and spinsters—could dictate the direction of their own lives. That was how she came to be at Harmony House, after all. But married women? They were subject to their husbands in all things. Scripture said so.

"For how long?" Katherine's grip on the counter tightened. "A year? Two? What about the Horsemen? Will you just leave them behind? Staying sounds like a good idea now, but what happens if you start feeling trapped? Your resentment would shred my heart." Her voice broke, and she turned her face away.

In an instant, he was in front of her, lifting her chin, seeking her gaze with his own. "I could *never* resent you, Kate. But it *is* about time you trust me to know my own mind."

The gentle jab hurt, but it also made her realize she was doing the exact same thing she'd done ten years ago—assuming she knew what was best for him, and letting her fear of holding him back get in the way of holding him close. His face started to blur in front of her eyes. She blinked to clear her vision.

"We aren't kids anymore," he said. "Both of us understand that choices have consequences and sacrifices have rewards. It's up to us to choose what we dwell on. Either what was left behind or what was gained. I, for one, plan to thank heaven every day for bringing you back into my life. The Horsemen are my brothers, and whenever they need me, I'll answer their call, just as they will answer mine. But they aren't my life. They aren't my future. Jonah, Preach, and I have been working with Captain Hanger at Gringolet, training horses and breeding stock, but the three of us know it's a temporary position, something to tide us over until we find our own calling. Well, I've found mine, Kate. It's you."

Her eyes misted again, and no amount of batting could keep the joyful tears from spilling down her cheeks. "Even if God keeps me at Harmony House for the next forty years?"

He smiled as he smoothed away her tears with the pad of his thumb. "Even then. Is it so hard to believe that I might find purpose here too? Maybe the Almighty brought me here not only to find you but to join in your work. As fine of a job as you and Miss Southerland are doing, the boys under your tutelage might benefit from a male perspective, someone who can teach them how to shoot, how to ride, how to"—he glanced at the window behind her—"replace a rotted railing."

A ripple of excitement lapped at Katherine's toes, then gained momentum as it rolled upward through her belly and her heart, until it crashed over her mind. Could he be right? Could the Lord have brought him here to join her ministry? As much as she and Eliza loved and supported the children here, she couldn't ignore the fact that there were some things they just couldn't give them. Certain practical knowledge such as Mark had mentioned, yes, but more than that. An example of godly manhood for the boys to emulate and for the girls to recognize in prospective suitors.

The scripture that had plagued her with doubts earlier returned to mind. Only this time, the next verse tagged along with it, offering a broader perspective. *Therefore as the church is subject unto Christ, so let the wives be to their own husbands in every thing. Husbands, love your wives, even as Christ also loved the church, and gave himself for it.*

Could it be that being subject to a husband who loved her with sacrificial dedication meant freedom instead of subjugation? That becoming one flesh extended to more than the bedroom? That her vows would be honored as if they were his own? That marriage would create a partnership marked by respect as well as love?

"I don't have all the answers," Mark admitted, his voice softening as he cupped the side of her face, "but I trust the Lord to find a way to make it work. Who knows," he said with a chuckle, "maybe I'll take over for that deputy who seems to think his job consists of manning an office and waiting for crime to find him."

Bubbles of possibilities fizzed through her like sweet soda water. "You could give music lessons in the evenings." If they were going to build their dream future, they might as well add all the trimmings.

Mark's eyes crinkled. "Maybe even start a community band." He slid his hand horizontally through the air as if painting a sign. "The Kingsland Calliope."

Katherine giggled. "That's a terrible name."

Mark shrugged. "Yeah, well, we'll probably sound terrible too. Just like a squeaky old steam organ with stops that stick and notes that play out of tune."

"Not exactly the Boston Symphony." The place where his talents would have truly shined.

"Nope. But it would be comprised of friends and neighbors, and we'd have a rousing good time." His playful grin softened into something deeper, more mature. "That's what music is all about. Spreading joy and touching hearts."

Her heart definitely felt touched. "Ask me again," she whispered.

His brow furrowed, then cleared a heartbeat later as if the sun had burst from behind a cloud. His hands closed around her waist, and he tugged her flush against his chest. She craned her neck back, her gaze glued to his, her heart thumping against her ribs like a percussionist performing a tympani roll.

"Marry me, Kate."

It was more demand than question, but there was something raw about the way his voice rasped the words that made her soul sing. The eloquent, detached Mark Wallace would have waxed poetic about her eyes or spouted flowery romantic words. But the man standing before her was anything but detached. His heart glowed in his eyes. Full of passion, commitment, and just a sliver of uncertainty. The charming rogue with all the right words might make a fine literary hero, but *this* was the man she could trust with her heart.

"Yes."

She barely got the word off her tongue before his lips crashed down over hers. Her arms twined around his neck. Her fingers combed through his hair. His palms climbed up her back. Holding her. Supporting her. Cherishing her.

When the kiss ended, he pressed his forehead to hers, their breathing heavy in the air between them.

"I'll make you happy," he whispered. "I swear it."

Dear, dear man. Happiness had never been her worry. "We'll make each other happy," she declared, "and trust God to make our joy complete."

Mark pulled away just enough to meet her eyes. "Amen."

— CHAPTER —
TWENTY-EIGHT

Eliza backed away from the kitchen doorway, not wanting to intrude on the private moment happening inside. She'd known this would happen. Had even tried to prepare herself for it. Yet hearing the abundant joy in Katherine's voice as she accepted Mr. Wallace's marriage proposal hurt. Eliza pressed a hand to her midsection, pivoted, and strode down the hall.

For heaven's sake, Eliza, quit feeling sorry for yourself. She fisted her hand and thumped it against her hip. *You should be happy for Katherine, finding love with the man she thought never to see again. What kind of friend hurts more over being demoted in relationship standing than rejoices in her sister's good fortune?*

Of course, if she were brutally honest, it wasn't the disintegrating vision of her and Katherine working together until they were a pair of old maids that brought the deepest ache to Eliza's heart. No, it was envy, plain and simple. Katherine had found love while Eliza remained alone.

Eliza thumped her hip again, harder this time. She wouldn't

let that seed of Satan take root. She would rejoice with those who rejoiced and count her blessings. Katherine wasn't leaving. Eliza had overheard enough to gain that assurance. Harmony House would continue ministering to outcast children. That was the important thing. But a husband would be a distraction. Even if he supported and participated in their mission. And what would happen when he and Katherine started having children of their own?

Leave tomorrow alone, girl. Her mother's oft-voiced scold echoed in Eliza's mind. *The Lord's the only one strong enough to carry the future. You'll wear yourself out tryin'.*

Mama was right, of course. Eliza lifted her chin and grabbed the newel post at the base of the staircase, resolved to focus on today's troubles instead of borrowing from tomorrow. There were children upstairs who needed to be readied for bed. Yet, as her foot trod the first stair, quiet murmurs from the other side of the front door tugged her in the opposite direction.

Abner and Jonah. She recognized the deep bass of the Horseman's voice, even though his words were impossible to distinguish through the wall. What were they discussing? A frown tightened her mouth. She hoped he wasn't filling the boy's head with whatever *hunting* plans he and Mr. Wallace had cooked up at the table tonight. Abner might think himself the man of the house, but he was only a boy.

Releasing her hold on the banister, she moved toward the door, thinking to insert herself into the conversation and redirect it if necessary. As she reached for the latch, however, caution stilled her hand. Neither of the people outside would thank her for interfering. Besides, she had no proof of what they were actually discussing. For all she knew, they could be talking about horses or how to shoot the best spitball. But if they *were* talking about the hunt for Miguel Ortega . . .

The matter required further investigation. Eliza crossed into the front parlor, picked up a chair with as much stealth as she could manage, and carried it on quiet feet to a place beside the window they had opened earlier to circulate air through the house. Taking care to position the chair on the left side to ensure Jonah wouldn't glimpse her should he look toward the parlor window, she slid into the seat and tuned her ears to the conversation outside.

"I wanna help." Abner's voice. "But I don't know what to say to keep her from runnin' away again."

They must be talking about Alice. Eliza leaned in, straining to hear over the crickets singing in the distance.

"Sometimes it ain't what you say but what you do that helps the most," Jonah answered. "Be a friend to her. And pray for her. God knows better than anyone what she needs."

Eliza sat back. He was recommending prayer? A man of action who rode a giant warhorse and solved problems with his gun was recommending prayer. It seemed out of character for some reason. Though she wasn't sure why. After all, this was the same man who carried his daddy's compass and quoted Bible verses. Jonah Brooks was a man of faith, so why shouldn't he urge a burdened young boy to pray?

"I ain't much of a pray-er," Abner admitted softly, surprising Eliza once again. The boy said his prayers dutifully every night before bed. Or at least she'd thought he did. Had he just been going through the motions?

"God don't need fancy words," Jonah encouraged, "just true ones."

"But he don't wanna hear nothin' from me."

Eliza's heart cracked at the sad certainty in the boy's tone. She started to rise, to go to him, but Jonah's voice stopped her.

"Why d'ya think that?"

"'Cause I'm a whoreson."

The ugly word stung Eliza like a hard slap to the face. Tears welled in her eyes. Cruel words from her own past clawed at her heart. Vile words hurled at her, at her mother. Words designed to degrade and humiliate. She clutched the chair arms in a bid to keep her anger and hurt under control.

Where had Abner heard such a horrible term? Certainly not around here. Had one of the railroad boys said something? No, more likely the word had followed him from the saloon brothel where Katherine had found him. Words like that tended to burrow deep into a person, leaving a stain that could be painted over but never removed.

Jonah didn't react to the obscenity at all, however. Not a bit of outrage warbled his voice as he spoke in the same measured tone as always. "That ain't what God sees, Abner. The Bible says he knew you even before you were in your mother's womb. Knew you and had a purpose for you. That makes *him* your Father. You're not the son of a whore, Abner. You're the son of the King."

Eliza's grip on the chair's armrests relaxed a fraction as Jonah's calm assessment soaked into her spirit and lifted her head. She was also a daughter of the King. Her earthly father might not claim her as his own, but her heavenly Father did. That was where her identity came from. Her value. Her purpose. She prayed Abner would see that too. That he'd hear the truth in Jonah's words and believe in his worth in God's eyes.

Yet the longer the silence outside her window stretched, the more she feared he was losing the struggle.

"You ever heard 'bout a fella in the Bible named Jephthah?" Jonah said, finally breaking the silence.

"No. Who was he?"

"The son of a harlot."

Eliza flinched at the bluntness. Jonah wasn't one to mince words, but maybe that was exactly what Abner needed. Those who had reviled him certainly hadn't sugarcoated *their* words.

"Did he do somethin' bad?" Abner's downcast voice sounded resigned, as if villainy were the only viable option for a man with such a beginning.

"He was a hero. One of the judges God chose to lead his people."

"What?" The sharp disbelief in Abner's voice contained a definite tinge of hope. Eliza smiled.

"Old Jep had it pretty rough growing up," Jonah said, getting into his tale. "His daddy married a different woman and had sons with her. Those boys didn't want Jep hanging around or getting any of their inheritance, since he was the son of a harlot. So they kicked him out of his father's house. Jep had nowhere to go, so he left Gilead and went to a place called Tob—a land full of scoundrels and rough men. I imagine Jep must've been a pretty big fellow and a good fighter, 'cause those scoundrels made him their leader. Pretty soon, Jep was known far and wide as a mighty warrior."

"But he was still a scoundrel."

"Yep. Until the Lord got ahold of him. Remember what I said about God knowin' us even before we were in our mamas' wombs? And having a purpose for us? Well, God had a purpose for Jep too, even though he was a scoundrel."

"What happened?"

"War happened." Jonah's voice tightened for a moment, but then he continued on as before. If Eliza hadn't been listening so intently, she probably would have missed it, but there had definitely been something there. Something dark. Painful. Something that haunted this man of faith.

"Back home in Gilead, Jep's brothers had grown up to take their place as the leaders of the land. Their land was under attack, and they were losing. That's when they remembered their brother. The one they'd cast out. They needed a warrior, and Jep was the best one they knew. So they rode down to Tob and asked him to come fight for them.

"Well, Jep wasn't exactly in the mood to help the brothers who'd been so mean to him, but when they promised to make him their leader, he agreed. Now Jep, even though he was a scoundrel, knew that any victory he won was only because of the Lord, not because of his own strength. So before he went to war, he prayed."

"And God listened to him?"

"Yep. Not only did God listen, but he helped. First, he helped him defeat the Amorites, who didn't want him crossin' their lands. After that, Jep wrote a letter to the king of Ammon, warning him that God was on Israel's side, hoping the king would back down. When that didn't happen, the Spirit of the Lord came upon Jephthah and helped him defeat the mighty Ammonite army. God made him a hero." A quiet clap sounded, and Eliza pictured Jonah's hand cupping Abner's shoulder. "God can do the same for you."

Boards creaked and bootheels tapped, signaling that Jonah had risen from the porch steps. "Now, why don't you go on inside? I'll take over the watch for the rest of the night."

"Mr. Brooks?"

"Yeah?"

"If that Jep fella was such a scoundrel, why did God still help him?"

Jonah took a long moment to answer. "All men are scoundrels in one way or another. We make mistakes. Bad choices. Sometimes ones with . . . hefty consequences."

That slight hesitation. Was he thinking of something specific? Something personal? Eliza's chest squeezed.

"That Jep fella made plenty of mistakes," Jonah continued. "One of 'em was so big, it cost his daughter her life. Yet God still used him to lead his people for another six years. I gotta think it's because even though the man wasn't perfect, he was still God's man at heart and did his best to follow where the Almighty led. That's all any of us can do."

"Even you?"

"Especially me." His voice rasped slightly. He fell silent, then cleared his throat before continuing. "Regrets are heavy, son. The fewer you cart around, the better off you'll be. But when they come, and they will, remember you got a Father who will carry them for you if you let him."

Eliza bit her lip, her heart melting. Maybe having a man around the place wasn't such a bad idea after all. Although, the man she wanted hanging around wasn't Katherine's beau, but his reserved partner. The man with deadly aim, secret regrets, and the patience to tell a hurting boy healing stories.

"Now get on in the house," Jonah said. "The young'uns are prob'ly lookin' for you."

"All right."

The front door opened and closed. Eliza leapt from her chair and pressed her back against the wall near the curtain, hoping Abner wouldn't notice her and realize she'd been listening to his private conversation. She needn't have worried, though. He charged straight up the stairs without a glance into the parlor.

Letting out a breath, she stepped away from the wall and turned back to the window, intending to close it for the night.

"Tradin' listening at doorways for listening at windows, now, are ya?"

Eliza gasped as Jonah stepped in front of the window and crouched down so she could see his face. He tipped his hat back on his head and aimed a sharp look her way, one that cut past her justifications and pierced a hole in her conscience.

"Why don't you come on out here and have a real conversation instead of stealing ones that belong to other folks?"

—CHAPTER—
TWENTY-NINE

Jonah hadn't known Eliza was there until the kid up and left and he caught movement at the parlor window. If he'd known, he never would've spoken in such crass terms. He'd done it to make a point, to help Abner understand that God loved *all* his children, no matter their origins. But to use such language in the hearing of a lady? His mama would've boxed his ears.

No telling what Miss Eliza thought of his character now. If he hadn't fully offended her with his frank talk, he'd no doubt finished the job when he'd snapped at her through the window. This was why he usually kept his mouth shut. It saved him from having to chew boot leather.

Sticking his feet someplace other than his mouth, Jonah stomped down the wraparound porch to the steps. He'd best focus on the job he was here to do and quit worrying about impressing a woman a mile out of his league. Eliza Southerland was educated. Refined. And about as beautiful as they came. Fiercely independent too. Probably didn't even want a man. At least not one like him. A Howard fella would suit her better. A man of letters. A scholar or maybe a minister. Not an ex-soldier with blood on his hands and sins on his soul.

"It's not polite to invite a lady to a conversation, then storm off before she has a chance to accept."

Jonah spun around. She stood in the doorway, eyes searching his, hands fiddling with the fabric of her skirt as if she were nervous. Or chastened.

Doggone it.

He strode back to the base of the stairs. "I had no call to say what I said." He snatched his hat off his head and banged it against his thigh. "I'm sorry for growlin' at you and for . . ." A few more thumps of the hat against his leg. "And for using inappropriate language in your hearing. I don't normally talk about . . ."

Shut up, Brooks, before you make it worse. He slammed his teeth together, then dropped his lips as an extra layer of protection against any other ill-advised explanations that might try to escape the stockade.

Eliza pulled the door closed behind her and sauntered down the steps, stopping on the next-to-last one so she could look him straight in the eye. "You had every right to call me out. As soon as I realized the personal nature of the conversation, I should have left the parlor. But I didn't." She glanced away. "I *am* sorry for invading your and Abner's privacy. However, I'm not sorry I heard what I did."

Slowly, her face came around again, and her gaze met his. His gut clenched when he noticed the moisture glimmering in her large brown eyes. "*Thank you.*" She touched his arm, her fingers squeezing against his bicep. His heart rate doubled. "I think you might have done more to raise that boy's opinion of himself with one candid conversation than Katherine and I have done with all of our mothering and instructing."

278

Jonah shook his head. "It's only because you've done such a good job makin' the boy feel safe that he opened up at all."

"Still, it was a conversation that needed to be had, and I doubt Abner would have brought it up to one of his female guardians." She shrugged, a self-conscious smile turning up the edge of her mouth. "To be honest, if he had, I probably would've invested more energy in trying to correct his assumption and his language than in truly hearing him. You heard him."

"Maybe that's 'cause I know what it's like to feel unworthy." The words slinked past the gate of his lips before he could lasso them back into the pen where they belonged.

Stupid moonlight, glistening in Eliza's eyes and turning them into glossy obsidian. It stripped a man of his defenses. Allowed hidden truths to sneak out into the open without his permission.

She circled around to his side and slid her hand into the crook of his elbow. She started walking across the yard between the house and the barn, forcing him to either pull away or take the hint and escort her on an evening stroll. Despite his exposing an unwanted thread she was sure to tug on, he slapped his hat on his head and stretched his legs into a stride that would match hers. He'd been trained for battle, after all, not cowardice. Besides, what man in his right mind *wouldn't* take a moonlight stroll with a lady he admired? Even in territory littered with verbal snares sure to trip a man. He'd just have to tread carefully.

Once they were about a dozen yards away from the house, she leaned her face close to his and murmured two small words. "Tell me."

No ducking or dodging that bullet.

Oddly enough, he *wanted* to tell her. Which made no

sense. Doubts and secrets lived in the depths, not in the light. He'd never spoken them aloud to anyone, not even Matt. Warriors carried their own burdens. And a warrior with black skin? Well, he hid his weaknesses even deeper, guarding them zealously, lest they be uncovered and used as ammunition against him.

So why were those same secrets scrambling up his throat and beating on the back of his teeth to be let out?

Jonah glanced down at Eliza's hand resting on his arm and felt the padlock inside him click open. Why not expose the worst of himself and test her reaction? If she pulled away, he'd know not to waste time pursuing what would never be his.

And if she didn't pull away?

He cleared his throat, not quite ready to ponder all the ramifications of that particular outcome.

Keeping his gaze trained on the packed earth in front of him as they walked the perimeter of the yard toward the barn, Jonah turned the key in the lock and let the words loose.

"Before I met up with Captain Hanger," he said, "I was assigned to the 10th Cavalry. My skill with a rifle moved me up through the ranks and landed me a position as sharpshooter. In three years, I earned a reputation as one of the best marksmen in the Army."

"I find that easy to believe." He heard the smile in her voice, but he didn't welcome it. Not when she didn't understand the price that came with the position.

"Snipers wage war . . . differently than other troopers."

How to explain? He blew out a breath as they reached the paddock. Pulling his arm away from hers, he moved to the fence and braced his back against the nearest post. He gazed into the sky and counted two stars near the moon, peeking through the still-early twilight to wink at him. Encouragement or mockery? Jonah thumped his heel against the fencepost at his back, feeling more apprehensive than he ever had fighting Apache with the 10th.

Eliza came alongside and leaned against the rails a foot or so to his left. Close enough that he could feel her nearness while remaining out of his direct line of sight. Supportive but not demanding.

"We plot our positions ahead of time. Lie in wait. Hide ourselves from our enemies instead of facin' them on the field of battle. We shoot from cover while our brothers fight in the open." Jonah's attention wandered to the barn where he'd set up a nest in the loft, exactly as he'd been trained to do. High ground. Line of sight. Protective cover. Everything he needed to stave off an attack, to eliminate the enemy before they could eliminate those he was charged to protect.

"I took pride in my skill, welcomed the praise of the officers who depended on my rifle to give us the advantage in battle. But takin' lives changes a man, hardens him, even when those lives are taken to preserve others." Jonah stared across the darkening yard. "Hand-to-hand combat is kill-or-be-killed. It's a level playing field. Honorable. Sharpshooting? It's all about stealth and distance. We're a necessary evil."

"You are *not* evil, Jonah."

He shrugged. "Maybe not. But what I do ain't exactly ethical neither. I think it messed me up . . . inside. Right and wrong blurred. God had made me good at somethin' that left me feeling like a murderer. So I turned everything off. Guilt, pride, fear. I shut it all down. Ceased being a man and became a weapon. Followed orders. Did the jobs I was called to do. Took enemy lives and protected my brothers. Until Wounded Knee."

A shiver ran through him as the horrors of that day replayed in his memory. So many dead. Warriors. Women. Children. And he'd played a part in the killing. Maybe not of the women and children, but the blood that stained the snow that day also stained his conscience.

His hand trembled as he rubbed it down his face. "It was a massacre," he choked out, not recognizing the gravelly sound of his voice. "That's when I knew I had to get out before my heart turned completely to stone. I couldn't be a soulless weapon. I couldn't just fire at whatever target my superiors placed in front of me without asking questions or considering consequences. So when Matthew Hanger invited me to join him and the others, to leave the ranks of the military and put our skills to work helping ordinary folks, I didn't hesitate. I'd worked with Captain Hanger on several special assignments through the years. Knew him to be a good man. A *godly* man. The kind of man who could help me reclaim the missing pieces of my soul before they were gone forever."

Although sometimes he wondered if he'd ever feel whole again. Even with as much as he and the Horsemen had done to right wrongs over the last few years, Jonah still saw battlefields in his dreams. Heard the cries of the wounded. Smelled blood and gunpowder. Saw each man who fell to one of his bullets.

"We took a vow against using lethal force," he said, "and swore only to use our weapons to defend the innocent against injustice."

He fell silent. Stood still in the night air. Breathing. Listening to Eliza breathing beside him. He hated exposing his bloodstained underbelly to her, but she needed to know the truth.

So, with a clench of his jaw, he made himself finish it. "Even with all the good we've done, my soul will always be scarred. Pieces will always be missing."

KAREN WITEMEYER

Finally, he pivoted to look at her. Tears glistened in her eyes, but he saw no anger, no horror. His heart throbbed with hope.

"Every day, I pray for the Lord to do in me what he promised to do for the house of Israel in the days of Ezekiel. To sprinkle clean water on me and cleanse me from my filthiness, to take away my stony heart and give me one of flesh. But until I came here," he said as his eyes caressed her face, "I hadn't realized how much flesh the Lord had already restored."

He pushed away from the fence and moved to stand directly in front of her. He yearned to reach for her, to stroke her cheek, to slide his fingers along her neck and take her face in his hand, to press a gentle kiss to her lips. But he did nothing. Just drank her in with his eyes.

"When I look at you, Eliza, I *feel*. More than I've felt in a long, long time. So I'm putting you on notice." He targeted a look at her that an officer would pin on a new recruit. No softness. No sugarcoating. Just the truth, shot straight and true with no frills to throw off the aim. "After Wallace and I find those missing kids and put things to rights, I'll be askin' permission to come courtin'. I ain't asking yet," he blurted when her mouth started to move. He held up a hand to halt whatever she meant to say. "The things I done told ya tonight need time to soak in before you answer. Lord knows you deserve a better man than me, and if you decide not to accept my suit, I'll have nothin' but respect for your wisdom in not saddling yourself with a banged-up old war dog."

Without conscious thought, the hand he'd held up to stop her from speaking found its way to her cheek. The backs of his knuckles stroked the side of her face, and the feel of her satiny skin on his fingers was the sweetest torture he'd ever known.

Her gaze locked on his, her eyes piercing in their intensity. Jonah's hand stilled. "But if you feel something when you look at me, the way I do when I look at you, and you're willing to explore what those feelings might mean despite everything you've heard tonight, then perhaps we can have more of these moonlit conversations and see where they lead."

Her breath caught at his caress. Jonah yanked his hand away from her face before he did something stupid like pull her against him and kiss her until the stars twinkled in full brightness overhead. With a sharp pivot, he strode away from her and did what snipers did best—watched his quarry from a distance as she slowly made her way back to the house.

THIRTY

As soon as the breakfast dishes were cleared away the following morning, Mark and Jonah saddled up and rode into Kingsland to question both the deputy and the livery owner about Miguel Ortega. Deputy Bronson had heard of Ortega but had no solid information on the suspect's whereabouts or who he might be working for. The livery owner proved more helpful when he identified Ortega's horse as a black Palouse. Ortega wasn't a frequent customer—Donaldson had only seen him once or twice—but a mount with distinctive, spotted markings tended to linger in a liveryman's memory.

"At least we have an idea of what we're looking for now," Mark said as he swung into the saddle and nudged Cooper into a walk.

Jonah came abreast of him as they left the livery but said nothing in response. Not that Mark had expected him to. Jonah was in scout mode. On the hunt. Only critical information warranted the use of words.

Impatient energy coiled within Mark's muscles, making

it difficult to hold Cooper to a walk. Wart had been missing for more than a week. An unknown number of other boys for even longer. This lead *had* to pan out. He didn't care how many unsavory rocks they had to turn over, they'd stick with it until Miguel Ortega crawled out from under one.

Lord, you are the Good Shepherd, the finder of lost sheep. Guide us today. Show us where—

"Mr. Wallace!" A female voice jerked him out of his prayer and brought his head around. Althea Gordon rushed down the school steps, waving her arm. "Mr. Wallace, wait. Please. I have news."

Mark reined Cooper in and hid his annoyance behind a manufactured smile, determined not to let her delay them more than a moment or two. He reminded himself that she was an ally in this fight. One who might have information to aid their search. Yet as he watched her weave between a pair of parked wagons, all he wanted to do was kick his horse into a gallop and get on to Honey Creek.

The teacher puffed slightly as she reached them. "I saw you from the window of my classroom and knew I had to catch you. I've been meaning to come by the foundling home, but I just couldn't seem to find the time."

Which meant the news probably wasn't too vital. Mark's annoyance level rose another notch, though he took pains not to let it show.

He tipped his hat. "Good morning, Miss Gordon. What news do you have?"

She glanced around, then lowered her voice so it wouldn't carry. "I've been watching for strange men, just as you instructed." She moved closer to him, craning her neck in order to meet his eyes. "I spotted one a couple of days ago. Loitering outside the schoolhouse, watching the children leave."

A gentleman would dismount and not force a crick into her neck, but Mark couldn't spare the time for gentlemanly manners this morning.

"What did he look like?"

Her face scrunched slightly, and her gaze moved upward as if she was searching her memory for details. "He wore a red shirt and tan trousers. Brown boots. A gun belt. He was chewing on a piece of straw."

Great details, but none of them helpful. If she'd just seen the man an hour ago, his clothing might be important. But two to three days after the fact? Pointless.

"Tall or short? Black, white, Mexican? What kind of hat did he wear?" A man might change his clothes, but most only wore one hat.

Her eyes widened. "I-I'm not sure. Nothing really struck me as unusual about him, so he must've been about average height. White, I think, though his skin was darker. Maybe tanned from the sun, or he might have been a vaquero. I'm not certain. His hat was brown, I think. Or maybe black. Definitely a dark color."

A dark-colored hat and a nonspecific skin tone. She could be describing eighty percent of the men in Llano County. "I don't suppose you recognized him or caught a name?" Mark asked, a dash of exasperation creeping into his tone.

Miss Gordon's face crumpled as she shook her head. "No. I thought it best not to approach him in case he was danger-ous, so I pretended as if I hadn't noticed him. Should I have spoken to him?"

"No. You did the right thing."

A touch of a smile returned to her face. "Oh, good. I so want to help. I can't stand the thought of children being taken. Unless your investigation has determined that this was, in fact, a misunderstanding?"

She looked so hopeful that he hated to disappoint her, but with children in her care, she needed to be on alert.

"Unfortunately, it's the exact opposite. We have confirmed at least one abduction and suspect several others. We've got a lead on a fellow from the Honey Creek area who might be involved."

"Honey Creek? Maybe Peggy knows something about him. Do you have a name? She's supposed to be in later today. I can ask her about him."

"Miguel Ortega."

She drew back and blinked, a bit nonplussed. "Ortega, you say? That name sounds vaguely familiar. I'll ask Peggy about him after school lets out. Will you be at the foundling home this afternoon? I assume that is where you're headed now."

Mark shook his head. "No. We're on to Honey Creek."

"But wouldn't it be better for me to talk to Peggy first? It could narrow your search. Save you some time." Miss Gordon nibbled on her lower lip.

"If we don't run him to ground today, I'll call on you to-morrow," Mark promised. "But we need to chase down this lead while it's hot. Those boys have been gone long enough."

Miss Gordon nodded. "You're right, of course. I've prayed this was all some kind of horrible misunderstanding. I didn't want to think it possible for someone to be stealing Kingsland children. The very idea makes me ill. If you have proof of this villainy, you must certainly search them out. At once." She backed away from him. "I'll hold you up no longer, Mr. Wallace. Godspeed."

"Thank you, ma'am." And with a tip of his hat, Mark nudged Cooper into a trot, more than ready to put the town behind him.

Jonah kept pace with him. "You think this other teacher might know something?"

Mark shrugged. "She's lives in the area, so it's possible, but I doubt Ortega is the type to get chummy with the neighbors."

Jonah retreated into thoughtful silence until they reached the edge of town. "Hold up," he said just as Mark was fixing to nudge Cooper into a canter.

Jonah steered Augustus to their right, toward the back corner of the mill, the building on Cedar Creek that marked the western border of Kingsland proper. "Come on out, Rawley," he called.

Mark hadn't seen any sign of the boy, but Jonah could spot a flea in a gravel pit, so Mark reined in and waited for the boy to appear.

Sure enough, Rawley stepped out from behind the mill, his face set in its usual defiant lines. "Ridin' off without updatin' me and the boys?" He crossed his arms over his chest and glared up at the two of them.

Jonah didn't miss a beat. "Trailin' us from the shadows instead of checkin' in at the house?"

Rawley shrugged. "Didn't have nuthin' to report." He jerked his chin in Mark's direction and smirked. "Heard you almost got flattened by the 6:50 yesterday, though."

"Yeah, well, dangling from a bridge pier without a speeding train on the tracks wasn't enough of a challenge for me." As much as Mark loved bantering with the hardheaded kid, this was not the time. "We got a lead on a man who might be involved in the kidnappings," he said. "Ever heard of a Miguel Ortega?"

All amusement dropped from Rawley's face. "That the fella who took Wart?"

Mark nodded. "We think so. We're heading out to Honey Creek now to see if we can run him to ground."

"I'll send the boys out to ask around town, see if anyone

knows who he hangs around with. Try to find you another name."

"Good plan. Just be careful." The closer they came to figuring out who the players were in these abductions, the less predictable those players would become. And unpredictable meant dangerous.

"You too," Rawley said with a small jerk of his chin. "And don't worry about Harmony House. I'll pop over from time to time to keep an eye on things while you're away."

Mark dipped his chin. "I appreciate that." Not that he thought it was necessary. But if Rawley tethered himself—even loosely—to the foundling home, it would limit the amount of trouble he could get himself into. "Miss Katherine and Miss Eliza will be glad to see you."

"Oh, they won't see me," the rapscallion said, right before he waved and disappeared behind the mill.

Mark chuckled and shook his head. "That kid's either going to be a master criminal or the best lawman this state has ever seen."

Jonah cracked a smile. "My money's on bounty hunter."

"Yep. I could picture that." Mark shifted in the saddle and touched his heels to Cooper's flanks. "Or maybe a Pinkerton."

Cooper responded and charged forward, leaving the conversation in the dust, as Mark and Jonah finally got out of Kingsland.

When they reached the first turn off the main road, something must have caught Jonah's attention, for he reined Augustus to a trot. Mark followed his lead, raising a brow in silent question.

"Rider comin'. Fast."

Mark glanced behind them. Listened. Pounding hoofbeats rumbled low, the sound growing louder, more distinct. His hand moved to his revolver as a precaution, but when the approaching rider appeared, he relaxed his stance. He recognized that pale gray hat.

"Looks like someone finally decided to leave the office." Mark drew Cooper to a walk, turning him around to face their company. "Deputy Bronson," he called, lifting his hand in a wave. "You looking for us?"

The man and his horse both looked winded as the deputy reined in his mount. "Wallace." He nodded toward Jonah but didn't actually greet him, a fact that grated on Mark's nerves. "Miss Gordon came to see me. Said something about you questioning folks out here about Miguel Ortega. She, ah, encouraged me to join you."

Shamed him into it, more likely.

"She was concerned that the folks around here might not be willing to answer the questions of a pair of outsiders. Thought a lawman might yield better results."

Mark shared a look with Jonah. His partner's stoic expression gave little away, but the slight tightening around his mouth made it clear that he was unenthused by the prospect of company. Mark concurred. However, he couldn't argue with the fact that locals *were* more likely to open up to a man with a badge.

"I'm glad you're finally showing some interest in this case," Mark said wryly.

The deputy's gaze narrowed. "You sayin' I've been derelict in my duty? I poked around in Honey Creek last week, just like Sheriff Porter asked. Found no evidence of increased outlaw activity. No reports of missing kids. What else did you expect me to do?"

Mark expected him to show a little more initiative. Ask more questions. Dig deeper. Though, to be fair, if Jonah hadn't been on hand when the snatchers attempted to take Rawley, the Horsemen probably wouldn't have much to go on at this point either. They'd been in the right place at the right time to gain valuable insight as well as a group of insider allies. Bronson hadn't had that advantage.

"You're right," Mark said. "You've done what was expected. I shouldn't have insinuated otherwise." Bronson looked slightly mollified at the apology. "And we appreciate your escort this morning. It will save us time to have someone along who knows the area."

Bronson wasted no time moving his mount to the front of the group. "Best if you let me do the talkin'."

"We'll let you take the lead," Mark hedged. He had little confidence in the deputy's interviewing skill. If he and Jonah had questions to ask, they'd ask them.

For the next four hours, Deputy Bronson led them up and down Honey Creek, knocking on every homesteader's door they came to. Unfortunately, they turned up nothing that pointed them toward Miguel Ortega.

When they stopped to water their horses, Jonah drew Mark aside, out of the deputy's earshot.

"We need to go farther west," Jonah said in a low voice as he lifted his canteen to his mouth and took a drink. He tossed a quick glance Bronson's way, then wiped his mouth with his sleeve. "Closer to Fern's cabin."

Mark patted Cooper's neck. Dust billowed out from the horse's light gray coat. "I agree. The settlers around here are too civilized. We need to find the rougher crowd. Men more of Ortega's ilk."

"Trouble is, men of that sort ain't too keen on bein' found."

Mark grinned. "So we find us some high ground and let you scout them out."

"I don't think the deputy there will be too keen on that plan," Jonah said as he turned in a slow circle, eyeing the landscape for possibilities. "Fella seems determined to avoid outlaw types. We've seen nothin' but respectable folks all mornin'." Something to the south caught his eye. "Highest ground is there." He nodded toward Packsaddle Mountain.

It was more of a large hill than a mountain, but it was the nearest elevation available. The dip in the middle mimicked the dip in a saddle, giving the local landmark its name. Traveling there would take them away from Honey Creek and in the opposite direction of Fern's cabin, which lay northwest toward Llano, but it offered the best visibility. The day was already more than half gone. If they were going to change tactics, they needed to do it now.

"Bronson." Mark waved the deputy over. "Jonah and I are going to head south, search out a rougher crowd."

"Ain't nothing south o' here except open country. You won't find anything that way. Best if we keep on to the north. There's a family a couple miles down the road. They got kids. They might know something."

"Good thought. Why don't we split up to cover more ground?" Mark suggested. "You check in with any other families you can think of in the area, and we'll hunt down whatever outlaws we can find."

Bronson shook his head. "Bad idea. Even if you did manage to find an outlaw den, I can't have you go stirrin' things up. I'm responsible for the safety of the folks back in Kingsland. The outlaws don't cause us no trouble so long as we leave them alone. That might change if you two start pokin' around."

"We'll be careful," Mark assured him even as he stuck his foot in the stirrup and mounted Cooper. They weren't asking for permission. Or company. A fact that seemed to register on the deputy's face when his scowl darkened.

Jonah mounted Augustus, and he and Mark set off to the south, leaving Deputy Bronson stewing at the creek.

After a quarter hour, they left the main road and followed a thin trail Jonah had spotted that led up one of the steeper sections of Packsaddle Mountain. The incline forced them to a slow pace, but the horses proved hardy and marched on without growing winded. After about twenty minutes, they came to a fork in the trail and reined in their mounts.

"Which way, do you think?" Mark asked.

The trail to the left looked overgrown, while the trail to the right sported flattened grass and well-worn dirt.

Jonah twisted in his saddle to scout the Honey Creek area below them, then glanced back at the mountain, examining each path. "Left," he finally decided. "Trail ain't as pretty, but it'll offer the better view."

Mark nodded and turned Cooper to the left. The two horses continued picking their way up the side of the mountain. The terrain grew steeper, with more rocks and less grass the higher they climbed. Mark shifted his weight forward in the saddle. Up ahead, the path widened enough for two horses to stand side by side. Mark signaled Jonah to come abreast of him, then moved to the inside of the path.

"This a good enough lookout point?"

Jonah scanned the valley below. "Should be. Aren't too many trees in this area to block rooflines or cook-fire smoke." He pointed to the landscape. "We already covered that eastern section, so I can ignore that. I see a few dots to the west that could be buildings." His hand shifted that direction, but Mark failed to see anything distinctive.

"I'll get the field glasses." As Mark turned and reached for his right saddlebag, a tiny shower of gravel rolled down the side of the mountain next to his leg.

He jerked his gaze upward, the brim of his hat tipping back just enough for him to catch a glimpse of a black horse with white, spotted hindquarters uphill from where a black-clad arm extended a rifle barrel over the top of a large rock thirty yards above them.

"Gun!"

His warning came too late. The first shot struck Jonah in the back and sent him plummeting from the saddle and over the side of the mountain.

"No!" Mark drew his pistol and fired overhead as he leapt off Cooper and plastered himself between his horse and the side of the mountain. His military training demanded he find cover. His heart demanded he find Jonah.

But he couldn't go after his friend until he dealt with the threat from above.

Flopping over to press his belly against the side of the mountain, he fired in the direction of the rock he'd seen the shooter sheltering behind. After exchanging a few shots each, the return fire seemed to switch direction, coming more from the right than the left.

A second shooter.

He was pinned down. Outgunned. No cover, and nowhere to run. His only chance was to surprise his attackers with the unexpected. To follow Jonah over the side of the mountain. Probable death was better than a sure thing. And if he survived, he'd be out of the gunmen's range and back with his partner.

The gunshots echoed closer. One grazed Cooper. The horse reared.

Taking advantage of the distraction, Mark lunged in front

of the horses. He shot left, then right, his last two bullets buying him precious seconds as he dove toward the ledge.

A gun cracked. His hat flew from his head. Pain ripped through his skull. He crashed to the ground inches from the ledge. His vision went black, and as consciousness departed, his last thought was of Kate.

Unable to stop his momentum, Jonah toppled end over end down the steep slope of Packsaddle Mountain. His head slammed the ground repeatedly as he rolled. Ribs cracked against rocks. Legs tangled in thick vegetation, tearing at his joints but not slowing his descent. Desperate to halt the fall, Jonah fought against the self-preservation instinct to curl in on himself and forced his knees away from his belly.

The more he unfolded, the more the mountain tore at his limbs. Gritting against the pain, he twisted with a jerk and sprawled onto his belly. Dirt filled his mouth. Prickly brush scraped his torso, pulling his shirt up to his armpits and exposing the tender skin beneath. Broken twigs jabbed at his chest and his belly, but instead of paying attention to the torture they wrought, he used it as a warning mechanism to alert him of brush that might be large enough to grasp. Thankful he'd worn his riding gloves, he grabbed wildly at anything within reach. Gradually, he slowed. And when his midsection bumped over a juniper bush big enough to punch a fist-sized jab into his stomach, he jerked his head up, laced his fingers, and lassoed the shrub with his arms.

He jerked to a stop. Finally.

He lay still for several minutes. Panting. Getting his bearings and thanking God he was alive. Though the first time he tried to move, that blessing seemed more like a curse. Everything throbbed. Except for the places that shot stabbing pain into him. Like his right shoulder. And left hip. And his head whenever he moved it. So he stopped trying. Just closed his eyes, lay still, and took inventory. A challenge when it felt like someone had tied him up, hung him from a meat hook, and turned a pair of bare-knuckle brawlers loose to tenderize him from both sides.

Slowly, senses other than his pain receptors started registering environmental details. Like the quiet. Jonah's eyes popped open. The gunfire had quit.

Wallace.

Jonah fought the urge to lift his head and look up the mountain. Had Mark been shot? Did he escape? Was he lying injured or dead somewhere on the mountain? Jonah swallowed hard against the emotion clogging his throat. He couldn't seek answers. He had to play dead. Convince their attackers he posed no threat.

Their attackers. Who were they? How many? He'd been too distracted by trying not to die during his plummet down the mountain to accurately assess the enemy. Coulda been just one man, but he doubted it. There'd been too many shots fired too quickly for a single attacker. Even if Wallace had returned fire. All he knew for sure was that they had shot from uphill and from cover. He would have seen them otherwise. Wouldn't he? True, his attention had been focused downward, on scouting the flatland below, but he would've caught movement from above if it had been there.

Had he missed something? Something that might have

gotten Wallace killed? Jonah groaned, his fist clenching at his side. No. He couldn't let his mind go there. Couldn't second-guess past choices. Had to focus on the present. On surviving. A dead man couldn't go after his partner. Couldn't fetch help.

So he lay in the dirt. Unmoving. Playing 'possum until birds started singing again, signaling that the danger had passed. Still, he took no chances. He lay there longer. Waiting for the sun to dip farther west. He spotted a rock a yard away from his face and determined not to move until his shadow touched it. And as he waited, his mind ran through the possibilities.

Had they accidentally stumbled across the snatchers here on the mountain? Or were the attackers just random outlaws protecting their territory? His gut rejected the outlaw theory. He and Wallace had not witnessed anything incriminating. Not even the men themselves. They would have no reason to attack when they could simply avoid their unwanted visitors. Why open fire and risk bringing the law down on their heads? Besides, those hadn't been warning shots designed to scare folks off. They'd been shooting to kill. And had almost succeeded.

The moment Wallace had shouted his warning, Jonah had kicked out of his stirrup and darted left to dismount. The bullet aimed at his back had only taken a chunk out of his shoulder, but the force and surprise of it had thrown him off-balance and sent him hurtling down the slope. Gravity and momentum had done the rest. Had he not dodged, the bullet would have hit vital territory, and he'd either be visiting the pearly gates right now or packin' his bags for the trip.

No, this attack had not been random. Not instigated by surprise. It had been stealthy. Almost as if the shooters had lain in wait. As if they'd been warned that he and Wallace were coming. But how could that be? He and Wallace hadn't known themselves they were coming out here until last night. Had they tipped off an accomplice during their search with Deputy Bronson this morning? It was possible someone from one of the first homesteads they visited had made a run for the mountain after they'd left, putting the men on their guard. Yet none of the people they'd met had raised any suspicions.

The throbbing in Jonah's head worsened, making it difficult to keep a grip on his thoughts. He needed to rest. Just for a few minutes. Then he'd be able to think clearly.

The next time his eyes opened, the sun's shadow had fully engulfed his marker rock. He'd dozed too long. Gathering himself, he pushed up from the ground, every inch of his body protesting loudly. A lizard napping next to his knee startled and darted off to find more stable shelter. Jonah envied the reptile's agility and speed. He felt like a half-dead armadillo mired in molasses. Probably looked like one too, all hunched over and wearing a layer of dirt thick enough to grow potatoes.

His shoulder hurt the worst, so as soon as he got his feet under him, he craned his neck to take stock of the damage. Blood stained his dust-encrusted coat. Hearing Dr. Jo's voice in his head, scolding about infection and keeping a wound clean, he hissed and moaned his way out of the coat, feeling decidedly light-headed as he battled the clinging garment. The shirt beneath carried less dirt but more blood—blood that was still oozing. Moving gingerly, he removed his riding gloves to expose hands that were somewhat clean. Next, he unbuttoned the placket on his shirt, then pulled his handkerchief from his trouser pocket. Lifting the shirt fabric away from the wound, he pressed the folded handkerchief against his right shoulder and pressed down hard for a count of fifty.

Then, praying the makeshift dressing would stay in place, he eased his hand away and fit the shirt back over it. He tugged the shirt down tight and tucked it as deep into his trousers as he could manage. Then he turned to face the climb.

Lord, save him. It had to be at least a quarter mile straight up. Well, not *straight* up. It wasn't a cliff face, after all. Just a robust incline with gravel, grass, and gopher holes to make the climb interestin'. A climb he'd have no trouble accomplishing if he didn't have a concussed head, shot shoulder, and battered everything else.

Jonah scowled at the mountain. Good thing his daddy hadn't raised no crybaby.

Concentrating on one grueling step at a time, Jonah ascended. In the steepest sections, he used his hands as well as his feet. He sought out roots for traction, grabbed grasses as handholds, and did his best to avoid the slippery rocky patches. He reached the halfway point by sheer force of will, but not even his will could keep his knees from buckling when his muscles gave out. Rolling onto his backside, he propped his spine against the mountain and closed his eyes against the mallet pounding the inside of his skull and the daggers stabbing his shoulder.

Then he heard a soft nicker.

Jonah's pain-filled grimace curved into a grin. Thank the Lord for stubborn horses.

Eyes still closed, Jonah tried to work up enough spit to whistle. No easy task when dust coated everything, even his innards. After two failed attempts, he finally managed the signal. A second nicker sounded in answer.

Augustus. Good old horse. The boys in the 10th used to give him a hard time about training his horse to refuse any rider other than him. In truth, there hadn't been much training involved.

Augustus had always been ornery. Wouldn't allow himself to be led or ridden without first giving his consent. And he was terribly finicky. To this day, Jonah had no idea why the horse had chosen him, but when he'd stepped inside that military remuda four years ago to select a mount, Augustus had stepped forward to claim him, nipping at any other horse who tried to interfere. They'd been inseparable ever since. The only time he'd known the horse to allow himself to be taken by a stranger was when the Horsemen's mounts had been stolen last year during the rescue of Dr. Jo's brother. Taggart and his outlaw gang probably would've shot the gelding if he'd put up a fuss, so Jonah was glad Gus had submitted on that occasion. But bless his cantankerous hide for being less than accommodating today. His stubbornness just might save Jonah's life.

Jonah opened his eyes when he heard the steady *clomp* of Augustus's hooves approaching on his left. Smart horse. Must've backtracked and come down a section where the incline was shallower.

"Good boy," he croaked as he struggled to rise.

He winced against the pain throbbing in his head as he turned to brace himself on hands and knees. The late-afternoon sun dipped toward the horizon, making it clear there weren't no time for lollygagging. Gritting his teeth, Jonah crawled to his horse, then pushed back onto his heels and lifted his torso.

"Sorry, Gus." He grabbed the stirrup and hoisted himself off the ground, climbing up the tack as if it were a rope until he finally found the saddle horn.

He leaned his face on the seat of the saddle, and his eyes slid closed again as he focused on keeping his legs beneath him. He locked his knees and leaned his weight forward, but he knew he could crumple at any moment.

And he still had to find a way to pull himself into the saddle.

God had done bigger miracles than gettin' a man on a horse. If he could bring a host of dry bones to life, he could get one dusty soldier into the saddle.

Focusing on the Almighty's strength instead of his own frailty, Jonah clicked to Augustus and urged him to back up one step at a time. Jonah hobbled along with him until they stood flush against the steepest slope of the mountain.

"Hold, Augustus."

Jonah gathered the dangling reins and lifted them over the horse's head. Then he eyed the stirrup.

You can do this. It ain't that high.

Even so, he backed himself up the slope a few inches, all while keeping a grip on the horn. Any shortening of the distance between his boot and the stirrup could only help.

Hanging his head against his good arm, Jonah gathered himself for the attempt. "If you got a minute, Lord, I sure could use a leg up."

Then, before he could lose what little momentum he'd gained, Jonah lifted his left leg as high as possible and strained against the horn to dip the saddle toward him.

Fire burned in his hip, but he pushed past the pain until the toe of his boot slid into the stirrup. Groaning aloud, Jonah pressed upward and swung his right leg over the saddle.

God be praised.

"Home, Augustus," he murmured as he slumped forward over the saddle horn, too depleted to sit upright.

As if he sensed his master's condition, Augustus kept to a walk, making slow but steady progress down the mountain. Jonah floated in and out of consciousness, haunted by thoughts of Wallace. Was he alive? Dead?

Jonah cursed his weakened condition. If only he were stronger. A Horseman never left a brother behind. But he'd do Wallace no good in his condition. The best chance for both of them was to fetch help. So he kept riding.

Until consciousness abandoned him for too long a spell, and he slid out of the saddle.

The collision with the ground woke him. They'd nearly made it to the base of Packsaddle Mountain, but they were still a long walk from the main road. He glanced up at Augustus and knew in his bones that he wouldn't be able to mount again. Not without significant rest. Rest that would steal time Wallace didn't have.

Jonah reached out and patted his horse's leg. "Run home, boy. Fast as you can." He slapped the horse's hock with the flat of his hand. "Yah!"

Augustus took off like a thoroughbred on race day, and Jonah prayed the right person would find him.

THIRTY-TWO

Katherine's stomach had been uneasy all afternoon. She knew fretting served no purpose beyond making her ill, but a heaviness had settled over her that she hadn't been able to shake. Hoping to distract herself with a change of scenery, she'd collected Alice and taken her to town to buy shoes. The battered, boy-style footwear the girl wore was at least one size too small and riddled with holes. They found a sturdy replacement pair in her size without much difficulty, which proved a blessing to Alice but a curse to Katherine. With her task now completed, her distraction dwindled, and Katherine's belly became a bowl of knots once again.

When they exited the mercantile, she couldn't keep her gaze from traveling down the road leading out of town to the west. *Where are you, Mark?* He'd warned they might be late coming home. Cautioned her not to worry. Yet she was doing exactly that.

She prayed for greater faith and less fear, but the knots remained. Even tightened.

Alice tugged on her hand. "Can we stop by the depot, Miss

Katherine? I want to see if Rawley is there. He might know something about Wart."

Surely the boy would have already reported any discoveries he had made on that front, but Katherine didn't have the heart to turn the girl down. Rawley was like a second big brother to her, and she'd be comforted in seeing him, whether or not he had any news to share.

"All right." She squeezed Alice's hand and forced a cheery smile to her face as she turned away from the road that led to Mark and, instead, marched toward the train station.

Alice led her around to the rear of the depot, where empty freight cars waited on a sidetrack for loading. None of the boxcar boys were in residence, however, and Alice's posture drooped like a flower with failing roots.

Determined to bolster the girl and herself, Katherine led Alice toward the platform. "Let's find Mr. Lopez. Maybe he's seen Rawley."

Alice's dragging feet quickened at the idea. She even beat Katherine up the steps and called out to the porter. "Mr. Lopez? Are ya here?"

A man ducked out of the baggage room and grinned at the sight of the little girl. "Al! Is that you? I look for a boy and here is a lovely niña."

Alice blushed and ducked her head, but a smile curled the edges of her mouth.

Mr. Lopez glanced at Katherine and winked. "And look what I happen to have in my pocket, eh? Candy! Would you like one? I have a few left over from yesterday."

Alice looked to Katherine. "Can I?"

Katherine smiled and nodded. "Yes, you may."

Mr. Lopez pulled a brown paper packet from his coat pocket and offered it to Alice. She pinched a candy between her thumb and forefinger and drew it out, the distinctive red and white stripes giving the flavor away.

Peppermint.

Katherine's abdomen went as hard as a rock. Hadn't one of the snatchers smelled of peppermint? The one who'd tried to take Rawley? Yes, she was sure of it. Mark and Jonah had rehashed all the possible identifying traits of the kidnappers so many times, she could probably recite the list in her sleep.

Katherine placed a hand on Alice's shoulder and drew her back to her side. The girl turned her head, her eyes questioning.

Doing her best to keep the alarm out of her voice, Katherine smiled at the porter. "Do you often eat peppermints, Mr. Lopez?" It seemed more of a child's treat than something a grown man would keep on hand. One of the reasons it distinguished Rawley's snatcher.

His brows rose slightly, but his cheerful disposition never flagged. "No." He chuckled softly as he put the packet back in his coat pocket. "Only when Señorita Gordon comes to see me. We started chatting after one of her trips to see her sick *padre* a couple months ago. I tried to lift her spirits. Her padre, I think, isn't long for this world. She's been coming to see me every week since then. Leaves candies with me after our chats." He grinned. "She knows about my sweet tooth, eh?"

"That's nice." Though something about it felt wrong. Althea Gordon had always seemed a very private sort of person. Eager enough to talk about her students and her love of history but rarely speaking of anything personal. The only reason Katherine knew about the teacher's ill father was because Althea had asked the church to pray for him. Katherine didn't even know where he resided, only that it was someplace near enough for Althea to make weekend visits by train.

"Sí. She treats me like one of her students," Mr. Lopez said, drawing Katherine back to the conversation. "Rewarding me for a job well done."

Katherine's heart pounded in her chest. "What job are you doing for her?"

Mr. Lopez shrugged. "Just chatting. You know how teachers are. They think boys should be in school, not roaming the streets. She comes by the depot to ask me about the boys who ride the rails. Have I seen them? Do I know where she might find them in the evenings? Where do they sleep? Can she take them food or blankets? She worries for their safety. Wants to get them in school. The candies are payment for the information I share." He winked. "If she ever catches up with Rawley, she'll need an entire jarful to bribe that wild one into a classroom." His face grew more serious. "But it's not good for him and the others to roam the rails like they do. They need schooling. And homes."

"I couldn't agree more." About the schooling and homes, anyway. The rest made her chest ache.

Had Althea Gordon rewarded another man for a job well done? A job involving snatching young boys? Surely the peppermints were a coincidence. Althea couldn't possibly be involved with the abductions. She was a teacher. A protector of children. Mark had trusted her and included her in their investigation.

Yet who else would be in a better position to know precisely which children in town had no families who would miss them? What if Althea's visits to Harmony House had not been a matter of professional curiosity, but as a way to take inventory of the children there? She was an expert on local history and geography. Those field trips she'd taken to Packsaddle Mountain to teach about the Moss brothers battling the Apache proved she knew the area. Would know where boys could be hidden. But for what purpose?

She must talk to Eliza. Get another opinion.

"We need to be getting back," she said, smiling at the porter even as she steered Alice toward the steps. "Have a lovely evening."

He waved. "You too, Señorita Palmer."

"Thank you for the candy, Mr. Lopez," Alice said around the peppermint in her mouth.

He pointed at her and winked. "You come see ol' Señor Lopez anytime, niña. You never know when he might have candy, eh?"

His warm chuckle should have soothed Katherine's anxiety, but it didn't.

"I wish we had found Rawley." Alice slurped at the candy in her mouth as she descended from the platform into the train yard.

Katherine should probably instruct her on not speaking with food in her mouth, but her mind was too busy sifting through a heaping pile of disturbing notions to care much about etiquette. "Me too."

"Well, ya did." Rawley popped out from behind a baggage car, startling a gasp out of Katherine.

Her hand flew to her chest to steady her wildly thumping heart. "Good grief, Rawley. You nearly scared the life out of me." She glanced down at Alice to make sure the girl hadn't sucked her candy down the wrong pipe, but she just grinned up at him with delight, completely unaffected by the suddenness of his appearance. Disgruntled, Katherine turned her attention back to Rawley. "Why didn't you make yourself known while we were talking to Mr. Lopez?"

"'Cause I didn't want him to hear what I have to say."

Rawley met Katherine's gaze, his expression a mix of cynicism and worry that put her immediately on edge. "He's a nice fella, and I don't want him to feel guilty."

"Because you think the teacher's involved?"

"Didn't 'til I heard Mr. Lopez talkin'. If Miz Gordon was so all-fired worried about us missin' school, how come she's never once invited me to her class? I seen her around town. Lots. Yet she's never tried to wrangle me or any o' my boys into goin' to school. Never so much as talked to us. She's been feeding Mr. Lopez a bunch of bunk."

Katherine's knees wobbled at the confirmation of her suspicions. *Lord, give me strength.* This was no time for weakness. Children's lives were at stake. "Are you certain Miss Gordon saw you?" She made herself ask the question even though she knew she was grasping at straws. "You are exceptionally good at avoiding being seen."

He gave her a look that insisted she cease insulting his intelligence. "I know boys in her class. I hang around the schoolhouse sometimes when they're about to be let out. I been as close to her as you are to me right now, and she never said a word. But her lyin' to Mr. Lopez ain't what's got me worried."

Katherine bit the edge of her tongue, dread sinking deeper into her belly. "No? Then what?"

"I saw her this mornin', talkin' to Wallace."

Mark?

"He told her about their search for Miguel Ortega. She tried to convince 'em to wait to do their searchin' until she could talk to a friend o' hers, but, o' course, they didn't. And after they rode off, she turned all her kids loose. Right in the middle of the day. I went to check it out. Caught up with Billy Fuller, who told me she had some kind of 'mergency. Sent the kids home. Not twenty minutes later, I spotted her on a horse, ridin' out o' town like a swarm of angry hornets was chasin' her." His dark-eyed gaze bored into Katherine. "She rode west."

The same direction Mark and Jonah had taken. If Althea was involved with the kidnappers and left to warn them, the Horsemen could have ridden straight into a trap.

Katherine snatched Alice's hand. "We've got to get back to Harmony House."

The girl's eyes flew wide. Without a word, she turned her head, spit out her candy, and nodded.

"I'll come with ya," Rawley said. "Help keep an eye on the place while your menfolk are away."

The way he said it made it sound like the men wouldn't be coming back soon. The thought spurred Katherine into a run. Ignoring the stares her unladylike haste garnered from passersby, she raced for home, restraining her speed only enough to avoid outpacing the girl at her side.

They had just reached the outskirts of town when a brown blur shot by them.

All three skidded to a halt.

"Was that . . . ?" Alice's voice trembled as her breath huffed.

"Mr. Jonah's horse." Rawley sounded shaken. Something Katherine had yet to hear from the street-toughened boy.

But then, the sight had shaken her too. To her core. Because the saddle had been empty. A regular mount without a rider spelled trouble. But a Horseman's mount? No minor mishap could unseat one of the famed Hanger's Horsemen. Only true disaster could separate a cavalry officer from his horse.

Rawley started to take off after Augustus, but Katherine shouted at him to wait.

She frantically dug in her reticule until she found the small tablet and pencil she kept among her spare hairpins, money purse, and door key.

"I need you to send a message to Matthew Hanger, Gringolet Farms, San Antonio," she said as she hunkered down and scribbled the direction at the top of the small page while bracing the tablet against her knee. She paused after getting the direction down and yanked her bag from her wrist. She tossed it at Alice's feet. "Get a dollar from my purse. Give it to Rawley." Not bothering to look up to make sure her instructions were being carried out, she resumed her scribbling.

Mark and Jonah in trouble.
Come at once.
Harmony House. Kingsland, TX.

She tore the page from the tablet and thrust it at Rawley. "There's a telegraph station at the depot. Have this sent immediately. If the telegraph operator doesn't take you seriously, get Mr. Lopez to help."

The boy's eyes glittered with determination. "I'll get it sent, Miss Katherine. They won't put me off."

"Thank you." Impulsively, she grabbed Rawley by the shoulders and pressed a kiss to his forehead. "I know I can count on you."

The shock on the Negro boy's face would have been comical had this been any other situation. As it was, she was glad to see the bewilderment quickly vanish beneath the hardened veneer he usually wore.

After stuffing the money Alice handed him into his trouser pocket, Rawley offered a sharp salute, then sprinted back into the depths of town.

Lifting silent prayers heavenward for Mark and Jonah, Katherine took up Alice's hand again and ran for home.

━━ CHAPTER ━━

THIRTY-THREE

With Priscilla on her lap, Quill wedged beside her on the parlor sofa, and Ted quietly building alphabet block walls at her feet, Eliza turned the page in Russell H. Conwell's *Bible Stories for Children* and continued reading about a shepherd boy who became a giant killer.

"David's faith in God was so great," she told the children, "that even when the king told him he was too young to help, he didn't give up. He might not have had any experience fighting giant warriors, but he had fought lions and bears to protect his father's sheep. He told the king, 'The Lord that delivered me out of the paw of the lion, and out of the paw of the bear, he will deliver me out of the hand of this Philistine.' All the fighting men of Israel were too afraid to face Goliath, but not David. He trusted God to help him." She tapped Pris on the nose and squeezed Quill's shoulders with the arm she'd wrapped around him earlier. "God will help you too, if you believe in him."

She glanced up from the book to make eye contact with Ted as well, but something other than the story had captured his attention. He launched off the carpet like a frog eager to try out a new lily pad. In his hurry to rush to the window, his foot collided with his carefully constructed wall. Blocks tumbled, but their builder paid them no mind.

"Come back to the rug, Ted," Eliza gently chided.

"But a horse just ran into our yard, Miss Eliza. A big one!" He plastered his nose and palms to the glass. "It looks like Mr. Jonah's horse, but there ain't nobody ridin' him."

Eliza dropped the book. Her throat constricted. "What?"

Ted had to be mistaken. She'd never met a man more confident in the saddle than Jonah Brooks. Whatever horse was out there, it couldn't be Augustus.

Heart quaking in her chest, she unhooked her arm from around Quill's shoulders, scooted Pris and the book onto the sofa cushion, then hurried to the window. She shoved the curtain aside and peered into the yard.

A giant chestnut horse reared, his front hooves pawing the air. A demanding whinny carried through the window glass and turned Eliza's blood to ice.

Augustus. It couldn't be.

Yet it was.

She dropped the curtain and ran for the front door. "Ruby! Abner!" she called, pausing at the foot of the stairs. "Something's happened. Come watch the little ones."

Her skirt billowed around her legs as she spun back toward the front door. Ted beat her there, his tiny hand already reaching for the handle. Eliza jumped forward and pulled him away from the door. "No, honey. You need to stay inside."

Who knew what horrible danger was afoot? Anything strong enough to tear Jonah out of the saddle boded ill for the rest of them. Even so, she had to go outside. See the horse. Figure out how to help the man who had crawled under her skin and into her heart.

The pounding of child-sized feet on the stairs announced Abner's arrival. "I've got him, Miss Eliza."

Taking the boy at his word, Eliza hurried out the door and slammed it closed behind her. Augustus's head snapped up at the sound. He snorted, tossed his mane, and charged toward the house as if he planned to race right up onto the porch.

Eliza lunged backward against the door, biting back a scream.

The giant warhorse did *not* charge onto the porch, of course. He simply eyed her from the base of the steps, pawing the dirt impatiently.

Get ahold of yourself, Eliza. It's just a horse. A well-trained one, at that. He won't trample you.

The logical arguments peeled her spine from the door and even convinced her feet to carry her to the edge of the porch. They couldn't quite get her down the steps, however. She clung to the balustrade, her breathing rapid and shallow.

The horse was too big. Too strong. Too . . . unpredictable. At least from the porch, she had the height advantage. And the protection of the railing. Down on the ground, she'd have neither.

The illustration from the Bible storybook she'd been reading to the children flashed in her mind. A boy facing a giant. A boy wearing no armor except his faith. A boy who refused to let fear keep him from doing what needed to be done. The Lord had granted that boy victory.

"God will help you too, if you believe in him."

The words she'd just spoken in the parlor thrust themselves into her mind in blatant challenge. Did she believe?

"For God hath not given us the spirit of fear," Eliza murmured, jutting her chin and releasing her grip on the balustrade, "but of power."

A spirit of power. She repeated the phrase in her mind

with each descending step that made her smaller and the horse larger.

A spirit of power. Coming alongside the shuddering beast, she lifted a trembling hand and placed her palm flat against Augustus's shoulder.

He didn't jerk from her touch. Didn't rear up in defiance. Just stood still. Waiting.

Eliza ran her hand along the saddle, over the stirrups, the saddlebags, searching for some clue to explain what had happened to Jonah. Unfortunately, the only clue was the horse itself.

As if sensing her reticence, Augustus curled his neck around and nudged her firmly with his nose. Eliza hopped back, a whimper catching in her throat.

A spirit of power.

Augustus followed her, stepping sideways until the empty left stirrup brushed her belly. He craned his head around again, his deep, dark eyes boring into hers. *Quit being a sissy and mount*, they seemed to say. *I'll take you to him.*

Lord, have mercy. She was going to have to ride this giant. If there was even the slightest chance Augustus could lead her to Jonah, she had to try.

"Abner?" she called without looking away from the saddle looming large in front of her face.

The parlor window scraped open behind her, confirming her assumption of having an avid audience.

"Yes, Miss Eliza?"

"You're in charge until Miss Katherine gets back from town. Keep everyone inside and lock the doors."

"Yes, ma'am." The window slid shut.

Eliza took a deep breath, then reached for the saddle horn. "You're going to have to help me, Auggie."

The horse snorted, probably in offense at the child's nickname she'd given him, but Auggie sounded far less fearsome than Augustus, Roman war commander and emperor.

"Don't give me any sass," she said, pretending a courage she did not feel.

She eyed the stirrup. Raised her foot. Nope. Too high. She needed a mounting block—which, of course, she didn't have. Botheration. The front steps would have to do.

"This way," she urged, tugging on the saddle horn as if she were actually strong enough to move the beast. Surprisingly, though, he complied, pivoting until his left side stood flush with the stairs. "Good boy."

She needed about three steps' worth of height but could only manage two without backing too far away from the horse.

"Steady, Auggie."

Hiking up her skirt and petticoats, she raised her left foot and, after a pair of unsuccessful attempts, managed to find the stirrup. Hopping on her right leg, she made a grab for the saddle and hoisted herself up and over. The most graceless mount of all time, but she was on.

The ground seemed impossibly far away. Dizziness assailed her, but she set her jaw and focused on Auggie's head. *Get settled and get Jonah.* With an awkward wiggle to adjust her seat, Eliza found the second stirrup, then took up the reins that had tangled in Auggie's mane.

David had a sling. She had a saddle horn. And she planned to hold on to it for all she was worth.

"All right, Auggie. Easy now." She clicked her tongue and tugged the reins to the right with one hand while clinging to the horn with the other.

The moment the horse's head faced the road, however,

something shifted in him. She could feel it. Tension. Energy. Purpose.

"Lord, please don't let me fallllll. . . ."

As if her prayer had been a starting gun, Augustus charged forward at the sound of her voice. Eliza's body was thrown backward from the surge. Releasing the reins, she grabbed the saddle horn with both hands and fought to regain her balance. The horse's raw power utterly terrified her. But, miraculously, she kept her seat.

As Augustus churned up the road beneath her, Eliza caught a distant call—Katherine, shouting her name. Eliza made no effort to investigate, however. Staying in the saddle required every iota of concentration she possessed.

Jonah's eyes snapped open. Horse hooves pounded the earth, growing louder, nearer. Someone was coming. After sending Augustus home, he'd managed to drag himself off the main path and into a cluster of juniper shrubs. Taking hold of the leafy limbs he'd hacked off with his knife, he arranged them as a camouflage shield in front of his face, then drew his revolver and waited.

Friend or foe?

He squinted through the brush, his normally keen vision hampered by the throbbing in his head. The horse was dark. Not black, though, so probably not Ortega's mount. The other snatcher had ridden a dun, too light for the horse cantering down the trail. Could be Augustus. Jonah's pulse hiccupped slightly at the thought, but he tamped down the unrealistic hope. Augustus was smart, the best horse he'd ever owned, but he was just an animal. Jonah had sent him home so that Eliza or Katherine would spot the riderless mount and notify

Bronson. Have the deputy organize a search party. It was too soon for a party to have formed. And that horse was traveling too fast to be carrying searchers.

Yet the nearer the horse came, the more similarities Jonah spotted. Size, color, stride. Everything matched. Except the rider. Whoever rode the horse sat hunched so far forward that Jonah couldn't see him past the gelding's head. Augustus had no patience with inexperienced riders—or *any* riders, for that matter—so the chances of Gus and the approaching horse being one and the same were slim to none.

Nevertheless, as the distance shrank, Jonah's eyes grew wider. Slim odds? Paper was too thick to describe the impossibility of what he was seeing. He dropped the branches shielding his face and blinked a few times to make sure he wasn't hallucinating.

Eliza Southerland, a woman terrified of the smallest ponies, was riding his seventeen-hand cavalry mount.

So stunned was he by the sight of her face bobbing up and down amidst Augustus's flying mane that he forgot to signal his position until woman and horse shot past his hiding place.

He whistled, then holstered his gun and crawled out from his juniper bunker, determined to stand on his own two feet before facing Eliza.

Augustus whinnied at Jonah's call and turned abruptly, catching his inexperienced rider unprepared. A muffled shriek, a flash of flying petticoats, and Eliza disappeared from view.

Manly pride forgotten, Jonah scrambled forward on hands and knees. "Eliza!"

Please, God. If she'd hit her head or twisted a leg in the fall . . .

Heart pounding, Jonah shooed Augustus out of the way

and lurched past the horse's hooves to reach the woman lying in a heap on the side of the path.

"Eliza!"

If she'd been wounded trying to help him . . . A dagger twisted in his chest, hurting more than all his injuries combined.

He'd just reached her feet when she gasped violently. "Eliza!"

She struggled to sit up. "All . . . right. Wind . . . out . . . me."

Thank God.

Jonah crumpled on the ground beside her, the few reserves he'd stored up depleted once again. Eliza rolled onto her side to face him, her breathing regulating as she got her wind back.

"Oh, Jonah." Her voice caressed him like soft leather, exquisitely tender but with an underlying strength that made a man feel like he didn't have to hide his vulnerabilities. "What happened to you?"

He cocked a wry grin. "Got shot off my horse."

"Shot!" Her gaze raked over him until it found the bloodstains on his shoulder.

"Just a graze. The tumble down the mountain did more damage than the bullet." His smile faded. "It's Wallace I'm worried about. I lost track of 'im."

"We'll muster a search party," Eliza promised. "*After* we get you home."

"I need to show 'em where to look."

She shook her head, and her eyes flashed fire. "You can *tell* them where to look. You'll only slow them down if you try to go with them."

She had a point. Jonah clenched his jaw. He hated being a liability. "Better send for the captain," he said. "He'll want to know."

"Of course. But first, we have to get you home."

Home. Why did that word sound so much better coming from her lips than anyone else's?

Eliza hovered over him, sliding her arm through his and reaching around to support his back. "I'll help you stand."

He nodded but didn't move. Her face was so close. So beautiful. Her eyes radiating concern. Her chin jutting with determination. Jonah reached up and cupped her cheek.

"I've witnessed heroic deeds on the battlefield, Eliza, but I've never seen anything braver than what you did today." She'd ridden Augustus, the monster horse that, until now, she'd refused even to touch. For him. "You're an amazing woman."

Her gaze locked with his, and her dark eyes softened. "You're worth the trouble."

THIRTY-FOUR

Mister! Please, mister. Ya gotta wake up!"

Mark's consciousness returned in tiny, excruciating increments. Scurrying echoed around him. And whispers. Both cut off abruptly, however, when he groaned. The back of his head felt as if he'd been kicked by a horse. Or rammed by a train. At least the insistent hands that had shaken him awake and rattled his brains in the process had released their grip.

Where was he?

Sandpaper eyelids scraped open only to find darkness on the other side. His chest clenched. Had he lost his sight? He peeled his eyes wide. Blackness. Solid, impenetrable night.

Panic shot through him. He tried to sit up, but his hands were bound. No, chained. He heard the links jangle, felt the bite of the iron manacles shackling his wrists. Rolling onto his side, he used his shoulder to lever himself up onto his knees. He sat up too quickly, though, and a wave of dizziness hit, disorienting him and sending him careening downward. Unable to halt his fall with his hands chained, he toppled over, the side of his face smashing against the hard ground.

"Ow."

A nervous giggle echoed from somewhere to his right, reminding him he wasn't alone.

"Who's there?" he demanded as he tried to get off his face and back onto his knees. "What do you want?"

Bits of memory started weaving together in his brain. The attack on Packsaddle Mountain. The black Palouse. Ortega. The kiddy-snatchers.

Kids. Boys who might giggle at a man who fell on his face. And the voice pleading with him to wake had been a child's voice. He was sure of it.

Had he found the missing children?

"Wart?" He latched on to the only name he knew, praying it would convince the boys he was friend not foe. "Wart, are you here? I'm Mark Wallace. We met at Donaldson's livery. My friend Jonah and I have been looking for you and the others. Rawley's been helping us. Al too." Mark tossed his sister's name into the dark like a poker player tossing in his last chip. "Al's safe at Harmony House, Wart. Safe and well."

Metal scraped against metal, and then a shaft of light pierced the darkness and diffused into a dim glow. *Thank God.* Mark swallowed hard, his chest tightening with gratitude. He wasn't blind. Just underground, judging by the cavelike passage he found himself in. Turning toward the light, he spied half a dozen faces staring at him. One in particular grabbed his attention, topped by a mop of matted curls that probably looked red in the sunlight.

"Al's all right?" The boy's voice wobbled but didn't crack. Wart stepped away from the group of boys huddled against the cavern wall, his eyes so full of hope, it hurt to look at him.

But Mark refused to look anywhere else. He knew the weight of responsibility and how heavy it grew when helplessness stole the power to protect those one cared for. The memory of Jonah tumbling over the side of the mountain flayed Mark's heart. His friend—no, his *brother*—needed him, and he could do nothing to help him. He *could* help Wart, though. Ease his burden at least a little.

"She's fine," he said. "I saw her just this morning." At least he thought it had been this morning. It was hard to tell how long he'd been out. "She's worried about you, but she's healthy and safe at Harmony House." He grinned. "Even wears dresses now."

"Wait." A new voice piped up from the shadows. "Al's a *girl?*"

Whoops. Well, it wasn't as if Rawley and the rest of the boxcar boys didn't already know the truth. Word of Al's feminine side was sure to have spread. Just not into underground caves in the middle of nowhere.

"So, where are we?" Mark asked, gingerly hoisting himself up to a kneeling position.

"Los Almagres," one of the boys answered.

The name didn't ring a bell. "That a town? Or a ranch, maybe? Are we still near Kingsland?" For all he knew, he could have been tossed onto a freight car and transported down to Mexico. He prayed that wasn't the case. It would make escaping with the kids twice as hard.

Wart didn't answer his questions. Just moved closer, frowning. He hunkered down in front of Mark and waved for another boy to bring the lantern closer. "Your face is all bloody."

"Yeah, well, that tends to happen when a bullet creases your scalp." Chains rattled as Mark reached around to the back of his head and probed the sore spot at his crown. He winced, the wound painful to touch. His hair was a matted mess too, most likely plastered with a combination of dried blood, dirt, and debris, but he didn't think his skull was actually cracked. A miracle for which he owed the Lord a debt of gratitude. Not to mention the fact that Ortega and his partner had dragged him here instead of shooting him.

"Los Almagres ain't a town." Another boy spoke up, his voice deeper and filled with derision. "It's a mine. In Pack-saddle Mountain. The lost San Saba. Or at least that's what I heard the lady tell Ortega." He spat on the ground, as if saying Ortega's name had contaminated his mouth. "The fools think they found buried treasure. They ordered us to dig up silver for 'em, but there ain't hardly any of it down here. Not enough to make anyone rich, anyways. I been workin' this blasted mine for near a month, pickin' and clawin' at every scrawny vein I can find. No silver means no supper, so we all search our hardest, but there's pitiful little to work with. We bring up just enough each day to keep us fed and keep them believin' the mother lode is around the corner. But I been 'round all the corners down here, and there ain't no vein wider than a blade of grass in this whole place." The heat left his voice, and his gaze flattened as it met Mark's. "At least we don't have to work the mine anymore after tonight."

Mark's gut tightened. Somehow he didn't think that statement was related to an unflagging faith in his ability to rescue them.

"Thanks to you stumblin' onto their operation, they decided to abandon their treasure hunt and cover their tracks." The kid folded his arms over his chest. "When they tossed you in, one of 'em stuck a note in your pocket." He pulled a wad of paper out of his trouser pocket and threw it at Mark's feet. "They're gonna dynamite the place at midnight."

Midnight? Mark bent to retrieve the paper, opened it, and read the words.

Take cover.
Mine will blow at midnight.

He rubbed his jaw on his shoulder. Could be that one of the snatchers had a conscience. Kidnapping children was one thing. Killing them was a different story. The fact that he'd snuck a warning to the boys could mean he planned to intervene somehow. Maybe at least sound the alarm in town to start a search. This could be good news.

Yet when his gaze measured the shadowed faces in the lantern's solemn glow, he saw no hope in any of them. Only futility. No tears. No trembling. No emotion at all. Just flat acceptance of death.

Well, he wouldn't be accepting death without a fight. He had a promise to fulfill to Kate. One involving a parson and at least fifty years of wedded bliss. And then there was Jonah. His injured partner was out there on the mountain somewhere. Not to mention the six young boys in here who deserved a chance to grow up. Surrender was not an option.

He patted his trouser pocket for his watch but felt nothing inside. Ortega probably swiped his valuables before tossing him into this pit.

"What time is it?" he barked as he examined his surroundings for a possible escape route. Did he have four hours to plan? Two? One?

"Dunno." The surly kid who'd taken charge of the explanations wrapped an arm around a concave stomach. "But it's long past supper, I can tell you that much."

Poor kid was half starved. "Was it dark when they tossed you down here with me?" The sun set around 8:00 or 8:30 this time of year. If the boys could estimate the time that had passed since night fell . . .

"We ain't been topside since breakfast. They never pulled us up. Just tossed you down. Along with the pulley rope." The ringleader pointed to a sloppy coil of rope about a foot behind Mark, directly beneath a dark hole in the ceiling that must be the vertical shaft leading to the mine's exit.

Mark frowned. It looked like going out the way they'd come in wouldn't be an option. Ortega and his partner were probably camped out by the entrance anyway. Mark shifted to get his feet under himself in a crouch.

"Can you estimate what time they lowered me down here? Was it around the same time they usually pull you out for supper? Or later?" Pushing to his feet, Mark studied the shaft above his head. Even when Wart followed with the lantern, it was too dark to see much. They were down pretty deep. Estimating the time was going to be nearly impossible.

"What difference does it make?" the spokesman huffed. "We're gonna be blown to smithereens either way. Who cares how long we got?"

"I care." Mark glared at the boy. "The more time we have, the more time I can take assessing our options. The more time I have to assess, the better our chances of getting out of this mess."

The belligerent boy scowled right back at him. "There ain't no way out, mister. The only thing that can save us is someone stopping them fellas from tossin' that dynamite down the shaft. And unless you got an army comin' that can see in the dark, there ain't no one around to stop 'em."

"I do have an army coming, actually." Mark squatted back down and grinned. "Ever heard of Hanger's Horsemen?"

All the boys' eyes grew wide. Well, all but those of the cynic in the front row. His eyes just narrowed into even thinner slits.

"I'm Mark Wallace. I ride with Matthew Hanger, Jonah Brooks, and Luke Davenport. By now, the ladies of Harmony House will have wired Matt for help." At least he hoped Kate had done so. They hadn't actually talked through contingency specifics, but she wasn't one to sit idle when someone she cared about was in trouble. "They'll likely be here by morning, which means we don't have to find a way out, we just have to find a way to survive the blast."

"Ya really think we can?" The tiniest stirring of hope lit Wart's gaze.

Mark turned his full attention to the stable boy. "Yes, I do." His chains clinked softly as he settled his wrists atop his hunkered knees. "When I first woke up, I wondered why Ortega and his partner hadn't just killed me outright. Why drag me back here and toss me into this mine?"

"Probably to save themselves the trouble of diggin' a grave to hide yer body."

Mark shrugged, glancing at the ringleader for a moment. "Maybe. But I think it was something else."

"What?" Wart asked.

"I think God brought me here. To help you."

"Ha!" Mr. Ray-of-Sunshine uncrossed his arms and waved them through the air in disgust. "And you expect us to trust a God who would shoot you up and drop you in a hole to die? Ain't happenin'."

Mark's patience thinned. "Ortega and his partner did the shooting and dropping. God did the preserving. My arms and legs are in good working order when the fall could have broken them. My head feels like a blacksmith used it as an anvil, but I'm awake and thinking clearly. I'm even well-rested, thanks to my little nap. I've been praying to find you boys, and now I have. That tells me God has a plan. All we gotta do is keep our eyes and ears open and follow where he leads."

"No, thanks."

Wart spun on the boy. "We ain't got time for this, Floyd. I got a sister out there. If there's a chance I can live to see her again, I'm gonna fight to make that happen. If you wanna sit here and whine, go ahead, but I'm gonna help Mr. Wallace." He turned back to Mark, chin set, hands fisted. "Where do we start?"

Now they were getting somewhere. Mark nodded at Wart, sealing the partnership. "I assume they'll plant the dynamite in the shaft near the entrance, so we'll need to get as far away from the blast as possible. If we can insulate ourselves from it, that would be even better. Build up a barrier of sorts. I just don't know if we have time for that."

One of the smaller boys pushed his way forward. He didn't quite meet Mark's gaze, but he thrust his hand out with purpose. "Here ya go, mister. I nipped it while you was nappin'." On his extended palm lay Mark's pocket watch.

"Thanks." Mark smiled as if the boy were giving him a gift instead of returning stolen property.

Stealing was how these kids survived. If they got out of here, he'd bring the lot of them to Harmony House. Try to convince them to trade in thievery for full bellies, education, and kindness. It just might turn them into reputable citizens.

He snapped the watch cover open and held it toward the light. Quarter 'til nine. That gave them a little over three hours. He glanced around the cavern, finally realizing what was missing from the picture. "Where are your tools?"

"In there." Wart pointed behind Mark.

He turned to find a narrow horizontal passage at the far side of the cavern. The ceiling sloped downward toward it, so even the boys would have to bend to get to it. The passage itself was nothing more than a crawl space, far too narrow for a man to fit through. Which explained why the boys had been snatched. They were the only ones small enough to get into the ore room.

Unfortunately, that meant Mark wouldn't be able to follow them and help find an exit. Therefore, their best chance for survival lay in insulating themselves from the blast.

"All right, boys. Here's what we're going to do. For the next two hours, you're going to bring me as many rocks as you can carry through that hole. If there is any loose or broken timber, bring that as well. We're going to build the biggest wall we can. Then, at eleven o'clock, all of you will go back through the passage and find the safest place you can to take shelter."

Mark looked past Wart to the glowering kid at the back of the group. "Floyd, you know this place best. Steer clear of weak spots, places where dirt and debris tend to shower down from the ceiling. Pick a place as far from the entrance as you can get. One close to the walls and support posts. If you find a large hole somewhere along the ceiling, stay close to that if possible. It might be a ventilation shaft. If there's a cave-in, fresh air will be important. Can you do that?"

Floyd shrugged.

It wasn't a no. Mark decided to take it as a yes. "Good." He turned to Wart. "You're in charge of keeping everyone together. Rescue will be easier if everyone's in one place. Can you do that?"

Wart nodded. "But where will you be? You can't fit through the *rat hole*."

Mark ruffled the kid's hair. "I'll be out here until the last minute, fortifying our wall. I'll need one of you to bring me a pickax. The biggest one you got in there."

He'd build the wall between the entrance shaft and the boys' passage, but he'd leave an opening on the other side for two reasons. First, it might redirect the blast in the opposite direction, taking the path of least resistance. Second, if Ortega took the lazy way out and just tossed the dynamite down the shaft, Mark might have time to grab it and hack off the fuse before it exploded. Not exactly the safest option for him, but it gave the boys their best chance at survival.

Mark and the boys worked the next two hours like a locomotive at full steam, Mark pounding out large chunks of rock from the back wall, and the boys bringing bucket after bucket of smaller pieces from the ore room. A pair of half-rotted beams wedged between the floor and the low ceiling near the entrance to the ore room served as their frame. They placed their rocks inside it, building their barrier higher and higher. By the time the boys took refuge, they had a decent wall in place. About four feet high and five feet wide. It would probably collapse in the blast, but if it helped redirect the explosion, even a little, it could give the boys a fighting chance. To increase their odds, Mark continued reinforcing the wall after the boys took shelter, wielding the pickax until his arms were too fatigued to lift it.

He checked his watch. Ten minutes to midnight. Stepping back from the barrier, he moved to the vertical shaft and lay beneath it. It was the best way he could think of to catch a glimpse of a lit fuse at the top of the shaft. He was too tired to stand much longer anyway. His wrists throbbed from the rubbing of the iron manacles, and his arms felt like rubber. He kept one hand on the pickax handle, though, ready to put it to use on the dynamite if given the chance. One act remained. Mark rolled to the side, closed the metal shield on the miner's lantern, and let the darkness engulf him.

He had done all he could do.

Keep those boys safe, Lord, he prayed as he stared into the blackness above him. *Lead rescuers to them in time. Take care of Jonah, and if I don't make it out of here, take care of Kate. Help her to know I loved her with my entire being, and that leaving her was the last thing I ever wanted to do.*

He dared not let his mind linger on Kate for more than a heartbeat. Thoughts of her in his arms, the kiss they'd shared, and the future they planned to build would steal his focus. A single pinprick of light was all the warning he would get. He couldn't afford distraction.

His left hand moved to his waist, feeling for the fallen pulley rope that he'd tied there earlier. He'd secured the other end to a support timber at the far side of the cavern. The nook he'd found there offered meager protection at best, but if the dynamite didn't fall down the shaft, he'd follow the rope and pray for the best.

Please let it fall. Please let it fall.

He could hear time ticking away on his watch. His heart thumped to the beat. His muscles tensed. His grip tightened on the ax.

Then all at once, it was there. A speck of light danced above him. Then it dropped. Mark launched to his feet, jumped back from the shaft, and raised the ax. But no bundle of dynamite landed at his feet. He glanced up the shaft and spotted the explosive swinging back and forth. It must be tethered with a rope or chain. Deep enough to collapse the mine, yet too shallow for anyone waiting below to interfere.

Mark dropped the ax, grabbed the rope at his waist, and reeled himself in as fast as he could while stumbling through the black cavern.

A deafening roar exploded in his ears. A herculean force picked him up and threw him forward, slamming his body into a wall. The earth quaked. Rocks fell like rain. And Mark's heart called out to his beloved.

━ CHAPTER ━
THIRTY-FIVE

Katherine sat bolt upright in bed. Her heart pounded, but she had no idea why. She glanced around the bedroom she shared with Eliza but spotted nothing that would have awakened her. Eliza wasn't even in the room. Katherine had left her tending to Jonah in the front parlor when she'd finally forced herself to try to get some sleep.

Thank you for bringing Jonah back to her. Katherine knew her friend was more than a little in love with Mr. Brooks. She'd never admit as much, not after only knowing him a couple of weeks, but only something as strong as love could have broken through her fear and gotten her on that horse.

Katherine threw off the covers and pivoted to dangle her legs off the side of the bed. *I'd do the same for Mark.* The thought froze her in place, her toes halting halfway to the carpet. Was that why she woke? Was there something she needed to do to help Mark? But what? What could she possibly do in the dead of night?

They'd already called Deputy Bronson to the house at Jonah's insistence. Jonah had refused any medical care until he'd told the lawman everything he knew about Mark and the men who had attacked them. Miguel Ortega and his spotted horse. His white partner who rode a dun mount with a nicked hoof and a recent injury to its flank. The precise location on Packsaddle Mountain where they'd been ambushed. A description of Mark's horse. The deputy had vowed to pull together a group of men and start searching at first light.

She'd also received a telegram from Matthew Hanger. He'd be arriving on the morning train. Help was coming from all over. Capable help. Experienced help. She'd prayed herself to sleep, believing that to be the best assistance she could contribute, but now an unsettling urgency drove her out of bed and toward the chair where she'd tossed her clothes a couple of hours ago.

Is this you, Lord, or is my worry goading me? Not sure of the answer, she hesitated, but the urge to dress was too strong to ignore. It had to be the Lord. Worry might have the power to keep her from falling asleep, but it had never woken her in such dramatic fashion. God must be calling her to action.

With hurried hands, she threw off her nightgown and grabbed her camisole and drawers. Not wanting to take the time to lace a corset, she left the undergarment on the back of the chair and pulled one of her looser dresses from the wardrobe. Petticoat, stockings, and shoes were essential, but she left her hair hanging down her back in her sleeping braid.

The door hinge squeaked as she exited into the hall. A shadow positioned between her and the stairs moved suddenly, causing her to clap a hand over her mouth to keep from waking the entire household with her fright.

"Miss Katherine?" a sleep-filled voice queried.

Her hand slid from her mouth to cover her pounding heart. "Good heavens, Abner. You gave me a scare. What are you doing lying in the hall?"

The boy pushed to his feet, something long dangling from his right hand. Mercy! Was that a fireplace poker?

"Someone's gotta watch out for the womenfolk with Mr. Wallace missing and Mr. Brooks all banged up."

Katherine's heart warmed at his concern. He was too young to carry such responsibility, yet she loved him for it. She hunkered down next to him and smiled. "You are very brave." She brushed the hair from his forehead. "Thank you for watching over us. I'm sure the men who attacked Mr. Wallace and Mr. Brooks are far away by now, though. Making their escape so the law won't catch them when the search party sets out in the morning. I think it's safe for you to go back to bed."

He didn't argue with her, but neither did he agree. He just held his tongue and tilted his chin in that stubborn way he had when planning to go his own way. Well, she had *her* own way to go at the moment too, so if he wanted to pass the rest of the night in the hall, she wouldn't stop him.

Straightening, she patted his shoulder and headed for the stairs. At the bottom, she diverted to the parlor and peeked inside. She needed to let Eliza know that she was leaving, especially since she had no idea how long she would be gone. But when she saw her friend dozing in a chair drawn close to the sofa where Jonah slept, she didn't have the heart to intrude. Jonah's sleep did not look easy. His mouth turned down and a muffled moan escaped him, as if the pain from his injuries impaired his rest. Or perhaps the discomfort stemmed from fretful dreams of the attack and what had happened to Mark. She could certainly relate to the latter.

At the sound of his moan, Eliza's hand moved to stroke his chest. He quieted immediately, his own hand finding hers in sleep and clutching her fingers close to his heart.

Stepping softly to the small table in the corner, Katherine found the telegram from Matthew Hanger right where she'd left it after showing it to Jonah. She flipped it over, pulled a pencil from the table drawer, and scribbled a short note to Eliza.

There was one person no one had taken the time to chase down after all the excitement this evening. One who might slip past the deputy's notice because of her gender. One who might actually know something about what had happened to Mark.

One who was about to entertain an uninvited midnight caller.

Katherine set the note in a visible place on the table, then slipped out into the night. The half-moon illuminated the yard enough for her to find her way to the barn to collect the lantern they kept ready by the door. A strike of a match later, she was armed with light and ready to trudge through the darkness to seek answers.

So full of purpose was she that she didn't even think to be afraid. Not until she entered town and heard a clatter behind her. She spun toward the sound and held her lantern aloft, but she saw no one. Telling herself it was probably just a coon getting into some nighttime mischief, she turned forward again and continued her march to Althea Gordon's residence. Yet her steps weren't quite as sure as they had been. Doubts seeped into her mind.

What was she doing, walking the streets in the middle of the night? The darkness that a moment ago had shrunk back from her light now seemed to creep forward, casting unsettling shadows. What wickedness loomed behind that building? What danger stalked her from the trees? She was just a woman. Unescorted. Unarmed.

Her hand trembled as she held the lantern in front of her. "Yea, though I walk through the valley of the shadow of death,'" she murmured softly, "'I will fear no evil: for thou art with me.'"

Thou art with me.

Katherine straightened her shoulders as she internalized the promise. Her stride lengthened. Her chin lifted.

I will fear no evil.

This was not the time for timidity. Mark was out there somewhere. Probably injured. Alone. He had sprinted directly toward a speeding train in order to save her life. She could walk through a bit of darkness for him.

Katherine clutched the lantern with renewed determination. God had awoken her. Sent her. She wouldn't quail in the valley of shadows. He was with her. And no darkness could withstand his light.

Yet when she reached the small house Althea Gordon rented on the south side of town, a different light drew Katherine up short. A light from the back of the house. From within. Katherine glanced around. No other houses occupied this section of town. A few businesses stood nearby, but they were closed up tight for the night. No one would notice her skulking about. She turned down the wick on her lantern and used the darkness as an ally to conceal her presence as she slipped around the corner of the building to investigate.

Althea was awake. And moving around, judging by the silhouette that occasionally darkened the bedroom curtain. Did she know someone suspected her of being involved with the snatchers? Did she plan to sneak out of town in the dead of night? If she succeeded, what would become of the missing children? Of Mark? Would they remain lost forever?

Katherine couldn't allow that to happen.

Setting her lantern on the ground by the back stoop, Katherine reached for the narrow railing and crept up the back stairs. She fit her hand to the latch. The door opened.

Katherine stepped inside the small kitchen and closed the door softly behind her.

"It's about time you got back," Althea called from another room. Her bedchamber, most likely. "I'm nearly packed. The smith didn't haggle over the amount again, did he? I don't mind paying extra for his discretion, but if he thinks to extort me, I'll send Miguel after him."

Miguel. Althea *was* involved! Katherine crossed the kitchen, taking care not to click her heels on the wooden floor. Not only involved, but the way she talked about ordering Miguel around, she might actually be the person in charge.

"He and Dorsey should have destroyed the evidence by now. I hated to collapse the mine, but it couldn't be helped. Production was pitiful anyway. Daddy will be disappointed, but he'll understand. I left enough raw ore at the site to cover the men's share, so we need never see them again. Everything's going to plan. We need only to—"

Althea appeared in the doorway, a pile of petticoats in her hands. Her eyes widened in surprise at seeing Katherine, but they normalized quickly. She tossed her armload of undergarments onto the bed, then casually stepped into the hall.

"Miss Palmer. Have you taken up housebreaking, then? I must say, I didn't think you had it in you."

"Where's Mark?" Katherine demanded, doing her best to ignore the gooseflesh prickling uneasily across her nape.

"You mean that handsome Mr. Wallace?" Althea smirked as she leaned a hip against the side wall. "Gone, I suppose. I saw him leave town this morning with that partner of his. I don't expect they'll be back."

Katherine's heart clenched. Her distress must have shown on her face, for a flash of triumph flared in Althea's eyes.

Something raw and fierce surged inside Katherine in response. "You're wrong, Althea. Mr. Brooks *did* return. And he had quite a tale to tell."

Uncertainty flickered in the teacher's eyes, but only for a moment. "Did he? And who exactly did he tell this tale to? You, I suppose?"

"And Deputy Bronson. A search party will be leaving at first light."

Althea smiled. "Oh, I don't think so, dear."

Katherine heard the scuff of shoe leather on wood a moment too late. A man grabbed her from behind, one hand snaking around her middle and lifting her off the ground as the other closed over her mouth to muffle her scream.

"You see," Althea said, pushing away from the wall to saunter forward like a tigress inspecting the injured prey her cub had just dropped at her feet, "Deputy Bronson works for *me*."

THIRTY-SIX

W hat d'ya want me to do with her, sis?"

Sis? Katherine's struggling stuttered to a halt. She looked up. Examined Althea's hair and eyes. The shape of her face. The deputy had similar coloring. Both were tall and slender. Their eyes were different, though. Deputy Bronson had brown eyes, while Althea's were green. His face was longer and more pointed too. Yet a resemblance existed . . . if one knew to look for it.

"Tie her up and stuff her in the pantry for now." Althea gestured toward the kitchen. "We'll have to take her with us. We can drop her off at Miguel's camp, let him deal with her."

"That'll add time to our trip," the deputy grumbled. "We're already gonna have to lead the team with lanterns all the way to Llano."

"Quit your complaining, Ernest. The train doesn't leave until nine, and we only have to use the lanterns until dawn. We've got time for a short side trip." Althea shot a glare at Katherine. "We can't leave her around to tell people what she knows." She shook her head and made a *tsk* sound. "You really shouldn't have stuck your nose where it didn't belong, Miss Palmer."

"How could you?" Katherine's angry question sounded more like *Ow ood oo* with the deputy's hand covering her mouth, but talking caused one of the deputy's fingers to slip between her lips. Katherine immediately bit down.

"Ow!" The deputy yanked his hand away from her face. Unfortunately, he had enough presence of mind to maintain his grip on her midsection. In fact, when she didn't start screaming, he opted to secure both her arms behind her with his hands.

Screaming would only lead to a gag being applied, and Katherine needed to learn as much information about Mark and the missing boys as possible. Escape could wait.

"You're a teacher," Katherine spat at Althea while Bronson dragged her backward. "You're supposed to protect children. Nurture them. How could you participate in their abduction?"

"Participate?" A humorless laugh erupted from Althea. "I'll have you know I never abducted a single child." Her arrogant smile turned Katherine's stomach. "I did, however, orchestrate the entire endeavor."

And was apparently proud of that shameful accomplishment.

"Why?" Katherine cried. "For money?" She'd mentioned a mine. And a smith. Was she using the boys to dig for gold? Silver?

"For my father!"

The passion behind that pronouncement surprised Katherine.

Althea advanced on her, eyes flashing. "He's searched for Los Almagres his entire adult life. It's his obsession. He raised me with stories of Bernardo de Miranda's discovery of rich ore in the *cerro de almagre* in 1756. Taught me about the Apache

341

mission and the presidio captain tasked with working the mine they found. About the giant pile of slag left behind by the Spaniards on the San Saba River near the presidio. About the destruction of the mission in 1758 and the Apache raids years later that discouraged treasure seekers."

Her arms gesticulated as if to add extra punctuation to her tale. "Father collected maps by Stephen F. Austin and Henry Tanner showing mines near the old Spanish fort, pamphlets promising silver to immigrants, and Texas information guides declaring the existence of Los Almagres. Finding that mine was his life's work, but no matter how carefully he searched, he never found it. The failure broke him." Her hands fell to her sides, and her shoulders hunched forward. "He took to his bed five years ago and has been slowly dying ever since, sure he's wasted his life on a fool's errand. Certain that Los Almagres never existed."

Althea's posture straightened, and she took a step closer to Katherine. "But it does exist, and I can prove it with the silver we've collected. All those years, he'd been looking in the wrong places," she said with a cynical laugh, "because the maps were *wrong*. I widened the search into Llano County. Studied local history. Combed through ore samples and assay reports. Everyone believed the mine was located near either the San Saba or Llano Rivers, but I began to suspect the true location was near Honey Creek. That led me to Packsaddle Mountain.

"I used my mother's maiden name, took a teaching job in Kingsland, and continued my search with no one the wiser. Ernest cozied up to the sheriff in Llano and got himself appointed deputy a few months later. We kept our familial relationship a secret, and no one suspected we were any-thing more than acquaintances. We searched on weekends and during the off-terms for more than a year, and then, six months ago, we found the mine's entrance on the southern slope of Packsaddle Mountain.

"We excavated the archaeological remains of spoil piles and shafts. Discovered the paths the Spaniards left behind. Some of those paths, however, proved too narrow for adults to navigate. Hence our need for smaller bodies. If the Spaniards used boys to work their mines, I'd do the same. But not for riches, Miss Palmer. For my father. I would not let him die thinking himself a failure."

Moisture glistened in Althea's eyes, but she ruthlessly blinked it away. Her gaze hardened. "Make no mistake," she said without a speck of compassion or conscience coloring her voice, "I'll do whatever it takes to see this through. No matter how many indigent children or interfering busybodies have to disappear."

A shiver coursed over Katherine's skin as Ernest yanked her wrists together behind her back and bound them with some kind of cloth strip. A movement at the back window drew her attention. Half a face appeared at the window. The *bottom* of the window. She couldn't see much of him in the dark, but she recognized the discolored section of skin on the top right side of his face.

Abner! He'd followed her.

She locked her gaze with his and shook her head. Just once, but hopefully it would be enough to keep him from doing anything rash like storming the house and taking on two criminal adults with only a fireplace poker. As she watched, a small, dark-skinned hand grabbed Abner from behind and pulled him away. Rawley? Thank heavens Abner wasn't alone. She didn't like the idea of either one of the boys so close to danger, but if they were close enough to overhear, they could pass the information on to Eliza and Jonah.

She had to keep Althea talking while she had the chance. Any minute now, she'd find herself stuffed in a pantry closet, no further good to anyone.

"Is that what happened to Mark?" Katherine pulled against her bindings, lurching toward Althea. Ernest jerked her back with a rough motion, gripping her arms to keep her still. But Ernest wasn't her concern. Althea was. "Did Mark interfere with your plans? Did he stumble across your mining operation in his search for the boys?"

"I tried to warn him off," Althea said. "Asked him to wait a day. But like most men, he wouldn't listen to a woman. And now he's paid the price." She shrugged. "Unfortunate waste of a good-looking man, but it couldn't be helped. He found his missing boys, though. He'll be happy about that. Just like my father, he'll die knowing he completed his mission. Small comfort, but it's better than nothing."

"So they're all in the mine together, then," Katherine guessed. She couldn't afford to let her heartbreaking fear for Mark steal her wits. Her job was to cull information. "Did you leave them there to starve?"

Please, Lord, let there be time to save them.

"Nothing so cruel, I assure you. Their end came swiftly. About an hour ago, as a matter of fact. You might have heard it. The quiet boom of distant thunder? Dynamite has much the same resonance, I'm told." She smiled, then turned her attention to her brother. "Enough of this chitchat, Ernest. Lock her in the pantry and help me with my trunk. We have a schedule to keep."

The deputy's grip tightened. Katherine struggled against his hold, desperate to get one final message to the boys she prayed were listening on the other side of the door. "You won't get away with this! Mark Wallace is one of Hanger's Horsemen. It'll take more than a stick of dynamite to bury him. Jonah and the rest of the Horsemen will find that Packsaddle mine, you'll see. They'll save Mark, then come after you."

Althea turned just as Ernest shoved Katherine backward into the pantry, banging her spine and skull against wooden shelves.

"Even if you're right, my dear, they'll have no proof that I did anything wrong. Miguel Ortega is the one with blood on his hands, not me. And I have my very own lawman to vouch for me in the unlikely event that your Horsemen capture Miguel and get him to talk. No one will believe a murderer over a deputy of the law. Your threats are pointless, Miss Palmer."

No, not pointless, Katherine thought as the pantry door slammed closed against her nose and the lock clicked into place. Not when her points were aimed at a pair of quick-witted boys hovering outside the window.

Show them what to do, Lord. Get word to Jonah and the others in time to save Mark and the children.

And maybe, when the Almighty was finished with that, he could send her a few ideas for an escape plan. Her experience in slipping free of criminal captors was regrettably thin.

THIRTY-SEVEN

J onah." A soft voice called to him. A gentle hand stroked his brow. "Jonah, wake up."

The darkness didn't want to let him go. He frowned, struggling to shake free of sleep's grip and answer her call.

"Jonah, *please*."

Something was wrong. The voice that had soothed him and eased his pain now called with urgency. Desperation.

Eliza! Why couldn't he get his eyes open? A cavalry officer always woke at the first sound of the bugle. Bugle . . . Mark . . . something about Mark . . .

A hand grabbed his shoulder. Shook him. "I know you're hurt, but I need you."

His strong, capable Eliza. With tears in her voice. She needed him. Jonah punched through the darkness and opened his eyes. "Liza?"

"Thank the Lord." Worry warred with relief on the beautiful face leaning over him. "They took Katherine. I have to go after her. I just need you to show me how to use your guns."

That woke him up. Shoving aside the lingering grogginess,

Jonah sat up, biting back a moan at the throbbing in his head. Pain didn't matter, though. Protecting the women did. And there was no way he was sending Eliza out into the dark of night with his guns.

"I'll go," he said, his voice filled with gravel.

"You're injured." Eliza tried to push him back down on the sofa, but he batted her hands away. "You're in no condition—"

"Quit your bossin', woman. I'm fine."

Determined to prove his words true, he rose to his feet, careful to keep his discomfort masked. He tugged the cuffs of his sleeves down to his wrists as he waited for the dizziness to pass. Falling on his face wouldn't exactly convince Eliza of his fitness for duty.

Shake it off, Brooks. You got a job to do.

And do it, he would. Starting with reclaiming his gun belt. The one buckled around the prettiest pair of hips he ever did see.

His hand trembled slightly as he reached for the buckle. Once there, he looked up into her eyes. Eyes wide with fear for her friend, fiery determination to enact a rescue, and frustration that Jonah wasn't staying where she'd put him. Yet as he slowly worked the belt loose, something else entered her eyes. Something soft, warm, and tentatively hopeful. Man, but he could get lost in those eyes.

The belt fell away, swinging behind her as he held one end steady. The tug of it against his hand sharpened his focus back on the job. Swallowing down the other thoughts and emotions swirling in his brain regarding the mesmerizing woman in front of him, he cleared his throat, took a step back, and murmured, "Tell me what happened."

"I don't know." Eliza sagged against the sofa arm, her gaze falling to the ground. "She left to confront Miss Gordon, and now they have her. Rawley thinks they mean to kill her." She glanced up, tears in her eyes. "Why would she do that? Leave in the middle of the night? With no protection?"

Jonah had never seen Eliza look so lost, so vulnerable. "Don't know. But she musta had a reason. She ain't the reckless type."

A movement near the doorway caught Jonah's eye. Rawley stepped inside the parlor. He looked haggard yet ready for action. "She did it fer Wallace. Whole time she was there, all she did was ask questions about him and the snatched boys. Acted like she weren't scared for herself at all. Never even asked 'em to let her go. And once she spotted Abner in the window, she made it clear we were to come fetch you. Not for her, though. For Wallace and the boys."

Eliza blew out a breath. "That sounds just like Katherine. Always worried about everyone else."

But if she'd found out where Mark was . . . Jonah swung his gun belt around his hips and worked the buckle from memory, his gaze zeroed in on Rawley. "You know where he is?"

The boy gave one sharp nod. "In a mine. South side of Packsaddle Mountain." He paused. "One they dynamited around midnight."

A soft gasp escaped Eliza. She pushed away from the sofa and clasped his hands, as if she knew what that news did to him, how it tore up his insides and left him raw and bleeding. Then again, maybe she *did* know. Her own insides must be shredded, knowing that her friend was in the hands of people who would callously bring a mountain down on the heads of children. He squeezed her hands back.

"We need to tell Deputy Bronson," she said. "Let him know where to focus his search—"

Rawley's shaking head cut her off. "The deputy's in on the whole thing. He was there at Miss Gordon's house. He's the one what captured Miss Katherine and tied her up. Said they was gonna turn her over to Ortega."

Jonah clenched his teeth. Nothing worse than a corrupt lawman. 'Cept maybe the unscrupulous fella he hired to do his dirty work.

"We have to hurry, then," Eliza declared. "Catch up to them before they leave the house. I'll fetch lanterns."

Jonah halted her with a touch to her arm. "No light. I'll track 'em in the dark." She started to protest, but he shook his head. "Can't afford to announce we're on their trail. Too dangerous for Kate."

"But if we stop them before they leave . . ."

Jonah looked to Rawley, who confirmed his suspicion with a wag of his head.

"It's too late for that, darlin'. They've already gone." He turned back to Rawley. "You know where they're headed?"

"Llano. To catch the train. But they're gonna drop her off at Ortega's camp first, and I doubt that's on the road."

Jonah's mouth tightened. His night vision was good, but not good enough to spot an off-road path cut through the brush without going at a snail's pace.

"Don't worry. Abner's following 'em."

Eliza spun around. "What?"

Rawley shrugged. "One of us had to, and I'm the faster runner. Better suited for fetching help. 'Sides, he wasn't about to leave Miss Katherine alone. I told him how to stay hidden, to keep his distance and follow the bobbin' lantern. He'll break off twigs from the brush to mark the path once they leave the road. I'm only worried that if we're too slow in comin', he'll take on Ortega himself."

"Then we best get going." Jonah found his boots at the end of the sofa and stuffed his feet into them. "I'll meet you at the barn."

Rawley nodded and left.

Jonah took Eliza's hand and squeezed it tight. "I'll bring her back to you. I swear it."

Tears misted her eyes, but she didn't let them fall. She held her head up like a queen. "I'll rouse the children at first light. We'll put together our own search party and leave word at the station for your partners in case you're not back in time to meet the train."

Jonah smiled. "Have I told you how much I love that practical streak of yours?"

Her lips twitched. She covered it up by dusting invisible lint from his shoulders and straightening his shirt buttons. "Yes, well, I'm counting on that mile-wide stubborn streak of *yours* to bring you back here in one piece. No more tumbling down mountainsides, you hear me?"

"Yes, ma'am."

Then, before he could think better of it, he clasped her face in his palm and drew her lips to his. The kiss was fast and far too short, but it was pure heaven. Breaking it off when he wanted to delve deeper, Jonah released her and left the room—heart pumping, senses alert, and mind fixed on accomplishing his mission so he could return to the woman who was quickly taking ownership of his heart.

"Deputy Bronson. Didn't expect to see you out here this time of night."

Katherine stilled at the unfamiliar male voice. Ever since Ernest Bronson had dragged her from the pantry, gagged her, and tossed her into the back of the wagon, she'd been trying to work free of her bindings. He'd covered her with a canvas tarp, so she could work without being seen, but all her efforts were for naught. Tiny splinters riddled her wrists, and her nails were chipped and broken, yet the ties were just as tight as they'd been before.

"Got one final job for you," Bronson said as the plodding wagon halted. "A witness who needs to disappear. She's in the back."

"She?" Interest laced the unfamiliar man's voice.

Katherine bit her lip. Maybe she could run. Catch the men off guard and lose them in the dark.

That slim hope died the moment Miguel Ortega threw back the tarp. Flickering light from his campfire lit him from behind and filled his face with fiendish shadows. His gaze raked over her, his eyes coldly assessing.

This man belonged to the darkness. There'd be no escaping him. Not on her own.

Help me, Lord.

"Gonna cost you. I don't usually do women."

"This ought to soothe your conscience. What there is of it." Bronson pulled a small sack of coins from inside his coat and tossed them to Ortega.

The outlaw caught it, inspected the contents, then tucked it away in his vest. Without warning, Ortega's hand closed over Katherine's ankle and yanked her down the wagon bed toward the tailgate.

She whimpered through the cloth gag. Tears gathered in her eyes. She tried to scramble away from him, but his right hand held her fast. His left moved to the tailgate latch. Her heart pounded like that of a rabbit caught in a snare.

Then, like a soothing breeze, a whisper blew across her

cheek, bringing with it the memory of a story. Of three men, trapped by those who wished them harm and facing a furnace of fire. Men who met their trial with dignity and absolute faith in their God. A God with the ability to deliver them, should that be his will. Yet even if deliverance did not fit God's plan, they resolved to face their fate with convicted hearts and peaceful spirits.

Katherine's heart slowed its frantic pounding. And when Ortega dragged her out of the wagon and set her on her feet, she met his gaze without flinching. He blinked, then looked away. His fingers bit into her arm in retaliation as he jerked her toward the front of the wagon.

Althea Gordon twisted to face them as Bronson moved back to the front of the team. "Wait an hour before you take care of this business, if you please, Miguel. Ernest and I need to be well away."

"Still tryin' to keep your pretty little hands clean? I got news for ya, lady. Just because the blood ain't on your hands don't mean the stain ain't on your soul. You'll get yours one day."

Althea smoothed her skirt as if nothing were amiss, but Katherine caught the slight tremor in her fingers. "Perhaps," she said, covering one hand with the other in her lap as she turned her gaze forward, "but not today. Ernest?" she called to her brother. "Let's be off."

Harness jangled and lantern light bobbed as Ernest turned the horses around and headed back toward the road.

Despite her legs feeling like jelly, Katherine held her chin high as Ortega dragged her toward his campsite, where her fiery furnace awaited.

Either God would deliver her, or she would meet her end with dignity.

Or spend an hour tethered to her captor like a dog on a

leash, tripping after him while he searched for the best place to do her in. A gully or shallow ravine, preferably, so the burying would already be half done.

"I suppose this spot is as good as any." Ortega set down his lantern and turned to face her. "It's a pretty place, don't ya think? Got some nice prairie grass. Even a few wildflowers. There are worse places to spend eternity."

Her eternity would *not* be spent here. She wanted to shout at him that glory awaited her. That her eternity would be spent with the God of heaven, singing with the angels in praise to the Lamb. But the gag kept her silent.

Ortega took hold of the rope that bound her to him and reeled her in, wrapping the hemp in a circle between his left elbow and palm. "I'll make sure it's quick," he promised as he wound another coil. "You won't feel much pain." He unsheathed a wicked-looking hunting knife. Its blade shimmered in the lantern's glow.

Katherine's courage evaporated. She screamed through the gag and pulled against the rope. She spun and ran. Or tried to. Ortega jerked on the rope and yanked her off balance. She crashed to the ground, her bound arms useless to break her fall.

She rolled and kicked out at him, but the blow glanced off his thigh, doing nothing to halt his charge. In a blink he was on her, pinning her to the ground. His knee planted against her chest. Breathing became nearly impossible. He thrust her chin up, exposing her throat.

Tears streamed down her face. Prayers cried from her soul. The knife lifted.

A yell suddenly echoed from the night. The knife paused its downward slice. A dark figure rushed forward and smashed Ortega across the shoulders. The blow would have collided with his skull if the man hadn't lurched up at the last second.

Her rescuer reared back for a second blow, his face close enough to see.

Abner! Dear God in heaven. The boy was no match for this man. Ortega blocked the second blow and knocked the metal rod out of Abner's hands. The boy backed away. Ortega advanced. Katherine screamed through her gag, praying for Abner to run, then pushed to her feet and launched herself at Ortega's knees. He cursed and fell forward, the knife falling from his grip. A heartbeat later, his gun cleared its holster. The barrel pointed at her head.

Crack!

Katherine flinched. But it was Ortega who fell to the ground. Dead.

Abner ran to her and buried his face in her side. She wrapped her body around him as well as she could, sheltering him from the gruesome sight of death.

Then came the sound of hoofbeats. Of her name being called. And the sight of a Horseman, rifle splayed across his lap. His stiff motions lacked their usual grace as he dismounted, but his steps were sure when he hurried forward.

Jonah Brooks. The Lord's deliverance.

J onah swallowed the bile that rose in his throat as he strode past Ortega's body. He hadn't killed a man since Wounded Knee. Had prayed never to have cause to do so again. But anything less than a kill shot would have left Katherine and Abner vulnerable. The weight of a life taken justly would be easier to bear than the weight of two innocents lost when he'd had the power to protect them.

Defend the poor and fatherless: do justice to the afflicted and needy. Deliver the poor and needy: rid them out of the hand of the wicked. The Horsemen had adopted the verses from Psalm 82 as their creed when they left the Army, vowing to preserve life whenever possible. Yet when Ortega had gotten a bead on Katherine, Jonah hadn't hesitated. There'd been only one way to rid her and the boy from the wickedness that threatened them, and Jonah thanked God his aim had been true.

Still, no woman or child should see such violence and death up close. Jonah placed himself between Ortega and

Katherine. Going down on one knee, he gently tugged the gag down over her chin, leaving it to dangle at her throat.

"Are you all right?"

Tears shimmered in her eyes. "Y-yes. I th-think so."

Jonah gave her a quick scan, then frowned at her bound arms. It looked like apron strings wrapped around her wrists. He slipped his knife from its sheath and met her eyes. "I'm gonna cut you free. Hold still."

She nodded.

Standing up, he bent over her shoulder and slid his blade between her wrists. One good slice, and she was free. He barely had time to sheath his knife and hunker back down before she snatched him around the neck and squeezed the breath out of him.

"Thank you, Jonah. Thank you."

Her body shook as if she were crying, but no sound emerged. Probably trying not to alarm Abner. The poor kid had been through enough already. Taking on a grown man. Nearly being killed. Then seeing the villain shot down right in front of him. The kid could do with some sheltering.

After giving Katherine's back an awkward pat, he slipped free of her hold and locked eyes with the boy. "You done good, Abner. Laid a good trail for me to follow. Protected Miss Katherine. Things coulda gone a lot worse if it weren't for you."

Katherine quickly swiped at her face before directing a big smile Abner's way. "He's my hero." She pulled him into her lap and hugged him tight.

After a moment, her attention landed on something behind Jonah. Jonah's hand went for his gun as he spun to face whatever approached. That *whatever* being Rawley.

"And there's the third hero of the night," Katherine said, a smile in her voice.

"One who was supposed to stay where I left him until I gave the all-clear signal," Jonah grumbled, hating the way the kid stared at Ortega, like he couldn't tear his gaze away. "Come on, then." He waved at Rawley, trying to divert his attention. "Let's get back to the camp. There's a horse there we can use." He turned back to Katherine. "Can you ride?"

She lifted Abner off her lap and pushed to her feet. "Well enough." She sidled past Jonah to place herself and the bell of her skirt between the wide-eyed Rawley and the unmoving man on the ground. "Time to get going, boys. There are others still in peril. We need to get to Packsaddle Mountain as quickly as we can."

Spell broken, Rawley nodded, jogged over to where Abner stood, and slapped the other boy's back in manly approval. The adventure of the night had apparently formed a bond of friendship between the two.

Jonah whistled, and Augustus trotted over. He took up the lead line and started walking. Wallace was still out there, along with a group of missing boys. "I wanna meet the mornin' train in Kingsland. Fetch Matt and Preach. They'll aid in the search and help corral Miss Gordon and the deputy before they get away."

Katherine shooed the boys ahead of her, falling into step beside Jonah. She rubbed her arms and wrists, as if trying to get the blood pumping through them again. Or maybe to ward off the same fear that plagued him.

Had Wallace and the boys survived the night?

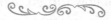

Eliza stood on the train platform, holding a schoolroom slate with the names *Matthew Hanger* and *Luke Davenport* chalked in bold letters. The minister's wife had been kind enough to watch Ruby, Ted, and the twins after Eliza banged on the parsonage door at first light to ask for the preacher's help in rounding up men to search for the caved-in mine. Alice, however, had refused to stay behind. She was determined to help find her brother, and as much as Eliza worried about what outcome they might encounter on Packsaddle Mountain, she knew it would be pointless to try to keep the child away. The little scamp would just escape and head out on her own. It was only Eliza's suggestion that they wait for Rawley's return that had kept Alice from traipsing after the search party when the men left town a half hour ago.

Passengers began disembarking the newly arrived train. Eliza held her sign over her head, praying the Horsemen would see it. A paunchy fellow with a drummer's case exited the train car, followed by a lady with a frustratingly large hat. Said lady apparently felt compelled to stop three steps from the train car to converse with the porter, completely blocking Eliza's view of the disembarking passengers. She rose up on tiptoes and craned her neck from one side to the other, trying to see behind the feathered monstrosity.

A giant of a fellow stepped down to the platform, too big for even that hat to hide. Behind him came a man with a touch of gray in his tightly trimmed beard. As they stepped around the woman with delusions of millinery grandeur, Eliza felt sure she'd found the Horsemen. They carried themselves the same way Jonah did—with authority and confidence. And with enough guns to start a small war. Her only hesitation lay in the fact that the second fellow turned to assist a lady down the steps, a lady who slid her arm into his as if it belonged there. Would Horsemen bound for battle travel with a woman?

"Look, Miss Eliza." Alice tugged on her skirt and pointed down the road. "Mr. Jonah is back."

Eliza's full attention riveted on the weary man on the giant horse walking toward the station. *Thank you, God, for keeping him safe.* And Katherine! *Oh, Lord, how good you are!* Eliza's heart galloped with joy at that sight of her friend alive and well, riding a strange black horse with speckled haunches. Abner sat safely on the saddle in front of her. Eliza had known Jonah would do whatever he could to save her and the boy, but she'd worried he might not be in time. Praise God for his mercy!

"Ma'am?" A deep voice brought her gaze back to the platform. The big man she'd spied earlier now stood in front of her, tipping his hat. "I'm Luke Davenport. You from Harmony House?"

Eliza nodded, pulling her arms down, and handed the slate to Alice. "Yes. I'm Eliza Southerland. Thank you for coming. Jonah's on his way in now." She nodded toward the road.

Jonah, of course, had already spotted his partner and had a hand raised in greeting. Mr. Davenport lifted his in response.

"Matt's seeing to the horses. Dr. Jo insisted on taggin' along too. In case anyone needs patchin' up." He frowned as Jonah reached the platform and gingerly dismounted. "Looks like Brooks could use her."

The lady was a doctor? That would be a blessing. Though Eliza doubted Jonah would submit to an examination any time soon. "His injuries are secondary right now. He won't stop until we find Mark."

"Nope. None of us will."

The big man's words held such deep promise, they eased a bit of Eliza's worry. At least the worry assigned to Mr. Wallace and the missing children. The worry assigned to Jonah and the likelihood of him working himself to death to save his friend held steady. Which was why she'd be going to Packsaddle with him. Even if it meant riding that giant horse of his again. She aimed to make sure he didn't push himself too hard. She wouldn't try to stop him, but she fully intended to ply him with food, water, and anything else he might need to keep him sustained.

Jonah helped Rawley off Augustus before crossing to the second horse and lowering first Abner then Katherine. Mr. Davenport strode forward to meet the group at the end of the platform. Alice dashed after him, making a beeline for Abner and Rawley. Eliza followed, not running, but not exactly walking either. By the time she caught up with the others, Jonah had already clasped Mr. Davenport's hand.

"Preach. Thanks for comin'."

Mr. Davenport nodded, then raised a brow in question. "Wallace?"

Jonah's face looked grim. "Buried in a collapsed mine somewhere on the south side of Packsaddle Mountain."

Eliza longed to ease his frown, take some of the load upon herself. "A search party set out thirty minutes ago. Hopefully they'll have found the entrance by the time we get out there."

Jonah's eyes met hers, gratitude shining out from behind the weariness. Heavens, but a woman could get used to such a look, knowing her man depended on her, appreciated her.

"We'll get him dug out in no time," Mr. Davenport vowed.

But Jonah shook his head. "Not you, Preach. I need you to get back on the train and ride to Llano."

The big man scowled. "Not while Wallace is buried under a mountain somewhere!"

"If you don't, the pair responsible for putting him there will get away scot-free."

Davenport's frown darkened.

Jonah exhaled, obviously not wanting to be at odds with

his fellow Horseman. "They intend to board this very train when it reaches Llano and make their escape. We can't let that happen."

"Then why don't *you* get on the train?" Davenport crossed his bulky arms over his chest. "You're the one who knows what these people look like. Besides, you can barely stand. I'll be more use at the dig site."

"It ain't that simple, Preach. I killed a man."

A shiver passed over Eliza at Jonah's statement. Not because of what he'd revealed—she had no doubt that his actions had been righteous. Whatever he'd done, he'd done to help Katherine escape. No, what caused the shiver was the flatness in his voice, as if he hated himself for what he'd been forced to do.

His pronouncement had a similar effect on Mr. Davenport. His arms uncrossed, and his expression lost its stubborn edge.

"Someone needs to report it to the sheriff, and if a black man shows up alone to confess to that kind of crime, there's no guarantee things won't take a nasty turn. Sheriff Porter seems like a fair-minded fellow—I spoke to him when Wallace and I started our investigation—but you never know who might overhear and decide to take justice into their own hands before all the facts are collected."

Eliza's shiver grew into an outright quake. She moved to Jonah's side and slid her arm around his, squeezing it close to her side. Lynchings were all too real, and the thought of something like that happening to Jonah . . . No. She wouldn't think of it. God had saved him from the attack on the mountain. God would save him from hotheaded fools. He had to. Eliza had just found him. She wasn't ready to lose him. She'd *never* be ready to lose him.

Davenport nodded. "I'll go. Just tell me what to do."

Eliza let out the breath she'd been holding.

"First order of business," Jonah said, "is to run Althea Gordon and Deputy Ernest Bronson to ground."

"A deputy?" Davenport let out a whistle. "That ain't right."

"Apparently they're brother and sister, but no one knew of the relation. They're the ones responsible for kidnapping the missing kids. Their hired guns attacked me and Wallace on Packsaddle yesterday, and it was their idea to dynamite the mine with Wallace and the boys inside to bury the evidence."

"I can testify to all of that," Katherine said, stepping forward. "Althea admitted her guilt to me face-to-face. Right before she and Deputy Bronson tied me up and delivered me to Miguel Ortega."

She extended her arms for Davenport's inspection. Eliza's heart ached at the angry red welts and bloody scrapes at the base of Katherine's arms.

"They paid Ortega to . . . dispose of me. Ortega's pistol was aimed at my head, his finger squeezing the trigger, when Mr. Brooks made the shot that saved my life. Make sure you tell Sheriff Porter that Ortega's death was justified. I'll answer any questions he has and sign whatever papers are needed. Jonah saved my life and Abner's life. He's a hero, not a killer."

Eliza slipped her hand into Jonah's, twining her fingers with his. "She's right," she murmured softly, her words meant for his ears alone. "You *are* a hero. A guardian of women and children. A valiant warrior. A man I'm proud to stand beside."

Jonah turned, his eyes searching hers with an intensity that left her with a different type of shiver coursing over her skin.

As if Katherine recognized their need for privacy, she steered Mr. Davenport a few feet away, catching him up on the abductions and giving him descriptions of Althea and Ernest.

"Do you mean it?" Jonah fit his free hand to her waist. "The blood I spilled today doesn't bother you?"

She placed her palm flat against his chest and felt the not-so-steady *thump* of his heart. "It bothers me insofar as any violent death bothers me," she admitted. "I hate that it happened. Hate that evil exists in this world and that good men must pay the price for fighting it. I hate that you carry a burden that no one should." She patted his chest and gazed straight into his eyes. "But I *love* that you have the courage and the skill to save those in need. I love that you value life and do everything in your power to preserve it. I love that Katherine and Abner's lives were spared, and I love you, Jonah Brooks. I love the man you are and the man you are striving to become."

His fingers twitched at her side. His eyes darkened.

She hadn't meant to blurt out her feelings like that, feelings that were new and untested. Yet she'd spoken the truth, and she didn't regret it. Especially not when the man in front of her stood a little taller and looked at her with a hunger so hot it nearly melted her spine. She had to clutch his shoulder to remain upright. When she did, his gaze dropped to her mouth and his hand drew her an inch closer. But then he blinked, glanced at the people bustling around the depot, and pulled back. She dipped her head and bit her bottom lip, their surroundings and circumstances coming back to mind.

"You and I need to have a serious conversation after all this is over." Jonah growled the words in a low, rumbly undertone that stole Eliza's breath. But not her sense. There were more urgent issues to deal with than kisses and intimate conversations.

One such thing being her partner. Katherine was shaking her head at something Mr. Davenport said and wrapping her arms around her middle like she did when her heart was hurting.

"It would be easier if you came with me," Davenport urged. "You could point them out to me. And give your statement to the sheriff."

"I can't." She sounded on the brink of tears. "I can't leave Mark. Not again. I have to *be* there."

"But—"

"Preach." Jonah shook his head. Davenport raised a brow in question. Jonah said simply, "Mark will want her there."

Apparently that explanation sufficed, for Davenport nodded.

Then a new voice piped up. "I'll go with you."

Abner? Eliza stepped away from Jonah and moved to Abner's left side while Katherine hunkered down on his right.

"No," Katherine protested, her maternal instincts flaring even when no true danger existed. Abner would be traveling in the company of a Horseman, for pity's sake.

Still, Eliza knew Katherine. Knew her tender heart. A heart bruised from the violence she'd just witnessed. Violence that had touched not only her, but the boy she loved like a son.

"You've done too much already, Abner," Katherine insisted. "You don't have to do this."

"I want to." Abner turned pleading eyes to Eliza. "I can point out Miss Gordon and Deputy Bronson. I can explain what happened with Ortega. Please. Let me help."

Eliza couldn't ignore his plea. Especially when he was right.

She cleared her throat and turned her gaze to the man in front of her. "I'm sure Mr. Davenport will guard the boy well. Won't you, sir?"

"Yes, ma'am. On my life, he'll come to no harm."

"Then I see no reason to keep him from going. Do you, Katherine?"

"No, I suppose not." Katherine wiped her eyes and stood, mimicking Eliza's stance as if Eliza were some kind of pillar of strength to imitate, when Katherine was already one of the strongest women Eliza knew. Maybe not in the conventional way, but her soft heart had a core of iron.

"Then I guess you and me better get some tickets before this train leaves without us." The big man smiled at Abner, and the smile transformed his face. The intimidating bear looked more like an oversized puppy when he patted Abner's shoulder. Abner didn't smile back, but he did nod and follow Davenport into the depot.

"Ain't that Wallace's horse?" Rawley called out from where he stood in the street, holding the mounts Katherine and Jonah had ridden. He pointed, and Eliza caught a glimpse of the man and woman she'd seen exiting the train behind Mr. Davenport.

The woman led four terrifyingly oversized horses, one of them a gray that looked just like Cooper, with the ease of a mother duck leading a string of ducklings. Eliza didn't know whether to be impressed by her control of the beasts or worried that they might break away without a man's strength to control them. Her companion, however, had his hands full with a more belligerent charge, a stranger who sported a bloody nose and reddened jaw. The man Eliza assumed to be Matthew Hanger shoved his captive forward, keeping a grip on the arm he'd bent behind the fellow's back.

Jonah moved to meet him. "Captain?"

Eliza followed, keeping an eye on the horses, relieved to see that the lady doctor had them well in hand.

"Found this fellow trying to load Cooper into the stock

car when we were unloading our mounts," the captain said. "Claimed the horse was his. I knew otherwise. Thought I'd deliver him to the local law for horse thievin'."

"Ain't no local law at the moment," Jonah said, "but I got a better idea." He strode up to the man and spoke in a voice so cold it could freeze the Mississippi. "Horse thieving's not his worst crime. See, the only way he could have come across this horse was to take it after ambushing me and Wallace out on Packsaddle Mountain yesterday. Which means that in addition to horse thievin' and back-shootin', he's also guilty of snatchin' kids and collapsin' a mine on top of their heads."

The stranger's face paled.

Jonah jabbed a finger into the man's chest. "If my partner or any of those kids die in that mine, you become guilty of capital murder—a hanging offense. But if Wallace and the kids are found alive, there's a good chance hangin' gets taken off the table. It's simple, really. If they live, you live. So why don't you increase your odds of survival by showing us where the mine is?"

The snatcher swallowed hard, then gave a jerky nod of assent.

━ CHAPTER ━
THIRTY-NINE

Mark closed his eyes and focused on breathing. No easy task with half the mountain piled atop his legs and belly. Any sense of time had left him hours ago. He'd prayed, dozed, and prayed some more. Not just for himself, but for the boys in the far passage. Boys with so much life left to live. So much potential yet to realize. And for Kate. He'd imagined her beside him. Even pretended to talk to her. Should they wed here or back home in Westfield? How many children would they have? What should they name them?

He did his best to stay positive, to hold on to his faith and his optimism, but the darkness wore on him. As did the pain. Falling rocks had pummeled him during the explosion, leaving him bruised and aching. Being pinned to the cavern floor didn't help matters. He couldn't stretch or move more than an inch or two. And the air seemed to grow thinner by the moment. Fear of suffocation prowled at the edge of his awareness, ready to pounce.

Stay strong, soldier. The cavalry's coming.

Oddly enough, he heard the admonition in Matt's voice, not his own. Maybe the thin air was starting to take its toll.

The melody of a hymn he'd learned a year or two ago

started playing in his mind. Music had always been his solace, so when he'd run out of words to pray during the night, he'd let symphonies run through his mind. Bach. Brahms. Beethoven. The chords filled his head. Lilting woodwinds. Reverberating brass. Singing strings. He'd imagined his own trumpet joining the orchestra, harmonizing with the instruments around him, getting swept up in a current of music that could take him away from his present reality.

Mark lacked the energy even to imagine a full orchestral arrangement now, but he might manage the simple melody of a hymn. He tapped out the rhythm with his thumb, the *clink* of his manacles forming the percussion section. The tempo fell more into the *adagio* range than the *andante* the march-like piece called for, but it was the best he could do.

At first he heard the melody as a trumpet call. Rich, majestic, regal. But when the chorus ended and he returned to the verse, it was Kate's voice he heard, singing the lyrics to him in her sweet mezzo soprano.

> 'Tis the grandest theme thro' the ages rung; 'Tis the
>   grandest theme for a mortal tongue;
> 'Tis the grandest theme that the world e'er sung: Our
>   God is able to deliver thee.
> He is able to deliver thee, He is able to deliver thee;
> Tho' by sin opprest, Go to Him for rest; Our God is
>   able to deliver thee.

Ah, Kate. A tear squeezed through the crease of Mark's closed eyelid. "The Lord giveth," he whispered, "and the Lord taketh away. Blessed be the name of the Lord."

He drifted back into a hazy semiconscious state until something penetrated his fog.

Pounding. Muffled voices.

Mark's eyes popped open. Were his ears playing tricks? Had he imagined—

No! There it was again. Pounding. Joined this time by scraping. Dirt shifted above him and showered his face.

"Here!" He yelled as loud as he could manage, which was a pathetic mewling cut off by a round of coughs. If only he had his bugle! Frustrated, he willed the hacking into submission, cleared his throat, and tried again. "Here! I'm here!"

Silence was his only answer.

Until . . .

"Wallace?"

Matt. Sweet Lord in heaven, it was Matt's voice. He was here. And close.

Mark lifted his head a few inches off the ground. "Here, Captain. I'm here!"

A tear or two slid down his dirt-encrusted temples as his head fell back. Matthew Hanger was here, and nothing would stop the captain. Mark had never met a more reliable man.

Thank you, God. Thank you.

It didn't take long for Captain Hanger to chop an air hole through the top of the debris blocking off the passage. It took longer for him, and those with him, to open it up wide enough to fit a man's shoulders while not risking the stability of the mine shaft. Eventually, however, the captain wiggled his way through the opening and crawled down to where Mark lay.

"Brooks!" Matt called. "Hand in a canteen."

At the sound of the name, Mark grabbed his former commander's forearm, the chain resting on his chest clinking softly. "Jonah's alive?"

The captain, his face streaked with dirt and sweat, nodded. "He is. Banged up enough that Josie raked him over the

369

coals when he wouldn't let her tend him before digging you out, but he's all in one piece."

Even as he gave the assurance, a brown hand with a canteen attached shoved through the hole. The captain patted Mark's shoulder, then stepped away to fetch the water.

"Those rocks better not have squashed your head, Wallace," Jonah said from the other side of the hole. "You're gonna need your wits to keep up with all the kids that'll be swarmin' Harmony House after this."

Mark lifted his head again and tried to wedge his elbows beneath him so he wouldn't be flat on his back. "The boys?" He searched the captain's face. "You got them out?"

Hanger nodded. "About an hour ago. All six survived. No serious injuries. Josephine's tending to them, and Miss Palmer is plying them with food and water. Speaking of water . . ." He held up the canteen. "Drink up, soldier. Can't have you passin' out in front of your woman. I understand there's a wedding in the works."

The grin he flashed brought a touch of heat to Mark's cheeks and a heap of pride to his heart. But before he could do more than nod, the captain had the canteen tipped and water flowing into Mark's mouth.

"She's fine, by the way. Your Katherine. Jonah got to her in time. Took out Ortega. And Preach likely has the others in custody by now as well."

Mark coughed on his water, then shoved the canteen aside. He reared up as far as his rock blanket would allow. "What happened to Kate?" he roared.

"Now you done it, Cap." Jonah's voice floated through the slowly widening hole. "Good luck getting *that* cat back in the bag."

"Calm down, Wallace. She's fine. Brave little thing," the captain said as he screwed the lid back on the canteen and frowned down at Mark's manacles. "Brooks? Get one of the men to search that Dorsey fellow up top for a key to these manacles."

"Yes, sir."

Mark didn't care about the chains. "Tell me what happened to Kate."

Hanger shrugged. "Don't know all the details. All I know is she figured out who was behind the snatching and went to confront them sometime in the middle of the night. It's 'cause of her that Jonah and Miss Southerland knew where to send the search party to start lookin' for the mine. Finding Gabe Dorsey at the depot with your horse just helped us pinpoint the passages. The townsfolk had already spotted the caved-in entrance and started digging out the debris by the time we dragged his sorry hide up here."

Mark's head fell back to the ground. Ortega had had Kate? Lord have mercy. "She could have been killed." The words escaped in a broken whisper. The very idea so terrified him, he could barely breathe.

Hanger grabbed his shoulder. "But she wasn't. The Good Lord took care of both of you last night. Now, what do you say we quit frettin' over what might have been and start workin' on gettin' you outta here?"

And back to Kate. So he could wring her neck. Or more likely kiss her senseless. Yeah, kissing was definitely the better option. Though Mark was probably the one who'd end up senseless. He was halfway there already.

After an hour of shifting, shoveling, and chiseling, Mark finally escaped the mountain's hold. His legs hurt like the dickens, but they worked, so with the captain propping him up on one side and Jonah on the other, Mark hobbled through the man-made tunnel to the base of the vertical shaft that led to freedom. As Captain Hanger worked on the rigging to haul him up, Mark turned to Jonah and wrapped his friend in a hug. He thumped his back twice, then stepped back.

"Glad you're alive, Brooks."

Jonah grinned. "Me too."

Mark chuckled, then grew serious. He clasped Jonah's shoulder. "There aren't words enough to thank you for what you did for Kate. I'll be wanting the full story later, but know that I'm in your debt for life."

Jonah dipped his chin. "Abner and Rawley did most of the heavy lifting. I just showed up for the last hurrah."

Mark knew what that meant, as well as the cost such an act would demand from his friend. All the Horsemen understood the price of war. "Well, I, for one, am glad you were there."

The captain extended him a rope tied into a harness of sorts. "Ready, Wallace?"

To get out of this pit? To see his beautiful Kate? To finally start their life together? "More than ready, sir."

He took the rope in his hands, and with Matt and Jonah keeping him from toppling over, he fit his legs through the holes and sat across the knotted middle. The captain called up to the surface, and the rope started hauling him upward. When he reached the top, a pair of men swung him to the side and extricated him from the harness. Donaldson from the livery wrapped an arm around Mark's waist and started walking him away from the mine while the others stayed to haul up the other men.

Applause suddenly broke out. Kids cheered. Wart and his sister ran toward him hand in hand. Abner. Rawley. Even Floyd looked relieved to see him. But it was Kate's voice shouting his name that riveted him in place.

"Mark!" She leapt up from where she'd been helping one of the boys, grabbed a handful of skirt, and ran straight for him.

He untangled himself from a chuckling Donaldson and limped forward on his own power, all his energy focused on Kate. Tears streaming down her cheeks, windblown hair frizzing around her face, clothes dust-laden, and quiet sobs hiccupping through her—she was the most beautiful thing he'd ever seen.

When she reached him, he didn't waste any energy on words. His mouth had much more important work to do. He wrapped one arm around her waist and used the other to cup her face and lift her lips to his. His mouth slanted over hers with desperation, with thanksgiving, and with pure joy over the two of them being alive. Her arms pressed into his back, holding him tight. She lifted up on her toes to meet him, her enthusiasm in returning his kiss kicking his pulse into a full gallop.

Whoops and whistles penetrated Mark's consciousness and, regretfully, he pulled back. Not far, though. He might be able to find the strength to stop kissing her while on public display, but he didn't have the strength to let go of her. Not yet. So he held her close, her face nestled against his chest, their breathing ragged yet perfectly synchronized.

He dipped his chin and laid a kiss on her hair. "I love you, Kate."

She tipped her face back to meet his gaze, her glistening blue eyes shining in the afternoon sun. "I love you too. And I'm never letting you go again. *Never.*"

He grinned. "That makes two of us."

Later that evening, Jonah slipped out of the crowded parlor of Harmony House and into the cool breeze. Hearing tales of today's exploits over and over was wearing his patience thin, though he knew the fault lay with him, not the dozen kids crammed into the parlor. He just needed a few minutes of quiet. He was tired. And sore. And to be honest, a little worried about how things had gone with the sheriff in Llano. Preach still hadn't made it back yet with his report.

Dr. Jo and Miss Katherine were upstairs fussing over Wallace, concerned he might have a fracture in his left leg. The leg continued to pain him hours after his rescue, but Dr. Jo was sure nothing was out of alignment. She wanted to splint it anyway and had ordered Wallace not to put weight on it for a couple of weeks. Poor bugger. No riding or even much walking. Jonah would go stir-crazy if it were him, but he doubted Wallace would mind having an excuse to hang around the house with Katherine for the next several days.

Jonah rested his arms on the porch railing and released a heavy breath. A movement in the shadows on the ground below him caught his attention. Rawley. The kid sat on the dirt with his back propped against one of the porch piers. He'd snuck out of the house a few minutes before Jonah. Truth be told, his leaving was what had given Jonah the idea to make his own escape. Jonah had been wanting to talk with the kid anyway. Preferably before Rawley's itchy feet drove him to leave town. With the snatcher situation dealt with, the boy had no reason to stick around.

Yet.

"You on the hunt for fresh air too?" Rawley asked, tipping his head back to meet Jonah's gaze.

"Yep." Jonah pushed away from the railing and took a seat on the steps. "And I wanted to talk to you. Got a proposition for ya."

"Yeah?" The boy rose and joined Jonah on the steps.

Jonah smiled inwardly even though his face remained impassive. "I'm thinkin' about buying the old Garvey spread a quarter mile north of here. Ain't nothin' fancy, but it's got a cabin, a barn, and a small bunkhouse. Was thinkin' of setting down some roots and maybe running a few head of cattle."

Rawley waggled his eyebrows. "You're fixin' to court Miss Eliza, aren't ya?"

Jonah didn't fight to hide his smile this time. "Yep."

"Thought so."

They shared a grin, and then Jonah braced his forearms across his knees and knit his hands together. "I was hopin' you might consider stickin' around," he said, turning his attention to his hands, not wanting the boy to feel pressured one way or the other. "I'll need a foreman. You're a mite young for the job at the moment, but you'd grow into it. I got a whopping lot of learnin' to do myself. Never ranched before. But two smart fellas like ourselves who ain't afraid of hard work ought to be able to figure out how to make a go of it."

Rawley was quiet for a long while. Jonah snuck a peek at him from the corner of his eye. The kid looked like someone had turned him to stone.

Finally, Rawley spoke. "W-what about my boys? I can't just leave 'em. . . ."

"A ranch can always use more hands. I wouldn't be able to pay 'em much, but they'd have food to eat, a roof over their heads, and honest work to keep 'em outta trouble." He shrugged. "'Course, Miss Eliza will probably insist on fillin' all of ya with book learning too. It may not be as fun as ridin' the rails, but education will take a man farther in life than any train."

Rawley twisted on the step. Jonah straightened and turned to meet his gaze. "Can I think about it?"

Jonah nodded. "Take as long as you need."

The boy nodded solemnly, grabbed the railing at his side, and hoisted himself up. "Thanks for the offer, Mr. Brooks."

"Thanks for considerin'."

Rawley wandered off toward the barn to ponder. Jonah stayed on the steps, thinking he'd pray for a bit. Maybe watch the sunset. The clouds were just starting to turn pink. A silhouette against the dusky sky, however, caught Jonah's eye and sharpened his attention. Toward the road. He stood in anticipation, his chest clutching slightly.

He raised a hand in greeting as Preach approached the house, a sleeping Abner tossed over one shoulder.

The quiet *click* of a shoe heel on the porch behind him brought Jonah's head around. Eliza stepped away from the shadows of the outside wall and came to stand on the step behind him. She placed her hands on his shoulders, the gentle, possessive touch sending waves of pleasure through him.

"You look good holding a sleeping child, Mr. Davenport," she said. "You practicing to be a family man?"

Preach chuckled softly. "Not me, ma'am. I'm too wild to settle down."

"Who says family men have to be tame?" Eliza responded. "The right woman might like a little wild in her man."

Preach stared at her as if she'd just spoken in a foreign language. All Jonah could think about was whether or not *she* liked a little wild in *her* man. It made him glad his complexion hid the fire flushing his face.

Determined to reroute the conversation before his blood warmed any further, Jonah jerked his chin toward Preach. "How'd it go in Llano?"

"Took a bit of doing, but Miss Gordon and her brother are in custody. Sheriff Porter is comin' to Kingsland tomorrow to get your statement and one from Miss Palmer. He'll collect the body and conduct an investigation, but with Ortega's reputation as an outlaw, the sheriff don't expect any trouble clearing you."

Eliza's hands tightened on Jonah's shoulders, and her heartfelt murmur echoed above him. "Thank the Lord."

Preach mounted the steps, thumping Jonah on the arm as he squeezed past. "I better get this boy to bed. He's tuckered out."

Jonah expected Eliza to show his fellow Horseman into the house and had already braced himself for the disappointment of her leaving, but she surprised him by simply giving Preach directions.

"First room at the top of the stairs. His bed is behind the door on the right. Katherine is upstairs with Mr. Wallace and Dr. Hanger. She can assist you."

Preach tipped his hat. "Thank ya, ma'am."

Once the door closed behind him, Eliza came around to Jonah's side and lowered herself to sit on the steps. Figuring he better follow suit, he bent his knees and joined her.

"How, ah, long you been out here?" Had she overheard his entire conversation with Rawley?

She dipped her chin, a shy smile curving her lips. "Nearly as long as you. I followed you out, hoping we might have that long conversation you alluded to earlier."

Jonah's gut tightened. The conversation prompted by her saying she loved him. His mind had replayed that moment about a thousand times today. But where to start? He hadn't a clue. Thankfully, Eliza was smart enough for the both of them.

"So, the old Garvey place, huh? Sounds almost permanent." She nudged his shoulder with hers.

He nudged her back, scooting his hips over in the process

so that the length of his right side pressed up against her left. Man, she felt good against him.

"Thought I'd make my daddy happy," he said. "Buy some land. Court a good woman. Lay down some roots."

Eliza lifted her face, the look in her deep brown eyes making his heart pound. "You got any particular woman in mind?"

"Maybe. Not sure she'll have me, though. She's my better in nearly every way."

Her brows lifted. "I find that hard to believe."

"Oh, it's true, all right. She's smarter, kinder, and a whole lot better lookin'."

She leaned close and whispered a secret in his ear, the breath of air sending shivers dancing across his skin. "I hear she's terrible with horses."

He turned his face toward her, his lips a mere hairsbreadth from hers. "I don't know. I have it on good authority she rode a cavalry officer's warhorse all the way to Packsaddle Mountain and back. A ride like that takes skill."

"Or massive motivation." Her gaze darted to his mouth then back up to his eyes. "A little birdie told me she only did it to save the man she loved."

Jonah angled his body toward her and reached for her face. "Same bird told me that fella's been fallin' for her since the day they shared a wagon ride out to Miss Georgia's homestead."

"That long, huh?" Her soft, husky voice fragmented his pulse.

"Yep. I hear tell he's so far gone, a minute can't pass without him thinkin' of her. Thinkin' about holding her." He ran his thumb over her cheekbone. "Kissing her." His thumb moved to her mouth and brushed over her bottom lip.

Her breath caught. "Maybe he should quit thinking and start doing."

Jonah grinned, slow and deep. "Have I told you how much I love that bossy streak of yours?"

Then, before she could answer, he closed the last inch of distance between them and kissed her with the culminated passion that had been building inside him since the day they met. This amazing, intelligent, courageous woman *loved* him. He didn't deserve her, but he'd spend his life loving her, supporting her, and protecting her if she'd let him.

As she grabbed the front of his shirt and pulled him closer, taking charge of the kiss and driving his pulse to unanticipated heights, Jonah thought she just might be amenable to the idea.

Christy Award finalist and winner of the ACFW Carol Award, HOLT Medallion, and Inspirational Reader's Choice Award, best-selling author **Karen Witemeyer** writes historical romances because she believes the world needs more happily-ever-afters. She is an avid cross-stitcher and shower singer, and she bakes a mean apple cobbler. Karen makes her home in Abilene, Texas, with her husband and three children.

To learn more about Karen and her books and to sign up for her free newsletter featuring special giveaways and behind-the-scenes information, please visit www.karenwitemeyer.com.

Sign Up for Karen's Newsletter

Keep up to date with news on Karen's upcoming book releases and events by signing up for her email list at karenwitemeyer.com.

More from Karen Witemeyer

Ex-cavalry officer Matthew Hanger leads a band of mercenaries who defend the innocent, but when a rustler's bullet leaves one of them at death's door, they seek out help from Dr. Josephine Burkett. When Josephine's brother is abducted and she is caught in the crossfire, Matthew may have to sacrifice everything— even his team—to save her.

At Love's Command • Hanger's Horsemen #1

You May Also Like . . .

After being railroaded by the city council, Abby needs a man's name on her bakery's deed, and a man she can control—not the stoic lumberman Zacharias, who always seems to exude silent confidence. She can't even control her pulse when she's around him. But as trust grows between them, she finds she wants more than his rescue. She wants his heart.

More Than Words Can Say by Karen Witemeyer
karenwitemeyer.com

Seeking justice against the man who destroyed his family, Logan Fowler arrives in Pecan Gap, Texas, to confront the person responsible. But his quest is derailed when, instead of a hardened criminal, he finds an ordinary man with a sister named Evangeline—an unusual beauty with mismatched eyes and a sweet spirit that he finds utterly captivating.

More Than Meets the Eye by Karen Witemeyer
karenwitemeyer.com

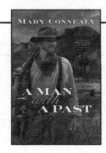

Falcon Hunt awakens without a past—or at least he doesn't recall one. When he makes a new start by claiming an inheritance, it cuts out frontierswoman Cheyenne from her ranch. Soon it's clear someone is gunning for him and his brothers, and as his affection for Cheyenne grows, he must piece together his past if they're to have any chance at a future.

A Man with a Past by Mary Connealy
BROTHERS IN ARMS #2
maryconnealy.com

◊ BETHANYHOUSE

More from Bethany House

After being robbed on her trip west to save her ailing sister, Greta Nilsson is left homeless and penniless. Struggling to get his new ranch running, Wyatt McQuaid is offered a bargain—the mayor will invest in a herd of cattle if Wyatt agrees to help the town become more respectable by marrying...and the mayor has the perfect woman in mind.

A Cowboy for Keeps by Jody Hedlund
COLORADO COWBOYS #1
jodyhedlund.com

Nate Long has always watched over his twin, even if it's led him to be an outlaw. When his brother is wounded in a shootout, it's their former prisoner, Laura, who ends up nursing his wounds at Settler's Fort. She knows Nate wants a fresh start, but struggles with how his devotion blinds him. Do the futures they seek include love, or is too much in the way?

Faith's Mountain Home by Misty M. Beller
HEARTS OF MONTANA #3
mistymbeller.com

In the midst of WWII, Jane Linder pours all of her dreams for a family into her career at the Toronto Children's Aid Society. Garrett Wilder has been hired to overhaul operations at the society and hopes to earn the vacant director's position. But when feelings begin to blossom and they come to a crossroads, can they discern the path to true happiness?

To Find Her Place by Susan Anne Mason
REDEMPTION'S LIGHT #2
susanannemason.net

ANYHOUSE